59372084371692   WDWD

HALF LIVES

HALF

LIVES

SARA GRANT

LITTLE, BROWN AND COMPANY
New York Boston

Half-life definition used by permission from *Merriam-Webster's Collegiate® Dictionary, 11th Edition* © 2012 by Merriam-Webster, Incorporated (www.Merriam-Webster.com)

Little, Brown and Company

Hachette Book Group
237 Park Avenue, New York, NY 10017
Visit our website at www.lb-teens.com

Little, Brown and Company is a division of Hachette Book Group, Inc. The Little, Brown name and logo are trademarks of Hachette Book Group, Inc.

The publisher is not responsible for websites (or their content) that are not owned by the publisher.

First Edition: July 2013

Library of Congress Cataloging-in-Publication Data

Grant, Sara, 1968–
Half lives / by Sara Grant.—First edition.
pages cm
Summary: Chronicles the mysteriously linked lives of two unlikely teenaged heroes living hundreds of years apart, as both struggle to survive and protect future generations from the terrible fate that awaits any who dare to climb the mountain.
ISBN 978-0-316-19493-8
[1. Science fiction. 2. Survival—Fiction. 3. Radioactive waste disposal—Fiction.]
I. Title.
PZ7.G7691Hal 2013 [Fic]—dc23 2012031405

10 9 8 7 6 5 4 3 2 1

RRD-C

Printed in the United States of America

To the memory of Margaret Carey—
writer, artist, and friend—
your inspiration lives on....

half-life:

1: the time required for half of something to undergo a process: as

  a: the time required for half of the atoms of a radioactive substance to become disintegrated

  b: the time required for half the amount of a substance (as a drug, radioactive tracer, or pesticide) in or introduced into a living system or ecosystem to be eliminated or disintegrated by natural processes

2: a period of usefulness or popularity preceding decline or obsolescence

—*Merriam-Webster's Collegiate Dictionary*, 11th ed.

ONE

If you'd asked me that day whether I could lie, cheat, steal, and kill, I would have said ab-so-lutely not. I've told little white lies to my parents to stay out of trouble. And, sure, I borrowed a few answers off Lola on that one chemistry test. (Who cares that U stands for Uranium or that it's number 92 on the periodic table of the elements?) I shop-lifted a Kit Kat when I was seven on a dare. That's not exactly grand larceny, but I'd never kill. *Not possible.* I'd relocate spiders rather than squash them. (And I hate those beasties!)

But now I've knowingly and willfully committed all those acts on the Richter scale of freaking horrible—

from lying to killing. I'm not proud of it. I learned that surviving isn't all it's cracked up to be. If you survive, you've got to live with the guilt, and that's more difficult than looking someone in the eye and pulling the trigger. Trust me. I've done both. Killing takes a twitch of the finger. Absolution takes several lifetimes.

When the final bell rang that last normal day of my life, I found Lola reclining next to our open locker, applying my Candy Corn Crush lip gloss with her pinky. Even in the Friday afternoon stampede, students and teachers steered clear of Lola as if she projected her own force field. With her combat boots and torn fishnets, the whole military-Goth thing she had going on could be kind of intimidating. But she was like a Tootsie Pop—hard on the outside but sweet and weirdly awesome on the inside.

"That bad, huh?" Lola asked the moment she spotted me.

"Bad would be an improvement," I replied, and stuffed my books in our locker.

On a scale of 1 to 10, where 1 equals "dumped by your boyfriend of three and a quarter months via text two weeks before senior prom" and 10 equals "winning a reality TV show and being insta-famous," my day was a big, ginormous 1.

Literally. Yep. Tristan ended our romance with a text:
I wan 2 brk up.
That's what he wrote. Didn't even bother with real words.

In my seventeen years, I'd learned that, no matter how heinous your life is, stay tuned for a *Psycho*-style surprise before the credits roll. And whatever higher power you worship—God, Jesus, Allah, Buddha, Zeus, or Lady Gaga—can't save you from the dull, rusty knife.

"So..." Lola looked me up and down, admiring my standard uniform of smart-ass T-shirt (today's: a smiley face with HAVE A MEDIOCRE DAY), cargo pants, and flip-flops. "You need a diversion. What should we do?"

I draped my messenger bag across my torso, tugging my dreadlocks free from the strap. "Starbucks?"

She shook her head. "Already shotgunned two Red Bulls to get through English."

"Movie? That theater down by that one place is showing Hitchcock—"

She raised her hand to interrupt. "Um, that's one of those black-and-white ones, right?"

I nodded.

She waved the idea away. "That's like playing a board game when you've got a Wii."

"But the man knows freepy."

"Freepy. I like that—freaking creepy." She fished the phone out of her faux military jacket and immediately started tweeting. "You have a gift," she said. Lo and I liked to create what we called "the Ripple"—not as in raspberry or caramel fudge—but a ripple of words.

Someone had been the first to utter *whatever* or *crupid*. My dad still periodically, and completely cringeworthily, said *dude*. It was Lola's and my mission to take our linguistic influence global. We'd come close with *borriffic*—terrifically boring. I'd proclaimed Mr. Kramer's third lecture on WWII *borriffic*. A day later I heard some freshman using it in the cafeteria, and three weeks after that one of Lola's friends' friends used the word on Facebook.

"I give it two days before Teek and Jackson are using it as if it were one of *Webster*'s own." Lola's fingers feverishly tapped her phone.

"Monument?" I suggested after she'd tweeted our newest Ripple. I loved D.C.'s morbid décor. I could barely flip my dreads without swatting some monument to dead people. We sometimes picked a D.C. landmark and saw how many tourists' snaps we could sneak into, or we would pretend to be tour guides and feed visitors false info: *Many people don't know this, but the Washington Monument is named for President George Washington's father and shaped like his unnaturally pointy head.*

"Nah. Too much effort." Lola looped her arm through mine and practically dragged me off school premises. "Mall," she decided. Our mecca. "You need a little retail therapy."

Once we'd outpaced all the other Capital Academy refugees, I confessed, "Tristan dumped me." Saying it was like reliving the dumpage all over again. He was my first serious boyfriend and what Lola and I called the trifecta of *G*s—gorgeous, geek, and giggle. He was equal parts good looks, smarts, and sense of humor, and that was a next-to-impossible combo. I wasn't going to marry him or anything, but I thought we might at least make it to graduation.

4

She wrapped me in a too-tight hug. "Icie, I'm soooooo sorry."

I wiggled free. "What a..." I felt the pre-sob throat clench. I wasn't going to lose it. "I mean he's a total..."

Lola squinted and puckered her lips as if she was thinking, then a wicked smile tugged at the corners of her mouth. "Totass."

It took me a second to dissect the word. "Jerzilla."

"Dumboid." She laughed and then glanced at me to make sure it was okay to laugh when my heart had been pulverized like a grande coffee frap hold the whip.

I smiled. "Fridiot."

"Yep, Tristan is the biggest fridiot in D.C."

"America."

"The world."

"Universe."

"Galaxy."

We exploded with laughter. We leaned on each other to steady ourselves. Tears streamed down my cheeks. My sides ached. Our laughter dwindled to sighs. My attitude shifted a smidge. With Lola as my life support, I no longer felt like I was going to die.

As we walked, Lola lit the cigarette she kept stashed in her bra. Even though she turned away to exhale, the cigarette smoke seemed to curl around me. I moved away to find fresh air and wished ditching Tristan's toxicity would be as easy. But his rejection clung to me like smoke. Why did he dump me? Was I so...so...But I couldn't find the right combo—ugly and disgusting? Stupid and revolting? I was never getting a date to prom now.

Lola paused and ground her cigarette into the sidewalk. She shifted all her weight onto the ball of her foot and shredded the stub.

"What's up?" I asked.

"Nothing."

"Nothing?" I nodded toward the cigarette confetti on the sidewalk.

She started walking. "I don't know if I should tell you."

"What?" I grabbed her arm and forced her to stop. I felt a hiccup of panic.

She wouldn't look at me. "Guess you'll find out sooner or later."

"What?" I asked again. The worst thing was not knowing, right?

"The fridiot already posted your breakup on Facebook with one of those winking smiley faces." She patted herself down, searching for another emergency cig. "Teek saw it and told Will, who told Tawn, who told me."

The gossip Ripple was way more powerful than the word Ripple.

Social death by Facebook. I take it back. Knowledge can suck.

I started walking, stomping really, in the general direction of the Metro. My life at Capital Academy was over. I fished out my phone from my cargo pants pocket. I tapped the FB app. My profile picture of Tristan and me stared back. It was taken on our seventh-and-a-half date. (Our first date only counted as half because he didn't take me to the dance, but we left together.) The picture was snapped after we'd seen a double feature of *American Psycho* and the original Hitchcock *Psycho*. He's pretending to stab me in the back with an imaginary knife and I'm mock-screaming in horror. A bit prophetic.

I changed my Facebook status to single and switched my picture to one of Lo and me last summer. We're trying on three-hundred-dollar sunglasses in this snooty boutique, right before the saleslady with the awful orange fake tan kicked us out. I was trying to think of the perfect snarky thing to post about Tristan when Lola caught up to me.

"Listen," she said. "Some things are just not meant to be."

Yeah, but how did you know? What if Tristan and I *were* meant to be? Maybe there was no such thing as meant to be, only shit happens and you make the best of it.

We stopped at the Metro entrance to consult our phones before we went underground. I scrolled through Twitter. Lola had, like, a thousand followers. #Freepy was already multiplying.

I checked Facebook again. Molly "Ho" Andersen had just "liked" Tristan's breakup post. She was such a...As my mind strained for the perfect combo-word, my phone buzzed and my dad's photo flashed on the screen. I'd programmed his ringtone to be the screeching noise from the shower scene in *Psycho*. I ignored it. I needed a proper sulk. I wasn't ready for Dad's platitudes: "Everything happens for a reason" or "See it as an opportunity." I didn't want to "make the best of it" yet.

Before I could put my phone away, those ominous notes from the movie *Jaws* played over and over. A text from Mum. I didn't need the "suck it up you're a Murray" lecture. "Stiff upper lip." "Brave face." "Chin up." "Keep calm and carry on." All that stoic British shit. I'd been dumped and I was entitled to feel like moldy gum on the bottom of last season's stilettos. I shoved the phone into my cargo pants pocket, double-checking that it wasn't the one with the hole. I'd lost about twenty dollars that way.

The telephonic harassment didn't relent. My pants sounded like a horror movie soundtrack. I dug the phone out and flicked to the text messages. They all said the same thing.

911 COME HOME ASAP.

Yeah, we'd come up with that oh-so-difficult-to-decipher code; 911 before any message meant an emergency for real. What family had a secret emergency code? Answer: a family whose mum worked for the federal government and whose dad was a nuclear physicist. We got one of those Barbie-posed, all-purpose holiday cards from the White House, and the president actually signed ours.

Mum and Dad were always getting threats from some activists who were a few crayons short of a sixty-four-pack—if you know what I mean. Mum assured me the threats were no big deal, but we'd still come up with our top secret code.

When I saw the 911 texts, my stomach dropped like it did when I rode Mega Coaster Rama at Flying Flags America. I'd only gotten one 911 from my parents ever, when Dad had his car accident. That message had said:

911 D.C. Mercy Hospital.

"I gotta go," I said to Lola. Suddenly, being dumped by fridiot Tristan didn't matter as much.

Lola paused her texting. "Seriously, Icie?"

"Sorry, Lo," I said with a shrug. "My parents have evoked the code. I'll call you later."

"It's going to be okay," Lola said, hugging me good-bye. "We will either get you another date for prom or you can stay home with me and we'll eat tubes of chocolate-chip cookie dough and watch classic horror movies until we vomit."

"Can I wear my prom dress and killer purple shoes?" I tried to joke. If I could make a joke, then things couldn't be that bad.

"Definitely."

"Later!" I called as I waved down a yellow taxi and texted my parents that I was:

ON MY WAY!

By the time the taxi pulled up in front of our three-story brownstone, I'd talked myself down from the ledge of worry my parents' texts had pushed me toward. Everything looked normal. Flames weren't shooting from our bedroom windows. The street was ambulance- and police-free. I relaxed a little. It couldn't be too terrible if the sun was still filtering through the trees that lined our street and flashing on the tinted windows of the BMWs, Jaguars, and Lexuses parked in a neat row. The nannies for the Smith-Wellses and the Pattersons chatted over strollers with sleeping toddlers. Mrs. Neusbaum in wedge heels that matched her helmet of snow-white hair clip-clopped after her pug, Sir Milo Winterbottom.

I stuffed twenty dollars through the taxi's payment slot and told the driver to keep the change. I climbed the steps to my house two at a time. The door swung open before I reached the top, and Mum pushed past me.

"Wait! Stop!" she shouted at the taxi.

Dad was slumped against the banister in the entryway. "Dad, what's going on?" I asked, and stepped inside. He didn't answer.

The backpack my parents bought for my one and only camping trip was resting at his feet. My SAVE THE PLANET, ROCK THE WORLD button was fastened to the front pocket. The last I remembered, my backpack was stuffed under my bed, and my parents adhered to the progressive parents' handbook and never, ever trespassed in my bedroom.

I scanned from my backpack past Dad's wrinkled khakis and polo to his face. His eyes were red and puffy, and his normally carefully brushed hair looked like he'd had a mishap with hair wax and a pack of wildcats.

"Dad?" My pinprick of worry was now a full-on jugular vein gush.

He wouldn't look at me.

"Dad, what is it? What's the matter?" I asked. My legs turned to rubber. I had to steady myself on the hall table, which caused a vase of white roses to wobble and a pile of mail to avalanche to our recently refinished mahogany floor. Neither Dad nor I made a move to stop the cascade of papers. The slick, glossy cover of Mum's *Modern Politics* mixed uneasily with the dull recycled pages of Dad's *Nuclear Energy Digest*.

Mum burst in. "Okay, the cab's sorted." She shut the door behind her. "Have you told her, Jack?" She looked from Dad to me and back again, tennis-match style. "No, clearly not."

This was the first time I'd seen my parents in the same room in about a month. Dad was a morning person, so he made me homemade granola with fresh blueberries every day for breakfast—because it was my favorite. Mum was the queen of the night, so she checked my homework after the ten o'clock news with a reward of Ben & Jerry's and whatever film was on the Horror Channel. We used to cross paths at dinner, but for the last few months our daily family time had slipped.

"Icie." Mum paused, and it was like watching the battery drain from a toy robot. Her voice and posture softened. "We need to leave D.C."

Dad handed me my backpack. I pushed it away. "Now?" I asked.

"Yes." She pressed an imaginary wrinkle from her skirt. I noticed the transfer of sweat from her palms to the black silk. "Please give me your phone." She held out her hand.

I protectively covered my cargo pants pocket. "But I need it to—" Mum flashed "Talk to the hand" before I could prioritize why I so desperately needed my iPhone: (1) to update Facebook, (2) to text Lola, (3) to listen to the playlists

Lola and I had created, with titles like "Wake Up 'n' Smell the Urine," "Songs to Slit Your Wrists By," and "Make-Out Mix (Virginity Blues)."

The look on her face told me that none of that was important anymore. I handed her my phone. She switched it off and laid it on the hall table. She smoothed a lock of hair that had escaped from the blonde uni-curl she called a bob. "This is serious, Icie. We need to go someplace safe," Mum continued, as if she hadn't just unplugged me from my life.

"What's going on, Mum?" I asked again. "You're scaring me."

"We need to get moving," Mum sort of barked.

"Mum, just because you're British doesn't make you, like, Jasmine Bond." I laughed nervously. My parents didn't.

"Jack, give her the money belt," Mum said, indicating the three-inch-wide beige cloth that lay coiled on the stairs. Dad didn't move. He stood there hugging my backpack. "Bloody hell!" Mum grabbed the belt. "There's ten thousand dollars in here."

Was it ransom? A bribe? I couldn't get my head around what was happening. She lifted my T-shirt and wrapped the money belt around me. I was having a total out-of-body experience. Had I hit my head? Traveled to a parallel universe? Eaten some bad Cheetos?

I stood, arms raised, like a two-year-old letting Mummy dress her. She fastened the belt at my spine. The cloth was cool and stiff. She pulled my shirt down and tugged the hem to straighten my smiley-face iron-on. The bricks of cash cinched my waist like a corset.

"Someone tell me what the hell is going on!" I demanded, and backed away, knocking the hall table again. The white roses toppled off. The vase shattered and water splashed on my cargo pants.

Mum took a deep breath. "You've got to trust us. We need to get out of here."

"We'll get through this, Isis," Dad said, squeezing me and my backpack together.

Mum pulled him off. "God, Jack, we agreed. Get a grip."

My brain didn't know how to process this. There was no combo-word for what I was feeling.

Mum glanced out the window as if she heard someone coming up the sidewalk, which made me look, too. But the scene hadn't changed from a few minutes ago.

"You and your dad get into the taxi and I'll get our bags," Mum said. That's when I noticed a second backpack and Mum's big Prada overnighter by the door.

"Come on, Dad," I said, shouldering my backpack. "It's going to be okay." I don't know why I said it. It clearly didn't feel true, but it's what you say, isn't it? When your life is falling apart, we utter stupid platitudes to make us believe it's not so bad. When I broke my arm when I was six, falling off the slide at the park, Dad had repeated the same phrase all the way to the hospital.

Now he looked at me with these incredibly sad eyes. "You are so brave."

It was easy to be brave-ish when I didn't exactly know what I should be afraid of.

Our home phone rang, making the three of us jump. We

turned toward the phone on the hall table, but none of us made a move to answer it. Mum shuffled through the pile of papers on the floor and pulled out a slightly soggy piece of white paper, spraying drops of water and shattered glass from the vase. She fanned it for a few seconds, drying the wet patches. She studied the now-smudged lines and dots on the page. It looked like some sort of hand-drawn map. She crammed it into the front netting of my backpack.

Mum's volume increased to be heard over the ringing phone. "Let's go." She slung Dad's backpack over one shoulder and clutched her handbag and matching luggage in the other. She looked around as if she had forgotten something.

The phone thankfully stopped ringing. But Dad's cell phone buzzed. He took it from the case clipped to his belt and checked the screen. He and Mum exchanged some coded look. They both switched off their phones and placed them next to mine. What was going on? Mum and Dad without cell phones was like Batman and Robin leaving their utility belts.

And then we all heard it. Sirens in the distance.

Mum opened the door and charged toward the taxi. Dad regained enough composure to snatch his navy blazer from the coatrack and follow me out the front door. We piled into the backseat of the taxi, luggage and all.

"Dulles Airport," Mum told the taxi driver, and slammed the car door. The taxi did a U-turn in the middle of the street.

The sirens were getting closer. Mum and Dad slumped low in the seat.

I opened my mouth to ask a bazillion questions, but Mum shook her head. I understood by the pleading look in her eyes that she needed me to keep quiet and trust her. I pushed back into the seat, wedged awkwardly between my parents.

The sirens were deafening now. Two black SUVs with blue lights on the dashboard blasted past us. I checked the rearview mirror. The SUVs screeched to a stop in front of our house. The taxi driver didn't seem to notice as he aggressively maneuvered around the growing afternoon traffic. What had my parents done? Were we felons fleeing the law?

Mum slipped her hand into mine, and I pried Dad's from his backpack. The sweat from our palms sealed our hands together. They couldn't have committed a crime. This was all some misunderstanding, or the best opening ever to a hidden-camera TV show.

The world looked the same. There was no alien spaceship hovering over the Washington Monument. No mushroom cloud emanating from the direction of the White House. The sky was bright blue, not even a wispy cloud in sight. But everything normal faded away. My life switched from *Glee* to *Drag Me to Hell* in one afternoon.

TWO

"Destiny is a choice, not an option."

—Just Saying 103

BECKETT

"Terrorists destroyed life Out There," Beckett begins as they began, with the end of everything. His heart aches every time he tells their creation story. He can't imagine such devastation or living without the Great I AM to protect and guide him.

"But the Great I AM…" His voice catches. "The Great I AM rose from the darkness and built the community of Forreal to guard the Mountain and its sacred Heart."

He stands near the fire at the center of the Mall, surrounded by his followers. He turns in a slow circle, admiring every face and every fault. They are a patchwork people, resurrected from the broken remains of the Time Before. The Mall is only pine poles and a roof tiled with ancient signs proclaiming fast food and cheap liquor an exit away.

"We are the descendants of Survivors." He keeps his voice low as if he's sharing a secret. "The blood of the Great I AM runs through our veins. We are lucky, but we must be ever vigilant. Evil does not die. It lingers, waiting for opportunity and weakness." He finds no pleasure in the fear that sparks in their wide eyes, but he can never let them forget that their history is not a happy one. They were forged from fear and survived through faith.

"What do Terrorists look like?" The voice is no louder than the crackling of the fire.

"Terrorists have fangs with poisonous venom," another voice booms from the darkness. It's Finch, shattering the stillness of Storytime. He limps on uneven legs around the perimeter beyond the firelight. "Their eagle-like talons are razor sharp for tearing the flesh of innocent victims." Finch curls his slim fingers and claws the air, creating long, grotesque shadows that flicker on the Mountainside.

Everyone shrinks into a tight circle, like the snap of a lasso around the neck of its target. They twist and turn, swatting one another with their dreadlocks, searching for Terrorists.

"Terrorists are black as night and sleek like a snake," Finch booms. He guards the Mountain, and everything about him serves to intimidate his unseen enemy. He coats his body with the Mountain's dull earth to camouflage himself on his patrols. His short dreadlocks stand like spikes. He wears a loincloth like Beckett, but his is stained with blood from hunting. A smile tugs at Finch's lips. Does he think frightening everyone is funny?

"Enough, Finch," Beckett says before Finch can continue with his scary story. "We have never seen a Terrorist, not in our eighteen years of life and not in the lifetimes of our dads and mums." Finch is only sharing the stories that have been passed from generation to generation.

"Just because we haven't seen them doesn't mean they aren't watching us even now." Finch laughs and fades back into the night.

"'Everything will be okay.' So Says the Great I AM." Beckett weaves among the Cheerleaders and rockstars seated on the rubber tires that surround the fire pit. Beckett lays a hand on one head and playfully tugs at another's dreadlocks. "The Great I AM will protect us like we have protected the Mountain for hundreds of years. And one day Mumenda will come and we will be free."

Beckett returns to the inner circle and stands with his back to the fire. "Let's form the sacred symbol and join in our Evening Tune."

Everyone takes his or her place in two connecting loops with Beckett at the center. He bows his head and closes his eyes. A calm like the moment before wake succumbs to sleep envelops him. He can feel the Great I AM's presence as sure as he feels his best friends beside him now—Harper on one side and Finch on the other.

Beckett leads Forreal in their Evening Tune. "Tonight's got promise," he calls.

Everyone repeats, "Promise!"

"Tonight's got faith," he sings.

"Faith!"

"Tonight's all we got." He is overwhelmed with the joy of song and the Great I AM's spirit. He wishes everyone could feel the Great I AM's presence like he does.

"For sure! For sure!" all of Forreal choruses.

As they continue the Tune, Beckett opens his eyes. He no longer needs to think about the words; they are like breathing. He looks up at Finch, who is a full head taller than everyone else. Like a stick figure drawn in the burned dust of the Mountain, Finch's bony body forms awkward, sharp angles.

One by one Beckett surveys each Cheerleader and rockstar lined up around him. The youngest only four. The oldest nearly forty. With bowed heads, their dreadlocks shade their bronze faces. Each person is unique, as if the Great I AM sculpted them from the Mountain's clay. Finch with his limp. His little sister Atti's wide-set eyes. Birdy born with only one arm. Tom with more toes than the others. May with her hunched back. Beckett believes the body has no true form.

Beckett's gaze finally rests on Harper. Even though Tom is holding her other hand, he keeps her at a rigid arm's length. She smiles when she catches Beckett's eye.

Harper stands out with her blue eyes, blonde hair that refuses to coil into dreadlocks, and pale skin that tans in blotches, leaving her with polka dots of white. She and Beckett were only five when she wandered onto the Mountain. Beckett found her. He believed that she was a Survivor and the Great I AM had led her to the Mountain. He held on to Harper and wouldn't let go, not even when the Cheerleaders tried to pull them apart. "If she goes, I go," he'd shouted. She's been at Beckett's side ever since. The others are afraid of her because her body is imperfectly perfect and she survived Out There among the Terrorists.

When the Evening Tune finishes, Beckett waits until all eyes are upon him. "Join me in our Saying of Dedication. Great I AM, protector of sacred Mountain..." His voice rings a beat before the others as they recite the Saying:

> *"Whatever!*
> *Whatever!*
> *The bad, the good.*
> *Whatever!*
> *I put my faith in the Great I AM.*
> *The Great I AM alone."*

Beckett raises his hand and twists his arm to expose the curved, red looping lines on his wrist. Beckett was born with the mark of the Great I AM. He is Cheer Captain, chosen to lead Forreal because the Great I AM etched this slim figure eight among the blue veins and the bump of his artery. The rest of Forreal similarly extend their arms. Everyone over twelve years old has a matching scar the size and shape of Beckett's birthmark.

"Whatever." Beckett proclaims the one-word Saying—so dense with meaning. With that simple word, he gives himself to the will of the Great I AM. It's Forreal's abbreviation for remembering that their lives are in service to their higher power. Whatever the Great I AM needs, wants, or desires. Beckett is at peace because whatever happens, the Great I AM will protect him. He feels the power of the Great I AM flow through him.

Everyone chants, "Whatever. Whatever. Whatever," declaring their love and rededicating themselves to the Great I AM.

Every Cheerleader and rockstar files past Beckett. He shakes each hand and smiles until his cheeks hurt.

Atti taps Beckett on the arm. "Cheer Captain," she says, and continues to tap. She is one of the most unique rockstars. Her eyes are permanently droopy and sad. Her torso is long, but her legs are short.

"You know you can call me Beckett." He takes her hand in his.

She giggles. "I like to say Cheer Captain."

"Okay," he says, and kneels down so they are eye to eye. "Did you have something to tell me?"

"Did Terrorists take my mum?" She blinks up at him.

Beckett is surprised and saddened by her question. Atti's mum disappeared a month ago. "I don't know what happened to your mum." Beckett always answers honestly no matter how much the truth hurts. "I have asked the Great I AM to protect her."

Atti slips her hand out of Beckett's. "Could you ask the Great I AM to send her back?"

"If it is the Great I AM's will, your mum will return to the Mountain." Beckett points to his best friend. "You know Harper, don't you?" Harper waves.

Atti nods and nods. "She's helping me study for my Walk of Enlightenment."

"Well, the Great I AM led Harper to the Mountain, so maybe the Great I AM will show your mum the way home too."

"Sorry, Beckett." Finch hugs his little sister away from Beckett. "Atti asks too many questions."

Beckett stands. "There are never too many questions." He winks at Atti.

"See," Atti singsongs. "What did I tell you? I was just asking about Mum—"

"We shouldn't bother the Cheer Captain with that now," Finch interrupts. "We have to patrol the Mountain soon."

As if on cue, the Timekeeper calls out, "Nine and twelve." Cheerleaders and rockstars disperse. Beckett loves Forreal's efficiency. Everyone has a role and responsibilities before Forreal can sleep.

Beckett, Harper, and Finch start their evening patrol at the base of the Mountain. Lucky is waiting for them. The black cat bounds ahead and then pauses to make sure they are following. Beckett is relieved to see Lucky. A black cat has always roamed the Mountain.

Beckett winds among the rocky burial mounds that create a barrier between the Mountain and Out There. He has memorized the name of each Cheerleader and rockstar buried there. Some graves are six feet long, some only two. He likes to believe that Forreal's ancestors are still keeping watch.

Beckett, Harper, Finch, and Lucky take the well-worn path up the Mountain. Huge boulders jet from the ground at odd angles as if tossed randomly from above. The ground levels as they make their way past the cave and rusty metal and pine structures that make up Forreal. They pause to drink from the Mountain spring bubbling in its stone-lined pool. It's an oasis of green in the Mountain's dull monotony. They check the nearby communal gardens and the trenches farther up the Mountain .that form the Necessary. They pick their way through scraggly scrub brush and prickly ankle-high cacti. The barren landscape conceals nothing. They often see rattlesnakes, scorpions, and coyotes making their own deadly rounds.

As they ascend, the air cools. Scrub brush gives way to Joshua trees that from a distance look as if they've been hand-drawn by a rockstar. Farther up, a band of pine trees create welcome cover. Beckett leads Finch and Harper to the Crown of thorns that circles the Mountain and marks the line that no one is allowed to cross. Beckett squints through the wall of twisted brambles as if he might glimpse the Heart of the Mountain. It's up there somewhere. It's what makes their Mountain special. It's what they guard and what the Great I AM died to protect.

Beckett follows the Crown to the Other Side of the Mountain with Harper close behind, but Finch takes his time, investigating every strange sound and shadow. The Man-Made Mountains come into view. Beckett can't believe Terrorists created those unnatural, jagged shapes that litter the valley below.

Something flashes in the distance. Beckett tells himself it's only a trick of moonlight. But there it is again. A light flickers in one of the Man-Made Mountains.

Harper gasps as another and another point of light dot the skyline like a plague of fireflies.

"What is it?" Harper asks, hugging herself and swaying slightly. The lights seem to have triggered a fear in Harper from long ago. She has no memory of her time before the Great I AM led her to the Mountain.

Beckett's eyes unfocus and the dozen lights scattered in the darkness transform into fuzzy balls, extending sparkling rays to one another.

"It's Terrorists...." Finch's voice makes Beckett and Harper jump. "They have returned as I knew they would." Finch scans the horizon as if he expects to see a Terrorist rising out of the darkness.

"Maybe it's Survivors," Harper whispers.

Beckett opens himself to the Great I AM. "Those lights are a sign," he says as the thought springs to his mind.

Beckett connects this new constellation of earthly stars, and they begin to take shape and meaning. "I see a heart." He traces the shape in the air.

"Where?" Harper asks.

He slips behind her so they are cheek to cheek. He shows her how to connect the dots. "See?" he asks. She leans into him. "Let us ask the Great I AM to direct us."

"And protect us," Finch adds.

Beckett repeats the Saying of Dedication. When he finishes, Harper and Finch chorus, "Whatever. Whatever. Whatever." Their volume increases with each word.

"We can't tell anyone about this," Beckett says, transfixed by the lights. He knows this will change everything. Harper is the only Survivor they've seen in generations. And what if Finch is right? What if the Terrorists have returned? "We don't want people to start panicking."

Finch cracks the knuckles on one hand and then the other. "We can't wait until Terrorists attack."

"We don't know for sure that it's Terrorists," Beckett says.

"Maybe it's just light," Harper mutters.

"We will guard our Mountain and ask the Great I AM for guidance." Beckett feels it all around him—an electricity he can't explain. *Endings are beginnings*, so Says the Great I AM. But he's not sure whether this is the beginning or the end.

THREE

.

None of us said a word all the way to the airport. The moment the taxi parked curbside, Mum pushed us out and gathered us into a huddle. Dad had sniffed in time to the Beatles song on the oldies station playing in the taxi. His eyes were bloodshot, but his face looked almost normal again.

"Here are your boarding passes," Dad said, pulling out three trifolded sheets of paper from his blazer pocket and handing one to me and one to Mum. My eyes zoomed in on the destination.

Vegas? What in the hell sent you running to the land of Elvis impersonators, slot machines, neon nightlife, and

Cirque du something? Was Dad's nuclear physicist gig only a cover for mob connections? Did Mum have a gambling problem? Were we in some sort of witness protection program? You could get lost in Vegas. From what I'd seen on the original *CSI*, weird was a way of life.

"We aren't sitting next to each other on the plane." Dad turned to me. "If anyone asks, you are traveling alone to meet your grandparents."

"Are Grandma and Grandpa Murray meeting us there?" I asked, hopeful that maybe this wasn't so horrible after all.

Dad swallowed hard. "No, but that's your story. Your mum is heading there for a conference, and I'm meeting some college buddies for the weekend."

Panic and confusion knotted in my brain.

"Let's just go, Jack," Mum blurted, and adjusted her purse strap on her shoulder.

"We should split up," Dad said. "At the gate and on the plane, don't acknowledge each other, okay?"

Wait. No. This is happening too fast. Brain malfunction.

"If anything happens..." Dad continued.

"Like. What?" I spoke slowly and enunciated each word. I needed everything to slow down.

"Just act like you don't know anything." Dad was breathing faster, talking faster.

"I *don't* know anything," I whisper-shouted.

Mum checked her watch. "It's time, Jack."

WTF! Seriously, WTF!

They both dropped their bags, and Dad pulled Mum into a fierce embrace. Mum's fingers clawed his back, creating

26

webs of wrinkles in his shirt. Mum's sudden flare of emotion scared me more than Dad's tears. Mum didn't believe in public displays of affection—or private ones, really.

"Go, Jack," Mum said, and pushed him away.

Dad hugged me until I thought my ribs might crack. "I love you, Icie. Always remember that."

Shit. Shit. SHIT! That sounded like good-bye.

"Dad?" I didn't even know what to say. I caught the sleeve of his shirt.

"It's going to be okay, Isis," Dad said, and did this weird laugh as if something was so funny. Then his face got all serious. "We are going to divide and conquer," he whispered. "I'll see you at the gate, and if not, then the bunker." He picked up his backpack, zigzagged through the traffic, and disappeared in the chaos of travelers.

"Bunker?" I looked from the spot where my everyday average dad used to stand to my wannabe superhero mum. "What's he talking about?"

Mum grabbed my elbow and ushered me through the airport. It looked like it always did, as if people had been poured in and stirred. My parents were freaking, but it didn't appear as if anyone else was. We headed straight for the security checkpoint.

"Mum, please tell me what's going on." I tried to stop, but she just kept dragging me forward. Now I was getting angry. She couldn't scoot me along the game board like that silver Scottie dog in Monopoly. I planted my feet. "I'm not going anywhere until you tell me—"

"Okay. Okay. Don't make a scene." She was looking

around wildly. "This way." She pointed to a sign with the universal symbol for bathroom. I followed Mum into the unisex/handicapped/diaper-changing bathroom. It smelled of bleach and lemon with a whiff of stinky baby diapers. She locked the door.

"Icie, please calm down, and I'll tell you what I know." Mum took a deep breath. "An attack is being planned for multiple cities." She looked as if it was causing her physical pain to say the next words. "We think D.C. is one. It's a credible threat."

"Do you mean bombs?" I paced from toilet to door.

She looked around as if they might have cameras in the bathroom. "No, the most recent intel is about a bioterrorist attack."

"A bio-what?"

"A fast-spreading and deadly virus. The initial projections are staggering. We need to get out of D.C."

Then it hit me. I mean really hit me. I was falling, drowning, and being electrocuted all at once. My mind flashed to every apocalyptic movie I'd ever seen—world wars, alien attacks, explosions, floods, tsunamis, bombs, plagues. My knees gave out and I plopped down on the toilet.

"Do you remember where your dad and I met?" Mum asked.

I nodded, confused about her sudden stroll down memory lane. They were on some committee that had to do with strategic planning—Mum's expertise—and nuclear waste—my dad's. It had some whacked name like *Preventing Inadvertent Intrusion into blah, blah, bleugh.* I always thought

28

it sounded like the slogan for a new contraceptive device. "You met on that mountain outside Las Vegas."

"That's right," she said. "We're going there."

I squinted, trying to let what she was saying sink in. "You mean we are going to Las Vegas." She certainly didn't mean the nuclear waste repository. The one that was the subject of the committee that brought my parents together. The one that was supposed to store all the nuclear waste generated by the nuclear power plants in the country. She couldn't mean that, because that would be beyond crupid.

"We're going to the bunker deep inside the mountain."

Mum was telling me we were going miles underground with the same tone she used to invite me shopping at Saks. My body started doing this weird earthquake thing.

"Seriously?" Had I joined the movie already in progress? Did I miss the part where my mum's body was probed by aliens or inhabited by a demon?

"Let me finish—"

But I didn't. "We are going underground with nuclear gunk."

"No. It's not like that. Construction was never finished on the facility," Mum stated matter-of-factly. "No one wants nuclear waste in their backyard. It's a political mine-field. Funding was cut, so the bunker inside the mountain has never been used."

"Is it safe?" It felt as if she was giving me the rock-and-hard-place option. Bio-attack or buried alive? Some choice.

"Now it's just a big, empty tunnel into the heart of the mountain. They dug part of the main tunnel and conducted lots of geological studies to make sure that the site would be safe for the long-term storage of nuclear waste. It was never more than a research site."

"But the nuclear waste..."

"Billions more dollars would have to be spent to make the mountain ready to store the waste. Nuclear waste isn't like shoving a box of old clothes in the attic. It takes a very complex system of—" Mum suddenly stopped midsentence and then seemed to switch channels. "Icie, I don't have time to tell you any more now. You have to trust me. I think it's the only place we'll be safe." Her voice quivered. "We need to forget about everything else and get to the mountain."

Get to the mountain, I repeated the phrase, zombielike, in my brain.

She removed the piece of paper that she'd stuffed in my backpack earlier. She placed it on my lap, smoothing out the wrinkles. "Las Vegas is here," she said, pointing off the side of the page toward my knee. "The bunker is in this mountain." She pointed her fire engine–red fingernail to the middle of a series of three upside-down *V*'s. If the paper were flipped upside down, it might look like a flock of pterodactyls. Two squiggly parallel lines ran across the page and were marked with a highway number. There were two dots with what might be names of cities.

I studied the map. "That's in the middle of nowhere, isn't it?" I asked.

"That's the way they designed it," she replied. "They didn't want people stumbling onto it by accident. We experimented with how to mark the site with 'Do Not Enter' signs that would last for hundreds of thousands of years. We'd need to make sure that everyone would know to stay away. These markers would have to say 'keep out' in a way that future generations might understand. There's a ring of thorns and a—"

"This is insane." I tried to push past her, but she didn't budge.

"Listen to me. I want you to know how to identify the mountain." She wasn't shouting, but her voice was forceful. I imagined that was the voice she used to talk to the president and all the other bigwigs. "Your dad and I used to call it the infinity project, so we marked the mountain and the tunnel entrance with an infinity symbol. You know what that is, don't you?"

"Yeah, it's a thin, horizontal figure eight." I drew the symbol in the air.

She folded the map in half and in half again and slipped it in my messenger bag. "If something happens to your dad and me—"

"What's going to happen to you and Dad?" I interjected.

"Nothing, but, if something does, do whatever you have to do to get to that spot. Okay?" She squared off with me, a hand on each shoulder. "Icie, promise me you'll do whatever you have to do to make it to the mountain."

There were two short, sharp knocks on the door. Mum froze.

"Can you hurry it up in there?" a female voice shouted through the door.

"Just a second," Mum called back. Then she pulled me

close and whispered, "Your dad and I have breached national security by running away. We weren't supposed to tell any-one what's going on, but we had to at least try to protect you. You can't tell anyone what I've just told you."

I thought I was going to vomit. I'd never felt terror like this before. It ripped through me like a—well, like an explosion.

Mum checked her watch. "We need to get going, Icie, or we'll miss our plane."

"Should we really be on a plane if—"

"We need to get out of D.C., and it's the fastest way. I think we have twenty-four hours before the initial attack. If it happens, it could take weeks for the virus to spread, and—"

She was interrupted by a pounding on the door. "Hurry up!" The voice was male this time.

"H-how l-long?" I stammered. "How long will we need to stay underground?" I couldn't believe I was saying it. It was admitting that all this was for real.

"A few months." Mum smoothed her hair. On my best day with my dreads and wrinkled T-shirts, I never looked as in control as my mum did right now with the world com-ing to an end. I wondered whether this would be the last memory I'd have of normal—a stinky airport toilet, the air heavy with what-ifs.

I had so many questions. "How do you and Dad know all this?" I knew she worked in the White House, but after that any job details got a little fuzzy. "If something was, you know, it would be on the news. People should—"

The pounding was nonstop now—both the fist on the bathroom door and the hammering of my heart.

"Icie, we can discuss all this later. For now, let's just think positive. We are going to get through this. At least we have a chance," Mum said as if she could read my mind.

I shouldered my backpack. I erased all the end-of-the-world scenarios that kept popping into my mind like annoying Internet ads. If only I could switch my brain off or download some firewall to prevent these images from causing my brain to crash. I needed to be strong. I wanted to be strong.

"Let's go," Mum said, and opened the bathroom door. Eight pairs of hateful eyes glared at us. "Sorry," Mum said as she muscled a path through them.

I diverted my eyes when I noticed that the old lady waiting had a cane. There was a red-faced mother holding her crying baby and a man resting his hand on a wheelchair with a young boy who had casts on both legs. I wondered if all these people would be dead soon. What right did I have to this secret, safe place? I added guilt to the whirlpool of feelings crashing through me.

We marched right up to the security checkpoint. When we were nearly next in line, the security guard's radio squawked. Mum's eyes widened as we both heard a description of Dad come over her radio. Maybe it wasn't him. His description matched that of nearly every middle-aged man in America. Mum took a compact out of her handbag. She flipped it open and used the mirror to look behind her. She dabbed the powder puff at the rays of wrinkles around her eyes. I couldn't see the reflection, but I could tell by Mum's expression that she'd seen something alarming. When she put the compact away, her hands were shaking.

"You get to the gate, and we'll meet you there," she whispered, so close that her lips touched my ear. She slipped a necklace over her head. It had been concealed under her shirt. A strange-looking key dangled on the end of a sturdy silver chain, not like the dainty kind Mum usually wore, but the kind security guards had hanging from their belts. She slipped it over my head and tucked it under my shirt. "This will open and lock the bunker."

I shook my head, dreads flapping. "No, no, no, no…" If she was giving me the key to the thingy whatsit, then that meant she wasn't sure if she and Dad were going to make the plane.

"This is just in case," Mum said.

"I can't, Mum." I couldn't move my body, as if it had hardened in concrete.

"You've got to, Icie." Mum had what Dad and I called her "Don't Mess With Me Face." Set jaw. Narrowed eyes. Flared nostrils. That's how she looked at me now. "Right now you are your biggest obstacle. You've got to think positive. You can do this. Go to the gate and get on the plane. Your dad has another key. If worst comes to worst, we'll meet you at the bunker."

"Mum…"

She leaned in again and whispered, "Icie, we stole the

keys to the bunker. We did all this for you. There's no turning back now. Don't let us down."

She dug around in her handbag. "How silly of me," she said with too much false enthusiasm. "I've left my driver's license at check-in." She seemed to be putting on a show for anyone watching.

"Next," the security lady said, extending her hand for my documents.

"Go ahead, and I'll meet you at the gate." She hugged me. "I love you."

"Love you too," I choked out. Everyone probably thought I was some stupid kid crying when I had to leave my mummy. All these lines and lines of people had no idea. They thought today was just like any other day—and maybe it was. Maybe Mum was wrong. Maybe someone would stop the attack.

Mum walked away. She didn't look back. Her shoulders straightened as she marched off.

I had to be strong. Mum and Dad had sacrificed too much for me to lose it now. I handed my boarding pass and driver's license to the security woman perched on a stool. She looked from the documents to me, circled something on my boarding pass, and then handed my stuff back. When my backpack and I were all scanned, I turned around hoping to catch a glimpse of Mum. But it wasn't the final farewell shot I'd imagined. She was surrounded by security and being led away.

FOUR

"Some things are just not meant to be."
—Just Saying 23

HARPER

"Race you to the spot," Harper says, but doesn't wait for Beckett's reply. She zigzags around the Mountain. Every inch of her skin is covered to protect her from the sun's burning rays. Scraps of material are twisted and tied around her body.

She leads Beckett and Lucky to the Other Side of the Mountain. She needs to get Beckett alone. She slows when she sees the rocky outcrop up ahead, the place where Beckett found her thirteen years ago.

"Are you okay?" Beckett asks when he catches up to her. Beckett's features are like chiseled rock—strong and solid. His deep brown eyes radiate warmth. He has a shock of white that splits his jet-black dreadlocks. His is the first face she looks for in the morning and the last image she sees before she falls asleep each night.

Harper shrugs.

He tugs at the frayed knots on her arms. "You looked like you were being attacked by butterflies with these pieces flapping as you ran."

She likes the image of butterflies lifting her off the Mountain.

"Why don't we find you some clothes that fit properly?" His finger finds a small patch of skin. She melts at his touch but elbows him away so maybe he won't notice the red rising in her cheeks.

"I don't mind using the scraps." She adjusts the material to cover any exposed skin.

They stare out at the Man-Made Mountains below. Lucky winds a figure eight around their legs. Harper recalls the lights in the valley the night before and shivers.

"What's the matter?" Beckett says, draping his arm across her shoulders.

She curls into him ever so slightly. "I can't believe I was Out There once, but…"

"You've remembered something, haven't you?"

She nods, too afraid to put these new memories into words.

She keeps staring straight ahead, even though she can feel his gaze upon her. "Last night, the lights in the Man-Made Mountains triggered something. I've been seeing flashes of images, nothing that makes sense. It's like fragments of a story."

"Maybe it's just a dream," Beckett says, and draws her in.

She closes her eyes so she can concentrate on his touch, but the visions start again. Something is emerging from the darkness.

It's coming after her. Her eyes spring open and search the landscape. *It's not real*, she tells herself, but it feels as if she's being watched.

"I think I'm remembering things from before," she says as the images come into focus. She's dreaming and remembering at the same time. "There are three bodies lying on the floor. There's blood everywhere. My ears ring with the most horrible bangs." She covers her ears because the sounds seem to ricochet inside her.

"You are safe," Beckett says. "The Great I AM will protect you." He pauses and places a kiss on her forehead. "I'll protect you."

She wants him to hold her and make everything else go away.

"Beckett," Harper says, "about those lights last night."

"Yeah," he murmurs, and scoops Lucky into his arms. The cat's fur looks chocolate brown in the bright sunlight.

"Beckett, I've been thinking…" Her voice trails off. Lucky squirms in Beckett's arms and Beckett releases her.

"Dangerous thing to do." He playfully knocks his shoulder into hers.

"I, well, it's just…" She glances at him out of the corner of her eye. He said those lights last night formed a heart. Maybe it is a sign. Maybe it's time for her to confess that her feelings for him have changed, deepened. Maybe he feels it too.

Suddenly Lucky crouches as if preparing to pounce. Her black pointy ears flatten against her head.

"Did you hear that?" Beckett whispers.

Harper sweeps Beckett behind her. Adrenaline erases everything except her need to protect him. Lucky races off.

"I thought I heard something," Beckett says calmly. He never panics, because he believes the Great I AM watches over him.

Harper hears it now. The faintest shuffle as foot displaces dirt. It could be Finch patrolling the Mountain, but his strides are usually swift and uneven.

There it is again. She triangulates the sound. It's coming from somewhere below. "Wait here while I check it out," she says, and heads down the Mountain. He doesn't obey; instead he follows her.

Harper notices swirls of dust dancing low to the ground. The path dead-ends at a nearly shear wall of rock. A Forreal-shaped figure is scrambling up the rock. Its long, golden curls are pasted with sweat to its neck and shoulders. Its hair is the color of Harper's when she bothers to wash it in the Mountain spring. It's wearing clothes like the others in Forreal do, salvaged from the Time Before, more holes than material. Its pale legs are scratched and bloody. When it reaches the highest point, it turns around and locks sparkling green eyes on Harper.

It transforms into a girl about the same age as Harper. Harper can't believe what she's seeing. It's almost like looking at her reflection in still water, but Harper is lean and fit and this girl is curvy and soft. Is she dreaming again?

Beckett is at Harper's side. A ray of sun illuminates the girl, casting a halo around her. He raises his hands to show he means her no harm. Her eyes scan him from his bare feet to his loincloth. Harper thinks the girl lingers on his nearly naked torso before focusing on the white streak in his jet-black hair.

The girl's lips twitch in a slight smile, and then she disappears down the other side. Beckett scales the rock, but Harper can't move. All these disparate images are falling into place. A picture is forming in her head. In this vision, she's no bigger than a rock-star. Shadows claim everything but the image of a girl so much like the one she's just seen. The girls—the one now and the one then—have the same features and coloring as Harper. But in the dream, the girl's face is contorted in anger. She's pointing something at Harper. It's a weapon of some sort. The air explodes with a flash and smoke and the most deafening bang.

"Beckett!" she screams, and climbs up after him. Her voice echoes among the hard surfaces. He doesn't know the girl is dangerous. She grabs his ankle.

"Harper, what are you doing?" He shakes free and pulls himself up on top of the rock. Harper catapults herself upward. She wraps her arms around him and anchors him to the spot. Her panic makes her stronger.

She buries her face in his back. "Thank the Great I AM."

"I have to go after her." He tries to wriggle out of Harper's grasp.

"It's not safe," she says. "Not with Terrorists Out There."

"She's not safe," he says, but stops fighting.

His eyes are trained on the blonde figure moving at a steady speed down the Mountain. They watch her until she disappears into the desert.

Beckett closes his eyes. His lips are moving. Harper knows he's sharing his secret hopes and fears with the Great I AM instead of with her.

"Beckett," she says, because she can't take the silence.

"The Great I AM has led another Survivor to the Mountain," he says. "You shouldn't have stopped me."

40

Part of her is jealous of this spirit that will always come first with him. The only thing she truly worships and trusts and believes in is Beckett.

"She looks..." Beckett doesn't finish his sentence. She knows what he was going to say: *The girl looks just like you.* She couldn't be the girl in Harper's vision, but Harper knows there's some connection.

"Let's continue our patrol," Beckett says, and heads up the Mountain, away from the girl and Harper.

"What should we do?" Harper asks, struggling to catch up to him.

"Nothing," Beckett says. "And we can't tell anyone else about the girl or the lights until we understand the significance of these events."

It's not like Beckett to keep secrets. "Why?"

"The Great I AM will reveal everything when it's time," Beckett says with an assurance that she suddenly finds irritating. The lights. These new images. The girl. Beckett can wait for the Great I AM's pronouncement, but Harper already knows— these are bad signs.

FIVE

My parents never showed. I waited as long as I could to board the plane. I'd kept my head down, afraid that the police, airport rent-a-cops, FBI, Secret Service, CIA, or some black-op commandos that were too top secret for a name might come after me. Once I was on the plane, I'd scanned every row for my mum's blonde bob and my dad's whacked do. I'd even asked for a glass of water in the back galley and tried to infiltrate the first-class toilets to get a second and third look at all the passengers.

I didn't cry until the wheels on flight 868 to Las Vegas left solid ground. I curled toward the porthole and watched Washington, D.C., transform into a grid of twinkle lights. I cried for what I was leaving behind and for what might lie ahead. My life had become a jigsaw puzzle dumped from an imageless box. I didn't know how I was ever going to be able to put it back together again. Tears dripped down my chin. I wasn't strong or smart enough for this bizarre treasure hunt my parents had concocted.

I felt a tap on my shoulder.

"You mind if I sit here?" The voice was young and female.

"Whatever." I scooted closer to the window.

"The guy next to me had eye-watering BO," she said, and dropped into the seat beside me. "You okay?"

I sniffed and then I did that thing, which I hadn't done since I was a little, where your face seems possessed; you gasp in tiny breaths and your lower lip quivers.

"Yeah, fine," I said in a pseudo-normal voice.

"Let me know if you'd like to talk to a total stranger about whatever is bugging you."

I sniffed back a ginormous wad of snot. "Thanks."

Inside I turned as black as the world outside my window. I cried until my body felt gooey. Somewhere over the Midwest, sleep hijacked my brain.

After what could have been minutes or hours, I felt another tap on my shoulder. "Something to drink?"

It took a moment for me to register where I was. My reality felt more like a dream. It was a simple question, but I had no answer. I shook my head.

"Come on. You've got to have something. It's a long flight," my seatmate said. "Two Diet Cokes," she told the flight attendant.

I shifted in my seat so my tray table could be lowered. I lifted my shirt collar to my forehead and wiped my face on the backside of the smiley logo on my T-shirt. I loosened a few dreadlocks by each temple and wrapped them around my spindly mass of hair, knotting them so air cooled my neck.

The flight attendant placed a plastic cup of ice and a can of Diet Coke in front of me. I poured some Diet Coke into the cup and watched the fizz bubble up. I took a sip.

Two snack-size bags were thrust in my field of vision. "I always bring my own snacks. Cheesy or salty?" my seat-mate said, and rattled the contents. "Or we could share." She ripped open both and set them on my tray table.

How could I be so hungry, yet feel as if I couldn't eat a thing? The last morsel of food to cross my lips was a bag of Cheetos at lunch.

"I usually like the sour cream and onion, but that makes my breath reek," the girl said. "The last thing you need is someone polluting your airspace. Am I right?"

I looked at her for the first time. She was bald, which for some strange reason made me avert my gaze. I tried not to stare, but I had seen zero bald-headed girls in real life. I wanted to reach out and touch her smooth scalp.

"Want one?" She pulled an orange squiggle from the bag marked CHEESOODLES. The word made me think of my and Lola's Ripples. Would I ever see Lola again? Tears threatened.

"It's not cheese and it's not a noodle, yet it's called a Cheesoodle," the girl said with a laugh. "Who comes up with this?" A solitary tear leaked from the corner of my eye. She must have noticed because she said, "Hey, hey. Don't get upset. It's only cheese—well, kind of sort of a cheese product." She plopped it in her mouth. The powdery orange from the Cheesoodle coated her lips and fingers. "Not so bad," she said, shoving a few more in her mouth. "Good for whatever's bringing you down and, if not, you'll die a year earlier from all the preservatives. That's win-win!"

Win-win. My mum said that all the time. I would see my mum again. Mum and Dad would meet me at the mountain. They just had to. I wiped one tear only to have another one replace it. "Sorry about..." I indicated the blubbering mess, which used to be a normal face.

"No problem," she said, stuffing a few more Cheesoodles in her mouth.

She was Asian American and had the most amazing deep brown, almond-shaped eyes rimmed with jet-black eyeliner that drew to a point at the corner. Her lashes were thick and matted together, giving her eyes a weight that made you forget her bare scalp. Countless earrings dotted each lobe as if providing a message in Braille. She wore a long-sleeved, button-down pink shirt that seemed out of place with her faded, ripped jeans. The words CHEER CAPTAIN were embroidered on the breast pocket of the shirt.

I forced myself to eat a potato chip. I ate another and then another. Before I knew it, the bag was empty. "Um, sorry. I didn't mean..."

"No problem. Food is the best medicine." She looked up as if there were something immensely fascinating about the ceiling. "Or, wait, is that laughter? Laughter is the best medicine, right after these." She nudged the Cheesoodles closer to me. "You need them more than I do."

"Thanks." I was a real conversationalist. "Beyond horrible day," I offered in way of explanation. I finished the rest of the Cheesoodles. "Are you from Vegas?" I asked when the carbs and artificial colors kicked in.

"Nope. I live with my dad in La La Land, you know, L.A. Los Angeles," she said. She fidgeted with the abnormally large pink watch on her wrist. The band was hot-pink rubber, and the square watch face was rimmed with diamonds. I could hear the seconds *tick, tick, tick*ing away. "But my mom lives near D.C. I was supposed to meet my cheer squad at a national competition there," she said finally. "State champs two years running. I got a message from the coach that the competition has been canceled."

"Weird."

"Mom and Dad had some fight over the phone about what to do with me. Mom was supposed to be dropping me off at the cheer competition hotel and then she was going to some convention. Dad wasn't expecting me home. I think he was having a slumber party with his new girlfriend. Mom bought me a ticket on the next plane—but she couldn't get a direct flight. I've got a two-hour layover before I get to ruin my dad's weekend. Fantastic, huh?" She gulped the rest of her Diet Coke. "I'm Marissa," she said, a cheerleader perkiness springing into her voice. I almost expected her to spell it with a double clap between each letter.

"I'm Isis, but everyone calls me Icie," I said, realizing for the bazillionth time how ridiculous both sounded.

"Suits you. The white hair. Dreadlocks. Blue eyes. I get it." She nodded her approval. "Or is it because you're like a mega-bitch from hell?"

"Not a *mega*-bitch," I joked.

We kept our conversation light and I almost forgot that something huge and horrible might be about to happen. I told her about being dumped after I'd already found the perfect dress for prom. Shimmering, silky lavender—sexy but not slutty. She shared her string of bad boyfriends. She caught one kissing another cheerleader. The next only had one thing on his mind; it was the traditional male preoccupation but with quite a pervy twist. The final in her string of breakups was the guy she thought was "the one," until she found out that he already had not one but two kids by different "ones."

"That's when I shaved my head." She raked her fist across her scalp as if she had the electric razor in her hand. "I thought it was getting in the way. All guys saw was the long black hair and these." She gestured to what must have been size quadruple-G breasts. "Can't do much about the rack, so I decided to simplify my life. Now I focus on my sport."

The captain came over the plane's intercom. Our flight was being diverted to Phoenix. The rest of his message was lost in the excited utterances of my fellow passengers.

The gods were giving me a cosmic smackdown. I'd almost begun to believe that my parents had been mistaken, but diverting planes couldn't be good. Mum had said attacks were planned for big cities, and Vegas was one of the biggest. All the panic from earlier came flooding back. I looked out my window. It was pitch-black. Anything could be happening down there. I gripped the armrests because real, raw fear took hold. The other passengers weren't happy, but they weren't terrified like I was.

If it was a virus, then any of these people could be infected. What if Mum was wrong about the timing? What if some deadly virus was being recirculated right now in the plane's stale air? I held my breath, like that might actually do some good. I held it for as long as I could before exhaling in one burst.

"You okay?" Marissa looked at me as if I were an escaped mental patient.

"Yeah" was all I could say. I moved as far away from her as my seat belt would allow. I decided right then that I wanted as little contact with other people as possible, not only because they might be infecting me but also because I had a secret and I wasn't sure how long I could keep it. Marissa was clueless. Maybe I should warn her, tell everybody, but who would believe me? I didn't want to be carted away in a straitjacket. My parents had risked everything to give me a fighting chance of survival. I didn't want to blow it.

"What are you going to do when we land?" Marissa asked.

I shrugged. I had no idea, but I couldn't have her tagging along or asking any more questions.

"They're probably rebooking everyone on flights to Vegas. Maybe we could try to get the same flight," she said.

On any other day, I would have friended Marissa on Facebook and probably made us squeeze together and snapped a photo that I could post and tag.

"They can probably get you a direct flight and I don't want to hold you up." I was speaking to the headrest in front of me more than to her.

She gave me this hurt-puppy look and twisted away from me. "Yeah, whatever."

As soon as we landed and the seat-belt light dinged, she bolted down the aisle. I waited for everyone to exit the aircraft. The more distance between me and all potential virus carriers the better.

I followed the signs to check-in. I struggled under the weight of whatever was in my backpack. All I needed was another flight to Vegas.

I decided to pretend I was in some teen version of *The Amazing Race*. If I thought of it as reality TV, instead of just plain reality, then my head and gut wouldn't go all supernova.

I'd made it as far as the food court, with the typical McDonald's, Starbucks, something Mexican, something Chinese, and a potato place, when an announcement rang out. The speakers crackled. The voice was garbled, like someone speaking while eating popcorn. I couldn't understand a word. After the announcement ended, everyone seemed to stop—as if suspended in Jell-O.

"What did it say?" I asked a man in a blue pin-striped suit who was standing near me. When he didn't respond, I asked a lady in a floral sundress and floppy hat. "What did they say?"

Before she could answer, everyone started talking at the same time. Tension in the airport increased by a factor of a bazillion. A plumpish, normal-looking mom snatched the ice-cream cone from her son's hand, dumped it in a trash can, and dragged him in the direction of check-in. Everyone moved in a pack, slowly and orderly at first, and then a few people started to do this race-walk thing. I was swept away like an extra in *Attack of the Killer Tomatoes*. I didn't resist. I needed to find another flight.

"What did the announcement say?" I asked an elderly couple. They were on a mission, and I had a difficult time keeping pace with them.

"All flights are grounded until further notice!" the white-haired man shouted without slowing down. At least that's what I thought he'd said as he raced away.

I stopped dead in my tracks.

9/11. The date popped spontaneously into my brain. Mum and I had watched some documentary about 9/11. One of the first things the government did was ground all the airplanes. I shoved that thought into the dark recesses of my gray matter and covered it with a healthy dose of Dad's platitudes: "It's never as bad as you think." "What you fear most never happens."

Then my mum kicked in: "Worrying doesn't do shit." "Control what you can control."

I did what I always did in times of extreme distress: I reached for my iPhone. Surely there was an app for being stranded in a strange airport after being kicked out of your home under some mysterious national-security threat. But my pocket was empty, and I grieved again for that missing handheld extension of me.

Someone plowed into me from behind and I fell to my hands and knees. Another guy leapt over me as if I were a hurdle instead of a human. He misjudged my height—or I might have *accidentally* arched my back at the precise moment he jumped. He knocked me to the floor, but at least I took him with me.

"Watch what you're doing!" the guy screamed as he staggered to his feet and hurried away. I was airport roadkill. My knees and palms stung. A woman with a bawling toddler in a stroller ran over my fingers and didn't even pause. I tried to stand, but my backpack made me top-heavy, so I wobbled back onto my butt. People huffed or muttered as they swerved around me. No one stopped.

Finally the corridor cleared. Only me and some surfer-looking guy on crutches remained. I regained my balance and stood. I tugged the hem of my shirt, brushed the dusty patches on my knees, and followed in the wake of the stampede.

By the time I reached the main check-in area, lines snaked into a spaghetti bowl of humanity. Airport staff in bright yellow vests tried to corral people, but they looked as sweaty and nervous as the rest of us. General announcements rang out that might as well have said: "Abandon hope all ye who are stranded here." Skirmishes erupted over positions in line. The airline staff shrugged and waved their hands. Nothing they could do. People exited the airport in droves. Marooned visitors staked out territory. A herd of college-age kids in matching orange T-shirts circled their Samsonite suitcases near the information booth. A gaggle in business suits huddled near the ticketing kiosks. Lone travelers rotated like those gooey hunks of meat in gyros shops, watching the arrivals and departures being canceled one by one. Alliances were forged. Battle lines drawn. Some surrendered. Others appeared all too eager to fight.

I weaved through the crowd, trying not to make eye contact or get too close to anyone. I was sure they could tell I had a safe place to go. I had a map and money strapped to me like a bulletproof vest. I couldn't tell if they were infected with some bio-sickness or if their pained expressions were just fear.

I decided to try another mode of transportation. I had to get out of here. By the time I hiked out to Avis and Hertz, their parking lots were empty. I meandered back via the parking garage. I heard people bartering to be the sixth man in a Ford Fiesta bound for Flagstaff.

Back in the terminal, I told myself to think short term, not long term. It was the opposite of what my mum was always trying to persuade me to do. I couldn't sit here and wait for the airport to reopen. I was itching to be on the road—away from all these people who now felt like nothing more than conduits of disease and death.

I focused on what I needed to do and not what was going on all around me. It was a gift. The Isis Ann Murray action figure came with built-in blinders. I refused to see the impending breakup, even when Lola told me she'd seen Tristan kissing Molly "Ho" Andersen. I wouldn't consider that my parents might divorce even though they'd had separate bedrooms for nearly a year. But it was hard, even for me, to overlook the fact that something ginormously horrific was going on.

The only way I was ever going to get through this was to pretend it wasn't happening. The world wouldn't end on some random Friday night. I mean, we were only a few weeks away from the *American Idol* finale. I had to graduate and have sex—at the very minimum.

Just get to Vegas, I told myself, *and it will all be okay. My parents will come get me and tell me this has been an extreme misunderstanding and my life will get back to normal.*

I didn't know it then, but *okay* and *normal* were already long gone.

SIX

"Everything happens for a reason.
You just may never know what it is."

—Just Saying 76

BECKETT

When Beckett wakes up the next day, his first thought is of the mysterious girl. Before his eyes open, he can see her there as if she is waiting for him. Like the sun, he travels a daily unalterable path from morning to night. Breakfast. Walk the Mountain with Harper. Sayings for the rockstars. Lunch. Meditation and counseling. Sayings for the sick. Dinner. Storytime. Patrol the Mountain with Harper and Finch. Every day he lives for others. But today for the first time in his life he is doing something for himself.

"I'm going to meditate near the Crown," he tells Harper, who is lying next to him. Harper rests between Beckett and Finch.

"I'll come with you." Harper is fully awake and wrapping a scarf around her neck.

"I want to be alone." He sees the hurt in her eyes. Recently he's found Harper's desire to protect him stifling.

"Do you think that's safe?" she whispers.

He glares at her, sending the message not to give away their secrets—the lights and the girl. "I want to be alone," he says again, a little too forcefully. "I've received a message from the Great I AM." And it's not a complete lie. This desire to see the girl again could be a message from the Great I AM. He has asked for guidance and understanding. An urge this powerful must be from the Great I AM.

Harper pokes Finch's blankets with her toe. "Finch, let's you and me..." He's not there. "Finch must be already on patrol."

Beckett grits his teeth. Will he ever be alone?

"See," he says, softening the angry edges of his voice. "I'll be perfectly safe." As he stands, he gives Harper a kiss on the forehead.

The cave air is sour with sleep, warm bodies, and stale smoke. Farther back in the cave, he can hear the rockstars beginning to wake. Atti is poking her face between the curtains that separate the Cheerleaders from the rockstars. Beckett wonders how long she has been waiting there. He waves to her, and she gives him one of her wonderfully wonky smiles.

"Hey, Cheer Captain!" Atti says too loudly. Beckett thinks the Great I AM packed too much energy in her little body.

He raises a finger to his lips to remind her to keep her voice down, but it's too late. The Cheerleaders are stirring. Atti races to him, treading on Cheerleaders as she goes. Her path is punctuated with grunts and squeals. She hugs him, and he feels guilty about wanting to sneak away. "Are you ready for your Walk of Enlightenment?" he asks her, demonstrating what a whisper sounds like.

She nods and keeps on nodding. She will be tested on the Great I AM's Just Sayings and her Facebook. If she passes, she will lead Forreal on a Walk of Enlightenment up the Mountain. She will be the first new Cheerleader they've had in nearly two years.

"Harper is helping you study, isn't she?" Beckett asks.

Atti nods and nods and nods again.

Beckett bends down and whispers in her ear, "I think you should go surprise Harper."

She giggles and practically dives onto Harper's pile of blankets. Harper gives Beckett a look that says she knows what he's done. He's catching two squirrels with one nut.

He makes his way to the cave's entrance before anyone can follow. The Cheerleaders shift in their blankets to clear a path for him. Their eyes track him as he exits. Beckett often feels like a bird soaring between the Great I AM and the Mountain, but today he feels like a spider trapped in its own web.

"Any news?" Beckett asks the two Cheerleaders who are guarding the cave.

"The Mountain was quiet. The Great I AM has blessed us with another beautiful sunrise," Heck says.

"Have a mediocre day!" Beckett says, and waves.

"Whatever," they reply as he passes.

Lucky scampers up beside Beckett. He sometimes wishes he could have Lucky's life. She comes and goes as she pleases. "Good morning, Lucky," he says, and lifts the cat into his arms.

She purrs and nuzzles the crook of his neck. She doesn't care that he has disrupted their routine. She's just happy to see him.

"Hey, Beckett," May calls, and stirs a meaty mixture that is suspended from a tripod over the fire. Her back is permanently hunched, as if she's always studying the ground. "What are you doing up so early?"

"Hey, May," he calls back. "I'm off to meditate." She's always up before dawn, cooking the morning meal.

"Whatever!" she says with a wave. Lucky leaps from Beckett's arms and runs to May. Lucky meows and May finds a few scraps to satisfy her.

Beckett sneaks out of Forreal, taking the path behind the Mall tiled with multicolored bits of plastic. He loops the Mountain before he heads to the place where he and Harper saw the girl. He feels light with his secret mission.

Disappointment settles in his chest when he rounds the corner where the trail they followed dead-ends and she's not there. He climbs the rocky wall and scans the valley below. He watches the shadows grow as the sun rises. How can he feel such a loss for something he never had in the first place?

The next day and the next he steals away as often as he can to the spot where he saw the girl. He makes excuses to Harper and takes great care to make sure no one follows him. Unlike the first time he looked for the girl, he slips these secret searches in among his responsibilities, but he can tell that a few of the Cheerleaders are starting to get suspicious.

He fills the days with thoughts of her. He etches her image in his memory. The shiny hair curling down her back, not matted in dreads. The full, figure-eight shape of her body. Those eyes a color he never knew eyes could be. He has conversations with her in his head. He tells her things he can't tell anyone in Forreal. He imagines how she would look at him if she didn't know his direct connection with the Great I AM. He's beginning to wonder if she was some sort of hallucination.

He holds his breath as he approaches the secluded spot. If she's not there today, he tells himself, he will stop coming here and waiting for her. Part of him wants to turn around. If he doesn't check, then he can imagine she's there, always there, waiting for him. But *Believing is seeing*, so Says the Great I AM.

He turns the corner to where the path dead-ends. And there she is. She's standing in front of him. He almost can't believe it. He wants to rush to her, but he knows this closeness he's created is only in his imagination.

She's wearing jean shorts. Loose white threads create a fringe at the jagged hem around her thighs. She's drawn a symbol on her dingy T-shirt. Three triangles form a sloppy circle. The triangles float near one another like three separate pieces of pie.

"You came back," he says. It takes every ounce of strength to keep his distance. She blinks those green eyes at him. They remind him of the lush oasis around the Mountain spring. That's what she is to him. "I'm Beckett."

As if in a trance, she walks over to him and touches his face. He closes his eyes. His attention narrows to the softness of her fingertips as she traces a line from his brow to his chin.

"Beckett." His name is like music on her lips. When he opens his eyes, she jerks her hand away. "I wanted to make sure you were real," she says shyly.

He cocks his head. Such a strange creature. "What did you think I was?"

"I don't know. A ghost or something. I've heard rumors that this mountain is haunted by strange..." She wipes her hand on her shorts. "Sorry."

She climbs up the rock. "Come on!" she calls, and he follows. The pair stand side by side and stare at the desert below.

He finally works up the courage to speak. "Where did you come from?" He realizes he is leaning forward, so eager to touch her.

"I live in Vega." She points to the Man-Made Mountains.

"Vega?"

"That city over there." She bites her lower lip.

He remembers the lights. This girl was the light in the Man-Made Mountains. "Is it safe in Vega? Our ancestors told us of horrible beasties that live Out There."

"I've seen mountain lions and coyotes," she says, and backs up to the rock's edge. "Is that what you mean?"

"Not exactly." He decides not to scare her with talk of Terrorists.

The girl sits cross-legged and pats the space next to her. Beckett suddenly feels vulnerable out in the open. He's been wishing for her and now she's here, but it doesn't feel right. He doesn't know what to say. She shouldn't be on the Mountain.

"Where are *you* from?" she asks, and cranes her neck to look up at him.

"I live in Forreal," he says. He's not sure how much to reveal. Suddenly this all seems like such a bad idea. What would Finch do if he found her?

"For real?" she says, breaking the word into two parts.

He doesn't correct her. "It's on the other side of the Mountain."

She tosses her hair over her shoulder, and Beckett marvels at how it bounces and falls down her back. He is mesmerized by her round face, rosy cheeks, and full pink lips.

He sits facing her. He can't hear the Great I AM over the pounding of his heart. He has so much he wants to ask. He's imagined this moment over and over, but now he's too afraid to break the spell. They take turns pretending not to stare at each other. He tests questions in his mind, but none of them seem right. And, as the Great I AM Says, *Knowledge can suck.*

"I probably should go," she says after a few more minutes of silence.

"Can we meet again?" he asks.

"I'd like that," she says, and places her hand on his leg. Her touch sparks something inside him. His attention focuses on her hand. "I'm Greta, by the way." She writes her name in the dust. "I'll come back tomorrow at sunset."

Beckett stares at the letters. He can't believe it. G-r-e-t-a. Great. It's a sign. The Great I AM has brought them together. It must mean something.

She stands and brushes herself off. "Why don't we meet down there?" she says, and points to a cluster of rocks that Beckett knows hide the entrance to a small alcove. It's the perfect secret meeting spot.

"I will see you there tomorrow," he says, but then wonders how she knows about that hiding place. How many times has she hid on his Mountain? He wipes those thoughts away. It doesn't matter. She's here and it's as if she was always destined to be here.

Even after she leaves, he can still feel the warmth of her touch. He can't wait to see her again and be a boy and a girl, nothing more and nothing less.

SEVEN

GRETA

Greta glances back one last time. Balanced on the rock tower and wearing nothing but this strange leather skirt, Beckett looks like one of those statues she found in Vega, except he's in one perfect piece—not broken like everything else. Every curve of muscle is carved into his glistening brown skin. As he climbs up the mountainside, the shock of white that splits his jet-black hair flashes like a bolt of lightning streaking across a stormy sky.

Her life has been about constant motion. Those moments with Beckett felt as if they were suspended in time. She imagined they were the only two people left on Earth. There were no meetings to draw up rules. No things to lug from here to there. No food to be gathered or cooked or served. No brothers to herd. She should have asked more questions. What will she report back to Da? Her first real mission and she has failed.

Greta lets gravity speed her pace down the mountain. Her legs are pumping almost faster than she can control. She can't stop her momentum, much like she can't stop Da. She's seen him assimilate other communities into the wheel and cog of their progress. She doesn't want that to happen to Beckett. She wants Beckett all to herself.

When she reaches the base of the Mountain she keeps running toward Vega. She wishes she could run away from her responsibilities. But she's learned no one can survive alone out here. She jogs through the endless maze of houses.

She hears laughing. That sickening bark her brothers make when their mouths gap and their fingers point and their fat bellies jiggle. She cups her hands around her mouth and calls, "Joe! Bungle! Tinker! Buzz! Time to go!"

Four boys twice her size come rushing toward her. The layer of dirt that perpetually covers them makes them almost indistinguishable from one another.

"Hi, Greta!" Bungle says with a wave.

"What took you so long?" Buzz asks, and shoves her into Tinker.

"Hey!" Tinker shouts, and pushes her into Joe.

Buzz, Tinker, and Joe jostle her between them while Bungle punches each one in turn, yelling, "Cut it out! Leave her alone!"

This type of teasing is new. They think she doesn't see their newfound interest in her recently developed body. She used to be one of them but now she's different, and there's a new awkwardness among them.

"It's all right," Greta says to Bungle. She dives under Buzz's arms and outside of the circle. "Let's go," she says, and takes off at a brisk pace. "We need to get back before it gets dark." She can hear them arguing and then there's the distinct sound of fist hitting gut. She doesn't turn around. She's through with their silly fights.

Bungle strides up next to her. "Don't worry about them," he says.

"I don't. I do worry about you." She rams her shoulder into his, and he knocks her right back. "What did you guys do besides wait for me?"

"Nothing," Bungle says, glancing back at the other three. "Tinker and Buzz saw how far they could throw stuff. Joe chased after those lizard things."

Greta shouldn't be surprised by their lack of brain function, but she is. Most days a pile of rocks would be more interesting than those three. The roar and scramble increases and soon Joe, Tinker, and Buzz are barging into Greta and Bungle as they pass.

"So, Regret, what did you find on the mountain?" Tinker asks, walking backward.

"Nothing," she says. She told only Da about seeing Beckett and the girl. She's supposed to determine if they are a threat or an asset. Da can't leave anyone alone.

"That smoke every night isn't coming from nothing," Buzz says. "Da's just going to send us back until we figure it out." She knows he's right. Next time she'll persuade Da to let her come alone. She doesn't need their protection or disruption. They don't know she's sneaked here once before and, if she needs to, she'll sneak out again.

"Maybe I should go to the mountain," Tinker says, and stops. "I will find the source of the smoke."

"You wouldn't know what to do if you found someone." She speaks too fast. It's too important. "You can't go to the mountain. Da sent me."

"He sent us," Tinker says, puffing himself up. "I can make first contact too, you know."

She changes tactics. "Tink, you're too big and scary." And he is. She hadn't really noticed before how much he's grown. He's always been her stupid younger brother. But he's already as hairy as Da, and she could hide in his shadow.

"I guess you're right." Tinker smiles a toothless smile and some of what makes him scary fades away.

Maybe that *is* why Da sends her. She doesn't look intimidating, but she's tougher than any of her brothers. They don't mess with her, not really. All she needed was to give Buzz one swift kick between the legs the first time he knocked her down. The others saw it and know she'd do it again.

The closer they get to Vega the tighter the buildings are packed together and the higher they climb. She can't believe that all these buildings used to have people. How did the world work with all those bodies crashing into one another? Even now, she feels trapped by the walls of her new home. Da claimed a building near the center of Vega. He liked that it was shaped like a big X.

Greta doesn't understand the ways of all the other people who have joined them. There's one family that only comes out at night. Another is trying to grow things on the roof of their building. She tried to tell them they'd have to cart water all the way up there, but they don't seem to mind. One family prefers to live in the basement. They've all survived, but in very different ways.

Greta's family searched for six years before they settled on

Vega. Da plans to set up lookouts on each of the surrounding mountains. He's trying to organize everyone. He says the only way they will survive is to work together. He says they need to play to their strengths. The group he calls the Fighters stand guard. They'd as soon punch you as look at you.

Greta's family are Gatherers. She and her brothers zigzag through streets they haven't traveled before. Tinker, Buzz, Joe, and Bungle can't help but explore the buildings and come out with broken bits and pieces. "We can use this!" Tinker says about a scrap of material with plastic loops clinking together on one end.

"Look at this!" Bungle shows Greta a metal pot with a broken handle. That is a rare find. Over the years these buildings have been picked clean like sun-bleached bones long after the vultures have stopped circling, but her family has discovered where people hid things way back then. They know how to take other's leftovers and build something new.

Greta calls to her brothers and keeps them moving. Without her they would get lost, wandering aimlessly, picking at shiny things like raccoons.

She runs the last mile to the heart of Vega. She wants to reach Da first. Da's standing on a glass bridge near the X building. He can see down the streets and keep an eye on everyone bustling about.

"Hey, you!" he shouts, and points his fat finger at a redheaded man who is piling wood for a fire in the middle of the street. "Dig a trench so the fire doesn't spread. We want it to be seen but not burn the place down."

The man nods.

"Are we going to have enough torches?" he yells at a blonde woman wrapping scraps of material around thick branches.

"I've sent Aaron and Blue to get some more," she yells without looking up at him.

"I want more lights in those buildings. I expect the Coasters and Valley folks to come soon. We need to make sure they can see our lights no matter which direction they come from."

"Yeah, yeah," the woman says. "You told me already."

Greta climbs the stairs and surprises Da with a hug. He shrugs her off. She places a kiss on his cheek and gets a rare smile from him. He makes a big show of wiping his cheek. "About time you and the lazy creatures returned."

"Will we raise the fires tonight?" Greta asks. The last time was magical. Vega was cold and lifeless and then everyone lit their torches at the main fire and carried their lights into the buildings. The Messengers taught everyone the words to a lullaby of light, and the song seemed to glow in the flickering flames. Da doesn't realize he's humming it now.

"Not tonight, Greta, but soon," he tells her, and then yells to her brothers, "Take your finds to the Collectors and help them organize the supplies." Her brothers are laden with treasure. Bungle has loaded everything he scavenged in a big blanket and is carrying it over his shoulder like a Traveler. The others haven't been so thoughtful and have to stop every few feet to pick up what they've dropped. Da and Greta share a laugh at their crazy procession.

"So, my darling daughter." Da turns his full attention to Greta. "What did you discover on that mountain of yours?"

Lying to Da isn't easy—or advisable. "I need more time. There are people who live on the mountain, but I need to find out more." She makes up her response as she goes along. She must give him a good reason to let her continue her contact. "They may have valuable knowledge about how to survive in this area. But they are as wary of me as we are of them."

"Did you meet with the leader?" Da asks this because it was his instruction.

"I am learning about their culture from a boy who is about my age. The more I learn the better equipped I will be to introduce you to their leader. As you say, patience leads to power."

"A boy," he says, and raises one eyebrow. She blushes. He knows. He always knows. "I trust you, Greta. You are going to lead us one day."

They look out over Vega, and she can see Da's vision. The city is coming to life again. Da said Vega had millions of people living here. Greta thinks he exaggerates. One day this place was alive with light and life—or so the story goes—and the next day everyone in it was dead.

Greta's ancestors survived because they lived on a farm miles away from anyone. Da says they can be stronger by joining with other survivors. He has the battle scars to prove that not everyone wants to rebuild what was broken so long ago. The people who survived the plague and the wars were outcasts in one way or another. Greta was starting to feel she didn't belong—not with Da and his quest to conquer and not with her brothers, who were happy to follow orders. She's never had someone to talk to, someone who wasn't related or scared of Da. But for the first time in a long time, she doesn't feel so alone.

EIGHT

I stared out the wall of windows overlooking the runways. Normally planes would be crisscrossing the sky like some airborne x-y graph. But all the airplanes were parked in neat rows. The airport terminal had grown strangely quiet.

I felt as if I was on the edge of my seat, but my seat was dangling by a dreadlock over the Grand Canyon. It was like a google times worse than the feeling I got when I watched horror movies. My insides were bunched up and a primal scream was permanently wedged at the back of my throat. All that was missing were those screeching violins. But I couldn't cover my eyes or switch off the TV. This horror story was my life.

I had to get out of here. I followed the exit signs. My spine felt as if the vertebrae were being crushed under the weight of my backpack. A line of people stretched through the sliding doors that led outside and slithered around a maze of barricades. They were checking and double-checking their phones. They all kept their heads down and their eyes averted. Women rummaged in their handbags. Businessmen removed their jackets. Kids my age bobbed their heads in prayer to the iPod gods.

Everyone was trying to act natural, but tension sparked in the air. No one had any info about what was happening. It was as if everyone knew this was a Darwinian test on a massive scale. Survival of the fittest. When I did inadvertently make eye contact, everyone's eyes were glazed with panic and their faces were tight, nearly twitching with fear. It felt as if one wrong word would transform this tenuous order into disaster-movie chaos.

Up ahead a vision in pink was jumping and waving wildly. It took me less than a second to recognize the bald head, the ears that were more metal than flesh, and the cat's eyes. Even though my predicament hadn't improved a fizzle, something inside me lightened a little. I realized that if I was going to survive, I was going to need a little help.

"Icie! Hey, Icie!"

Damn, that girl could project.

She was nearly at the front of the line, which I could see was marked TAXI. I swallowed back my fear of all these conduits for disease. I weaved my way toward her. "She's with me," she said to the people scowling at me. I handed her my backpack and then slipped between the metal bars of the barrier. I had to nudge a man in a purple golf shirt to make some room. He begrudgingly shifted his golf bag a whole five inches.

She placed my stuff on the ground between us and wheeled her fuchsia suitcase closer. "Got some supplies," Marissa said, opening a canvas bag, which was stuffed with bottled water, a year's supply of breath mints, and every snack food available at the airport travel mart. She had mad survival skills. I noticed the slogan on the bag: ARIZONA IS DEHYDRIFFIC! Another Ripple.

I couldn't think of Lola right now.

"Thanks for the assist," I said. "Sorry about earlier. On the plane, you know. I didn't mean to be rude."

"No problem," she said, spinning on the heels of her sneakers and clearing us a few more inches of space. "Desperate times call for outrageous actions."

"Desperate measures," I corrected. The saying was: Desperate times call for desperate measures.

"Yeah, whatever. You know what I mean." She whipped her phone from her jeans pocket and poked the screen. "Your cell working?"

"Don't have one."

A look of sheer horror crossed her face.

"I mean I have one, but I didn't bring it with me," I explained, but that didn't change her expression.

"My cell died," Marissa said. "It was working a minute

71

ago and now nothing. It's not out-of-juice-or-minutes dead, but, like, no signal. Everyone is having the same problem. Look at them. You'd think they lost children."

She was right. Everyone was switching phones off and on and punching buttons. Panic gurgled in my gut again. I remember Mum mentioning once that the government could jam the phone lines so cell phones couldn't be used to detonate devices of mass destruction. It—whatever it was—was starting already.

Conversations would twinkle around us. "Do you think all the airports are closed?" "Are more taxis coming?" "Can anyone get cell phone reception?" "What's going on?" "I wish they'd give us more information." Everyone was dancing around the real topic. No one wanted to be the first to say the words *terrorist* or *attack*.

Everyone was standing too close to me. Breathing on me. I could feel heat rising from their bodies and fear emanating from their pores. Everyone was a breath away from freaking out. A few more police and airport security patrolled the crowd. They eyed us, almost willing us to break the fragile calm.

When we reached the front of the taxi line, some fridiot airport employee decided now was the moment to make an announcement. "Everyone," the voice rang out, and static reverberated through the speakers. "Everyone please remain calm." *Wasn't that the worst thing to say in a situation like this?* "There's no reason to panic." *Nope, that was the worst thing to say.* Everyone began to fidget. "We don't have details, but all airports are closing due to an incident on the East Coast. This is a national-security measure. Please leave the airport in an orderly fashion." He might as well have said, "Run! Save yourself!"

Someone screamed. The man with the golf bag slumped to the ground. Had he fainted? People started to cry.

Marissa tugged on my shirt as our taxi pulled to the curb. She lunged for the car. "Come on, Icie!"

Then someone shouted something that included the word *bomb*, and all hell broke loose. People transformed from human to animal. What I can only describe as an electrical current shot through me. The fight-or-flight survival instinct kicked in all around me. For me it was fight *and* flight.

Marissa hip-checked a man in a business suit when he tried to open the taxi door. To clear the space around her, she swung her D&G handbag, which was big enough to comfortably hold a family of dachshunds.

I shouldered my backpack and pushed through the crowd as it surged forward. It was *us* or *them*. "Out of my way!" I shouted as I cleared the space around me, my backpack now a deadly weapon.

An announcement rang out from the speakers and the security personnel were shouting. The gist was *calm the hell down*, but it was too late for that.

Marissa had managed to open the back door of the taxi. She tossed her suitcase and goodie bag inside and dived into the backseat. "Get off!" she screamed, and bicycled her legs, kicking people away. "Icie, hurry!"

I bent over like a linebacker and charged headfirst toward the taxi. People were climbing on top of the car. I grabbed a handful of Hawaiian shirt and yanked some college kid out of my way. I heard his shirt rip and the guy scream as his body clunked to the ground, but I didn't stop. I kicked and punched and tore myself free until I was safely inside the taxi. Two people had climbed in the taxi from the other side. Marissa drew herself into a ball and kicked what might have been a husband and wife away from the taxi. We both yanked the doors shut and locked them.

"Drive! Damn it! Drive!" she screamed at the taxi driver, and slapped the Plexiglas that separated us from the front seat.

The car lurched forward. The driver laid on the horn. Faces were pressed against the glass. The roar of fists on the car was deafening. The driver eased forward.

"I don't think I can go." He gripped the steering wheel at ten and two. "Maybe I should take a few more passengers." The car rocked back and forth. It was like those shots from inside some famous band's limo, except these weren't screaming fans; these were adults dressed like reasonable human beings, but with faces red and contorted from shouting. Their eyes were wild, and I didn't know what they would do if they got their hands on me.

I fumbled in my money belt and grabbed a fistful of cash. "Here!" I shoved bills through the money slot. "There's more if you get us out of here."

The driver surveyed the waterfall of crumpled fifties collecting on the seat next to him. "You got it!" He honked the horn and hit the gas. I closed my eyes. Marissa and I bounced like paddleballs in the backseat as the taxi freed itself from the crowd.

I opened my eyes when the ride smoothed. I wasn't proud that I had left all those people behind, but I had to, right?

"Where do you want to go?" the taxi driver asked, facing us and swerving slightly. Cars honked. He honked back and screamed obscenities at them. He had greasy black hair that was combed in well-defined lines from his forehead and curled in soppy ringlets at his neck. He kept checking us out in the rearview mirror and raising his eyebrows. I was thankful the scratched and graying screen separated us.

"Las Vegas?" I said. Would he really take us that far?

The taxi pulled onto the shoulder and skidded to a stop. Marissa and I were slammed into the front seat. Water bottles and breath mints exploded from Marissa's goodie bag and rolled on the floor, knocking against my flip-flops. The air was once again filled with honking.

"Are you crazy?" He shook his head.

"How much?" Marissa asked, sitting cross-legged in the seat.

He tilted the SatNav that was suctioned to his windshield and tapped the screen with an unusually long fingernail. "That's nearly three hundred miles. It will take six hours, and then I have to drive back."

"How much?" Marissa persisted.

He scribbled on a candy bar wrapper, scratching his head with the pencil point and staring out the window at the passing traffic.

"Three thousand dollars," he said, turning to profile and glaring at us with one eye.

I nodded. I'd pay whatever it took. All that money

strapped to my waist wouldn't save me if I couldn't make it to the mountain.

"Wait." He reached for his pad of receipts and pretended to scribble something. I knew too late that he'd gauged my reaction and realized his fee was too low. "I mean five thousand dollars."

"That's almost seventeen dollars per mile. You're crazy," Marissa said.

I had to make this work. The traffic was growing by the minute. Each passing vehicle was packed with people and stuff bulging over the window line. I couldn't give this guy half of my money. "All I've got is thirty-six hundred dollars." I don't know why I picked that figure. I wanted to make it believable, I guess.

"Okay, but I want half up front. You buy all the gas." He shook his head. "And meals. You buy me food too. There and back."

Marissa settled back in the seat. "I can swing the gas and food as long as we go places that accept plastic," she told me.

"Deal," I said.

"I'm not moving until I see more money." He crossed his arms.

Marissa turned away to give me the privacy she could sense I wanted. I noticed the taxi driver leering at me in the rearview mirror. I lifted my backpack and held it with my knee against the partition.

I lifted my shirt and counted out eighteen hundred dollars twice. I clutched one wad in my hand and tucked the other eighteen hundred in my bra, nine hundred dollars nestled under each breast. *How's that for a boob job?*

I let my backpack fall to the floor. "Here," I said as I shoved the wad of cash at him.

"Where in Vegas? It's a big place," he asked as he counted the money.

I struggled to come up with an answer. I didn't want to tell him about my secret hideout, not that I knew exactly where it was. I told him to use the road Mum had pointed to on the map. "I need an address and zip code," he said with a twang of annoyance in his voice.

"I'll tell you the exact location when we get closer." I snuggled back in my seat as if I made these types of transactions all the time, but it felt like this was happening to someone else.

"I owe you big-time, Icie," Marissa said, extending her arms to give me a hug. The gesture exposed ragged circles that were a darker shade of pink under each armpit.

"I'd say we're even," I said, and dodged her embrace.

"What are we gonna do in Vegas?" Marissa asked, bouncing nervously on the seat. "I was just going to get a hotel in Phoenix and wait it out, but Vegas is closer to home."

"I'll get you to Vegas and then we'll go our separate ways." I hated that I was ditching her again, but I had to, didn't I? Mum said to tell no one.

Her eyes narrowed. "Whatever," she said after an awkwardly long pause. "If that's the way you want it." She turned toward the window. I liked Marissa. I liked her a lot. She probably saved my life back there. But I'd watched enough horror movies to know that, no matter how big the cast, only one person survives to the credits and lives to fight another sequel.

We were stranded in gridlock traffic leaving Phoenix. I read every inch of copy in the taxi. I memorized his taxi driver ID number. I was told I couldn't smoke in seven languages—as well as by the universal circle-slash no-smoking symbol. The car's air-conditioning couldn't keep up with the humid night air and three nervous bodies. I felt trapped in an Easy-Bake Oven of body odor, cheap aftershave, and the lingering hint of farts embedded in the cracked vinyl seat.

Marissa tapped on the Plexiglas. "How about some music?"

"Everyone calls me Lobo," our driver responded, shifting on his wood-beaded seat cover.

"Okay, Lobo," Marissa said, "how about some tunes?"

"No radio," Lobo said.

"What?" Marissa scooted up and pointed to the dashboard radio. "Come on, man, I mean, Lobo. Help a girl out. I'm going mental."

"No, I mean there's only static." He switched on the radio and turned up the volume so we could hear the white noise. He flipped through the stations. Static. Static and more static. Marissa and I exchanged panicked expressions. All I could think of was that scene from *Poltergeist* where the little blonde girl stares into the flashing TV screen and says "They're here" in a singsong voice.

"Uh, that's not good," Marissa whispered to me.

We scanned the horizon, looking for fighter planes or flying saucers. But beyond the stream of traffic, the landscape was dark.

"Do you know what's going on?" Marissa asked him. I shot her a dirty look. If I was going to get through this, I couldn't think about what was happening out there. I couldn't do anything about it. I couldn't think about Mum or Dad or Lola or anyone on the East Coast. I told myself that it was going to be okay. I didn't want Lobo to tell me anything to the contrary.

"Before the radio went funny, there was a national bulletin about solar or electrical storms or something, but I don't believe any of it. Someone else said that an asteroid was heading for Earth. Another station reported that the military was being deployed. Officials said satellite problems. Who knows? We are too close to Hollywood. Everyone has big imaginations. Everyone panics." He glanced at us in the rearview mirror. "Like you two. Why are you going to Vegas? Why not sit by the pool? If it is the end, I'd rather have a beer in one hand and a lady in the other."

I didn't like the way he was sizing us up as if he were Dracula and we were O negative. We didn't look like the type of girls men wanted at the end of days—Marissa with her bald head and piercings and me with my dreadlocks. I'd rather die a virgin than be this guy's apocalyptic sweetheart. Marissa and I pushed ourselves as far back into the seat, and as far away from Lobo, as we could.

"You're safe," Lobo said with a chuckle. "I don't believe

it's the end of the world." He winked at us in the rearview mirror and I noticed he was missing one of his front teeth— one that would be pointy if he were a vampire.

We drove in silence. Marissa and I tried to sleep. The temperature rose with the sun. The white-hot sunlight felt like a laser on my skin. It wasn't only the rays bouncing off the barren landscape; it was also the anxiety that was triangulating among the three of us. Lobo kept switching the radio on and off. "Just checking," he'd always say. Static would blare through the speakers and mimic my nerves.

We stopped at a gas station with huge lines at every pump. The guys working the pumps didn't look official, but they demanded and we paid five hundred dollars to fill our tanks. Inside the shop there was a guy with a gun who was threatening anyone who tried to steal anything. Marissa and I took turns guarding our stuff and going to the bathroom. People were acting crazy. Mum and Dad were right. Hiding out was the best option.

"Did you hear what they're saying?" Marissa asked when we were back on the road. Her skin was pale, as if she'd applied a lighter shade of foundation. "A few people said that terrorists had released a virus. That can't be happening, right? I mean, that's nuts." She dug around in her handbag and pulled out a mini pump bottle of hand gel. She squirted some in her own hands. I held up my hand and she squirted a huge glob in my palm. We both rubbed our hands together like comic henchmen. Did she really think some lethal virus was going to be stopped with hand gel?

Should I tell her what I knew? I spotted Lobo checking us out in the rearview mirror again, probably listening to every word we said. I might not mind being stuck with Marissa underground, but I wasn't about to be buried alive with Lobo.

I gave my new friend the gift of ignorance. "It's all rumors. Everything will be fine tomorrow. Could be some computer virus. That could shut everything down, couldn't it?"

She accepted my feeble explanation. She distributed cheese and crackers, chips, and cans of Coke we'd purchased for a mere two hundred dollars.

When we finally passed the road sign that said we were only thirty miles from Las Vegas, I began to think I might make it after all. The billboards changed from food to boobs and gambling. The closer we got to Vegas the more I got the distinct impression that we were headed in the wrong direction. Everyone appeared to be going the other way. Marissa was pretending to sleep. I could tell she wasn't sleeping, because earlier her snore had sounded like a hog riding a Harley.

I slipped the map Mum had given me from my messenger bag and uncrumpled it as quietly as I could. I turned the map to orient myself. I realized that my mountain wasn't far from here. I noted the name written near the dot closest to the mountain. I tucked the map back in my bag and watched the road signs for my dot.

As soon as I spotted the exit with the name from the map, I yelled, "Stop the car!" Lobo ignored me in his highway-induced coma. "Stop the damn car!" I yelled louder. "Stop the car. Stop the car. Stop the car." I kicked the back of his seat until he pulled over.

Marissa and Lobo stared at me as if I had morphed into an alien. "I'm getting out here," I said. I dug the money out from my bra. "Here." I gave nine hundred dollars to Lobo and the other sweaty wad of nine hundred to Marissa. "Take her wherever she wants to go." I opened the taxi door. I slung my messenger bag over my body and shouldered my backpack.

"Where are you going?" Lobo asked, stuffing my money in his pants pockets. "I don't care, but this is the middle of nowhere. You're not safe alone out here."

Marissa grabbed a fistful of my T-shirt. "Icie, don't leave me?"

"Marissa, I can't help you," I said, and prized her fingers from my shirt. God, it hurt to leave her. I zigzagged up the roadside, trying to regain the use of my legs and simultaneously balance the weight in my pack. A car zoomed by, sending a turbo blast through my dreadlocks and a grit-filled shower over my body. I could see mountains up a head. One of them was my mountain.

"Icie, wait." Marissa raced to me saddled with her goodie bag on one shoulder and her handbag on the other. "Please get back in the car. You will die out here."

We heard the sound of a slamming door followed swiftly by a gunning motor and tires screaming against asphalt. The bastard was leaving.

"My luggage!" Marissa shrieked, and bolted after the taxi as it veered off the highway onto the exit road. The girl could run, but there was no way she was catching Lobo.

Marissa let out a god-awful scream that rattled my nerves like windowpanes in a thunderstorm. That kind of scream was felt as well as heard. We'd been stripped of our home and our security and now she'd lost most of her worldly possessions. How much could one cheer captain take?

She stood, her chest heaving, but she didn't cry. I was impressed. She jogged back to me. "You know what they say?" she said, and slapped on a cheer-101 sort of smile. "Destiny is a choice, not an option."

What? That made absolutely no sense. But I sort of understood what she was saying. Maybe in a weird way she was right. Maybe Marissa and I were destined to be together.

NINE

"Believing is seeing."
—Just Saying 46

FINCH

Since the Terrorists' lights, Finch has increased his Mountain patrols. He's been up since sunrise, winding his way up and down the Mountain. He knows every pebble and pine needle. Today he must make sure the Mountain is safe for Atti's Walk of Enlightenment at sundown. The incline of the Mountain matches Finch's uneven legs. Beckett says the Great I AM created Finch perfectly for his life's work. Others patrol, but Finch can feel the Mountain in his bones. He knows someone or something has been on his Mountain. It's just a feeling. A glimpse out of the corner of his eye. A shadow. A sound.

Finch's job is to protect the Mountain, and he is failing. With every step, Finch hears the Great I AM chastising him: *Failure.*

Failure. Failure. He walks faster and faster to blur the taunts his feet unearth from the ground below.

Here. Here. Here. The Mountain birds squawk as he circles to the Other Side of the Mountain. He looks where they call, but the intruder has vanished before he can hobble there.

"How?" Finch asks himself as the Man-Made Mountains come into view. "How can you hide on my Mountain? My Mountain." He mumbles until the words bleed into each other. "Mymountain."

The sun bleaches his vision. Finch stumbles and falls. He's rolling down the Mountainside, bumping over rocks and flattening shrubs. He tumbles nearly to the base of the Mountain. His body wedges under a rocky ledge. He opens his eyes and finds the sun to determine which way is up. He presses his ear to the Mountain and listens carefully for the beat of the Heart. He wishes he could hear it. Beckett says it's there. It's what makes their Mountain special. He always seems so sure.

But on days like today, when the sky is so bright it almost hurts to open his eyes and the heat makes it hard to breathe, Finch doubts that there's a Great I AM watching over him. How can his faith be so weak? He begs for the Great I AM's forgiveness.

When Finch's mum disappeared and left him to take care of Atti. When another Cheerleader dies slowly and painfully. When a baby is born and they wait to see what will be missing or damaged, Beckett sees a gift where Finch sees a challenge. Finch desperately wants to believe, because without the Mountain what is he?

Whatever. Whatever. Whatever. Finch tries to find the peace that comes with giving himself to the Great I AM and the Mountain, but the words echo in his head and leave him hollow.

In this stillness, Finch hears the careful steps of someone with a secret. Maybe it's a Terrorist at long last. Every day Finch asks the Great I AM to deliver his enemy. He longs to do battle. How can he call himself brave if he is never truly tested? How does he know he is right if there is no wrong?

The footfalls are light and pause every few steps. Terrorists slither, not tiptoe. They are hunters and destroyers. Finch believes the Terrorists and the Great I AM are linked. Terrorists destroyed everything and the Great I AM rose from the ashes. They seed fear so the Great I AM can comfort. Without Terrorists, would there be a Great I AM?

Someone is coming. Someone who doesn't want to be seen.

Finch tucks himself further under the rock. The footsteps are louder and closer. Finch's body pulses with the energy of this dance with the enemy. His body coils, ready to strike.

The moment he sees the dirty feet, his body flushes with disappointment. It's not a Terrorist. Those feet know the Mountain as well as Finch's do.

Finch begins to crawl out of his hiding place when he hears Beckett whisper something. At first he thinks it's an abbreviation of "Great I AM." When he listens more carefully he realizes Beckett is calling "Greta. Greta. Greta." Finch slips back under the stone and hides. What is Beckett doing?

Beckett continues down the Mountain and Finch follows. Soon the landscape clears, making it difficult to follow unseen. Finch finds a cluster of boulders and ducks behind them. Beckett is heading to the alcove where they used to play as rockstars. It was their secret hiding spot.

As Beckett nears the alcove, Finch sees him wave to someone

who appears to materialize out of the dust and haze. Finch sees a flash of blonde hair and pale white skin. Was that Harper? Why would Beckett and Harper meet in secret? Unless…

Finch is overwhelmed with anger. Why does Beckett get everything? Harper isn't like the other girls in Forreal. She's the only one with strength of mind and spirit to match Finch's. But Harper doesn't see him, not really. It has always been Beckett. He and Beckett spotted Harper at the same time on the Mountain. Finch ran to get the Cheerleaders. When either Beckett or Harper recounts the story, they always leave him out.

Finch peeks around the boulder for a better look. He sees the blonde again, but it's not Harper. This girl is wearing loose clothes that obscure her shape. Harper ties rags around her body that cling to her muscles. But if it's not Harper, then who is it? Harper is the only Cheerleader with hair and skin like that.

Has the Great I AM led another Survivor to the Mountain? Finch clenches his fists. Beckett will return triumphant with someone else to feed and protect.

Beckett and the girl slip into the alcove. This isn't their first meeting, Finch realizes. Neither of them was surprised to see the other. They must have planned to meet. How long has Beckett been secretly meeting with the girl who lives Out There among the Terrorists?

Finch waits for another glimpse of the girl. Heat and exhaustion muddle his mind, until he is asleep. Finch's dreams and reality mix. He creates a story that connects the lights in the Man-Made Mountains with this girl and the Terrorists. When he opens his eyes, he's unsure what's real and what's imagined.

The sky is painted lavender as the sun ebbs away. Finch

remembers in a flash—Atti's Walk of Enlightenment. He runs around the Mountain. He instinctively takes the shortest route. As he approaches Forreal, he hears the low rumble of voices.

He strides into the Mall. The murmurs thin to silence and all heads turn. When they realize it's Finch and not Beckett, they return to conversation. The crowd would part if it were Beckett. Cheerleaders would reach out to him as if even his skin were special.

Umph! Atti collides with Finch, reaching one arm around his middle. The other clutches the thin pine slab that is her Facebook. How can two such opposites be siblings? Her short, stumpy legs; his long, skinny ones. Her boundless enthusiasm; his stoic standoffishness.

"Finch!" she shouts, her voice a blend of relief and joy. Atti's hair looks like the matted fur of a wildcat. Her dreads are more like bumps, growing only an inch before they break off. "I knew you wouldn't forget. They said you were too busy patrolling the Mountain, but I said, 'No, Finch is my brother and he will come. He will be here.'" She squeezes him harder, and he pats her on the top of her scraggly head.

"You know I wouldn't miss it." The stickiness of skin touching skin sets his teeth on edge. He grabs her shoulders and holds her at arm's length. "This is a ginormous day. You will be a Cheerleader."

"And I will be the best Cheerleader in the history of Forreal." Her too-big, droopy eyes sparkle. "Well, second-best, next to you, or third-best if you count Harper. I will make you proud. You'll see. I have been studying my Facebook and the Just Sayings." Harper walks up and Finch's attention shifts to her. "Harper has been helping me...." Atti keeps talking in the way she always does, until her words blend into a constant hum that Finch tunes out.

"Harper." He acknowledges her with a nod. He's still perplexed by seeing her double with Beckett.

Atti is chattering away: "...there hasn't been a walk in so long. I hope everyone will remember what to do...."

"We all remember," Harper reassures her, but Atti doesn't stop talking. Harper whispers to Finch, "Have you seen Beckett?" The hairs on the back of his neck quiver at the near touch of her lips. "Finch," she snaps, "do you know where Beckett is?"

He shakes his head. He doesn't know anymore. She's so close that he can smell the sweet mixture of sweat and dirt that lingers on her skin. He doesn't know what Beckett is doing. Beckett has never ever kept secrets. Or maybe he has. Maybe he's been lying and sneaking around all the time.

Harper's eyes scan the Mountain. What would she think of her precious Beckett if she knew about his secret meetings?

They can't start the ceremony without Beckett. He's not here and yet he still commands the attention of Forreal. As Harper paces the perimeter, Finch sows seeds of suspicion. He circles the crowd, asking one Cheerleader after another if they've seen Beckett. Atti nervously twists her dreads.

"Whatever!" Beckett calls, as if nothing is strange about him arriving late. He steps onto the platform in the center of the Mall. Bodies shift and faces lift to greet him. Sweat drips off Beckett's body. Lucky races up and knocks her head against his leg.

"Let's make the sacred symbol," Beckett calls, and takes his place between Harper and Finch. Two loops of people fan out on either side of Beckett. Atti stands in front of him and presents her Facebook. Lucky dips in and out of the circles as if inspecting their formation.

Finch studies the rows and rows of wobbly round faces Atti has carved into her Facebook. She has shaded the lines with the ashes from Storytime. These simply drawn faces smile and frown. Eyes squint and wink. Thin eyebrows arch and slant. There's even a face with a stuck-out tongue.

"Your Facebook is wonderful, Atti," Beckett says.

"Thanks!" Atti's fingers fumble from one dread to another.

"We are going to start with a reading from the CQ," Beckett says.

Cal, the Twitter, walks to their makeshift altar, which is made of rusty parts salvaged long ago from the Black River and hammered together to create a four-foot-high altar. Fragments of sacred texts have been preserved between scavenged sheets of plastic. The image on the cover has faded, but Finch can make out most of the old headline: *Cheerleader Quar.* There are also smaller pages with ragged edges, as if these sheets have been ripped from another book. Interspersed among the plastic is handmade paper with Just Sayings and stories of the Great I AM. They were committed to paper years after the Great I AM became one with the Mountain. Each Just Saying is numbered and corresponds to a face. Each story has been given a title: "The Savior and the Serpent" and "The Knock on the Door."

Cal opens the slippery pages of the CQ with her gnarled fingers. She uses her knuckles to flip to a page written in glittery green ink. "'The Journey to the Heart.'" She pauses dramatically and then recounts a story they each have committed to memory. When she is finished, the crowd choruses, "Whatever." She closes the book. "Let's meditate on number one hundred and eighty-eight."

Cheerleaders and rockstars bow their heads, except Finch. He stares at Beckett. The sun has set, but it's as if Finch can see clearly now. He sees through Beckett's holy facade.

The Timekeeper whispers a countdown from ten. "That's enough," he shouts when he gets to one.

"Atti has turned twelve. We are pleased that she is ready to become a Cheerleader," Cal says, and takes her place in their human symbol.

Beckett takes Atti's Facebook. "First we will test your knowledge of the Great I AM's Just Sayings." He catches Harper's eye and winks. Their connection feels like a slap in Finch's face. Even though he is in the inner symbol, he's an outsider. How has he not realized this before?

Beckett points to the twin smiley faces on Atti's Facebook. Atti bounces on her tiptoes. In a shaky, squeaky voice she begins, "Just Saying…" She clears her throat and tries again. "You can't really know somebody until you consider things from their perspective, like slipping under their skin and seeing stuff through their eyes."

She glances at Finch, and he forces a smile on his lips. She's not quoted it verbatim, but she's gotten the idea right. She beams at Finch's approval. Beckett will never have that. Atti is all Finch has. Beckett may have Harper, but Atti is Finch's flesh and blood.

Beckett whispers in Atti's ear, "Really fab, Atti."

Finch cracks his knuckles. He won't be sidelined anymore. Finch steps out of formation and places his hands on Atti's shoulders. She squirms under his grasp. He has broken protocol.

Wide eyes focus on Finch, and he likes the way that feels. Beckett doesn't seem to notice.

Beckett points to one image on Atti's Facebook and then another. Each time Atti picks a different spiky dread and twists it between her fingers and then recites the correct Saying. "Can you tell me Just Saying one ninety-two?" Beckett points to a smiley face with two arrows for eyes.

"I know this one." Atti grins at the real faces smiling down on her. She lifts to her tiptoes and practically shouts, "Your attitude determines your altitude!"

Everyone cheers. Finch gives his sister's back one swift, sharp pat. Atti lunges and wraps Harper in a hug. "We did it," she says, not realizing that her action has stifled the applause.

"You did it," Harper says, and quickly pushes Atti away. Atti gives Harper a confused, almost hurt, look. Finch understands. Forreal is watching and Harper doesn't want Atti to be tainted by their connection. She doesn't want Atti to feel the halfhearted acceptance she's always felt.

Finch thinks he should hug his sister. He pulls her in, and she falls the rest of the way. "Congratulations, sis," he says loud enough so everyone can hear.

"Atti, are you ready to lead us on your Walk of Enlightenment?" Beckett asks.

Atti nods.

"Onward and upward," Beckett says.

"Whatever!" Atti shouts, and then takes off up the Mountain. Atti is moving as fast as her awkward short legs will take her.

Each Cheerleader raises a torch to light the way. Lucky meanders among the Cheerleaders and rockstars, who reach down to pet the cat. They form a snake of fire, winding their way up the Mountain. The torches flicker and make the trees dance. Finch is always the last in line.

Atti waits at the sacred spot halfway between the Mall and the Crown. She strokes the pale patch of wood on the tree trunk. The actual indentions have long since disappeared, but the Great I AM marked this tree. The patch is worn smooth from so many Walks of Enlightenment.

Beckett rests his hand over Atti's. "Whatever," he murmurs. The procession continues.

By the time Finch reaches the Crown, everyone has gathered around Atti. He can hear her chattering nonstop. He fights his way through the crowd. Atti is standing with her back to the thorny hedge with Beckett at her side. Finch kneels down and turns her to face him.

"I am very proud of you," he tells her.

"You've never said that before," Atti says quietly. "Mum said it. She told me before she disappeared."

Finch doesn't want her talking about Mum. Finch told everyone that their mum vanished from the Mountain. But he saw her go. She walked down the Mountain and just kept walking. He should have tried to stop her. He kept thinking she would turn around. But she never even looked back. No one can know that his mum deserted Forreal. Atti hopes she's Out There somewhere. Finch hopes she is dead.

"Congratulations to you both!" Beckett says. They stare up at him, Atti with admiration and Finch with a new suspicion.

She shuts one eye and tries to peer through the Crown's tangled mass. "Why can't we cross?" Atti asks.

"You know why, Atti," Finch chastises her. She asks too many questions.

"Yeah, I know. The Heart's up there somewhere. Don't you want to see it? Don't you want to know what it is? I mean, is it an actual beating heart or some sort of jewel or a—"

"Secrets are okay sometimes," Beckett says, talking over Atti. Finch feels powerful knowing Beckett's secret.

"Yeah, yeah, but why…" Atti thinks about it for a second. "And how will we die if we cross the Crown?"

Everyone huddles around, listening for Beckett's answer. Finch itches to tell Beckett's secret, but he must use this knowledge carefully.

"We can't always understand the ways of the Great I AM. We trust and believe," Beckett replies. "Atti, you memorized the Just Sayings. You've made your Walk of Enlightenment. You are now a Cheerleader." He faces Atti. "Do you promise to protect the Mountain and live by the Just Sayings of the Great I AM?"

Atti nods. "Oh, I mean, yeah."

Beckett extends his hand, palm up, and Cal rushes forward, presenting Beckett with the ceremonial knife. Its shiny red shell and white cross seem magical in this dull desert. Finch thinks he should wield the knife. Beckett flicks open the blade. Atti presents her wrist without being asked. Beckett closes Atti's hand into a fist and holds it still. She chews her lower lip and looks away. He uses the tip of the knife to trace a thin figure in the same place and shape as his birthmark. Beckett's precision is almost surgical. He must leave a scar, but not cut too deep. Atti's face is pinched tight with pain.

When Beckett is finished, he places his wrist on top of hers so their infinity symbols are pressed together. "Whatever," Beckett says, and the audience repeats the one-word Saying.

Finch remembers six years ago when he, Harper, and Beckett stood together and took the oath. Beckett didn't have to be marked. He was born with the Mountain's symbol. From that day on, Beckett was proclaimed Cheer Captain. He took the ceremonial knife for the first time and carved the mark on Finch. His touch was too light, only a scratch. Finch had to deepen the mark later.

Beckett raises his arm over his head, exposing his wrist, covered in Atti's blood. Every Cheerleader does the same.

"Let us repeat the Saying of Dedication," Beckett says.

> *"Whatever!*
> *Whatever!*
> *The bad, the good.*
> *Whatever!*
> *I put my faith in the Great I AM.*
> *The Great I AM alone."*

"Please join me in congratulating Atti on becoming a Cheerleader," Beckett says. Finch applauds louder and longer than anyone else.

They linger at the Crown and enjoy this break from the normal routine of Forreal life. Only the patrols are allowed this high up the Mountain at night. The moon is full and seems to direct its light on the Man-Made Mountains.

Finch notices it first—a bright light glowing at the heart of the Man-Made Mountains.

Atti elbows him. "What is that?"

"Is it…" someone starts. Finch knows the end of the sentence. Everyone must be thinking the same thing. Terrorists.

"Remain calm," Beckett says, stepping up to block their view. Everyone readjusts his or her position to see the tiny points of light that are now dotting the Man-Made Mountains.

"There are more than last time," Finch tells Beckett.

"Last time?" Tom says. He pulls at his misshapen earlobes.

"You've seen the lights before?" Cal asks. And then everyone is talking at once. Finch steps toward Beckett and watches the line of Cheerleaders move with him. The small rockstars tuck themselves behind the Cheerleaders. Finch leads them closer and closer to Beckett until he is surrounded.

"Terrorists," Finch whispers to no one and everyone. He interjects the word again and again. Until the crowd is buzzing with it.

Beckett raises his hand, exposing his birthmark. "We do not know who or what it is."

"Could it be Mumenda coming at last?" May asks, gathering the smallest rockstar in her arms. Her hunched back curves lower under the weight.

"Don't be crupid," Finch mutters. "Mumenda will journey to the Mountain and then we will be free. Mumenda will join us on the Mountain, not appear in flashing lights in the distance."

"Let's return to Forreal and ask the Great I AM for guidance." Beckett walks away from the lights. Harper is right behind him, but no one else follows.

"Do you think it's Terrorists, Finch?" someone asks. Finch assumes Beckett's place in the center of the crowd.

"I think we need to be prepared. I have increased my patrols, but I will organize a new rotation of Cheerleaders to guard the Mountain, beginning tonight." Finch finds Cal's face in the crowd. "Cal, you take the rockstars back to Forreal and pick one or two other Cheerleaders to help you."

"We are only to protect the Mountain," Beckett says.

Who is this girl he's protecting?

"It could be other Survivors who are trying to make contact," Beckett adds, glancing at Harper.

Atti's tugging on her brother's arm. "Maybe it's Mum."

"It's not Mum," he says, and elbows her aside.

"She's Out There!" Atti shouts, twisting the root of each dread. "Maybe she wants to come home."

"Mum is never coming back," Finch blurts, and Atti bursts into tears. The faces around them soften from fierce determination to concern for Atti and a slight fear of Finch.

Harper scoops Atti in her arms, glaring at Finch. "I survived Out There," Harper tells Atti. "Your mum could too." Beckett and Harper usher Atti down the Mountain. A few others follow.

"Mum is so coming back," Atti calls to Finch. He tries to ignore her and the ache the word *mum* triggers inside him.

He gathers the Cheerleaders around him. They make a schedule to patrol the Mountain, but he secretly makes a plan to investigate and extinguish that light.

TEN

As we walked along the highway toward the mountain, I told Marissa everything—about the alleged bio-attack, the bunker, and my plans to hide out there until it was safe to come out.

"Damn, Icie," Marissa exclaimed when I'd finished. "Are you sure? I mean, that's crazy."

"You don't have to come, but please don't tell anyone, okay?"

"Yeah, yeah. I mean, no, I wouldn't. I won't. I've got to think about it."

The two lanes heading away from Vegas looked like an endless parking lot being drawn slowly forward on a conveyor belt. The two lanes on our side of the road were vacant. Every once in a while a car would zoom by at some ungodly speed. The sound and the gust would shove us toward the ditch on the side of the road, but we kept walking. We didn't seem to be making any progress toward the mountains.

Up ahead I saw a biggish lump on the side of the road. I wasn't used to seeing animals that were my size on the roadside. I hadn't considered that there would be wildlife when I jumped out of the taxi. I scanned the landscape. What scary creatures lived out here? Bears? Lions? Tigers? Man-eating gorillas? I didn't know. I'd napped or sneak-texted through most of biology and geography. I was starting to think I'd slept through most of my short, insignificant life.

I didn't need some half-dead hyena taking a bite out of me. I'd seen *Aliens*—or was it *Predator?*—where they thought the thing was dead only to have it rear up and attack. And my dad said I was wasting my time watching all those horror movies! He could never have imagined they would become more of a handy survival guide.

The lump on the roadside twitched. Marissa and I screamed and grabbed for each other.

Wait a minute. Was that animal wearing a polo shirt?

The thing groaned. It wasn't the growl of a polar bear. It was human, but in this scenario, humans were probably the most deadly creatures of all. I had to get away from whatever it was. I looked for oncoming traffic. The coast was clear. I started to cross.

"Shouldn't we try to help?" Marissa asked, holding me back.

Normally I'd agree, but right now everything and everyone was my enemy. I wasn't taking any chances.

"Hey, are you okay?" she shouted to the lump.

Between video games, *CSI*s, and horror movies, I probably averaged fifty dead bodies a day. This was different. Flies were collecting and covering the body while a buzzard, an actual buzzard, circled overhead.

"What...the...hell...do...you...think?" The voice was weak and the words were spoken painstakingly slow. "Help me." It was a boy, maybe twelve or thirteen, and he was trying to push himself up. Rusty-brown patches of blood covered his body. His curly hair was blond under a layer of dust. His face was badly bruised, but everything seemed to be attached, thank God. He blinked up at us. His eyes were blue, but not a pale, watery blue like mine. His eyes were a bright blue, like a neon sign.

Marissa went into some sort of rescue mode. She took one of the bottles of water from her goodie bag, unscrewed the lid, and tilted the bottle to his lips. He half drank, half spat the water. He unfolded a little, becoming more human.

"I'm Tate Chamberlain." He said the name as if it should mean something to us, to everyone. "Tate Cham-ber-lain." He said it again slowly as if we might not have heard him the first time. "My dad owns Ozuye. You know, the big new casino on the Strip."

Even though he was covered with blood and dirt and had

a stain down his leg that I was pretty sure was urine, his tan trousers still had a crisp crease down the center. His golf-course-green polo shirt was branded by some designer.

"I'm Marissa and this is Icie," Marissa said as if we were tied together: Marissa-and-Icie 4 eva.

I maintained a safe distance. My calves were tight and ready to flee. "Are you sick?" I asked, praying for him to give the right answer.

"No," he said as if that was a stupid question.

I relaxed a little, even though the boy was the eye in a tornado of flies.

"So what are you doing out here in the middle of nowhere looking like the losing end of a prizefight?" Marissa asked.

"Don't you know?" he said, perking up a bit more. "Everything is out of control. I mean there are rumors of terrorist attacks. My dad heard one report on a private security channel that thousands of people were already infected with some deadly virus and people were dying."

Marissa gasped. Nausea overwhelmed me. Mum was right. I clutched my stomach and doubled over. I couldn't catch my breath.

The boy didn't notice our reaction and kept right on talking. "My dad paid some guys a million dollars to get me out of the city and someplace safe. He loaded the casino's VIP RV with a bunch of food and weapons and stuff."

I wasn't the only one with parents who'd do anything to give their kid a chance of survival.

"So what are you doing here, looking like that?" Marissa asked.

His big baby blues brimmed with tears. "The guys dumped me." The boy wiped dirt, snot, and tears from his face. "They threw me out while the RV was still moving. I've been trying to walk home. My dad trusted those guys. They'd been working for him forever. They did security at my birthday parties since I was two. How could they?"

"People do all kinds of crazy stuff when they think it's the end of..." Marissa rumpled his hair.

I felt as if we were in some massive hourglass and time was slipping away one precious grain of sand at a time. I'd broken my promise to Mum and spilled to Marissa, but I couldn't be responsible for anyone else. I could barely take care of myself. "Let's flag down a car and see if we can get *you* a ride back to Vegas," I said.

I walked a few feet away, raised my arms over my head, and waved when I saw a car materialize in the hazy distance. When the driver spotted me he seemed to speed up.

"Do you think Vegas is a good idea?" Marissa asked, stepping up next to me. "I mean, if it's some sort of virus thingy, wouldn't Vegas be one of the worst places to go?"

"Hey! Hey, you!" Tate called. "Dread! Baldy!" Tate was shouting but somehow managing to keep a whiny tone to his voice. "Can one of you help me up? I need some more water. Do either of you have any food? I'm starving."

Marissa and I—or should I say Dread and Baldy—glared at him. We found him near death by the roadside and he thought we owed him? *Seriously?*

"Keep on doing whatever you're doing," he shouted. His voice cracked with the effort. "Don't worry about me. I'm fine down here with all the bugs. I could use a clean shirt. Either of you got any painkillers? I think I may have broken something."

Marissa strolled over to Tate. "Let me explain a little something to you. Dread and Baldy saved your sorry ass, and we expect a little respect. My name is Marissa and that is Icie. You are not the boss of us. You'll do as you're told. Got it?"

He nodded and raised his arms like a toddler asking for a hug. He blinked those big blue eyes, which I was sure usually helped him get his way.

"Help me get him up, Ice," Marissa said, slipping her hands under his arms, like a forklift.

I couldn't move. I wanted to help, but this was too much, too real.

"Okay, take a breath and then I'll lift on your exhale," she told him. As Marissa lifted him, he took a deep breath and screamed like those pregnant girls did on that MTV *16 and Pregnant* show. As he got to his feet he staggered into me; I flinched at the feel of his sticky body on mine and the smell of urine that wafted off him.

"Thanks." He breathed the warm and wet word into my ear.

He wrapped his arm around my neck, and I reluctantly placed my arm on top of Marissa's, which was already slung around his middle. I whipped my free arm in a wide arc to shoo the flies.

We stood frozen like one of those stone sculptures that litter the D.C. landscape. We could be soldiers helping a fallen comrade off the battlefield—minus the steely looks of determination and matching uniforms. If there was some higher power—and I was having some significant doubts—then he or she was having a serious chuckle with this choose-your-own-adventure story.

"Marissa thinks it would be safer if we go somewhere away from Vegas," I told Tate.

"Yeah, I guess." He shrugged.

"We'll help get you across the road," Marissa explained. "It doesn't look like you've broken anything, so after that you'll need to suck it up and walk on your own. It's too hot and we're too tired."

He slouched in our grip. "But I'm really hurt," he whined. He was banged up. I could see that, but it was clear to me that he was exaggerating a little for effect. He was used to being taken care of.

"You'll be fine," Marissa said in a way that meant *end of discussion*, and surprisingly, Tate straightened a bit.

We had to time it just right. A few cars were zipping past on our side of the highway, heading to Vegas. It was hard to gauge their speed. By the time we could make out a car in the glare of the sun, it was too late to cross. It was like watching some sports-car event. The three of us tracked the cars from the distance and followed them as they passed. It looked like about a bazillion miles to the concrete barricade that separated the lanes of traffic.

"We're gonna have to make a run for it," Marissa said. "It's clear after this car. Ready?"

As the car passed, we synchronized our jog. Marissa and

I battled for the lead a bit, banging Tate between us with our ill-timed steps, but we finally got the pace right.

When we reached the median, we lifted Tate over the triangular barricade. I hauled myself up and over and helped Marissa do the same.

Tate was standing on his own, shaking his arms and legs as if making sure everything still worked.

"Looks like you're feeling better," Marissa said to Tate. Her scalp was shiny with sweat, but other than that she didn't look as if she'd exerted one calorie of energy.

"Oh," Tate groaned. "I'm really hurt." He slouched and screwed his face up in pain.

"Cut the dramatics. We need you to toughen up," Marissa said, giving him a playful shove. "Let's find a ride."

Marissa and Tate studied each car. Tate wanted to pick the most expensive vehicle. Marissa thought they should find an elderly couple or someone that needed their help. By looking at her you'd never guess she was like a bald, teen Mother Teresa. Tate was trying to convince her that people with money would give them the best chance of survival. To Tate money equaled freedom and happiness and a get-out-of-a-national-disaster-free card. I rolled my eyes but felt the tiniest wave of sympathy for him. He was only a kid.

Don't get attached, I told myself. I had to mentally prepare to say good-bye to Roadkill, and maybe Baldy too. I wasn't cut out to be a hero. I wasn't the best or the brightest at anything. They'd be better off without me.

As Tate and Marissa discussed the strategy for selecting a

getaway car, I felt a darkness descend. Was I really going to be all alone? I didn't think I'd ever been truly alone. In D.C., even when I was alone in my house, I could hear life going on outside my window. Lola was only a text away. If I screamed, I was pretty sure the neighbors would come running.

This was really it. Maybe I should just slip away. I summoned all my courage. But I couldn't do it. I'd left too much behind already. I couldn't stop the terrorists. I couldn't go back and save Lola. Maybe saving Marissa and Tate was the least I could do.

"Guys, there's another option." I opened the map and found a few rocks to pin down the four corners. I crouched next to it and waved Marissa and Tate over. "This is where I'm going." I pointed to the spot on the map and then the mountains in the distance. "You can come with me or whatever."

"But there's nothing there," Tate said.

I hesitated. My parents had entrusted me with a secret and not even twenty-four hours later I was blabbing it to everyone I met. But I couldn't leave them here and I realized I didn't want to be alone. "There's an underground—"

But before I could finish, Tate interrupted, "You mean that nuclear waste repository. That was never finished. I know because my dad got the casino owners to lobby against it. He made his employees go to demonstrations and distribute flyers."

"That's the point," I said, and shoved the map in my pocket. "It's an empty bunker. You can come with me or stay here. It's up to you."

"I don't know," Marissa said, appearing to mentally weigh her options: hop in a car with complete strangers or go underground with only slightly less strange strangers.

"We could at least go check it out," I continued. "Maybe you could get a phone signal once we're up on the mountain," I said to Marissa. "Maybe we wait it out a few days. I don't know." I was feeling pretty vulnerable out here in the hot sun with a mass of humanity rolling by. "I don't care what you do, but you need to make a decision."

"No offense, Ice, but I think I'll hitchhike to the next town," Marissa said.

"Yeah, I'm with Baldy." Tate moved closer to Marissa.

"Okay, whatever," I said. This felt a bazillion times worse than being dumped by Tristan. Was that only yesterday?

I picked a minivan with two kids watching movies on the screens embedded in their parents' headrests. There was room in the very back for Tate and Marissa. I tapped on the passenger-side window. The woman, who was the Wikipedia definition of soccer mom, stared straight ahead. I forgot what I must've looked like with my dreadlocks and mismatched set of bald and bloody.

I tapped on the window again. "Can you help us?" I shouted through the glass. She cringed, so I knew she could hear me. "Please," I called to her.

She lowered the window less than an inch. A wisp of cool air exhaled across my face. Oh, how I wanted to climb in her air-conditioned heaven and let someone else take me far, far away.

"What are you doing, Denise?" the driver yelled, and

stabbed at the window controls on his side. "You're going to get us killed," he said as the window gap closed.

She looked at me. Tears had drawn white and black tracks through the woman's bronzer. She mouthed the word *sorry*.

I pressed my palm against the window.

She shook her head. The driver was shouting at her. She turned toward the windshield and the minivan eased forward a foot.

"My turn," Tate said, and led Marissa and me to the most expensive car he could find. He hobbled over to a shiny red sports car occupied by a man in a black suit with his hair slicked back. Tate knocked on the window.

There wasn't really enough room for both of them in the car. The tiny backseat was strewn with a laptop, a brown leather briefcase, and a matching overnight satchel gaping open with clothes spilling out.

The man reached over and extracted something from his glove compartment. I didn't even need to look. I already knew what he'd be holding. He pointed the handgun at Tate and said calmly and clearly, "Get the hell away from my car."

Tate's face blanched. He raised his hands in surrender and backed away.

Marissa decided it was her turn. She picked one of those old tanklike sedans. Even though it had to be fifteen years old, its denim-blue paint job was pristine. As we approached the car from behind, we spotted two heads of silvery white hair. "I don't want to sneak up on them," she told to us. She wiped her face and head on her shirttail and plastered on a big cheerleader smile as she stepped in front of the long hood. She opened her mouth to say something but stopped. Her face scrunched as if she might cry. She rushed back to us.

"What is it?" Tate asked.

Marissa couldn't speak. She shook her head manically, half screaming and half sobbing.

"Marissa?" I asked, and put my arm around her shoulders.

"It-it's..." she stammered. "It's..." She took a deep breath. "It's awful." She curled into me and sobbed.

Tate rushed over to the car, looked in, and walked back. "Oh, man," he said. "That's disgusting. I bet that car must really stink."

"What?" I wanted and didn't want to know. "What?"

Marissa freed herself and clipped Tate on the back of the head. "How can you be so insensitive?"

"She's old" was Tate's explanation.

"What? What?" I asked Marissa and then Tate.

Marissa raked her sleeve across her face, smearing her perfectly outlined eyes. "The woman is...she was..." She sniffed.

"Dead," Tate said a little too enthusiastically. "Yeah, and the guy's bawling."

"What?"

Tate continued, "She's slumped over, and she got these—"

But before Tate could give me what I'm sure were the gory details, Marissa whacked him again. "Have some respect."

"The man's got these..." Tate flinched when he saw

109

Marissa raise her arm, but it was only to wipe her face. "He's sick too," Tate whispered to me.

"How can you be sure?" I asked.

"Trust me. You can tell," he said.

We stood there, scanning the vehicles around us. I didn't see people in those cars; I saw killers. No one and nothing felt safe. Someone could shoot us for staring at them. Some of these people were already infected. That was it.

"I'm out of here," I said, and found the straightest line to the roadside.

"I'm coming with you," Marissa said. She raced up next to me and looped her arm through mine.

"Yeah, okay. Okay. Wait up," Tate called. "I guess I'm going too. We can check it out, but I'm not saying I'm going in."

"Come on," I said, and led them toward the mountain range. One of them was my mountain, and I was going to make it there or die trying. My story wasn't going to end with my corpse decaying by the roadside like fast-food litter chucked out of some SUV.

ELEVEN

"There is no such thing as a good death."

—Just Saying 66

ATTI

All the rockstars are clustered around Atti like a litter of kittens. They slept all night in this jumbled pile with their arms and legs tangled together. Seeing those lights in the Man-Made Mountains had scared them. Atti's the oldest and a Cheerleader now. The rockstars look up to her like she does to Finch. She has to show him, show all of them, that she isn't a rockstar anymore. Last night she could hear the Cheer Captain talking to the Great I AM. He asked for guidance and strength and wisdom. Then he started all over again. Atti heard Finch come back. He didn't even check on her. There was this kind of buzz all night. The rockstars kept crying. She stroked their dreads just like her mum used to do. Mum. Her mum. It was her mum Out There. She knows it. The Cheer Captain always talks about signs. Atti's never really understood it before, but when those lights came on, she said to herself, *That's my mum. She's Out There. She's lost and scared, and she's signaling me and Finch to come help her.* Why can't Finch read the signs like she can? When the light outside the cave changes from black to a soft gray, Atti makes up her mind. She will go find her mum, even if no one else will. Even if it gets her into big trouble on her first full day as a Cheerleader. That's what Cheerleaders do. They are leaders. That is part of the name. Part of the word that she now is. She nudges one rockstar and pokes another, and they roll away. Now she's cold. She rubs her arms and legs. Harper says she generates her own energy. She wishes Harper could come with her, but she thinks she needs to do this all by herself. Show them that she is a Cheerleader. She crawls over to the mess of clothes along the back wall. She was supposed to wash them in the Mountain spring yesterday or the day before, but she doesn't like to wash. It's boring. She pulls on a few shirts and a skirt that fits. They're supposed to share, but she tries to wear the same things all the time. She rips the material and ties a few knots to make the clothes fit better. Her body is different from everyone else's, and their bodies aren't the same shape as those of the people who first wore these clothes years ago. They all know it but no one says. She has to roll up the waistband and cuffs. Her feet fit the shoes and her head fits in the hats, but she doesn't look like the people in the pictures from the Time Before. The bracelet her mum gave her slips off her wrist because her hands are too small. She takes the silver loop from where she keeps it safe and slips it all the way up her arm until it gets stuck. She kisses the metal and tells her mum that she's coming. She tells the two Cheerleaders guarding the cave that she's going to the Necessary. Lucky is waiting for her right by the Mall. She's flicking her tail back and forth as if she's keeping time to her own special song. Atti gives Lucky a tickle behind the ear and a kiss on her head. She spits out the thin cat hairs that stick to the cracks in her dry lips. "You can come on this adventure with me," she whispers to Lucky. She imagines that the Cheer Captain will tell her heroic story. Att and the Cat. She likes the sound of that. She sneaks out of Forreal with Lucky at her heels. She's pretty good at sneaking and Lucky is too, but it's easier because most everyone is asleep. She bets Finch has people patrolling now, so she better be careful. She can't get caught. Not until she has brought Mum back. Finch will be so surprised. She will probably be given her very own title, like Rescue Captain or something like that. At the edge of Forreal, right at the place where she thinks Forreal ends and everything else begins, there are these boulders that have the sacred symbol. Lucky leaps from one rock to another until she is sitting on the tallest one. "Cheer Captain Lucky," Atti says, and laughs at the cat looking down at her with her big yellow eyes. The way Lucky sits with her back straight and her head held high, she could be a leader. Atti will lead like a cat. "Come on, Lucky," she calls to her, and claps her hands. She takes off running because if Harper is right and she makes her own energy, then she must be making too much. She needs to go! Go! Go! She hesitates when she gets to the Black River. She's never been this far before. She's not supposed to be here. It's as if Lucky knows, because she sits on the edge of the Black River and meows at Atti. Lucky's so loud that Atti thinks someone might hear her.

They can only leave the Mountain with the permission of the Cheer Captain, and he only lets a few people leave every so often to find stuff they can use. Atti races down the Black River and hopes Lucky will follow, but the cat just sits there. Atti keeps turning back to check, which makes her stagger off course. Lucky's still there and still there and still there until she's a black dot that fades into the landscape. Atti runs and runs and runs. The sun is directly over her head now. Her legs feel wobbly because they aren't used to all this flat. She runs by rusting hunks of metal. She zigzags from side to side, looking in these big metal containers. Finch said the rubber rings they sit on at Storytime came off these things. He said they used to move, but she doesn't see how. Some even have bushes growing inside them. One has a nest, but she doesn't wait around to see which animal lives there. Being out here on her own is a bit screepy. She wishes she remembered to bring water and food. She should search for some of those plants they eat. She races off the River and looks high and low. But everything is brown. Just brown all around. She spots a chuck and wally. She races after them. She's caught them before, but there are too many places to hide here. She loses chuck and then wally. She's hungry and hot and tired. She thought it would be easy to find the Man-Made Mountains. They are right there in the middle of the valley. She figured she could walk in a straight line. The Black River looks like it leads there, but now she's not so sure which way the Black River is. She walks one way for a while and then another. The sun is mixing up her head and this flat nothingness all around her doesn't feel real anymore. Her feet keep walking. Maybe she should just go home. The sun is escaping behind those mountains over there. "Mum!"

she calls. "Mum!" Maybe Mum can come find her. Atti's getting
so tired. "Mum!" she screams. She's got to hear her. "Mum!"
She's gone and Atti's lost and she's really, really scared. She runs
as fast as she can. *Just run*, she tells herself. She's looking up for
the lights in the Man-Made Mountain but all she sees are stars.
Her foot rams into something hard and she sprawls flat on her
face. It's the Black River. Maybe she's safe. One way leads to the
Man-Made Mountains and the other to Forreal. She just needs
to get up, but her body feels so heavy. She hears a low growl.
She shuts her eyes tight and curls into a ball. Maybe it can't find
her if she's so small. She offers up her humble Saying to the Great
I AM. *Whatever...*

TWELVE

At first our pace was slow, but then I looked in the car windows. I didn't mean to, but they were a few feet away and curiosity got the better of me. Maybe I wanted to check for myself. I suppose a part of me was clinging to the tiniest shred of hope that this wasn't for real. I still wanted to believe that terrorists hadn't unleashed some horrible ripple that was spreading and killing quicker than the speed of a tweet.

The people in some cars looked fine, except for panicked expressions and their inability to turn their heads and look at us. They were as afraid of us as we were of them. In other cars, I saw people with skin of a pale greenish color. Others had blotches and splotches that looked like the combination of a bruise and a blister. I saw one guy vomit, just spew right over the dashboard and coat the windshield. I gagged and then started running along the roadside. I wanted to get as far away from what was left of humanity as fast as possible. Marissa and Tate were soon keeping pace at my heels.

All doubt about what to do vanished. I channeled all my fear into action and ran. I spotted a path that looked like it might have once been used as a road. I pointed and tore off down the path. Sweat was washing down my body and I was slip-sliding in my flip-flops. When the cars behind me blurred into the landscape, I skidded to a stop. I hunched over and panted for air. Marissa and Tate caught up to me. Neither of them looked as near to collapse as I felt.

"Take it easy, Icie," Marissa said. She rubbed my back, but her touch felt icky and contaminated. I ducked from her hand. "I got heat stroke one summer at cheer camp. It's nasty. I think we should take a second and prepare for our hike."

Marissa made us cover our heads. At the airport, she'd pinched two baseball caps with the words *Grand Canyon* stitched in rainbow thread. I found my favorite black hat in my backpack. It had the silhouette of *Jaws* and the line *You're Gonna Need a Bigger Boat* embroidered on it. Marissa slathered us with lotion, which she pulled from her massive handbag. It was an expensive face moisturizer, but the label said it had some sort of protection against the desert sun's harsh rays. I traded my flip-flops for my grubby old tennis shoes, which were stuffed at the bottom of my backpack. While rummaging through, I spotted Nutri-power Bars, a flashlight, vitamins, and a first-aid kit. From my quick inventory, it appeared that my parents had included the main stuff I'd need to survive.

As soon as we were protected from the sun, I took off. I was doing this race-walk thingy. Mum and I had made fun of the momodels at the Mother-Daughter Breast Cancer 10K for doing exactly what I was doing. That's what we called the women with faces plastered with makeup, wearing matching workout wear and doing this wiggle walk.

The heat was like a fist shoving me into the hard, rocky ground. We walked in a blessed silence. Then, for no reason I could discern, the Tate tap started to drip, drip, drip. "What if it's chemical warfare, you know, like deadly gases that deep-fry your lungs and melt your eyeballs. That grandma looked like..." He glanced at Marissa, who only had to look back and raise one eyebrow to indicate her disapproval, and Tate changed the subject. "My dad said that D.C. and New York were targeted first. Man, all those poor slobs in D.C. and NYC. They are probably just a big oozing pile of flesh now."

Marissa stopped. Tate was too busy with his gory tale to notice, and he smacked right into her. She gritted her teeth and whipped around to face him.

"What?" he whined. "I'm just saying—"

"Well, don't. Don't just say. My mom and Icie's parents live in D.C. This isn't some video game, you..."

"Fridiot," I filled in the gap.

"Man, Baldy has a bit of a temper," Tate muttered. He walked ahead of us now. He wasn't really talking to us anymore; he was just talking. "I was just saying that my dad says that no matter what kind of attack it is, the world's going to go freaking insane. I heard him telling his head of security to lock everything down because there would probably be riots and looting. He also said the U.S. might retaliate with bombs and shit and they might—"

"Tate!" I screamed to get his attention. He turned and walked backward. "I need you to stop talking." I spoke every word slowly, so even Tate, with his limited IQ, would understand. "If you say one more word, I swear I will kill you with my bare hands."

He pinned his lips together, turned back around, and kept right on walking.

We put one foot in front of the other and headed toward the spot Mum had pointed to on the map. The landscape looked like a mix between an old Western and a sci-fi flick. Scary and creepy. Screepy. I thought I must remember to tell Lola that one. She'd like it, but then it hit me. I might never see Lola again.

Don't think about Lola, I told myself. Don't think about anything but getting to the mountain.

As we approached the first mountain, I scanned for any sign. It looked big and barren. Was this the one? Mum had pointed to the middle mountain in the series of three. From this vantage point the mountain range stretched out forever. One mountain blended into the next.

We kept walking. How was I supposed to recognize it?

Mum said something about an infinity symbol. Now the idea sounded crupid. I begin to doubt my memory.

I noticed two clusters of boulders up ahead where the first mountain merged into a valley before ramping up to the next mountain. As we drew closer, I could see the rocks had been tagged with graffiti. I stopped to study the markings. Someone had drawn a cartoon face in white paint. Maybe it was supposed to be that fat kid from that cartoon Lola liked. The heat and sun seemed to be eating my brain. I couldn't remember the name of it.

This Rocks! was painted in green. But there was something painted in silver underneath all the rest of the scribbles. It was hard to tell with the overlapping graffiti and the weatherworn paint. I walked up to the rock. Glittery flecks in the stone glimmered in the sunlight. I placed my finger on the silver paint. The rock felt dry and warm. I traced the line through crisscrossing splotches of paint. My finger looped as the silver paint snaked in a thin, horizontal figure eight that was as big as my outstretched arms.

"Infinity," I said. I pressed my palm on the rock as if I might be able to feel ancient vibrations traveling up through the stone. Its message had been received. This was my mountain.

"This way," I told Marissa and Tate, who were sipping water and sharing a can of honey-roasted peanuts.

"How do you know?" Tate asked, munching and spewing peanuts.

"This is the symbol my mum said would mark the mountain." I ate a handful of peanuts.

"Infinity," Marissa said. "I hope that means we'll live forever."

Or at least through the night, I thought, and snatched the water bottle from Tate before he downed the last few inches.

The initial power surge I'd felt to get to the bunker eased a little. We were well away from the main road and there wasn't another person or animal in sight.

The boulders formed a gateway to what I realized was a dirt road that twisted between the two mountains and then snaked up and out of sight. This had to be it. To build tunnels underground they would have needed to drive trucks and equipment up the mountainside. "Let's go," I said, and marched ahead. They followed. The weight of their survival weighed me down more than my backpack and sweat-soaked clothes.

Mounds of trash bordered the dirt road. It was mostly smashed wood and bits of plastic, but there was also a burned-out washing machine and a pile that contained two rusty bedsprings and a roll of orange shag carpet. Tate inspected each pile, kicking at the stray bits and calling out what he could recognize.

"Old tin Spam container."

"Leather shoes."

"Beer can."

"Coke bottle."

Broken glass crunched beneath our feet. I imagined a group of people our age drinking and laughing around a bonfire. This secluded spot would be great for a secret party.

The farther we got from the highway the less I felt as if we were in the U.S. or any earthly civilization. We picked our way through low-lying shrubs and spiky cacti. Marissa screamed and clung to Tate when a brown lizard no more than a foot long and a few inches high darted in front of her.

"Chuckwalla," Tate said. "They're harmless."

Marissa peeled herself off. "Yeah, whatever."

Tate would call out "Chuck" or "Wally" when he spotted one of the brown lizards. I would jump a little every time he shouted. I didn't even like the zoo and thought roughing it was taking the Metro. I tried to shake the image of six-foot hairy spiders and mountain lions that would consider city-girl a delicacy.

Tate plugged himself into his iPod. He drummed his fingers on his leg or thumped his hands on his chest. He clicked. He hummed. He shuffled to his own beat. We found out later he had cradled his prized possession in his hand while his captors literally gave him the boot out the back of the RV.

Tears stung the back of my eyes. How were we ever going to survive? I didn't have enough food for the three of us for very long. What about a clean supply of water? Nevada is a desert, after all. Were Marissa and Tate and I really going to be the last survivors on Earth? And, if I didn't get sick or melt or burn or die in one of Tate's end-of-time scenarios, how could I possibly live in some bunker while everything else was destroyed?

I pushed all those questions out of my head. All I had to

do was find the bunker. That's it. I wouldn't think beyond getting to someplace safe. If I found my parents' bunker, then I'd figure out how to live one more day. I raced ahead and started the gradual ascent up the mountain.

Getting to the mountain had not been easy, but finding the entrance to this top secret bunker was going to be next to impossible. The mountain was ginormous, and I had no idea what we were looking for exactly. We wound our way around the mountain. It could take us days to find the entrance this way. Marissa checked her phone a few times but still no signal.

"Hey, is this it?" Tate asked when he spotted an entrance to a cave.

I tentatively peeked my head inside. It was a decent-size cave, but it wasn't marked by an infinity symbol. It didn't look man-made. "No, this isn't it."

"Look!" Marissa shouted. A big-horned sheep darted away as she pointed. I walked closer to the spot it had vacated. The sheep had been drinking from a small pool. Water was bubbling from a triangle in the mountainside created by two rocks tilting into each other. The water was framed by three flat stones to create a natural paddling pool. I knelt down. The pool was swarming with wasps and these beautiful blue dragonflies. I cupped the water in my hands and took a huge drink. The water was cool and fresh.

"There are a few of these natural springs in the mountains around here," Tate said, as if he had somehow become our nature guide. "Weird, huh?"

"Let's refill our water bottles," Marissa said, and started right to work.

"Nah," Tate said, standing a few feet away. "I don't like wasps, sheep spit, or whatever else might be swimming in that water. I don't even drink tap water."

The boy didn't fully understand our dire situation yet, and I didn't feel like enlightening him.

After a brief rest, we walked on. Complete and utter exhaustion usurped my overwhelming anxiety. I recognized the same cluster of what Tate said were Joshua trees. I thought we'd passed them before, but I couldn't be sure.

"We need to mark where we've been," I said when we reached a line of pine trees. Marissa and Tate parked themselves in the first shade we'd seen all day. Marissa stretched out on a bed of pine needles.

"What?" Tate asked, plucking the earphones out of his ears.

"I said I think we need to mark where we've been," I repeated. "Listen to your music and give me a minute."

He turned his silver iPod over in his hands as if it were the first time he'd seen it. It was the brand-new version that could hold a millionish songs and play movies, probably had some sort of global positioning, and, for all I knew, actually stored the boy's brain. "It hasn't been on," Tate said. "I've been saving my battery—even though I probably shouldn't worry. Dad had this custom made for me. Its battery life is, like, insane. I've been creating playlists in my head or trying to remember every tune on a CD in the right order. That kind of thing."

"Oh." My heart sank. The boy was a walking noisemaker.

"I've got a pocketknife." He dug in his pocket and fished out a red Swiss Army knife. "You said you wanted to mark where we've been. You could use this to carve something on trees."

I took the knife from him and flipped out the blade. I scooted next to the nearest tree and carved my initials. It felt good to dig the knife into the fleshy bark. I dug the letters deep into the tree. I walked a few feet to another tree and carved the letters again. "I'm going to look around. I'll be right back." I needed to think.

I wandered from tree to tree, making my mark. I'm sure it wasn't good for the trees, but it was a matter of life and death. I found a patch of dirt and sat cross-legged. I slipped the pocketknife in my phone pocket.

It was quiet up here. I mean a quiet like I had never really experienced before. Our fridge buzzed. Our air conditioner hummed. The traffic rumbled. This kind of quiet was unnatural and unnerved me.

Something furry brushed against my arm. I sprang to my feet.

My panic fizzled when I realized I wasn't going to be eaten by a grizzly bear or mauled by a coyote. Bears and coyotes don't really brush up against you before they devour you. The closest I ever came to an animal attack was a squirrel stealing my sandwich at the Lincoln Memorial Reflecting Pool.

I looked at the source of my terror. A black cat. A domestic cat, not a jaguar. It rubbed up against my legs and purred.

The cat was a sign. In the middle of nowhere, a friendly black cat sauntered over for a cuddle. It had to be a sign. But superstitions were relative. My American dad thought a black cat meant bad luck, but if you were British like my mother, black cats were good luck. Or maybe this was heat stroke and I was hallucinating house pets. I knelt down and petted the cat's head with one finger in slow, metered strokes. It flopped on its side at my feet, stretched its paws, and rolled from side to side.

"You're a good sign," I said out loud to the cat.

"I see you've met Midnight." A deep voice startled me.

I fell back on my butt. Only a few feet away stood a guy, maybe my age, dressed in a white T-shirt and jeans. I scrambled away from him. Adrenaline surged through my body and every part of me trembled.

Even in my full-out horror-movie fright, I still registered that he was handsome in a Times Square billboard model way: silky jet-black hair tied back in a slick, low ponytail. Possibly Native American heritage. Dark, nearly black eyes. Tall, probably a head taller than me if I were able to stand up. I bet there was a six-pack under that tight white T. You'd think his underwear-model looks might make me relax, but again, the horror-movie handbook clearly states that the better looking they are, the more deadly they can be.

"What are you doing here?" His voice was so low it resonated in my chest.

I couldn't speak, only spider-walk, like the chick from

The Exorcist, farther away from him. The air seemed to rattle, as if my meltdown were in surround sound.

The cat leapt to her feet. Her back arched and every hair on her body stood at attention. Her tail sprang up in a straight line. She opened her mouth and hissed, exposing needlelike fangs. The tiny domestic cat was possessed and, believe it or not, incredibly scary. My brain told me to run, but it was as if the air around me had thickened to caramel.

The guy's body tensed. "Shut up and stay still," he barked. He moved in slow motion. He twisted his arm behind his back. When his hand reappeared, it was holding a gun. I'd seen bazillions of guns, but none this up close and personal until today, and now I'd seen two. If you've ever read any murder mysteries, you know the author will tell you what kind of gun the bad guy is holding. All I could tell was that it was pointed right at me. I didn't care if it was a 747 Magnum, a shotgun, or a semiautomatic. All he needed was one bullet, which I assumed he had; reasonable aim; and the slightest twitch of his pointer finger.

"Please. No." I was babbling and pleading in this baby-whisper kind of way. I'd like to say I had some profound final words, but all I could say was "No. No. No."

"Don't move!" he shouted. I drew myself into a tight ball, wrapping my arms around my legs. I squeezed my eyes shut tightly.

"Shit!" the guy bellowed. "Shit. Shit. Shit."

The air exploded with a deafening *bang*!

THIRTEEN

"Your attitude determines your altitude."

—Just Saying 192

BECKETT

Greta is all Beckett can think about as he patrols the Mountain or leads the Evening Tune. Her face and touch come to him even as he's instructing the rockstars on a Just Saying.

But this has to be the last time they meet. Now that everyone has seen the lights, these secret meetings are too risky. Finch has Cheerleaders constantly patrolling the Mountain, searching for Terrorists. Beckett isn't helping by keeping his meetings with Greta a secret. He should tell Harper or Finch, but they have a new paranoia about Terrorists and everything Out There. Beckett doesn't know what would happen if anyone found him and Greta hidden away. The only way Greta will be safe is to keep her and her people off the Mountain.

Sneaking out this morning was tricky. Beckett followed the early morning patrol and peeled off when they returned to Forreal. He won't have much time with Greta, but how long can it take to say good-bye?

He holds his breath as he nears their meeting place. He pauses and clings to the sweet anticipation before looking up to the spot where he first saw her, facing the Man-Made Mountains with the sun kissing her cheeks.

"Hi," she says shyly, and waves down at him.

"Hey," Beckett says as he climbs up the rock and takes his place next to her.

"So," she says, and slips her hand in his.

How can she do that with such ease, as if their hands were always meant to clasp? He smiles with what feels like his whole body.

"I missed you," she says. The same words were on his tongue, there ready and waiting, but she speaks them.

"I missed you too." He feels the warmth of a blush rise into his cheeks. He thinks the words sound silly when he says them.

They stand there, suspended in the morning sun. He wants to stay like this forever.

"Someday you are going to have to tell me more about Forreal," she says as if starting in the middle of a conversation. He wonders if, like he does, she keeps a running list of the things she wants to tell him. He has this ongoing monologue to her in his head. It's similar to the dialogue he has with the Great I AM. Thoughts of Greta keep edging into his meditation time. That's another reason that this has to be good-bye.

She continues, "I mean, I know there are less than fifty of you and you live together on the other side of the mountain. Those mounds that surround the mountain are your ancestors. I think it's amazing you have lived here for so long." She sighs. He didn't realize he'd told her so much. "I feel as if I've moved more than I've stayed."

"Why is that? Why don't your people stay?" he asks, trying to change the subject. He doesn't want her to know he's the Cheer Captain. He doesn't want to tell her about the Great I AM. He doesn't want her to look at him any differently than she does right now.

"That's not fair. I answer your questions and you never answer mine." She tugs her hand free and his hand feels naked. "I'll answer this one last question, then you have to talk. Okay?"

"Okay," he says.

Greta takes a deep breath, as if her answer may take a while. "My family lived on a farm far away from everyone else. That's how they survived after, you know."

Beckett doesn't know. He knows Terrorists destroyed everything in the Time Before, but none of his ancestors created a story about the Plague or the Battles. The Great I AM said, *It's better to look forward than back.* He knows fragments, but he gets the sense Greta's people could fill in the gaps.

"My family stayed on the farm as long as they could until we ran out of resources. We've been moving around ever since I was born." She has a faraway look. "Now it's your turn."

What can he tell her? "The Mountain has been good to us. It provides what we need. We survive because we work together."

She takes his hand again and gently swings. "Maybe you should consider joining us. Move to Vega. Wouldn't it be great to see each other all the time? We could combine our resources."

"Yes, I mean, no. I mean it's fromplicated," Beckett says. He feels as if she's setting a trap, trying to get him to expose what he's painstakingly kept hidden.

"What?" Greta asks.

"Fromplicated," he says again, as if repeating it will make her understand. She shrugs. He tries a different way. "It's very difficult and complex."

"Oh." Greta nods. "Complicated."

"I guess," he says, even though she's saying it wrong.

"Go on," Greta encourages.

"The Mountain is special to us. It's hard to explain to someone who hasn't grown up here. We belong here. We can't leave."

"Do you mean you've never left the Mountain?" Greta's mouth gapes open in surprise.

"No, not really." Beckett can feel his face getting hot. "We send teams out every so often to salvage things, but I never get to go." He explains how Forreal creates a chain of people so everyone can see the person just ahead and just behind. They have scouts who shuttle things back and forth. They have lookouts. They leave when the sun rises and return well before it sets. He doesn't say they do this elaborate gathering maneuver to defend against a Terrorist attack. He doesn't want to frighten her with talk of beasties.

"There's so much more out there." She spins around with her arms open wide. "How can you not be curious?"

Her face is alive with life. It makes him realize how little they smile in Forreal. They work and worship and every day is like the last—until she showed up. For a second he wishes he could leave the Mountain with Greta. He immediately asks the Great I AM to forgive him. He didn't mean it.

"You know there's a big wide world beyond these mountains?" she says when she stops spinning. She staggers a bit and he grabs her elbow to steady her. "We picked Vega because the mountains are a natural barrier to keep people out."

So she's scared of others too.

Greta pinches the front of her shirt and pulls the sweat-wet material away.

"I keep forgetting to ask…." He points to Greta's shirt, with its hand-drawn circle with an inverted *Y* in the middle. The pie pieces are floating free. "What does it mean?"

"It's the ancient symbol for peace," she says, peeling the shirt from her skin again so he can get a better look. "I don't know if I've drawn it right."

"Peace," he repeats, and likes the thought of it. While there are Terrorists Out There, he doesn't think Forreal will ever truly have peace.

Greta moves in front of him. His arms hover and then slip around her waist. He smells the tang of sweat and the tart of the earth that coats everyone, but there's a hint of something floral. He drinks it in. She presses her cheek to his and they stay like this, suspended between two places. He holds his body very still. His mind mellows. People aren't looking to him, waiting for answers. He's just a boy lost in a girl.

"This is nice," Greta murmurs. He rests his head on hers. No matter what happens, he will always have this one perfect moment.

He senses movement in his peripheral vision. He glances in that direction, but he doesn't see anything. Finch's paranoia is rubbing off. Then he feels something tickle his leg. He jumps, surprised at his surprise, but it's only Lucky. She meows as if she's trying to tell him something.

"Who is this?" Greta asks, and strokes the cat between her pointy ears. Lucky flops on her side and rolls on her back. She extends her front paws in the air, exposing the soft fur on her chest.

"That's Lucky," he says, knowing exactly what the cat wants. He scratches her furry stomach.

"I've never seen a black cat before," Greta says, kneeling beside the cat. "She's beautiful."

"There has always been a black cat on the Mountain," Beckett says. "We have a special reverence for cats."

"You mean you worship cats?" Greta asks, touching the black pad of the cat's outstretched paw.

"No," he says. "But cats have a special connection to Forreal." He won't tell Greta how important this cat is. He realizes it might sound odd that Forreal believes some great calamity will befall them if there is not a black cat on the Mountain. Other cats roam the Mountain, but Lucky has always been special. A black cat saved the Great I AM.

There's a sound like the clack of rock on rock. Lucky darts back the way she came. Greta must hear it too because she and Beckett shift so they are standing back-to-back, turning in a tight circle, scanning their surroundings.

"Follow me," she whispers. She's holding his hand again and leading him down the Mountain.

"I can't," he says, and digs his heels into the rock, but there's no foothold. Pebbles roll under his feet. Something flashes out of the corner of his eye and now he's clambering down the rocks alongside her.

He sees it again, movement in his peripheral vision. He senses it too. Someone is watching. Maybe it's his guilt creating this sensation. Or is it the Great I AM's watchful eye?

"Come on," she says, pulling Beckett forward. Beckett wonders if the Great I AM can see him if he leaves the Mountain.

They begin to run. He trips and tries to regain his balance, but he stumbles and hits the ground hard. His body keeps rolling and collecting debris. He crashes into one of his ancient ancestor's burial mounds and pain radiates through his body.

Greta is at his side. "Are you hurt?" she asks.

He shakes his head and rises to his elbows. Nothing is broken or bleeding. He sends thanks to the Great I AM. Was the trip telling him not to leave the Mountain? Or was the roll, the inertia, the Great I AM's way of sending him off the Mountain? Before Greta, the Great I AM's messages were clear. He can't decipher the Great I AM's wishes through the muddle of his feelings for Greta.

Greta tucks his dreadlocks behind each ear. "I'm sorry, Beckett, this is my fault. I thought if I got you off the mountain…" Her voice trails off.

"What?" He props himself against the rock.

She sits down next to him and bows her head. "You're always looking around, preoccupied. I thought if I got you off the mountain, we could truly be alone. It was stupid and I'm sorry."

He is overcome with emotion. He kneels beside her. He takes her face in his hands and kisses her. His tightly puckered lips press her half-open mouth.

She pulls away, blinking in surprise. Then she kneels in front of him. She slowly, gently touches her lips to his. She tilts her head and nudges his lips apart with hers, showing him how to respond. He mirrors her every move. His heart is racing. They are falling into each other. He can't be close enough to her. His hands grope, wanting to hold and explore her simultaneously. Every part of her is so soft: her hair, her skin, her curves, her lips. He realizes his fingers are tangled in her hair.

What is he doing? He wrenches himself away and wipes at his lips.

"Beckett." Greta crawls toward him, but he scrambles away. It's too much. This is all too much.

"I've got to go," he says, and stands. If he stays one more moment, if she kisses him again, he will never be able to tell her good-bye.

"What?" Greta is fumbling to her feet. She's tugging at the hem of her T-shirt, which has risen up to expose her creamy-white stomach. "When can I see you again?" she asks, and slips into his arms.

"You can't. You can't stay and I can't leave." He can't keep risking everything for secret conversation and kisses. And it can never be more than that.

She kisses him again. It feels as if they've been doing this forever, as if her lips were always meant to meet his. He's never felt a force so strong. He's got to go. But his body is alive with the feel of her.

Beckett somehow finds the strength to walk away, but he looks back. She is standing there, mesmerized by his kiss. "You can never come back to the Mountain," he tells her. He hates to walk away, but it's the only way to keep her safe.

FOURTEEN

"Sometimes we are our biggest obstacle."

—Just Saying 200

HARPER

Tears stream down Harper's face but she doesn't wipe them away. The sensation surprises her. She hasn't cried since Beckett found her wandering on the Mountain.

He's racing up the Mountain away from her, away from that girl. Harper is hidden behind one of the burial mounds.

"He kissed HER," she says to herself, but it can't be real. That girl haunts her dreams. These flashes from Harper's past have gotten more violent and disturbing. The girl in her dreams has been replaced by the image of this girl. The memory is still cloudy but the meaning is clear. It's a warning to stay away from her.

"HE kissed her," Harper says again, and feels pain tighten in her gut. He's been sneaking behind her back and keeping secrets.

"He KISSED her." She saw the way he lunged for the girl and swept her in his arms. Their bodies pressed together, writhing like snakes. "He kissed her." She lets the pain bruise and harden.

She wasn't looking for him. She was looking for Atti. Harper hasn't seen her since her ceremony and the lights last night. One of the Cheerleaders says he might have seen her go to the Necessary early this morning, but he's not sure. Atti loves a game of hide-and-seek. They've played it since she was a little rockstar. But Harper's checked all her hiding spots. Atti is never any good at the game. She usually springs out of her hiding place to surprise Harper. Harper's been searching all morning.

Harper must keep looking. She wipes her face and sniffs back her sadness at Beckett's betrayal. She's tracked Atti to the base of the Mountain. She thought she might be hiding among the burial mounds. She likes to visit her dad's grave and tell Harper stories about him, even though he died a few months before she was born. Atti tells the stories her mum and Finch told to her. She paints him as this great hunter and loving father, but Harper knew Dill and he wasn't. He was the same as everyone else on the Mountain. He did his assigned jobs and died a slow and painful death. But Atti needs to believe he was special.

Harper glances up the Mountain. Beckett has disappeared. Harper climbs the mound of rocks without dislodging a single one. She tries not to think about the bones that are rotting below her. She presses herself flat and looks to the spot where she saw Beckett kiss the girl. The girl is still standing there. She hasn't spotted Harper because she's staring up the Mountain. The girl touches her lips and something inside Harper snaps.

Harper screams as she leaps off the pile and sprints toward

the girl. Harper doesn't know what she'll do when she reaches her. When the girl sees Harper, she bolts. Harper hesitates before she heads across the desert. Harper hasn't been off the Mountain since Beckett saved her. She's always been too scared, but now she doesn't care. Let the Terrorists come.

When she reaches the first row of buildings, the girl's pace slows. She glances back. Harper's close enough to see the fear in her eyes. The girl dodges behind one of the endless rows of houses. When Harper makes the same turn, the girl's gone. Harper skids to a stop and looks down the empty spaces between the buildings. She walks to the corner of the next house and checks left and then right. The girl has disappeared. Harper screams, a sound more like a roar. It erupts out of her and she can't contain it. Hot tears spill from her eyes.

Harper falls against the side of a house and collapses to the ground, sobbing. She will find the girl. She just needs to calm down and listen. In the hunt, the ears are as important as the eyes.

Harper takes a deep breath and then another. She closes her eyes and erases the image of Beckett kissing that girl. She focuses on the blackness behind her eyes. She listens for the girl and the approach of Terrorists. Finch has recounted how their scaly bodies rustle like dried leaves and how they growl and hiss. Harper's body is contracted and ready for battle.

She hears voices. Male voices. Her eyes spring open.

"What was that?"

"I think it was some sort of animal."

"I think we should go."

"What if it's waiting for us?"

It's difficult to determine where the voices are coming from. She crawls to the front of the house and looks around. All the doors stand open. The windows have jagged teeth of glass. Cheerleaders might have searched these or they may have been gutted from the Time Before.

"Are you sure Greta came this way?" one voice says.

There's mumbling and then another voice. "Let's just go back. There's nothing good here."

"But what was that noise?" There are at least three separate voices and they aren't far away.

Up ahead there's the burned-out remains of the machines that took people from place to place. Harper stays low and slips inside one, hoping to get a better look at the source of the voices. She rubs her hands in the charred remains and wipes the ash on her face and in her hair. She colors herself in black camouflage, still listening and watching.

She hears a *bang* to her left. She rises so only her eyes peek out of the blackened frame. Four boys are pounding down the front steps of a house. They are knocking into one another and laughing. They are too big and bulky to be from Forreal.

The boys are heading straight for her. She sinks down and pulls herself into a tight ball. Their voices get louder.

"Where is Greta? I thought you said she came this way, Tink."

"She's gone to the mountain again, hasn't she?"

Greta. Is that the girl's name?

"Da sent her to investigate the mountain, stupid."

"She told you what she's doing, didn't she?"

"You better tell us."

There's shuffling and sounds that must be the boys hitting one another, not hard but shoving enough to make one of them stumble.

"Stop it."

"Talk."

They are so close. Harper clenches her fists to stop her hands from shaking.

"She's supposed to find out about the people who live on that mountain."

"She told us she didn't find anything. She's such a liar."

Harper's breath is coming faster and faster. The more she tries to calm herself, the harder it is to breathe.

"Maybe we should go check it out."

"She said those people might be dangerous. They guard the mountain."

They stop right beside Harper. One leans on her hiding spot and jostles her.

"Maybe they have more food."

"We can't go up there. Da and Greta would kill us."

"Greta is going to report back to Da and then they will decide what to do about the mountain people."

Harper understands. Greta's a spy. She's using Beckett.

"You need to grow up and think for yourself and not always follow Greta."

Harper looks up just as one of them is shoved toward her. The brittle, burned metal breaks under his weight and he is on top of her.

He screams a high-pitched squeal when he sees her. She springs to her feet and kicks him with all her might.

"What the—?" but Harper doesn't let the guy finish. Before

they have time to react, she punches him square in the jaw, kicks another in the chest, and swings around and shoves another one to the ground.

The fourth one comes at Harper, but a swift kick between his legs sends him crumpled to the ground. Harper raises her fists, begging one of them to make a move.

"What is it?" asks the one still flailing inside the metal frame.

Harper pumps her fists in the air and screams, "Stay away from the Mountain!" Her voice is raw and gravelly from the crying and running and screaming.

Harper runs, laughing at the black lithe creature she's become. She doesn't look back, because she knows they won't follow her. Their fear will keep them rooted to the spot. She hopes they deliver her message to Greta and the others who want to take the Mountain.

She passes row after row of houses. This suddenly seems familiar to her, as if she's been here before or someplace very much like it. She knows she shouldn't take the time, but she peeks in one of the windows. Harper can imagine what it must have looked like before the grit, sand, and sun invaded. She closes her eyes and a memory comes flooding back. She sees a boy and two girls. They must be about the same age as she is now. The ache in her gut tells her these people were her family, maybe a brother and sisters, but certainly people who loved her and took care of her. They are fighting with the girl who reminds Harper of the girl Beckett kissed. They are shouting and shoving and arguing about a can. That's all. One blackened silver can with rust crusting at the lid. Harper knows there's food inside. She can see the fight but she's safe, hidden in a pile of rags. One of her sisters glances at her. Her eyes say, *Stay safe, stay hidden.* She hears three bangs. She hadn't noticed the weapon in the girl's hands. Harper watches her brother and sisters fall to the floor; pools of blood spread and connect. The girl peels her brother's fingers off the can.

Harper opens her eyes, but she can't shake the image or crushing sense of loss. She runs as fast as she can.

As Harper approaches the Mountain, she sees several Cheerleaders dotting the Mountainside. It's far too many for a normal patrol and then she remembers Atti. They must be looking for her.

Harper spots Finch's unmistakable walk. She rushes toward him. When he sees Harper, he lets out a yell and tackles her. Harper can't speak while dodging his fists.

"F-F-Finch," she finally manages to stammer. What is he doing?

He stops with his fist drawn for another blow.

"It's me. It's Harper."

His eyes narrow. His face still contorted with rage.

"What's the matter with you?" Harper struggles beneath him, but he keeps her pinned there, studying her as if he doesn't believe it's her.

"Harper?"

She doesn't respond. She realizes what she must look like painted black.

"I thought you were a Terrorist." He calls her the name that was just forming in her brain.

And he's right. How has she not seen it before?

"Why are you covered in ash?" He relaxes and lies beside her.

She's turned herself black, inside and out. She became a beastie the moment she lashed out at Greta and those boys.

"Harper, what's the matter?" He rolls on his elbow and stares at her. Maybe he's seeing her for the first time, maybe he understands now too.

All her visions make sense. A girl like Greta killed her family. The girl was a person, no different from a Cheerleader.

There are no beasties Out There—not the kind Finch describes with scales and claws and fangs. No, Terrorists are better disguised and more deadly. She is a Terrorist. She hates and destroys. Greta and her people, they are Terrorists too. What Forreal has feared all along is a myth to protect them from the knowledge that they did this to one another. And if she doesn't do something, they will continue to destroy one another.

"Finch." Harper rolls over to face him. She knows how to keep Greta off the Mountain and Beckett safe. "I've seen Terrorists."

FIFTEEN

I'd read scary stories where people said crupid stuff like: (1) That's when I realized I was holding my breath. *Really?* I never bought that anyone could forget to breathe. How many times do you think about breathing? *Um, never.* And (2) I heard screaming and then realized it was me. *Yeah, right.* When I scream I know for damn sure it's me.

But when the hot guy shot the gun, I did both—just not in that order.

There was one long, bloodcurdling outburst that made Jamie Lee Curtis's screams in the original *Halloween* and *H2O* sound more like my grandma's disapproving mews when her tea gets cold. I heard the sound and realized I was screaming.

My eyelids snapped open as wet red bits rained down on me. This all happened in nanoseconds. The guy's eyes were fixed straight ahead with the gun still extended in front of him, but he hadn't been looking *at* me. He was focused on something behind me.

I sprang to my feet, whipped around, and saw what the guy had shot. That's when I did that thing where I realized I wasn't breathing. I took a ginormous gulp of air and then I screamed again and again and again and again. I couldn't stop. I wiped the red flecks from my arms, still screaming. These bloody chunks were all over me. They dotted my clothes and were lodged in my dreads. I flipped the baseball cap off and shook my head like some Rastafarian on crack. I had to get every piece off me.

The guy tucked the gun in the back of his jeans and came over and flicked away the pieces I couldn't reach. His fingernails were rough and scratched my bare skin.

"You're okay," he said between my screams, which were dying down to a whimper. He circled his arms around me in an air hug and then slowly lowered them. I fell into him, sobbing uncontrollably. His body was rock solid and his grip like steel.

Until I'd seen the bloody bits and mentally reassembled them, I'd forgotten that Nevada had snakes. Rattlesnakes.

I'd shut the TV off if an image of a snake flashed on the screen. I never saw *Snakes on a Plane,* because even the title had given me nightmares. Snakes in a confined space, slithering under seats and dangling like oxygen masks from overhead compartments. *Uh, no, but thanks for asking.*

I wrapped my arms around this stranger and slobbered and snotted into the crook of his neck. A moment ago he was a serial killer who was going to blow my brains out. Now he was my hero and I didn't plan to let go of him—ever. I wanted to climb his frame and have him carry me on his hip like a mother holding a toddler. I didn't want my feet to touch a ground that could be covered with snakes. I now knew what it meant to have your skin crawl. I felt as if I were covered in snake bits and the clan of the dead snake was collecting its posse to come after me. I imagined the scaly bodies skimming along the mountain, collecting snake comrades as they raced to finish the job their rattler friend had started.

"Icie! Icie!"

Marissa burst through the pines with Tate right behind her. Seeing Marissa and Tate, I was reminded and overwhelmed again with the unknown end-of-the-world scenario I was living. As horrible as snakes were, they were only slimy little creatures, which this guy proved could be defeated with a gun.

"Ice, are you okay? What's wrong?" Marissa yelled. I couldn't answer. She jerked me free of my tall, dark, handsome rescuer. I couldn't stop crying.

Then she did it. She did that thing that I've always wanted to do. She did that thing that you think is the most terrible, yet appropriate, thing to do to a hysterical person.

She slapped me. Open palm. Square on the cheek.

Horror-flick cliché or not—it worked. The shock and burn of her hand switched off my tears like an abrupt cut in a movie.

"Ice...are....you....o...kay?" she asked.

I nodded and struggled to catch my breath. I was being baked by the sun and fried inside by fear.

"Who are you?" Marissa wrapped a protective arm around my shoulder and turned her attention to my mystery man. She scanned his body from head to toe.

"I'm Chaske," he said, and then as if he knew my brain hadn't processed this new name, he repeated it slowly so I could take it in, pronouncing it *Chas-kay.*

Marissa didn't move. She must have noticed that I was covered in blood spatter, or maybe she spotted the mangled snake leftovers. "What did you do?" Marissa's tone was cold and threatening.

Chaske surveyed his kill. As he did, Marissa and I both spotted the butt of his gun tucked in the back of his jeans.

"Listen," Marissa barked, her muscles flexing as she swept me behind her. "Leave us alone."

"It's okay, Marissa," I said, finally able to speak. "He saved me."

Marissa turned to face only me. "But he's got a gun," she whispered, as if that explained everything I needed to know.

"If he wanted to shoot us, we'd be dead already," I said, regaining my normal voice.

"Did you kill this?" Tate nudged the snake bits with the toe of—I kid you not—his tasseled loafers.

Chaske shrugged.

I noticed a red blob on my yellow smiley face, which made it look as if smiley had been shot right between the eyes. I stripped off my shirt and wadded it in a ball. I'd forgotten about the key around my neck. I wrapped my fist around it. I didn't want them to see it.

I twisted the chain so the fob hung down my back and the silver chain strained at my neck like a choker fit for a dominatrix. I didn't care that Chaske, Tate, and probably even Marissa were staring at my electric-purple bra and the money belt cinched to my waist. I wasn't what you'd call a girly girl, but I did like matching bra and underwear. After being called "Granny" all through middle school thanks to my white cotton panties in seventh-grade gym, I knew the power of Victoria's Secret.

I sucked in my gut when my eyes met Chaske's. He raised his eyebrows a little in approval.

"Where's our stuff?" I asked Marissa.

Tate dumped my backpack and Marissa's goodie bag at my feet but never took his eyes off my boobs. I tossed my shirt on the ground and snatched a bottle of water from the bag. Even then, I knew I shouldn't do it, shouldn't waste water. I unscrewed the lid and poured the whole bottle over me. I used my hands like squeegees and wiped the water off. I shook like a dog, my dreadlocks thudding against my face and back. My dreads stung, like I was being flicked with a wet towel in gym. I slipped on the first shirt I found in my backpack. It was bright yellow with black silhouettes of monkeys with wings and the slogan BEWARE OF THE

FLYING MONKEYS. In my current situation, flying monkeys no longer seemed that implausible.

Everyone was staring at me as if I'd grown two heads, but the hysterical terror was subsiding to mere mind-blowing fear. I realized what was missing from this scene. "Where's your cat?" I asked Chaske.

"She's not my cat, really. She found me when I found this mountain. She must be around here somewhere." Chaske glanced around, but there was no sign of the black cat.

"Where did you come from?" Tate sized him up as if he was determining if he could take him in a fight.

Chaske shrugged. "I could ask you guys the same." Ah, the question-with-a-question diversion. Who was this guy?

"What's with the gun?" Tate asked, and stepped in front of me and Marissa. Was he really getting all mini-macho on us? It was kind of cute.

When Chaske didn't answer, Tate did that thing that people do when speaking to foreigners. He slowed down and spoke up. "Where. Did. You. Get. The. Gun?"

Chaske smiled this wonderful cheeky smile, which was so slight that I felt privileged to notice it. "What's with all the questions?" It was a rhetorical question, but Tate didn't quite get it.

"Well, you have a gun, which you shot at Dread, and it's not the first gun that has been pointed at me today so I'm a bit freaked out, and you shot it once so I'm wondering if you'll shoot it again but this time at one of us and I mean I've been through a lot today with being thrown out of the back of an RV..." On and on Tate went in this stream-of-consciousness way, and everything he'd been holding back came spewing out like a spit-take in one of my dad's stupid sitcoms.

The tension that had solidified in my veins seemed to shatter. I glanced at Marissa and we busted up laughing. When he said it all like that in one massive run-on sentence, it sounded so unbelievable and, for some unknown reason, incredibly, hysterically funny.

"Hey, that's not funny." The whine was back in Tate's voice. "The guy's got a gun."

This only made Marissa and me laugh harder. My laughter had an uncontrollable edge, like crying. Chaske looked at us like we were mental patients.

"How can you laugh?" Tate asked Marissa and me, who were now doubled over in convulsions of laughter. "It's not funny," he told Chaske. "I'm just saying there's some crazy shit going on." Tate went on to tell Chaske every gory detail. Tate's commentary ended my laughter like the snap of a flyswatter on bug then glass. I tried to tune him out. I didn't want to hear Tate describe it like a TV newscaster would an event on the other side of the universe.

How could Tate be so casual about it? He couldn't really understand, could he? How could any of us? None of us had ever experienced anything in the same zip code—or galaxy—as this. How could we possibly imagine what this meant?

Each time I crawled out of the funk and horror of it all—even if it was just the tips of my fingernails breaking the surface—I was immediately sucked back under. As Tate talked, Chaske's face paled and everything about him slumped.

"Is this for real?" Chaske asked, looking from Marissa to me. We both nodded.

"We need to get moving," Marissa said to keep Tate from saying anything else.

Tate added, "And Icie here says there's some underground bunker we can stay in until this blows over. Isn't that right, Dread?"

"I'm not sure where the entrance is exactly," I said. "My mum said it was marked with an infinity symbol."

Chaske raked his fingers through his hair, pulling out the nude rubber band. He seemed to withdraw inside himself as he retied his ponytail. It was like those before-and-after pictures where the main difference is the person's facial expression and posture. He was looking "before" and less, well, less the hero.

"I think I might be able to help you find it," he said. He disappeared through the trees. I stuffed my hat and shirt in the goodie bag. Chaske returned a minute later with a proper camper's backpack, complete with sleeping roll at the bottom and two canteens crisscrossing his torso—and, to my relief, Midnight. "Onward and upward," Chaske said.

Marissa and I followed Chaske and Tate up the mountain. Tate was giving this monologue about everything from his love of cinnamon-flavored chewing gum to how to win at blackjack. Chaske listened and let Tate fill the space that was once occupied by normal.

Marissa tried her phone again, but there was no signal. Maybe the phones were working again, but we couldn't get reception on this godforsaken mountain. The sun was setting, but it felt more like darkness was rising, transforming every boulder and clump of trees into some sort of beastie. It was like a non-lame haunted house, except it wasn't a house and these screepy illusions weren't props. I tried to tell myself the shadows and shuffling were just my imagination. I wondered if I had days, hours, minutes, or seconds to live.

I tried not to imagine the bazillion different heinous scenarios that could be playing out around the globe. Would the survivors stack the bodies like layers of lasagna, bury them in Grand Canyon–size pits, or set them adrift in the oceans Viking-style and watch them bob on the waves until they sank out of sight? Or maybe there would be no survivors. I had to stop thinking about it, but I couldn't. My parents, Lola, and even Tristan had to be alive. I wouldn't let myself think that they were, well, you know.

"Careful," Chaske said, pointing with the toe of his hiking boots. It was a thorny, knee-high hedge. Midnight was cradled in his arms like a sleeping baby. She peeked open one of her bright yellow eyes when he started talking and almost immediately closed it again. "This thing circles the mountain."

"There's no way this occurred naturally," Marissa says, glancing at Chaske as if for approval.

Was this supposed to make us turn back? Like those people who had "Beware of Dog" signs but no dog? I hoped my mum hadn't used her Oxford education and taxpayers' hard-earned cash to come up with this "Do Not Disturb" sign. You can't just write KEEP OUT! It's like when my parents locked their top dresser drawer. They might as well have put a sign that said SOMETHING REALLY AWESOME IS IN HERE. I picked the lock and sure wished I hadn't. I was like ten and didn't quite understand what all the gadgets and gunk were, but when I finally figured it out...major emotional scarring. The only proof—well, besides me— that my parents had sex. *Um, gross.*

If this tiny hedge was supposed to be a warning sign for when the nuclear waste repository was finished, then future generations had no hope. That is, if there were going to be any future generations.

Chaske helped Midnight over and then took a flying leap and easily cleared the hedge. Tate tried to mimic Chaske, but his jump was less graceful and he fell hard on all fours. Chaske hauled Tate to his feet as effortlessly as he'd picked up Midnight. Marissa jumped, practically doing a split in midair. I climbed over it, but my feet got tangled in the brambles and the thorns slashed at my ankles. I started to fall, but Chaske swooped in and caught me. I could smell the musky fragrance of his body and long hair. I wiggled free, landing on one knee. I popped back up, not wanting to look like the total klutz I was. "Let's keep moving."

The air seemed thinner and cooler the higher we climbed. There was no infinity symbol that led to a secret hideout. Maybe someone had filled in my parents' top secret bunker.

Midnight scampered between our legs, racing ahead and then waiting for us to catch up. The terrain was rocky. Spindly shrubs and massive boulders dotted the landscape. More chucks and wallies scuttled and darted out of our way. I could swear I saw a scorpion. After my near–snake attack, I strained my ears for rattling and slithering and hissing.

Tate incessantly asked Chaske questions, and he expertly evaded every single one.

"Where do you live?"

"Around."

"Why aren't you in school?"

"Why aren't you?"

"What sports do you like?"

"Same as you, I guess."

"Are you in the military?"

"What do you think?"

It reminded me of when we were forced to watch the presidential debates in history class. Chaske was well schooled in the nonanswer. It was as if he had magically appeared on the mountain.

The mountain leveled. The ground looked like it had been bulldozed flat to create a ring around the mountain. This must have been part of the path I'd spotted from the ground. And things just kept getting weirder and weirder. A wall materialized in front of us. It was the same earthy color as the rocky ground, so it took a 3-D form only when we walked closer. Stones of various sizes were piled in a huge, continuous cairn maybe ten feet high. It appeared to circle the mountain. The rocks were dumped in a rough line that was maybe five feet thick. This must have been erected by humans—or possibly aliens. We had to be getting closer.

"It's like Stonehenge or something," Tate said, chasing Midnight, who was climbing up the pile.

Midnight had scaled to the top and was sitting pretty, her yellow eyes squinting in the setting sun. Midnight's pink tongue flicked across her whiskers and then she meowed. The sound didn't sound like *me-ow*. She had a hoarse voice. She made the sound again, like *mrrrroooow*, and disappeared over the wall. We followed her, clambering up on all fours and half sliding, half surfing down the rocks on the other side.

With every step, I became more and more despondent. We were never going to find the bunker. I'd brought these people here and we were all going to die. Our heads swiveled like searchlights scanning for the symbol. Part of me wasn't sure if I really wanted to find it. Was I really going to lock myself underground? Was that really necessary? Maybe we could camp out on the mountain until my parents showed up.

"Look," Chaske called us over. "Is this what you mean?" He was pointing to a huge round stone that looked like a prehistoric giant's dinner plate. It was propped against a rocky wall. The boulders stacked behind it resembled a large square about the size of a two-car garage. "I wondered what this was," Chaske said. Marissa, Tate, and I filed in next to him. An infinity symbol was chiseled in the center of the stone.

This was it.

I stroked the rock face with my hand. I wanted to laugh, cry, and scream all at once. We'd found it. Maybe we were going to make it. But it also meant this whole bizarre not-so-1950s-bomb-shelter scenario was for real. I had to have faith in my parents. They'd gotten me this far.

"Help me roll it away," I said, pushing on one side of the stone. It was heavy but I think it budged. Chaske found a strong branch from somewhere and wedged it under the rock.

Marissa moved in next to Chaske and gripped the branch so her hands were touching his. "Why'd they mark it with infinity?" she asked.

Tate watched. " 'Cause that's how long that nuclear waste stuff lasts. That's why my dad didn't want it anywhere near here."

"A half-life of up to ten thousand years or longer," I said. "That's how long the stuff is deadly." My dad and I had had this argument many times. How can we create something that's hazardous for generations? He believed nuclear was the safest, cleanest form of energy. It doesn't create carbon dioxide and other stuff that wrecks the ozone. He said it was the only real option to meet the world's electricity needs. "Just be happy they never got around to storing any nuclear waste here."

Chaske, Marissa, and I scrunched next to one another, pushing and prodding with all our might.

"Yeah, well, I'm thankful for the stuff," Chaske said. We looked at him as if he had sprouted a clown nose, rainbow hair, and a pair of deely-boppers. "No nuclear waste. No underground bunker. No safe place for us."

"So thank God for nuclear waste," Marissa said with a fake laugh.

"Amen to that!" Tate chimed in, and finally joined us.

I found it a bit odd that Chaske was so willing to take our word for what was going on. But I didn't question. Not then, anyway. I was glad he was there. Maybe it was because he saved me, but I trusted him and I definitely felt as if I owed him.

The stone rolled away inch by inch. I held my breath until I saw rock give way to a black hole. When we'd created a space big enough for me, I squeezed into the opening.

"Why don't I investigate first?" I said, feeling protective of this place my parents had found for me.

"Here." Chaske handed me a flashlight from his backpack. Midnight hopped from her perch on a nearby rock and peered inside. She sniffed the stale air, gave a loud meow, and darted a safe distance away.

I switched on the flashlight and shimmied through the hole. I tried not to think of snake holes or being buried alive. The space was filled with an airless heat, like I'd crawled into one of those big clay ovens that fancy pizza places have. I stood frozen in the shaft of dusty light that was filtering in from the outside. It was as if I'd been beamed into deepest outer space.

"Everything okay in there, Icie?" Chaske called.

The darkness was closing in.

"Ice?" Marissa called.

"Yeah." My voice cracked. "I'm fine." I remembered my flashlight and directed the beam ahead of me. What was hiding from me in this cave? My imagination exploded with creepy-crawlies, beasties, aliens, and even the distorted white mask from *Scream*. My hand shook and the light flickered with a strobe effect.

Get a grip, I told myself. My parents wouldn't send me here if it wasn't safe. I took in the space one circle of light at a time. The room was empty except for a steel door on the far side that looked like an old-fashioned bank vault. I walked over and examined the door.

I slipped the key from around my neck. There was only one place it could go. I slotted it in and the door opened with the clunk of metal. I grabbed the door handle. It took all my strength to inch it open enough for me to slip through. Cool air washed over me. It was as if the place had central air-conditioning. I shivered.

I stepped, flashlight first, into the pitch-black. The light from outside dissipated to a thin slice of gray. I swept the flashlight beam around a cavernous room of solid rock. It was impossible to determine the exact dimensions. I didn't want to venture too far away from the door. The darkness felt as if it might swallow me up.

But then an eerie calm descended over me.

We might survive, buried safely in the heart of the mountain. We had a chance. I sent my thanks to my parents—wherever they were. "I made it," I whispered, and hoped I would see them again soon. If we could make it, maybe others could too. There were bank vaults and subbasements all over the place, right? The president had some sort of subterranean hideaway.

I scrambled back out again. "This is it," I said, trying to sound confident. Midnight was the first to greet me, gently knocking her head against my legs.

"Can we do this? I mean, can we survive in there?" Marissa asked.

"I've got some food and water, which should last a little while," Chaske said, shrugging his shoulders and jostling the contents of his massive backpack.

"I've got lots of supplies too," I said.

"I have some water and stuff that I"—Marissa blushed—"liberated from the airport."

We all looked at Tate.

"Yeah. Yeah, I know. I got nothing, but it's not my fault," Tate whined.

"So." Marissa bounced. "Are we going in or what?"

Tate cleared his throat. "I don't think we should take the cat." Chaske shot Tate the most hateful look. "Well"—Tate's voice rose an octave—"how will we feed it and stuff?"

"Uh, pretty sure that's not your problem," I said, and scratched the cat behind her ear.

"Do you think we really need to do it?" Tate asked. "Why don't we camp out here for a while?"

"But what if the virus is airborne?" Marissa asked, as if we might know the answer.

"I think we need to hide out from other people. People are sick and dying. We've seen it," I told Chaske. "Locking ourselves away is the only way we will survive. We don't have to decide right now how long we're going to stay. We can just hide out for a while."

"I think I agree," Marissa said.

"Yeah, okay, I guess," Tate said.

"We can go inside in a second, but, I mean..." What was I trying to say? "I'm just saying we don't know how long we're going to be trapped...I mean, um, it's getting late and we're exhausted, but, I mean, um..."

"How about one last look?" Chaske asked, as if he knew what I was thinking. "Follow me." We walked down and around the mountain. We weren't far from the rocky wall. Chaske led us to a stony outlook. He climbed up first and then instructed the rest of us on where to find the footholds. He had to help us the final few feet, taking each of us by the hand and hauling us onto the ledge. I was momentarily blinded by the glare of the setting sun. As my eyes adjusted, the skyline of Vegas took shape. It reminded me of the LEGO towers I'd constructed with my dad, creating multicolored and strangely shaped buildings. There were Xs and Os. Bronze blocks and thin needles pointing skyward. But something wasn't right.

"The lights," Marissa whispered as if her voice might have blown them out.

She was right. The buildings were there, but the normally brilliant skyline etched in rainbow colors had been snuffed out—every last one. A nearly solid line of white lights led away from the city. There were no red lights heading in anymore.

"What do you think it means?" I asked.

"Nothing good," Tate said.

We watched the last flashes of the sun sink behind the mountains in the west. The sky beyond glowed the most brilliant shade of pink. Midnight rubbed against my legs.

"The city looks dead." I didn't mean to say it, but it was true. I loved the skyline of D.C. at night. The way the city looked fresh and sparkly, framed by the dark sky. I always thought there was something magical about the city after sunset. It was as if the darkness erased the rough edges and all you could see was the bright sparkling promise. Las Vegas was disappearing below us.

"Everyone should decide for themselves," I said, "but I'm going underground, at least for a little while."

Marissa turned her back to us. She was taking deep breaths. I wasn't sure if she was crying or having some sort of panic attack. I reached out to touch her, but she stormed off.

Tate started drumming his fingers against something. I could hear his *tap, tap, tap*. It was as if he was counting down our last minutes.

"Will you please cut it out?" I shouted. Tate's cheeks glistened, wet with tears. He ran the way we came, right behind Marissa. "Sorry, Tate," I called after him. How could I be so insensitive? He was just a kid, after all.

"You ready?" Chaske asked.

NO! I thought. How could anyone ever be ready for this?

I peered over the edge. Below was a sheer drop to a rocky ravine. "Just one more minute." I inhaled deeply, drinking in the fresh air. No hint of exhaust or Dumpsters or urine or the million other smells that blended together on the streets of D.C.

It was nearly dark now and I could see the first twinkle of stars overhead. I memorized the sight before me. I rarely saw the stars in the city. How long would it be before I saw the sky and the stars again? What was going to happen to my world? What was going to happen to me? The sadness that gathered in my chest was overwhelming.

If I was going to survive, there would be more bad days ahead. I was burying myself alive with three people I barely knew for reasons that weren't completely clear and for an indefinite period of time.

But it wasn't death. It wasn't forever. My parents would come for me. It's hard to explain the feeling that came over me. I was watching but wasn't part of the drama that was about to unfold.

A distant rumble filled the air. Within seconds, the roar was upon us, exploding in our ears and rattling our bones. Chaske and I dropped to the ground. We flattened ourselves on the rock, Chaske protectively covering me, as fighter jets zoomed overhead. They passed us in a flash. As we got to our feet, we could see the V formation disappear at the horizon.

I ran as fast as I could. Soon I was flanked by Chaske, Marissa, Tate, and Midnight. We didn't talk. It was unanimous. We were going underground.

SIXTEEN

"What you fear most sometimes happens,
and it's worse than you could ever imagine."
—Just Saying 187

FINCH

Finch calls out to the other Cheerleaders, "Gather everyone at the Mall!" Finch isn't scared. He's euphoric.

In no time, every wooden bench in the Mall is crammed with Cheerleaders more wedged than seated. The rockstars are huddled together at the front, sitting on the ground. The tension in the Mall is like smoldering embers; one breath could ignite Forreal.

As Finch enters the Mall, he takes Harper's hand. She resists. "For Atti," he says, and her hand relaxes in his grip. The crowd parts as they make their way through. The Cheerleaders look at Finch, really look at him now. *At last,* Finch thinks. He must disguise his true feelings. They can't see his happiness. They wouldn't understand. He channels his excitement into a calm confidence. He helps Harper onto the platform that is usually occupied only by Beckett and the Twitter.

"The time is twelve and five," the Timekeeper calls, raising his hand above his head. The chunky silver watch dangles on his wrist.

Beckett is one of the last to the Mall. He makes his way to the front, but people aren't focused on him like they usually are. They are looking to Finch.

Beckett climbs onto the stage next to Harper. He whispers, "What's going on?"

Harper turns away from him. Finch puts a protective arm around her.

"Atti has disappeared, and Harper has seen Terrorists," Finch announces in a booming voice, and the Mall erupts. Cheerleaders find their rockstars. Finch raises his hands to quiet the crowd. "Terrorists have taken Atti. I'm sure of it."

Everyone is talking at once and Finch's voice strains to be heard. "We must organize a search party. If Terrorists have taken my sister, they will pay!"

There's a low rumble from the gathered crowd as people mumble their agreement. He lets their anger fill him.

Beckett steps to the front of the stage. "We don't know what's happened to Atti. The Great I AM preaches peace, compassion, and common sense. We must not react with anger before we have all the facts."

Finch won't let Beckett ruin it. "Tell them, Harper," he says, and shoves her forward, next to Beckett. "Tell them what you told me."

Harper and Beckett exchange a look that Finch can't quite decipher.

"Harper, don't," Beckett says, but Finch nudges him aside.

"I was searching for Atti." Harper's voice is trembling. She's looking from Finch to Beckett.

"Go on," Finch says.

"I went to the buildings near the base of the Mountain." She bows her head. "I shouldn't have done that, but I thought Atti might have wandered off the Mountain. I saw something Out There." She lets that thought linger as she glances toward Beckett.

The crowd's red shiny faces remind Finch of Atti's Facebook. He spots fear and anger and hate and even rage on the round faces in front of him.

"I saw four." She pauses and swallows. "Four creatures Out There. I came back as quickly as I could and told Finch what I'd seen."

Finch puts his arm around her shoulders again and pulls her away from Beckett. "We must protect our Mountain," he says. "And the only way to do that is to attack!"

Cheerleaders shout their support and punch the air.

Beckett raises his arm, the one with the birthmark. Finch hates that he has the advantage of a birth defect. "Enough!" Beckett bellows.

And it's as if Forreal has been switched off. Beckett never raises his voice. He has their full attention now. Forty faces tight with anger soften one by one. Beckett looks Finch square in the eyes. Finch holds his gaze. He knows Beckett's secret. He's conspiring with the enemy. The girl may not look like a Terrorist, but she must be working with them. How else could she survive Out There?

"I am sorry Atti is missing," Beckett says with his usual calm. "We will do everything in our power to return her to the Mountain. But we are not helping Atti by letting fear and anger take over. We must turn to the Great I AM." Beckett bows his head and all eyes lower. "Great I AM, protector of sacred Mountain, please watch over Atti and, if it's your will, return her to the Mountain. Whatever your will. We trust in you. Whatever happens. We know you watch over us. Whatever you decide. We know it will be okay."

He pauses and Forreal joins in the Saying: "Whatever. Whatever. Whatever."

But Finch remains silent. Where was Beckett when Atti went missing and the Terrorists came?

Beckett raises his head. "Why don't we have a reading from the CQ?" he says, and walks to the altar. He riffles through the CQ, letting the smooth plastic slip between his fingers.

Finch lets out an exasperated sigh. Beckett is a man of thought, of waiting and Saying. Finch is a man of action. Words will not save his sister. They are wasting time.

Finch tenses every muscle in his body. Harper must feel his muscles pulse because she places her hand on his bicep and pulls him toward her.

Beckett's fingers pause and the CQ slips open to a page. He flips ahead to another page. He says the Great I AM leads him to the appropriate message from the 303 Just Sayings captured on scraps of paper, but it's obvious to Finch that Beckett is selecting one himself.

Finch has been misled by Beckett his entire life. He's no conduit for the Great I AM. Finch can't follow this man anymore.

Beckett reads what is written in glittery green ink. "'Before I can worry about other people, I've got to be able to live with myself. A person's conscience is not guided by majority rule.'"

Beckett pauses and the crowd choruses, "Whatever."

Finch pinches his lips together. Not whatever. He cannot give his sister's life and his future over to Forreal's false prophet, not this time.

Beckett closes the book. "The Great I AM—"

Finch has had enough. "The Great I AM calls us to act." Finch rises on the tiptoe of his shorter leg so his legs are level. He towers over Beckett. "The Great I AM showed us the lights, showed us our enemy."

"You have suffered another loss. We"—Beckett sweeps his arms wide to indicate everyone gathered—"understand your pain, but we cannot turn our backs on the teachings of the Great I AM."

"We can't be passive anymore." Finch feels tension in his hands. He laces his fingers together and flexes them. His knuckles crack with satisfying clicks. "Terrorists are Out There. We can't wait for them to attack."

"Fighting only leads to more fighting, never to a solution!" Beckett shouts to be heard.

"The Terrorists are Out There," Harper says quietly. Her voice builds. "We must find Atti. We must protect our Mountain."

"My sister is gone. Who will be next?" Finch stands toe-to-toe with Beckett. Finch has had enough of Beckett's secrets and lies.

"We will organize a search for Atti," Beckett says, glaring at Finch. "You may continue to patrol, but we will not attack. We will only protect the Mountain."

Now is Finch's moment. "I can't keep your secrets anymore, Beckett," Finch says, and shoves him hard in the chest. Beckett falls to the ground. A collective gasp fills the air. "I saw you with a girl from Out There."

"A Terrorist," Harper adds. "I saw you too," she whispers to Beckett. "How could you?"

Beckett doesn't get up.

"It's not like that. She's not a Terrorist," Beckett says to Finch, and then repeats his confession to the gathered crowd.

"So you admit that you've been secretly meeting someone from Out There. Beckett, you have betrayed your own people. Take him!" Finch shouts to Tom and Cal. No one moves.

"Tom. Cal. You know me. I would not betray Forreal." Beckett stands and scans the crowd. All heads are bowed. "Harper, tell them. If you saw her, you know she's not a Terrorist. She's just a girl."

Harper steps behind Finch. She's choosing him. Finch stands taller and shifts to block Beckett when he reaches for her.

"Is it true?" Cal says. "Have you been secretly meeting with someone from Out There?"

Beckett nods.

Finch takes his rightful place behind the altar. "Beckett admits his treachery, and my sister has paid the price for his deceit. We are wasting time." He motions to Tom and Cal. "Take him to the cave and guard him." He waves them away like pesky flies disturbing dinner. "We cannot risk that he will signal our enemy." He locks eyes with Beckett. "We will deal with your betrayal later."

Tom and Cal each take an arm. Beckett doesn't struggle as they haul him away. "This is not the will of the Great I AM," Beckett calls as they lead him away.

"The Great I AM has chosen me to lead in this time of great conflict," Finch shouts, and he's beginning to believe it. "Onward and upward!"

Finch hears Atti's name echoing around the Mountain as Harper leads her search. A dozen of the strongest Cheerleaders circle around Finch. He has found a stick and drawn a rough map of the Man-Made Mountains. "The lights were about here." He marks the spot with an X. "This will be the target of our mission. We will send teams in from both sides and one straight up the middle. We will surprise them." This plan has been formulating in his brain ever since he first saw the lights with Beckett and Harper. He knew this day would come. "If they like fire, we will give them fire. They can't scare us with their pathetic light display. Fire will rain down the Mountain and cleanse Out There of Terrorists." Finch's chest swells as the Cheerleaders nod their agreement.

Finch's moment of triumph is suddenly stifled.

"Finch!" Harper screams. His name pierces a ragged arrow through his heart.

"Finch!" Her voice is sluggish with tears.

Chills prickle his skin as he prepares for the loss he knew was coming.

"Finch!"

Harper staggers into the Mall. "It's Atti," Harper says, and throws herself into his arms. "She's dead." Harper is sobbing.

"Are you sure?" Finch asks.

Harper nods. "They found her on the Black River. She'd been attacked." She covers her mouth as if she can't continue. "She's been ripped apart."

Grief flashes through him. Atti is gone. And for a moment, he hopes that Beckett is right. He hopes the Great I AM has gathered Atti and made her one with the Mountain. Finch hopes that Atti is with those who have gone before.

"Terrorists," Finch says, and erases all other possibilities. It must have been a ruthless attack by the clawed and fanged beastie.

Now is his moment. Harper is in his arms. Forreal is looking to him. Soon they will attack their lifelong enemy. Finch has hungered for a fight because only the heat of battle can forge a hero.

SEVENTEEN

The bunker door shut with an ominous thud. No one said a word, but I knew we were all wondering when that door would open again. Chaske swept the beam of his flashlight across the vast cavern in broad strokes. Marissa and Tate stood wide-eyed, taking it in. While they were occupied, I slipped the key from under my shirt and slotted it into the lock on this side of the door. The locking mechanism clunked and sealed with a thud and a *whoosh*. I tucked the key away.

"Ice?" Marissa's voice echoed in the space with a note of alarm. "What did you do?"

I had to handle this right. I'd locked them in and I had

the only key. "Uh, we have to lock whatever's out there out there. Right?" I swallowed. "I mean, we can't keep the door open. If it's locked, we're safe." I didn't even understand what I was saying.

Tate's voice rang out in the darkness. "Dread, so you have the only key?"

Chaske's flashlight illuminated my face. My eye twitched. I was conscious of every muscle in my face and I didn't know what to do with any of them. I nodded.

"What if something happens to her?" Tate's voice again, but the carefree, boyish tone had vanished. Maybe I'd misjudged him. Maybe there was a brain in that over-gelled head of his. "I mean if she, like, chokes on some gum or something, I don't want to die here because she can't chew and swallow."

"It pains me to say this, but Tate's right," Marissa said.

Even in the dim light, I could feel their eyes drilling into me. I was the gatekeeper to the real world. It wasn't a feeling of power as much as security. I'd seen movies where confined people go mental and kill each other. This way, they needed me.

"Where's the key?" Tate wasn't going to give up. Note to self: *Don't underestimate Tate Chamberlain.*

My parents and my expensive private education had prepared me for college, for more thinking and yakking about abstract issues and political ideas. For taking tests. For following rules. Nothing had prepared me for this. "I don't know what's going on out there. None of us does. But I intend to stay here until my parents show up. My mum and dad said they would come get me when it's safe. We'll be safe here until then."

"Maybe we should check outside once a day or something," Tate said.

I thought that might be a good idea, but Chaske said, "I think it's better if we completely isolate ourselves for a while. That way nothing and no one can get to us."

I didn't want to force anyone to do anything, but I'd made up my mind. "If you want to go, I'll open the door right now, but if you stay, I won't open the door until my parents come and tell me it's okay."

"Or we run out of food," Tate added.

"I'm staying here with Icie," Chaske said, and shifted to my side. "If we're wrong, then we've had an underground vacation, and if we're right, then..."

"It's our best chance of survival. I'm staying too," Marissa said. We turned toward Tate.

"Yeah, whatever. What choice do I have?" Tate shoved his hands deep in his pockets.

"It's better than dying by the side of the road," Marissa muttered.

"So..." Chaske let the word dangle. "Maybe we should try to get some sleep." He lowered his backpack to the ground. "We can check out this place tomorrow."

I wanted to explore it now, shine a bright light into every corner, but I was exhausted. I hadn't really slept in twenty-four hours, and I had hiked miles. Escaping into sleep and leaving reality until morning made much more sense.

We agreed that we would sleep together near the door.

We'd all take turns keeping watch—just in case. Marissa and Tate exuded a coldness. I had changed from friendly savior to calculated captor. I didn't mean to. They had to understand. They would have done the same thing—if they were the ones with the key.

Chaske spread out his sleeping bag. He and Tate slept half on, half off the edges and Marissa and I were sandwiched in the middle. Midnight curled up between Chaske and me. My head buzzed with rattlesnakes, nuclear bombs, and plague-like sickness. My heart ached with thoughts of everyone I loved being trapped on the other side of that door. Strange that I thought of them as trapped and me as somehow free. Eventually I fell into a dreamless sleep.

"Rise and shine, you sleepyheads," Marissa said with a little too much perkiness. She was no longer lying next to me. Her voice emanated, godlike, from a location unknown.

"Oh, man, what time is it?" Tate moaned. "It's not even light out." He rolled over and right into me.

"Um, we are underground," Marissa replied. "There is no light."

Her words struck a nerve. My eyes opened to no effect. It was pitch-black. I sat bolt upright. I felt Midnight jump to her feet. There was so much I hadn't considered. I'd worried about how we would eat and keep clean. I'd wondered about being lonely. But now I could add no sunlight and no sense of time to my ever-growing list of reasons to panic. What about fresh air and water?

"It's nearly noon," Marissa said. The glowing face of her massive watch floated disembodied above us. "We need to explore and map out this place and take an inventory of our stuff. Until we know what we're dealing with, we need to conserve." Marissa's glowing watch bounced as if it were speaking.

"How long are we really going to have to stay here?" Tate asked.

"I read once that during the Cold War, people built bomb shelters prepared for fifteen years underground." Chaske's voice was low, calm, and reassuring even when he was basically talking about being stuck down here for about as long as I'd been alive.

"If it's some sort of bio-threat, like my mum thought, we could probably go outside in a few months," I said. That is if we didn't go all *Lord of the Flies*.

"Months?" Tate repeated.

"Yeah, well, we'd have to wait for everyone to die off and the air to clear so whatever the hell it is ain't contagious anymore." Marissa said it so matter-of-factly. If she was feeling as freaked out as I was, she sure wasn't showing it.

"Does that mean we will have to have sex so we can repopulate the Earth?" Tate's voice sounded hopeful. " 'Cause if so, I call Marissa. No offense, Icie."

"None taken," I said with a nervous laugh, but it wasn't really funny. What chance did the human race have if the four of us were the progenitors?

"Even if you were the last man on Earth, I would not procreate with you. Your gene pool should stop here,"

Marissa said in her staccato tone. Gotta love the cheer captain.

"Harsh," Tate muttered. "I was just saying…"

As if by magic Chaske's face appeared in a beam of light. "I think maybe you shouldn't 'just say' right now."

The flashlight was positioned under his chin, illuminating a slice of his face. He had deep sleep lines etched along his cheek and a scar that cut diagonally through his left eyebrow. Tate was stretched out on his back with his arms crisscrossed over his face. Marissa was sitting at the end of the sleeping bag, and Chaske and I were sitting with our backs against the cool metal door.

"I'm hungry," came Tate's muffled voice. Was he crying?

"I could eat," I said, and gave Tate a playful shove. Marissa shouldn't be so hard on him. "Marissa had some juice and cereal bars in that bag you carried all day yesterday, Tate." I nudged Marissa. "How about you serve us up some breakfast?"

Marissa tossed me three cereal bars. "Here, Tate," Marissa said, and handed him a small box of apple juice. I laid a cereal bar on his chest. He sniffed and wiped his face. He took the juice and cereal bar and sat with his back to us.

I gave Chaske his breakfast. He switched off the light, and we ate in silence. I nibbled the cereal bar, savoring every bite. My stomach felt like a bottomless pit and each little bite hit with the tiniest ping—a grain of sand in the Grand Canyon. I jumped a little when Midnight rubbed against me and purred. I broke off a piece of my bar and crumbled it in my palm. She licked my hand with her rough tongue. As much as I hated to admit it, Tate was probably right. Midnight might have had a better chance of survival on the outside. But I couldn't say good-bye to anything else.

"Why don't Tate and I explore the rest of this place and you guys sort out our supplies and stuff?" Chaske said when the chewing and drinking sounds subsided.

"Oh, right, the men should go hunting while the women-folk gather berries," Marissa said with a sting in her tone.

"Um, no," Chaske corrected. "I thought you might want a little cooling-off period from your new lover boy."

"Whatever," Marissa said with a laugh. "You boys go off and kill us a bear, or better yet, find water, food, and four king-size beds."

Chaske switched on his flashlight again and slowly swept it around. The place was massive. You could fit three semis parked side by side and three more stacked on top in the entryway and still have room to spare. In the pitch-black, the space had felt much smaller, claustrophobic. I took a deep breath. It was as if I could breathe again in this big open space.

The walls were solid rock. Chaske's light paused on the far wall. I could see there were parallel, horizontal lines maybe six feet apart, as if someone had chiseled out the rock in large rectangular blocks. The entrance narrowed to one tunnel. The floor sloped at a sharp, steady decline.

"Let's go, Tate." Chaske stood and directed his flashlight at Tate.

Marissa checked her big pink watch again. "If you're gone any longer than two hours..."

"You'll come looking for us," Chaske finished her sentence.

"No." Marissa paused. "I was going to say that's more food for us."

I swallowed hard, recognizing the nugget of truth in what she said. Would we turn on one another like in every postapocalyptic movie I'd ever seen?

"Here's all I got." Chaske handed me his backpack. He removed the gun from under the corner of the sleeping bag where he had slept and tucked it into the back of his jeans.

"Where'd you get the gun?" Tate asked, picking up his line of inquisition from yesterday.

Chaske shrugged, untucking his shirt to cover the weapon.

"I bet it was your dad's. He's a cop or maybe an FBI agent, isn't he?" Tate stood.

"As far as you know, yeah," Chaske said. He put a brotherly arm around Tate. "Come on, Tate. Onward and, well"—he pointed to the sloping tunnel—"downward, I guess."

Midnight raced after Chaske but paused at the tunnel's entrance, glancing back at me before scampering off.

"First we need light," I said, reaching for my backpack.

"Wait. Wait. I think I got something." Marissa rummaged around in her ginormous handbag. "Most of my good stuff drove away with that that damn thieving taxi driver, but…" More rummaging. "I do have a few things to contribute."

There was a *pop* and then we were bathed in a faint yellowish-green light. She held up a glow stick with the words BARRY MANILOW written on the side.

"Never pictured you as a Fanilow," I said.

"I took my gran to the concert. Everyone got one of these." She shook the glow stick. "I couldn't bear to wave it around while the entire audience sang 'Daybreak,' but I thought it might come in handy sometime, you know, at a drunken party in some state park, but whatever." She emptied the contents of her D&G and started humming what I thought was "Copacabana."

Marissa's worldly possessions included an issue of *Cheerleader Quarterly*, a purse-size antibacterial hand gel, a Hello Kitty wallet, an avalanche of makeup, a nearly full bottle of Clinique Happy, a confetti of loose change, foil gum wrappers, abandoned breath mints, and a scrap of paper with the name *Cruz* and a phone number.

We dumped the contents of my and Chaske's backpacks, my messenger bag, and Marissa's goodie bag in the center of Chaske's sleeping bag. I handed her a pink gel pen and took a green glitter one from my messenger bag. I ripped out a few pages from the blank notebook that was supposed to be my journal for English class. We started organizing and cataloging. Soon she had me humming along. My dad liked a bit of the Manilow too. That song lodged itself in my brain like a splinter that hurt like hell but was impossible to remove.

I made a separate list of the feminine hygiene products. The boys didn't need to worry their pretty little heads about our girl issues. I wanted to get this list finished and the products hidden before the boys came back. Marissa had six ultra tampons, two partially unwrapped regular tampons she found in the inner lining of her purse, a half packet of contraceptive pills, and three condoms. I was less prepared. I only kept one tampon bullet in the zipper compartment of my bag. Mom had packed three washable sanitary pads and two menstrual cups, which looked sort of like the diaphragms the health teacher showed us in our lecture on contraception. *Um, disgust-o-rama.* They were in brown, recycled envelopes from someplace called Organic Feminine Care. There were diagrams and instructions. To be honest, I grieved more for the loss of disposable feminine hygiene products than I had for every senior—except Lola—at Capital Academy.

I showed my find to Marissa. "Now that's what I call roughing it," she said, and shook her head.

We quickly had everything organized in piles and documented on our inventory sheets. We didn't have a ton of clothes. With everything combined, we each had two complete outfits, with a few T-shirts and sweatshirts to spare. I'd have to share with Marissa. I was bigger than she was in every area but the one that mattered most to boys. Chaske was easily twice Tate's size. They looked like David and Goliath walking down the tunnel earlier. Guess it wouldn't matter if our clothes fit down here. It wasn't like we were going to host a subterranean fashion show.

My parents had done an amazing job of packing everything I would need. There was a first-aid kit. Plus Mum must have emptied their medicine cabinet. I had a variety of painkillers and penicillin, as well as a nearly full prescription of Dad's Valium. A thousand multivitamins, each big enough to choke a linebacker. A few lighters as well as four Maglites with extra batteries. They also had packed disposable face masks and rubber gloves.

These supplies hadn't been gathered in a rush. The packaging had been removed and everything was crammed in clear plastic bags. Some of these items had been ordered and acquired from survival stores. My parents had created a survival kit after 9/11. Mum tried to sit me down once and tell me what to do in case of some national disaster, but Dad told her not to worry me. I think they told me where the kit was, but I hadn't paid any attention. I thought she was being, well, Mum. I figured it was just a flashlight, radio, and candy bar, but she'd really thought it through.

Chaske had a hammer, a small collapsible shovel, and one of those multipurpose pocket gadgets that had every kind of tool, including a toothpick. He also had a coverless copy of *To Kill a Mockingbird*, two canteens, a pack of cards, four boxes of matches, a box of ammunition for his gun, two signal flares, and a one-man pop-up tent.

"Whoa, get a load of this," Marissa said, unwrapping a screepy hunting knife from one of Chaske's shirts. "Are you sure we can trust this guy? I mean, look at the size of this." She pinched the handle between her fingers and let the four-inch blade dangle and reflect green in our Manilow light.

"Maybe he's out here hunting or camping or, I don't know, just hiking. People do that all the time." My stomach rolled, not because of hunger this time. Everything about the knife, from the curve of its handle to the jagged notches on the blade, was designed to kill.

"Yeah, maybe, but it's weird him being out here on his own, and he's not Mr. Chatty," Marissa said, glancing down the tunnel to make sure they weren't listening. "What's the deal with him?"

I shrugged. "All I know is that he saved my life, and he seems pretty normal, except for the man-of-mystery routine. I'm sure he'll talk when he's ready and he will be some average guy from some average place. It will make perfect sense why he's alone on the mountain with all this survival gear."

"Let's hope you are right," Marissa said as she placed the knife next to Tate's Swiss Army knife. Tate's knife with its shiny red exterior and white cross logo looked like a children's toy next to Chaske's massive hunting knife. "I plan to keep a close eye on him just in case he's escaped from some nuthouse."

I knew less than a Facebook profile about these people. I added fear of Marissa, Tate, and Chaske to my "Reasons to Panic" list—not only fear of who they really were and what they were capable of today, but of what they might do after a few months locked in a bunker.

We turned our attention back to the inventory. My parents had sent hundreds of Nutri-power Bars in every flavor imaginable. That was all Mum ate when she was busy. I'd tried one once. It had the taste and consistency of mud and sand mixed with Jell-O. Chaske had exactly eighty-one of these vacuum-packed, army-issued Meals, Ready-to-Eat. MREs. Cheesy tortellini from a packet I could live with, but I wasn't sure about eating vacuum-packed meat products like Mediterranean chicken or spicy penne pasta with some sort of sausage. He also had a big Sam's Club bag of beef and turkey jerky. Marissa had twenty-three packs of breath mints and assorted travel-size snacks.

We had nearly finished organizing our supplies into food, medical, tools, and miscellaneous when the place was suddenly flooded with light. I squinted at the brightness. Marissa and I leapt to our feet. My head swam from the sudden action and lack of food. Two parallel lines of those energy-efficient lights lined the ceiling.

"This place is massive," Chaske hollered to us. We rushed toward one another. Midnight raced between us, as if following the conversation. "I think the lighting must be solar powered. There's also some sort of air-filtration system. We switched everything on."

"Oh, that's fab!" Marissa clapped. Her enthusiasm was a bit over the top. Maybe the latent cheerleader in her was coming to life. I wonder if she had a cheer for not suffocating in a bunker.

"This tunnel spirals down about a mile," Chaske said.

"It would be great for skateboarding," Tate interjected.

"The tunnel gets narrower as you go down. There's a part at the back that's not finished. No lights or anything. We should stay away from that part," Chaske said. "All right?"

Marissa and I nodded.

Chaske raised his eyebrows at Tate.

"Yeah, yeah, whatever." He kicked at the dirt floor.

"Well, I've got good news and bad news," Chaske said.

"What's the bad news?" I asked.

"You're supposed to ask for the good news first," Marissa said.

"I'm glass half-empty at the moment," I replied.

"Well, you're getting the good news first. We found a few dusty gallon jugs of water in this huge room near the back of the tunnel. That should last us for a little while, but there are also a few places where water is pooling from cracks in the walls. We should be able to collect that water somehow."

"And..." I prompted.

"There are even a few cots. The construction crew must have slept here sometimes," Tate jumped in.

"So what's the bad news?" I said, getting more anxious by the minute. "Is the place infested with nasty beasties?" I hopped on the balls of my feet at the thought of more snakes or rats or alligators or mountain lions or zombies or werewolves...."

"Nope, we didn't see any creatures, did we, Tate?"

"Nope," Tate said.

"Just tell us the bad news already," I demanded.

"No toilets," Tate announced.

"No plumbing of any kind that we could see."

I suddenly had the overpowering urge to pee.

"We'll figure out something. It's not that big of a deal really." Chaske was trying to sound reassuring.

It felt like a big, ginormous, urgent problem. Mum always said she was going to "the necessary." She hated any of the words—British or American—for toilet. Now the title seemed 100 percent appropriate.

Until now the worst thing that had ever happened to me

was Tristan Carmichael breaking up with me before prom. I felt light-headed from my dramatic change in priorities. If I survived this, I promised whatever god was listening that I would never complain about anything ever again.

After I'd worked up the nerve to go to the necessary, which in the short term consisted of an empty plastic bag and two tissues from my messenger bag, we gathered at the entrance. Midnight slept on my lap with one paw covering her eyes, like she was some melodramatic actress in one of those silent movies. "The only way we are going to make it is if we work together." I sounded like my mother.

"We need to make a plan," Marissa piped up. Was Mum inhabiting her too?

"Can't we eat?" Tate whined. "I'm starving."

"Yeah, in a minute. We need to agree on a few things first." Chaske kept any hint of annoyance out of his voice. I was impressed at his self-control.

"We need roles and responsibilities." Marissa studied each of us carefully. "Tate." At the sound of his name, he sat up. "Tate, you will be our timekeeper."

"What? Why me?" he moaned.

"You've got the most expensive watch." Marissa continued, "I'm assuming it's one of those that doesn't need a battery. It keeps time using your body's movement, right?"

Tate proffered his wrist so we could see our official timepiece, a big chunky silver Rolex. "Yeah, right. What do I have to do?"

"Our days and nights could easily get mixed up. It would be great if you could give us a regular account of the time and also find some central place to tally the days. What do you say?" She had that unique combination of soothing and condescension in her voice. Was she giving him a compliment or making fun of him? It was hard to tell.

"Yeah, sure. Whatever," Tate said. "Can we eat now?"

"We are making some pretty important decisions and you are a part of this team," Marissa said.

Tate shrugged and slouched back, reclining on his elbows. "So get on with it."

"Chaske, can you be responsible for toilets and sleeping quarters?" Marissa stated it as a question but it was clear she was handing out orders. It felt strange all of a sudden that Marissa had decided she was boss. I mean, she was right, but I didn't like the feeling of being told what to do.

"I'll manage all our supplies," I said. It was the most important job and I decided no one was going to do it but me. "Tomorrow I'll divide up the resources and make sure we have enough to keep us going for as long as possible."

"That's fab, Ice," Marissa said. Her tone was that of someone rewarding a dog for a simple trick. Up until now, I'd seen mostly the "cheer" part. Now I thought I was meeting the "captain."

"What about you?" Chaske asked Marissa.

"I'll help you with the physical stuff tomorrow," she said, and put her hand on Chaske's knee. What was she doing? Was she holding her friends close and her enemies closer? She did say she was going to keep an eye on him, didn't she?

"Yeah, okay," Chaske said, and stretched his legs, which caused Marissa's hand to shift off him. "We should move everything farther down into the tunnel. But we can sleep here again tonight."

"That's fab, Chaske," Marissa said. She batted her eyelashes at him. I think his cheeks went a little pink with embarrassment. Was she flirting or playing him? Marissa was much more complex than I'd originally thought. Chaske wouldn't fall for her giggly-lack-of-hair-flip cheerleader routine. Would he?

Then it hit me. I felt a fluttering in my stomach and this feeling like an emotional hiccup when I looked at Chaske. The guy saved my life and I was crushing on him, big-time. I was jealous of Marissa's girlish ease around him. I needed to get a grip. This was reality, not reality TV.

EIGHTEEN

"Stuff that doesn't kill me, makes me way better."
—Just Saying 222

HARPER

Finch and Harper spend the morning digging Atti's grave at the base of the Mountain near Finch and Atti's father's burial mound. Sometime overnight Finch shaved his head. Harper doesn't ask him why. This isn't about him, no matter how much he's trying to use Atti's death to gain attention. Today is about saying good-bye to a dear, sweet little girl who was a ray of sunshine in their dull existence. They place her remains in the misshapen hole. Harper can't bring herself to cover Atti with dirt. Finch does that on his own. It's horrible seeing dirt fill in Atti's missing pieces. Harper helps him cover the grave with a blanket of stones. A sob is permanently wedged in her throat. She can't believe Atti's gone.

As the Cheerleaders gather, Harper sprinkles Atti's grave with the tiny white and yellow flowers that grow wild on the Mountain.

Atti would have loved it. They have picked flowers together before and made crowns. A warm breeze stirs the air, creating spirals of petals that rise and fall as if her spirit is swaying among them.

Lucky is perched on a boulder looking down at the scene. Finch scrambles up next to her. His newly shaven head glows pink from the sun. Without his hair, he looks menacing. Maybe that was his intention. All faces are tilted toward him. He stands taller. Speaks louder. Moves swifter. It's as if he has been inflated by this new respect from Forreal. It's making him a bigger man. Harper's not sure it's making him a better one.

Harper misses Beckett. It's more than just his physical presence. She feels as if she's extinguised Forreal's light somehow. It's not right to have Beckett locked away. This is all her fault. She was heartbroken seeing Beckett kiss that girl, but she should have known what her words would inspire. She's told a frustrated hunter that she spotted his prey. She wishes she could take it all back. She should never have called those people Terrorists, no matter what people like them did to her family.

Cheerleaders have rocks cupped in their hands. "It's twelve and twelve," the Timekeeper calls. It's time to begin.

"Everyone, gather around," the Twitter, Cal, says. "We are going to start our tribute to Atti with a reading from the CQ."

Harper turns a stone over and over in her hands. Its smooth, flat surface gives way to sharp edges. She found it when she was looking for Atti. It was buried among her meager pile of belongings. She had her Facebook and another lump of carved wood, which she said was a sheep her father had whittled. The wood was worn smooth and shapeless by Atti's fidgeting fingers. There were the remains of the flowers she and Harper had collected a few days ago. A scrap of blue material with yellow flowers from a dress her mum used to wear. A silver, sparkling loop that Finch found on one of his scavenges. Atti said she thought it was special and sacred, but Harper knew it was an earring from when people used to put holes in their ears.

Harper rubs the rough edges of the stone where it was once a part of something bigger. She imagines the hole it left. As they dug Atti's grave, she was amazed how the ground broke in large chunks, which looked solid and felt heavy in her hands, but she could easily smash those clods into dust with one swift whack of her shovel.

"No death is a good death," the Twitter proclaims the Just Saying. "Atti has left us too soon. We can't bring her back. We can't say 'what if.' We need to celebrate her life and then move forward."

Cal pauses and the crowd choruses, "Whatever." The Cheerleaders look at one another, lost without their Cheer Captain.

Finch climbs off the boulder and as he speaks he walks among those who have gathered. "We will miss Atti, but this is not a sad occasion. Atti has become one with the Mountain. As the Great I AM says, 'We custom-make our afterlife.' And if I know Atti, she will be reunited with our parents and her ever-after will be filled with flowers and kittens and rainbows, but no more questions." Finch chuckles to himself. Harper thinks his speech is strange. Atti was so full of questions. Each one seemed to irritate Finch. Now he's acting as if they were endearing.

"We will miss you, Atti," Finch shouts, raising his fists to the sky. Harper hates how he's taking advantage of Atti's death, using her to elevate his place in Forreal. "Your smile and your giggle. We ask that the Great I AM watch over you." Finch places his rock on Atti's grave. The flower petals stir. "And by the power of Victoria's Secret, we will avenge your death!"

He cracks his knuckles as if punctuating his speech. Harper reluctantly steps up next to him. She kisses the stone and then places it on Atti's grave. Her stone has dark drops on its sandy surface and she realizes those are her tears. Harper wants to tell them about the real Atti. The one who had so much to say that words spilled out of her and filled the silence, but Harper is too overwhelmed with sadness to speak. Harper walks to a place just outside the circle of Cheerleaders.

Each rock falls with a sharp click against the others as the pile builds. Voices raise as each Cheerleader talks about Atti, bringing her alive in their memories for these last few precious moments. Then she will be gone, and the CQ encourages Forreal to look forward, not back. But Harper will never forget Atti.

"Please join with me in our Farewell Tune," Finch says, and begins to sing:

> *"Don't hold on to hate.*
> *Accept your fate.*
> *We had time.*
> *All you got is time.*
> *Till it's gone."*

Everyone cheers and claps and sings along, and Harper's heart lightens a little. When the last note rings out and wafts away, Finch climbs up onto the new mound of rocks over his sister's grave. "Tomorrow we will attack the Man-Made Mountains at sunset, and we will burn what the Terrorists have built."

Harper thinks about the girl Beckett kissed and the four boys she attacked. Part of her wants them to pay for what their ancestors did. She wishes Forreal had never seen the lights. She wishes that girl would have stayed away. Forreal will never be the same, but if Forreal attacks these Survivors, they will become no better than the Terrorists they have feared for so long.

As Finch bellows on about his plans, the Cheerleaders' grief and fear turn to anger. Harper understands. Grief and fear are helpless emotions. They are thrust upon you and all you can do is suffer. But anger has power and purpose. Anger gives a victim control. Forreal has been scared for so long. The Cheerleaders are ready to blame and hate. Finch turns that girl and her people into beasties. Forreal believes him because they want an enemy, someone they can destroy so that their fear can subside.

Harper's impulsive, thoughtless words have caused this confrontation. When she blurted them, this wasn't what she wanted. Harper has to stop Finch. Beckett is her only hope.

Harper edges away slowly, keeping her eyes trained on Finch. He doesn't notice her movement. She's not sure he's seeing any of them right now. His focus is on the Man-Made Mountains and the Terrorists she has helped him bring to life. Harper has to make this right.

Tom is guarding Beckett. He is pacing back and forth across the entrance of the cave. Beckett is slouched at the back of the cave. His hands and feet are bound. His eyes are closed but his lips are moving. He's Saying. Of course he's Saying, and this time *I am the answer*, Harper thinks. Her heart breaks at what she's done. He will never look at her the same. They will always have this scar of betrayal between them.

"Finch asked me to relieve you," Harper lies to Tom. He

squints and studies her. Years of distrust can't be overcome by one Terrorist sighting. Harper has been "other" too long for him to trust her. "Finch thought you might like to say good-bye to Atti." Wait. That's not what will convince Tom, Harper realizes. "Oh, and Finch is making plans for the attack and he wants the best Cheerleaders to help with the planning," Harper explains.

Tom dashes off without a word. Like so many of the Cheerleaders, he is now anxious to do battle.

When Tom is out of sight, Harper unties Beckett, but she can't meet his gaze. "We've got to get out of here. We can hide in the desert until this blows over, or maybe we could wander and find a new home."

He rubs the red raw patches on his wrists and ankles where the ropes have dug into his skin. "I will never leave the Mountain. You know that, Harper." She helps him stand. He's trying to look her in the eyes and they do this strange dance as she looks anywhere but at him. "What is Finch planning?" he asks.

If she tells him, he will try to stop Finch. Harper doesn't know what Finch might do if Beckett interferes. "Beckett, please. . Come away with me just for a little while."

"Harper." Even her name sounds different, like an accusation.

He places his hand on her shoulder and she melts. "Finch plans to attack the Man-Made Mountains at sunset tomorrow," Harper blurts.

Harper walks to the cave's entrance and checks around. Forreal is empty, but soon everyone will return. "We need to go."

"I forgive you," Beckett says. He's right beside her. And for a moment, she is home once again in his presence.

Then the image of him kissing that girl flashes into her mind and she moves away. She's that five-year-old wandering in the desert. How can he forgive when he doesn't even understand?

"I saw you kiss her." She looks him in the eye.

"Her name's Greta."

That's what those boys called her. "I remember now, Beckett. I know what happened to me before I came to your Mountain, and it was people like her who killed my family. Don't you see? There are no beasties. We destroy each other. We are all Terrorists."

"Don't be ridiculous."

Harper shakes her head. "I overheard some of her people talking. They want to take over our Mountain." That's not exactly what they said, but she's got to make Beckett listen. "She's a spy. She's using you. Can't you see that?"

"She is just a girl trying to survive," Beckett says. He hasn't heard a word she's said. "I have to warn Greta."

"Don't go." Harper blocks his way.

"I have to. I can't stand by and let Finch destroy Vega."

"I'll come with you," Harper says. Maybe she can change his mind. Maybe she can confront the girl and make Beckett see her lies.

"I will meet you at our spot, after I've gotten a message to Greta."

Harper's heart aches. He has shared secrets and stolen kisses with that girl. He's putting her safety over everything else.

"Once I'm sure Greta is safe, we'll figure out how to stop Finch," Beckett says.

She watches him race down the Mountain. She's lost him. She wants to blame the girl, but she knows she's pushed him away, and that's what hurts most of all.

NINETEEN

The rest of the first day, we kept busy. Chaske took us on a tour. The walls looked like jumbo graph paper with score marks from what must have been blasting. Rock fragments were scattered everywhere. The tunnel narrowed to the width of a two-lane highway. The ceiling was as high as my high school gym's.

"Ice, keep up!" Marissa called. I had stopped, eyes fixed heavenward. What was happening out there? Through all that rock was there still blue sky and sunshine?

"Dread! Seriously!" Tate bellowed.

I had to stop thinking like that. Stop thinking, period.

When I lowered my gaze, they had vanished. I was

surrounded by sandy-brown rock—and nothing else. I was alone.

All alone.

"Where are you?" I screamed, panic creating ragged, hoarse edges to my voice.

"We're right here." Chaske appeared ahead of me. In these monotonous surroundings, it was hard to see any definition. The tunnel spiraled down at a steady decline. The others had simply made the first turn.

My body was jittery from my thinking I'd been deserted—it was only for a few seconds, but that feeling was lodged in my brain. I rushed to Chaske and had to stop myself from hugging him. He led me to the others.

As we rounded the first turn, Chaske pointed to a metal box the size of a laptop computer bolted to the rock wall. Two thick cables led from the box to the ceiling. "Here are the main light switches," he said. "If we can stand the pitch black, I think we should turn the lighting off every night. We're not sure how the lights are powered, so maybe it's best to conserve."

I didn't like the idea of shutting off the lights ever again, but I didn't say anything.

Marissa clapped. "Excellent. Awesome." I didn't understand where this overenthusiasm was coming from. Maybe that's how she dealt with fear—she buried it behind a wall of perky.

Chaske kept walking until he reached this cubbyhole. "We can each pick one of these for our own room."

"Oh," Marissa said, stepping closer to Chaske. "I thought

we might"—she paused—"we might sleep in the same place, like last night."

"You can if you want, but I want a little space." Chaske backed away from the rest of us. I agreed with him. I wasn't completely sure I trusted them yet. Also, after seeing the effects of the virus, I thought a little distance might not be a bad thing. It wasn't a logical thought. If they were already infected, then I would know it by now, wouldn't I?

I peeked in the first room. The space was high enough for me to stand up straight and lie down spread eagle. Several pipes of various sizes were piled in the middle. "I'll take this one." I thought I should be closest to the door. I wanted to be the first one to hear the knock when my parents arrived.

Chaske walked to the next cubbyhole and said, "I'll take this one." The space looked like a carved-out, human-size mouse hole. His room was roundish. It was about two feet taller than he was. It could fit a bed and a couch—if he'd had them.

"I'll take the next one," Marissa said, and pointed to the next opening maybe ten feet away. She picked it without even looking inside.

Both Tate and Midnight poked their heads in every cubbyhole they encountered. Tate even dropped to his hands and knees and crawled down a munchkin-size tunnel. He flipped his body around so he was facing us. "Maybe I'll take this one."

"Don't you want a bigger one? Aren't you going to feel…" I was going to say trapped, but how could he possibly feel more trapped?

"Yeah, maybe." He wiggled so his face poked back outside the hole—like a groundhog looking for his shadow. Midnight pranced over to Tate and tilted her head and arched her neck until Tate butted heads gently with the cat.

The tunnel kept spiraling down forever. One spiral from my new bedroom was the room where Chaske and Tate found the water and cots. The main tunnel and the lighting system ended in a square about the same dimensions as my entire house. The main tunnel split in two. One tunnel was covered in thick, smoky plastic sheeting hung on a metal frame. We agreed that this was the perfect space for our necessary. This far down the tunnel would allow a little privacy and maybe even keep the stench factor to a minimum. Chaske said he would hang one of the Maglites somehow so we could have at least a little light behind the plastic curtain.

I walked over to the other tunnel entrance.

"That dead-ends after maybe twenty feet," Chaske said.

The square of light quickly faded into blackness.

"I explored it earlier," Tate said proudly. "It's like there was a cave-in or something."

My stomach lurched, but the others appeared to be unfazed by the mention of rocks crashing down.

Tate continued, "The tunnel ends in a pile of rocks."

"And we agreed." Chaske waited until he caught Tate's eye. "We agreed that we should stay out of that tunnel."

"Fine by me," I said.

"Hey, Chaske!" Tate called, straddling the line where light turned to dark. He swayed in and out of the light. "What if I use your tent and sleep right here?"

"I don't know," Chaske said.

"I think it's okay," I told Tate. Keeping the noisemaker as far from me as possible seemed like a great idea. I also had to admit I was impressed by Tate's courage. I wouldn't want to sleep all the way back here by myself.

"Okay," Chaske reluctantly agreed. "Well, that's it. That's all there is."

I don't know what I'd expected—satellite TV, maybe a radio, skylights—but it wasn't this. I guess I'd pictured one of those bomb shelters like they show in the movies. The ones stocked with food and entertainment and a bare swinging lightbulb. I was thankful to my parents for the food in my backpack and the water, but somehow I thought they might have rigged something like a five-star hotel crossed with an amusement park underground.

"All right, team. We better get to work," Marissa said, and hooked her arm through Chaske's. "As my coach always says, 'Team equals together everyone achieves a lot.'"

"More," I said. I'd heard that quote before, or maybe saw it on a bulletin board with some picture of skydivers hand in hand in a free fall. "Otherwise it spells *teal*."

"Whatever. Chaske and I will work on the...what did you call it, Ice? Oh, yeah, the necessary. Maybe you and Tate go back up and get our supplies stored in one of those extra rooms," she said to me.

I bristled again at being told what to do. I had to assume Marissa meant well. She was getting us organized. She was the cheer captain and maybe she couldn't help it. But this was my bunker and I'd saved her, all of them. I wasn't proud of myself for thinking this way. I couldn't deny that something had already changed between us.

"Race you, Dread!" Tate called, and legged it up the tunnel.

I resisted the urge to roll my eyes and followed Tate at a considerably reduced speed.

Tate and I dumped the food and medical supplies in Chaske's sleeping bag and headed for what would become our supply room. He held two corners and I held the other two. We stretched the sleeping bag between us and sidestepped down the long incline.

As we walked deeper and deeper underground, I felt farther and farther from my normal life. It was as if everything outside had ended already.

Tate began to sing, "*Quit yo cryin' be-otch. No time for lyin' we-otch.*" He sang the same lyrics over and over.

I gritted my teeth, determined not to say anything. This was his coping mechanism. I knew the song. It was "Outta Time" by In Complete Faith. It didn't help that it was one of Tristan's favorite songs.

He mumbled through the next part of the song but hit the chorus with gusto. "*Don't hold on to hate. Accept your fate. We had time. Not so much time. All you got is time till it's gone.*"

I'd never really listened to the lyrics before. "Hey, Tate," I said when we'd navigated the first turn and I couldn't take it any longer. "How about we switch stations?"

"Yeah, sure. You got a request?" He honestly asked me that question.

My body was tight with a terror that I didn't think would ever go away, but somehow this kid was managing to have a little bit of fun. I couldn't take that away. "Whatever you want," I said. "You have a really nice voice."

"Thanks," Tate said. "I'm going to be a rock star someday."

Didn't he get it? There were no more rock stars. No more music. Probably no more nothing. Nothing. Nothing. Nothing.

Stop it. I told myself as Tate started to sing another rock song. *"Wha Eva. Wha Eva. The bad, the good. Wha Eva. I put my faith in Wha Eva. Wha Eva alone."* I pretended to sing along with him, and to my unbelievable surprise, by the time we reached the supply room, I'd forgotten our dire situation for a few seconds.

"I'm going to deliver the cots to everyone's rooms, okay, Dread?" Tate said when we'd laid the sleeping bag and its contents out on the floor of the supply room. "You can handle this organizing stuff."

As soon as I'd said "Sure," the boy was out the door and up the tunnel.

My head was fuzzy with exhaustion. It was only the first day and I could feel the claustrophobia playing around the edges of my mind. Stay busy, I told myself. No time to think. I got right to work, stacking and piling and then restacking and sorting. Whenever I paused, my brain would pluck the faces of Mum, Dad, Lola, Tristan, and other people and things from my life before. Those images flicked like a PowerPoint presentation to random people, like my English teacher Mrs. Lord or the president of the United States or the old guy at the corner shop who gave me one of those mini Peppermint Patties every time I dropped by.

I finally figured out some sort of system for our supplies. Everything was stacked neatly first by category: food, medicine, tools, and so on, and then by alphabetical order. I'm not sure it would make any sense to anyone else, but it kept my brain occupied.

Tate was singing at the top of his lungs, probably hysterically excited for a place where no one would tell him to turn his music down or shut up. I could hear a constant clink and tap of Chaske and Marissa chiseling out a trench for our toilet. The idea, Chaske had explained, was to dig a new hole every few days and fill the old one in. I sort of gagged at the thought of our "necessary" situation.

Tate called out six twenty-two and added, "Time to eat!" Everyone gathered for dinner. Chaske and Marissa were covered in a fine, rocky powder. We were almost too tired to eat our half power bar and stick of beef jerky. Only Midnight was delighted by our dinner. She gobbled down the jerky as if it were a double pepperoni pizza with extra cheese. We nibbled our dry and greasy dinner.

"If we ration carefully, I figure we have enough food for maybe three months," I told them after we'd finished eating. "Half a power bar for breakfast and lunch and half an MRE for dinner. We can substitute jerky and Marissa's snacks for a few meals each week."

"Okay, that's totally doable. I survived my first cheer camp on one yogurt and two bananas a day."

"That doesn't sound like a lot to me," Tate said, surveying the empty wrappers tossed in the middle of our circle. "I'm still hungry."

"I know," I said. "But we've got to try, okay?"

Tate shrugged.

We retired to our cubbyholes when Tate told us it was nine o'clock. No one made a move to turn out the lights, and I was glad. I curled up in my cot with Midnight. I clutched the key in my fist. Holding it made me feel as if I had the power to leave anytime. I knew that wasn't true, but it made me feel the tiniest bit less trapped. I didn't want to think any more about toilets or MREs or how we were going to survive.

One day down. How many more did we have to go?

We slept most of the next day. It was easier to lie on my cot and doze in and out of consciousness. Then we were like Ping-Pong balls in a swimming pool. We'd float on our own for a while and then bump into one another. We didn't know what to say or how to act. The novelty had worn off and reality had set in. We were hungry and tired. None of us wanted to talk about our situation or about anything that would remind us of what we'd lost.

Late that night I walked to the entrance with only a flashlight to illuminate my way. I thought about leaving. I even held the key up to the lock. But I couldn't open the door.

The infected, vampires, zombies, soldiers, aliens, serial killers, snakes, spiders, and even sharks now inhabited the space outside that door. Or, worse yet, there was nothing out there. A vast gray space with everything burned to ash.

It's hard to explain how you grieve for the loss of the world as you knew it. One day Lola and I were sipping cappuccinos at Starbucks, me indecisive about a Bountiful Blueberry Muffin or Chocolate Chunk Cookie and Lola giving me the scoop on Wyatt and Saleha's Facebook flaming. The next day, everyone and everything was stripped away.

I'd close my eyes and see my parents screaming in pain. Then I'd see them in coffins. I countered every horrible image with a mundane one of me and Dad licking fingers full of brownie batter and laughing when there wasn't enough left to bake. Or Mum and I watching *An American Werewolf in London* and screaming at the scary parts even though we'd seen them all before. My parents would be coming to get me. They would. That's the thought I clung to with all of my might.

I woke up to Tate calling out that it was nine in the morning, but it could have been afternoon or evening. I was already losing track of time.

I didn't feel like getting up. What was the point? I spotted the coverless copy of *To Kill a Mockingbird* peeking out of my messenger bag. I'd nicked it from the supply room. It was the only personal thing Chaske had in his backpack. I wondered why. I turned it over and over in my hands. I wondered what the cover looked like and where it was.

You can't judge a book by its cover.

That's how my brain was functioning. I had nothing to do but couldn't concentrate on anything.

Midnight curled up on my chest, tucking herself right under my chin. I raised the book higher and flicked through the pages. I could feel the thrum of her purrs. I stroked her and she made this tiny squeaking sound. I felt the tiniest twinge of something.

Something. Something.

Whatever.

This was one of the books on the summer reading list my sophomore year. My English teacher Mrs. Storms told us that Harper Lee, the author of *To Kill a Mockingbird*, won some major award and sold a bazillion copies and then never wrote another book. I wondered why. Did she say everything she needed to say? Or was putting yourself out there on paper like walking naked down senior row at Capital Academy? Once was more than enough.

I flipped to the last page. I wanted to see how this story ended. I didn't understand it all. It was about some guy reading to a little girl, his daughter maybe. Someone had underlined the line that said something about nothing being scary except in books.

I laughed out loud. Midnight dug her claws into my chest as she sprang off the bed, startled from the unnatural sound I'd just made. What did the narrator know about scary?

I kept reading. The characters were reading a book about

someone who was accused of doing some bad things. The dad character was saying that most people are real nice once you finally see them. I didn't think he was right. All evidence to the contrary. I bet those terrorist people who did this weren't nice deep down. How could they be? And what about the guy who pulled a gun on Tate? Was it just the situation that brought out the worst in people? Then I thought of Marissa, Tate, and Chaske. We'd pitched in to help one another. They were good, weren't they?

I closed the book and clutched it to my chest, missing the warmth of Midnight. The book made me feel closer to Chaske. Someone who liked literary stuff like that had to be okay, right? I felt guilty about taking the book. It must be special to him. I'd put it back in the supply room later.

I studied the patterns in the uneven dirt ceiling. I was like a worm burrowed deep underground. The only time I ever saw worms was when it poured down rain. The sidewalk in front of my house would be scattered with dead ones—like some battlefield of Worm War III.

Floods.

War.

Don't think.

But it was too late. It was like Mum switching on the overhead light in my room when I overslept. Memories bombarded me. But what was worse were the overwhelming emotions that each memory triggered. The happier the memory the more sad it made me. It felt as if a giant hand had reached into my chest and grabbed a fistful of my organs and was trying to jerk them out of my body.

Don't think of end-of-the-world scenarios or anything from outside.

But that was impossible.

I leapt up. My head swam. I tottered as if I was on a cliff's edge. I shut my eyes and pulled myself back.

Find Midnight, I told myself. If I could find her, then everything would be all right.

I smelled a hint of citrus and the eye-watering stench of gym socks. And then Marissa stopped right in front of me.

"Hey, Ice!" Her voice a bouncing ball.

"Hey." I sounded like a gooey, underdone pancake.

"Let's do something. We can't keep lying around all the time." She jogged in place. "I've finished my run. I've got to stay in shape, you know? I'm getting bored. The four of us should do something together."

I wasn't in the mood for Marissa's brand of extreme perky, but what excuse could I possibly give? I didn't have any plans for the foreseeable future. "Sure."

"Let's get the guys and, oh, I don't know, play twenty questions."

I felt as if I'd stepped into some strange combo episode of the old *Star Trek* and *Little House on the Prairie*. She led me straight to Chaske's room.

Right before we reached his doorway, she stopped. "How do I look?" she asked.

Um, really? Seriously? Was she angling for the Miss Apocalypse crown?

I wanted to respond: *What does it matter?* But instead I gave her the elevator eyes like the freshman boys gave the girls in gym class. Her head had a hint of black stubble. Her eyes were bordered by dark circles, as if she'd been punched. Her skin was more yellow than brown, from the lack of self-tanning product, I assumed. She hadn't changed her clothes since we'd met. She seemed like a recycled version of herself. Her sleeves were rolled up and scrunched past her elbows. She unbuttoned her pink shirt and flashed her hot-pink sports bra. She knotted the shirt right under her breasts. The effect was better than a boob job for accentuating the positive.

"You look good," I said, and finally understood a little more about Marissa. It was all about the guy. Yeah, she shaved her head, but she couldn't give up flirting. It was an addiction. I'd had girlfriends like Marissa before. They'd be your BFF until some boy came along.

I swear to the power of Victoria's Secret that the girl sashayed into Chaske's room. And I hoped my mum—a card-carrying member of the bra burners' society—would forgive me, but I fluffed my dreadlocks, gave my pits a sniff—not too rank—and scratched at the flaky, beige spot that had crusted on my purple BE NICE TO YOUR CHILDREN— THEY CHOOSE YOUR NURSING HOME shirt.

When I walked, okay, shuffled, into the room, Marissa was all "Oh, Chaske" this and "Ooo, Chaske" that. She was all touchy-feely and he was like a kung fu master trying to deflect her advances. Her vow to swear off boys was beyond broken. I guess Chaske was way more interesting than I was—seeing as I'd been comatose more than awake since we met.

"You agree, don't you, Ice?" Marissa cooed in my direction.

"Yeah, um, what?" I had to shift my brain into conversation mode.

"I was telling Chaske that we thought it might be fun to play a little twenty questions, or truth or dare. You know, something to get our minds off of..."

"I'm not sure... maybe we could..." I started to form a response, but Marissa had slipped her arm through Chaske's and was leading him out of his room.

I followed like a band groupie.

"Tate!" Marissa shouted with every ounce of her cheer-powered lungs. "Meeting up front!"

Tate came racing by and beat all of us up to the entry-way. We sat in a circle—well, a square. Midnight curled up by the door. She was giving herself a tongue bath. Her big pink tongue looked brighter against her black fur. I suddenly felt the layer of grit coating my skin.

"Okay," Marissa bounced. "Truth or dare?" Her attitude, her smile, everything felt too forced. She was trying too hard to make this seem like no big deal.

"Truth," Tate said when no one responded.

"Oh, okay," Marissa said, and looked at the ceiling, thinking of a question. "What did you want to be when you grew up?"

Chaske and I noticed her verb choice—past tense—and glared at Marissa.

"Um, I mean..." She fake-giggled. It was screepy. "What do you want to be when you grow up?"

Tate didn't notice the shift in verb tense or in the atmosphere. He didn't hesitate. "Rock star, of course." He played a little air guitar. "A guitarist, like the next Jimi Hendrix, or maybe a drummer, like Neil Peart. My dad took me to a Rush concert, and man, could that guy wail. It was like…" Tate flailed his arms like an octopus in heat, banging on an imaginary drum set. "He was in, like, some three-sixty surround-sound drummer's trance. It was wicked."

"All right," Marissa said, unimpressed.

"I'm taking lessons, you know. I got mad skills," he said with a flourish of his imaginary ride cymbal.

My life had suddenly gone from black-and-white to 3-D. It was overwhelming to be around them at once and Tate and Marissa being so wired. I was suddenly tired again.

"Okay, Chaske," Tate said. "Truth or dare." But he didn't wait for Chaske to choose. "What were you doing out there? Why were you on the mountain? Where did you come from?"

"Whoa, there, rock star," Chaske said, his face flushing.

"It's truth or dare, not twenty questions, Tate," I said on Chaske's behalf.

"It's okay." Chaske placed his hand on my leg and just as swiftly moved it.

Marissa and Tate leaned in, eager to hear Chaske's response and solve the mystery of this guy once and for all.

"I'm nothing special. Just a guy who was at the right or wrong place at the right or wrong time, you know."

"Ah, come on, man. You've got to give us more than that," Tate whined.

"Your last name at least or something," Marissa added.

"Eastman," Chaske said flatly.

Awkward.

Tate started tapping his fingers in what I'm sure was the opening beats to "Wipe Out." Marissa's mouth twitched. I couldn't figure out if it was a tic or if she kept starting to say something.

"I was graduating in a few months and I had no clue what I wanted to be," I blurted, unable to take the silence any longer.

They stared at me as if I'd proclaimed myself radioactive.

"I was probably going to be a doctor. Science comes really easy for me." Marissa shrugged. "Runs in the family. My mom's a surgeon and my dad's a shrink. What about you, Chaske?"

"Doesn't matter anymore, does it?" Chaske said. "Everything's changed. All we have is the here and now."

He was right. Nothing before this moment mattered anymore. That was a strangely comforting thought. My senior year was all about getting the best grades and figuring out what college to attend. Tristan was pressuring me to go all the way. None of that mattered anymore. I needed to survive. I may not have gotten an offer from Harvard, but maybe I could survive one more day and then another and another.

"I say from now on we forget the shit from outside," Chaske continued. "Start over." His hand went to his mouth and he chewed on the jagged edge of his thumbnail. I hadn't noticed before, but all his fingernails were bitten down to the quick. The skin around each nail was peeling and raw. When he realized what he was doing he shoved his hands under his thighs.

He was right. It was too painful to remember everything I'd lost. I had to stop hoping that there would be some made-for-TV moment when we went outside and everything would be exactly as we left it. I didn't feel like the same person I had been a few days ago.

"I mean, we're alive. We're safe. That's not too bad," Chaske said, and absentmindedly chewed one of his nails again. "Now I say we play some cards." He pulled a pack of cards from his back pocket.

"I can teach you Texas Hold'em," Tate said.

"Great," Chaske replied.

"I'm in," Marissa said, bouncing a little.

"Why not?" I added.

Tate's lips curled into a cheeky grin. "Strip poker?"

"Not on your life," Marissa said, giving him a playful slap.

"Nice try, man," Chaske said with the faintest hint of a smile.

"I ain't dead yet," Tate said.

I choked back the "yet." I mentally shook off the cobwebs, slapped on a fake smile, and said, "Quit yakking and deal."

TWENTY

"See everything as an opportunity for improvement."

—Just Saying 129

BECKETT

He waits for Greta at the spot where they hid away. How crupid he was to think he could keep Greta secret. It was never going to end any other way. Beckett thinks he should be Saying to the Great I AM, but instead he's begging and hoping to see Greta one more time.

And then she's standing in front of him. He almost can't believe it. He thanks the Great I AM. He kisses her with a passion that makes him tremble.

"Beckett." She tries to pull away, but his lips are on hers again. He slips his hands in the space between her shirt and shorts and feels her warm, smooth skin. His connection with the Great I AM is pure and spiritual, but this is physical and overwhelming.

He tears himself away. He scans every inch of her. She has a smear of dirt on her cheek. He goes to rub it off, but instead he traces it with his finger.

Their lives are colliding in so many ways. He kisses her lips tenderly. He cups the back of her neck and holds her there, drinking in everything he will never have again.

"Greta…" He can't find the words. How can he explain in a way that won't make her hate him?

"I came to warn you," she blurts.

"What?" She's warning him? It doesn't make sense.

"My brothers saw something out there." She points to the valley below. He can tell she's scared. And yet she's come to warn him. His heart swells. She's risking everything for him too.

"A black creature attacked them," Greta continues. "They saw it climb this mountain."

The realization of what she's saying clicks. "Terrorists?" He can't believe it. Harper is wrong. There are real Terrorists, beasties just like his ancestors believed. It's as if he's been doused with cold water, washing away the haze of emotion for Greta that has made him so happy but clouded his judgment.

"What did you say?" Greta squints at him.

"Terrorists. We've always feared their return." He starts to pace. This is worse than he thought. Finch is going to attack Vega and Terrorists have returned.

"No, this was some sort of monster."

"Yeah, with claws and fangs. The beasties that brought about the end of everything."

She studies him as if he's a puzzle she can't solve. "With these monsters running wild, I think you need to persuade your people to join with us," she says. "We can protect you."

They can protect us? He needs no protection other than the Great I AM. Beckett remembers Harper's warning: Greta's people want our Mountain. This doesn't mean Harper was right. He won't believe Greta has ulterior motives. She came to warn him. She wants to protect him. She risked Terrorists to come here. And even if she's a spy, what does it matter? His people are planning to attack her home.

He stops pacing, but his thoughts continue to go round and round. He faces her. He can't wait any longer. "Greta, I came to warn you too." He doesn't want to say it. He doesn't want to believe it's true. He knows it will kill whatever it is that's blossomed between them and he grieves for the loss of her. "Some people in Forreal believe," he starts slowly, "someone from Vega killed a young girl from Forreal."

"We could never—"

He's got to tell her. He's got to say it now or he may never be able to find the courage. "These people plan to attack Vega at sundown tomorrow. They know we've been meeting, and they think I've been conspiring with you."

"Oh, God, Beckett, no." She looks at Beckett and then out toward Vega.

He reaches for her, for one last embrace, but she backs away. Her eyes are locked on his but she's shaking her head and moving farther and farther away. "What have we done?"

For that, there is no answer.

Greta turns and runs away.

215

And now he has lost her for good.

Without so much as a backward glance, she's gone.

Maybe Harper was right. Maybe Greta has been using him all along.

Beckett lies stretched like a star on the hard, rocky soil. If it weren't for the thousands of tiny pebbles digging their sharp edges into his flesh, he would feel nothing. He's waiting for Harper as agreed. He's been Saying to the Great I AM, but he feels abandoned—by Harper, by Greta. The Great I AM seems to have abandoned him too.

He presses himself into the Mountain and Says to the Great I AM, *Whatever. Whatever. Whatever.*

He feels the grit on his skin and imagines that he is becoming one with the Mountain, slowly blending and then disintegrating until the fragments of him are blown away on the hot desert air.

Whatever. Whatever. Whatever. The Saying rolls around in Beckett's brain, but it doesn't give him peace. The Great I AM can't want him to stand by and watch them destroy one another. But what can he do?

Whatever.

The word, usually so solemn, so meaningful, now feels almost unknown on his tongue. His eyes squeeze shut tightly in frustration. *What am I supposed to do?*

Beckett's skin prickles with goose bumps, as if the temperature on the Mountain has changed. Someone is coming. He can feel it. He tries to relax and tune in to every molecule around him.

He keeps his eyes closed and Says to the Great I AM, *What-*

ever. Beckett hopes that whoever it is will simply go away. The person is so close now that Beckett feels his skin flush with the heat radiating off him.

He waits until he feels hate hover on the blade of a knife above his throat. He opens his eyes. The defining features of the figure looming above him are obscured in shadow. The silhouette materializes, a tall, lanky frame, a beaklike face, and a bald head.

Finch.

Beckett looks him in the eyes, demanding an explanation.

Finch clears his throat. "You have betrayed Forreal." Beckett can feel the blade quiver in Finch's hand. "It is my destiny to avenge Atti's death and kill the Terrorists once and for all. I won't let you stop me." Finch's eyes are wild.

Beckett can almost picture it. Blood draining from his body and staining the earth below. *Has the Great I AM sent Finch?* Beckett wonders. Is this his destiny?

Finch straddles Beckett's torso, keeping the knife poised over Beckett's throat. He kneels on Beckett's arms and sits on his chest. Finch's legs are like steel rods, cutting Beckett's arms in half. Beckett whispers the Saying of Dedication.

"Stop that." Finch presses the flat of the knife into Beckett's neck. It stings as the blade breaks the skin. Finch tenses his grip on the knife. Beckett sees doubt in Finch's eyes. It only lasts a split second, but Beckett interprets it as a sign from the Great I AM. He bucks Finch off and snatches the knife from him. He recognizes the knife, its red handle and white cross.

Beckett kicks Finch's legs out from under him. Now Beckett and Finch have switched places. Finch lies stunned on the ground. How dare he look up with fear in his eyes after everything he's done? He is destroying years of peace and disobeying the Great I AM. Beckett's vision tints red. He lunges for Finch's throat, leading with the tip of the knife. Finch rolls out of the way and the knife slashes his bicep. A teardrop of red drips down Finch's arm. Beckett staggers back with the shock of what he's done.

Finch levels a kick at Beckett's wrist, causing the knife to arc through the air. Finch scrambles for the knife. Beckett zigzags up the Mountain, dodging boulders and threading through a maze of pine trees.

Beckett knows he can't run forever and the Mountain's landscape doesn't offer many hiding places. He checks behind him. Finch is gaining on him. The knife in Finch's hand blinks in the sun.

Up ahead Beckett spots the Crown. The Great I AM warned that anyone who crosses the Crown will die.

Beckett's thoughts loop in an endless figure eight. If he doesn't cross the Crown, Finch will finish the job. If it is the Great I AM's will that he die today, then let it be the Great I AM who takes his life. He accelerates and heads straight for the Crown. His Saying echoes in every footfall. *Whatever. Whatever. Whatever.*

He springs into the air. Branches break under his weight and he is impaled on the thicket. Hundreds of thorns pierce his body, and he screams, caught in a spiderweb of pain. He crawls up the Crown. Thorns claw at his bare chest and snag his loincloth. When he reaches the top, he half dives, half falls over. The second his hands hit the ground he tucks and rolls.

Maybe it's his imagination, but his skin tingles. He's on sacred ground. He waits for the Great I AM to exact the ultimate punishment.

Finch stops in front of the Crown, panting from the effort of the chase. "Beckett," Finch calls through the brambles, "you have betrayed Forreal and disobeyed the Great I AM. I am the Cheer Captain now."

Beckett stays silent even though his lungs beg for air. He believes that he is moments away from death—either by the force of the spirit or Finch's hands.

The anticipation is torture. Every cell in his body feels stretched and ready to burst.

Finch straightens his tall, lanky frame, his body a mosaic through the twisted branches. "May you be at peace with the Mountain," Finch whispers, and sprints away.

Beckett waits for death. He lies flat, watching the daylight fade. Tears threaten when he thinks of Greta and Harper. What will happen to them? He will watch over them if he's able. He clings to every second of life the Great I AM allows him.

Nothing happens.

Not a lightning bolt or a rattlesnake, not even a breeze disturbs him.

.And he's relieved and devastated. He's dedicated his life to the Mountain. He breaks the most sacred rule of the Great I AM. *If death does not come*…but he won't let himself finish that thought.

The air cools, and the sounds of night crackle around him.

"Great I AM," Beckett says, nearly pleads. He's said *Whatever* so many times. *Whatever* doesn't feel like an answer, so he asks, "What now?"

TWENTY-ONE

Midnight never left my side. She was small but had started to occupy a ginormous space in my life. I'd sit and watch her for hours. I'd wonder why she'd suddenly decide to clean her back left paw. I loved the little mew sound she'd make when I woke her with a scratch under her chin. She liked to play with my gel pens. I'd twirl them above her and she'd bat at them. I'd smash up rubble to make her a litter tray at the very back of the necessary and spend hours creating cat toys from scraps of material and foil wrappers. She'd chase the foil balls I made her up and down the tunnel, but sit on them if I caught her playing. I'd almost laugh when she'd have her wacky fifteen minutes at about the same time every night. She'd do this hop and skip up and down the tunnel. Or she'd stare at a spot on the wall as if she were admiring a Picasso. Sometimes I'd sit and stare with her and find patterns in the dirt that could rival some of those famous abstract paintings in the National Gallery of Art. Being with Midnight was easier than being with people.

Tate incessantly made noise. He was either drumming his fingers, tapping his toes, or humming. His jaw even popped when he ate. He snored and sometimes called out in his sleep. You never had to worry about him sneaking up on you. He was like always having the TV on in the background. I sometimes wished Tate had a mute button.

Chaske kept to himself. I'd glimpse him when he'd pass my room. I timed it right sometimes so I'd bump into him in the supply room and offer to split a power bar. I'd spend hours creating scenarios that consisted of him and me in the real world doing everyday stuff. He didn't like to talk about himself. I didn't know what kind of movies he liked or what kind of coffee he drank. Did he even drink coffee? I didn't think he was the type for organized sports. He had that book; maybe he liked museums and art galleries. But maybe he liked to make skin suits from the carcasses of dead animals for all I knew.

And I guess it didn't matter if he liked coffee or any of the rest of that stuff. We'd probably never have any of it again. I'd probably never see my favorite horror movies. What would remain when we resurfaced, if we resurfaced? No TV. No electricity. Running water? Even our attempts at mundane conversations seemed pointless in a way and only reinforced what we'd lost.

I'd fantasize about who he was before: the youngest and only American MI6 agent, a boy genius who sold some dot-com for millions, an Indian chief. Maybe he ran away because he saw a mob hit. Then I'd see those tiny slits of fingernails he had with their jagged edges. I'd catch the way he chewed them when the conversation went quiet and hide his hands when he'd see me looking at them. Maybe he was an ordinary guy on a camping trip. It still didn't explain why he had so much food or why he came to this mountain—and then there was the gun....

Marissa was obsessed with staying in shape. She had a daily workout routine. She covered her body odor with a dose of Clinique Happy. You could smell her before you saw her, like walking into a citrus grove and discovering the orange trees were planted in cow dung.

"Hey, Ice!" Marissa called as she passed on her early morning run. Marissa had turned the lights on in the tunnel. Her D&G bag slung over her shoulder with everything she owned—as if Lobo were going to drive away again with the rest of her stuff. The bag banged into her back as she ran.

In my half-dozing state, I rubbed my eyes and propped myself up on my elbows. I checked my watch—it was six thirty-seven in the morning. *Seriously, Marissa?* I'd started sleeping about ten hours a day. It helped pass the time and I was weary from our new apocalyptic diet.

I reached for my comforter, wanting to cocoon myself

away. Funny that I still did things like that. I'd forget where I was for a minute and think that I was somehow tucked in my king-size bed at home. I had this fluffy comforter that was like being snuggled in a bed of marshmallows—minus the stickiness. Mum had let me and Lola tie-dye the comforter cover black and red. It hadn't turned out exactly like we planned. The red and black sunbursts looked more like gunshot wounds. I reached for it again but grasped thin air.

I tucked myself in a ball to find a degree or two more warmth in this cool, dark space. I usually wore a pair of jeans and my cargo pants, a T-shirt, and a sweatshirt to bed. But I still felt a chill. I buried my head under the pile of clothes I used as a pillow.

I easily dipped back into sleep. I was dreaming that Lola and I were at the mall but the shops were closed. One minute people were everywhere, crashing into me, and the next minute everyone was gone and I was alone in the middle of the mall, calling for my mum and dad.

"Ice." Someone was poking me. I batted them away.

"Ice." It was Marissa and I couldn't figure out what she was doing at the mall. "Ice, you were calling out in your sleep."

"Yeah, so?" I turned over and tried to make like I accidentally pushed her away.

She regained her balance and moved back to the entrance of my room. "You sounded upset. You were calling out for your mom and dad." She started twisting the studs up and down her ear one by one.

"My *mum*," I corrected. "My *mum* is British and that's

what I call her, *Mum*." Why I needed to make sure she understood this distinction, I didn't know exactly. "Why are you waking everyone up?" Annoyance was scratching my insides. I wanted my dream back. She'd woken me before my parents had a chance to even make a dream appearance. "Let us sleep. Do you have to be so perky all the time? What in the hell do we have to be happy about?"

She looked as if my words had punctured the blow-up Marissa doll. Her shoulders sagged. I thought she might cry.

"I was just trying to help," she muttered.

"Yeah, I know. Sorry." It was bad enough without me tapping into my inner bitch. None of this was her fault, but her obsessive need to exercise partnered with this exaggerated positive attitude was bugging the shit out of me.

She started running in place. The flash of sadness from a moment ago was gone.

"Are you going to join us for poker later?" she asked, backing out of my room. "Your moping isn't helping anyone. Your attitude determines your—"

Argh! She was always doing that. She was like some famous quote app on acid. She had some sort of saying for everything, but she never got it quite right. At first it was funny, maybe even a little charming, but now it just agitated me.

"Altitude. Yeah, I know."

"So, poker later?" she asked again, still running in place.

"I'll have to check my schedule."

"We're playing right after lunch."

I let out an exasperated groan. "We've done the same thing for the past ten days."

"I know. Whatever." She raced away.

I went to the door and waited until she disappeared around the first bend. I knew I probably only had ten minutes before she'd pass this way again. I marched over to Chaske's room. We had to do something about Marissa.

When I peeked into his room, he was standing with his back to me wearing only this tatty white pair of boxers. The elastic band was wavy and they hung off his hips. There was a hole on one butt cheek. But that wasn't the most shocking thing. His body was a road map of wounds. His lovely brown skin had round, dark dots and lighter lines. When he bent over to rummage around in his backpack, I saw that the skin behind his knees was a spaghetti bowl of scars.

I stifled a gasp and ducked to one side of his door, out of sight. Maybe he was in a car accident. Maybe there were more scary things for him outside than deadly viruses or chemical attacks. Maybe that's why he didn't care that the world could be ending. He looked like he'd already survived a war.

"Chaske, can I come in?" I called. I heard him shuffling around in his room.

"Yeah, one second." More shuffling. "All right."

When I entered his room, he was sitting on his bed, fully clothed in his uniform of plain T-shirt and jeans. "Hey, Icie," he said in his low baritone voice, any hint of sleep long gone. "Everything okay? You're up early."

I completely forgot why I was here. My mind was filled

with the image of those awful scars. He removed the rubber band from the end of his long braid and combed his fingers through his shiny, thick black hair. Ever since we'd locked ourselves in, he was my rock, my hero. This perfectly mysterious man who seemed so in control. Now he seemed broken somehow.

"Icie?" he said. He started to chew one of his nails but thought better of it.

"Yeah, I'm fine," I said, shaking off his secret. "It's Marissa. She's driving me crazy."

"She's dealing the best she can." He gestured to his cot and I plopped down next to him.

"Yeah, I know." I felt the overwhelming need to tell *him* everything was going to be all right, that whoever or whatever hurt him was out there and couldn't hurt him anymore, but I couldn't. I finally understood why he didn't want to talk about anything from before.

"Can't you talk to her about waking up everyone so early? I need my beauty sleep," I said, tossing my dreads behind my shoulder and batting my eyes at him. "If I'm going to be Miss Apocalypse America when we get out, I've got to get my rest."

He sort of smiled.

"And all that exercise can't be good with as little as we have to eat," I continued. "I am worried about her. Something's not right. She acts too perky and I think she's going to blow one day."

"We should just give her time and space," he said.

He was probably right. I needed to lighten up. Maybe it

226

was me, not her. Without realizing what I was doing, I leaned into him. He slipped his arm around me. I rested my head on his shoulder as if it was the most natural thing for me to do. This closeness surprised me, but I surrendered to it. And for a moment, I was content. All my anger and frustration faded.

"Icie." He touched my face and I flinched. What was he doing? "Icie," he said again more quietly, and turned my face toward his. He was looking into my eyes, directly into my soul. Was he going to kiss me? I closed my eyes, willing it to happen. I could feel his breath on my face.

"Hey, guys!"

My eyes sprang open. It was Tate. I scrambled away from Chaske, nearly falling off his cot. I got to my feet.

"I thought since we were up already we might start the poker tournament early." He was oblivious that he'd wrecked the best moment I'd had since I got the texts from my parents. But maybe I had misread the situation. Maybe Tate had saved me from completely embarrassing myself.

"So what do you say? You two losers ready to lose?" Tate was clutching what looked like one of Chaske's black T-shirts in his hand, except it rattled when he shook it. "I collected four hundred pebbles from that avalanched wall."

"I thought we agreed that you wouldn't go back there." Chaske's voice was low and loud again.

"Chillax there, big man. I thought poker would be way more fun if we had more stuff to bet with." We had been playing with the hundredish fifty-dollar bills left in my money belt.

"How about after breakfast?" Chaske said. "I'm starving." Midnight appeared in the doorway and gave one short, sharp meow, as if she was hungry too.

"You've also got to catch Marissa," I said as I picked up Midnight. I cradled her in my arms like a baby. She wriggled a bit to get comfortable, but she loved being held close. I kissed her on the top of the head.

"Yeah, Baldy's in. I already asked. She can't stand that I'm whipping her in poker." Tate tossed the deck of cards to Chaske. "I'll go get breakfast and meet you up top."

"Okay," Chaske and I said at once.

Tate darted down the tunnel, leaving Chaske and me alone again. There was a new strangeness between us.

"I'll go get the..." He paused as if he had to think of something. He was brushing past me. "I'll go set up things up there."

"I'll, um, see you up there. I've got to, well..." I stammered, but thankfully he was gone before I had to finish that unfinishable sentence.

I waited in my room, snuggling with Midnight. I felt even weirder than I normally did. There were these new feelings about Chaske. I thought about all the scars covering his body and about that magical moment when I think he almost kissed me.

Marissa and Tate passed by. "What are you waiting for, Dread?" Tate called when he saw me sitting on my cot.

"Yeah, coming." Midnight jumped out of my arms and raced up the tunnel.

The entryway near the metal door had become our social spot—like the Starbucks of the unfinished nuclear waste repository. It was the biggest space. I felt less confined here. I also thought we could hear my parents when they finally arrived. It had only been about two weeks. That wasn't that long. I'd seen the traffic leaving Vegas. The highways were probably crammed. My mind flashed to the woman's face in the minivan. The image of a family locked behind glass, frozen in time. And the image of that old woman slumped in her seat, the awkward tilt of her neck and how her hair was flattened to the back of her head. Then there was the guy with the gun. My mind always zoomed in on the barrel and what looked like an unblinking eye staring at us. The hole that housed a bullet. I couldn't picture the guy's face, but for some reason I could picture the bullet. Mum and Dad were out there among all that, but they were smart. They would survive.

By the time I reached the entryway, the cards were dealt and four piles of one hundred pebbles had been distributed. Marissa was handing out our breakfast. Midnight was already snoozing by the door. We sat cross-legged on Chaske's sleeping bag. The red, green, and blue plaid flannel made our pebble chips hard to see. I placed my palm flat on the threadbare material. Chaske must have had this since he was a kid. I rubbed my hand back and forth across the soft flannel and imagined a seven-year-old Chaske tucked inside for his first camping trip. Then I remembered the scars on his back and that idyllic childhood vanished.

"You in, Dread?" Tate asked. His legs flapped. I'd quickly learned that was Tate's tell. When he had a good hand, he bounced nervously; when he had a bad hand, he sat perfectly still.

I checked my cards: a four of clubs and a seven of diamonds. "I fold," I said.

Marissa sat next to me. She wore her sunglasses when we played. She held her cards close to her chest and peered at them again. She placed them facedown on the blanket, then began to twist her big pink watch on her wrist around and around. "I'll see your two and raise you two," she said, dropping four pebbles in the center of the blanket. Her hand shot immediately to her ear and twisted the diamond stud in her earlobe, then the next two hoops, and on up the ear she went. This fidgeting behavior had started a few days ago. She was always twisting or pulling or tugging at her jewelry or her buttons or clothes. I glanced at Chaske and the look he gave me said he'd noticed it too.

"That's too rich for my blood," Chaske said, slipping his cards under the pile of pebbles.

"Guess it's me and you, Baldy," Tate said, legs wiggling. The bidding continued and the final cards were revealed.

"I win!" Marissa shouted, a little too loudly. She raked the pebbles in front of her. "I win. I win. I win." Her fingers stroked her pile of pebbles, making them rattle like a piggy bank full of pennies.

"Yeah, all right, already," Tate shouted. "It was just dumb luck."

Even with sunglasses, I could tell Marissa was giving Tate a hateful stare. "Watch out, rich boy," Marissa said. She poked her finger in Tate's chest.

"Hey!" Tate said, rubbing the spot she'd poked. "That hurt."

Chaske brushed her hand away.

"This is supposed to be a *friendly* game," Chaske said to Tate and Marissa. I almost expected him to say something like, "If you kids can't play nice, I'll put the game away." That's what my mum always said if Lola and I ever got too rowdy playing *Super Street Fighter IV*. We'd gone through a phase when we were ten when we would lock ourselves away for the weekend and survive on nothing but video games, Red Bull, and peanut butter M&M'S. Being in here felt kind of like that.

Marissa slipped her sunglasses on the top of her bald head. She rubbed her eyes and cracked her neck from side to side. "Sorry, Tate," she said. "It's just I haven't been able to sleep, you know, and it's all a bit, whatever, and I, well, I can't, you know what I mean."

"Yeah, I know," I said. That's how my head felt too most of the time. All jumbled. My body was always in a heightened sense of alert. It was hard to live not knowing, but always fearing.

"Just deal." Marissa dug around in her handbag and whipped out a roll of peppermint Life Savers. "Mint?" She offered one to each of us. Even though she was the queen of body odor, fresh breath was a priority. She made sure we got one breath mint a day. I sucked on the mint very slowly, savoring the cool sweetness.

We played for the rest of the morning, upping the ante every half hour. That's a trick Tate taught us from Vegas poker tournaments. It kept the game moving. The first time we played poker the game lasted for hours. It wasn't like we had anything better to do, but the game lost its luster after about three hours.

The last hand was down to Tate and Marissa. Tate's legs were bouncing and he was even drumming his fingers on his thighs. He must've had a really good hand. I'd been the first one out of pebbles. I was only starting to get the hang of it—looking at my hand and figuring out my odds of winning. Chaske lost his pebbles next.

I couldn't be sure, because he never showed us his cards, but I think he'd intentionally thrown the game. I got the sense that, if he wanted to, Chaske would win every time. Tate bragged about his poker skills, but Chaske had the cool, calm demeanor of the poker players on those all-night poker channels.

Chaske flipped the last card over. Tate's lips twitched for only a split second into a smile and then he tried to make his expression blank.

"I'm all in," Marissa said, and pushed her pile of chips into the center.

"Me too," Tate said, and did the same.

"It's winner take all," I said in my best TV poker announcer voice. You'd think a safe bunker underground trumps being outside with a possible WWIII scenario, but looking at Marissa's bloodshot eyes and Tate's pale skin, I wasn't so sure. This place was taking its toll.

Marissa showed her cards. She had two queens in her hand and there was a queen and two fours on the blanket. She had a full house. Tate beamed and slapped his cards down—he used the same two fours on the table, but he had the other two fours in his hand. "Four of a kind," he shouted, and jumped to his feet. "I win. You lose." He whooped and hollered. You'd think he'd won the lottery, not a pile of pebbles.

"Who gives a shit about this stupid game!" Marissa shook her corner of the sleeping bag, causing the cards and pebbles to scatter. She stormed off.

"Whoa," Tate said, freezing mid–victory dance. "I was just saying…I mean, it's no big deal." He called after her, "I'm sure you'll win next time, Baldy!"

There would be no next time. When Tate brought the cards the next morning for poker, the queen of hearts was missing and no matter where we looked, we couldn't find it.

TWENTY-TWO

"Don't think, just do."
—Just Saying 15

HARPER

Harper squints through the snarled brambles. "Beckett!" Harper calls, but part of her hopes he won't answer. If he's crossed the Crown, then his fate is sealed. "Beckett, where are you?" He wasn't waiting at their spot like he promised. She followed a trail of footprints here.

She can't imagine life without him. He is not only the air in her lungs but the reason she breathes. She will spend her whole life searching for him. She already grieves the loss. "Beckett." She whispers his name like a Saying. She closes her eyes and for the first time, she Says to the Great I AM. It's more bargain than worship. "Please, Great I AM, return him to me. I will be your servant, your greatest Cheerleader, if only you keep him safe."

"Harper?"

She stumbles away from the Crown. Is that the voice of the Great I AM?

"Harper." The voice is human and makes her heart sing.

"Beckett, where are you?" She spins in a crazy circle.

"I'm right here." Through the Crown he looks broken into a hundred pieces.

"Beckett?" She exhales her thanks to the Great I AM. "How?" she asks. How has he crossed? How has he survived?

"The Great I AM has spared me."

She tries to weave her hand through the brambles. If she can touch him, she'll know he's okay. But the thicket is too dense and wide.

"Finch tried to kill me," Beckett says.

This is all her fault. She punches her fists through the Crown. She cries out as the thorns rake her skin away in fine red welts. She hooks her arms through the vines. She rattles the Crown like a cage. It crackles, almost groans, but doesn't give. She needs to reach him. He will make everything all right. He always has. She can survive anything as long as she has Beckett. "I'm crossing too."

"Harper," Beckett says softly, and waits for her to calm down. "Harper, I'm not sure it's safe."

"I don't care," she says. "It's not safe for me here. Please, Beckett, please let me in."

"Okay," he says finally. He must know she wouldn't accept any other answer.

"If you go, I go, remember?" Harper says, recalling what he'd said so long ago.

"Harper, you're going to have to climb over. Do you think you can do that?"

"No problem," she says without hesitation.

"Are you sure?" he asks. "I mean I can't guarantee…"

Harper scans the hedge, looking for the best place to cross. "Move away. Give me some room." She strides back several paces. Beckett backs away from the Crown.

Harper launches herself at the hedge. The Crown wobbles as she plants her foot halfway up. The bramble bounces as she springs to the top. And then it's as if she's flying. Her arms sweep from her side and stretch over her head. Harper wishes she could take flight and fly them far, far away. She can't protect him anymore—not from Finch or Greta or herself. She lands with an *ooph*.

Harper stands and dusts herself off. She slicks back her hair and knots it at the base of her neck. She feels a twinge of fear. Will the Great I AM punish her for crossing the Crown, for lying about Terrorists, for betraying Beckett? She holds her breath.

Nothing.

She was desperate to reach him and now that he's an arm's length away she doesn't know what to do.

"The Great I AM has spared us for a reason," Beckett says.

Is that true? There is another explanation, which means Beckett's entire life is based on a lie. But Harper doesn't mention it.

Harper spots the black cat on the other side of the Crown. "Look, Beckett." She points.

Lucky flattens her body and crawls under the Crown. Her ears are drawn back nearly flat on her head. Once inside the Crown, she carefully rises to all fours, contorting her body to fit a gap in the branches. She appears to tiptoe, lifting one foot slowly and testing a branch before she slips her paw in a triangle of space. When she pulls her body free of the Crown, she shakes from the tip of her black nose to the point of her tail.

"She makes it looks easy." Beckett laughs and then grimaces.

That's when Harper notices the hundreds of scabs dotting Beckett's body. "What happened?" She moves to comfort him but he waves her away.

"I wasn't as graceful as you." He gingerly kneels to greet Lucky. She saunters over and nuzzles his side. He strokes her furry head and she purrs. Harper wishes it were that easy to make everyone happy.

She expected this forbidden land to be different from the land below. But it's just dirt and rock with a sprinkling of green. She wanders up the Mountain. The moon is hiding behind clouds. The landscape is painted in shades of gray. She's looking up ahead, searching for why this place is so special. The ball of her foot feels the edge before her heel makes contact with the broken ground. She waves wildly to keep from falling headlong into the deep hole in front of her. "Beckett," she calls, and lands hard on her back.

She flops over and finds herself looking into a pit. The clouds must shift because suddenly she can see clearly what's below. Beckett dives next to her. "Are you okay?"

Harper's focus is fixed on the pit. Bone fragments, lots of them. She counts maybe a dozen of what might be skulls. She wonders if these are the remains of others who have defied the Great I AM and crossed the Crown. Half buried among the scrambled bone fragments are flashes of metal. She thinks she sees the broken blade of a knife. There's a fragment of pink rubber and a big, square watch face that would barely fit in her closed fist. The glass is cracked but its edges sparkle in the same way the Mountain spring does when the sun catches it just right. "What's that?" Harper points at the pink. Beckett doesn't respond. He has a faraway look, as if his body is here but his mind is somewhere else.

"What is it?" Harper asks.

"Crossing the Crown has brought me closer to the Great I AM," Beckett says. "I can feel it. The Great I AM is trying to tell me something. But it's just out of reach."

The sky darkens again. Harper feels a wet drop on her head and another on her body. Raindrops dot Beckett's upturned face. The rain pours from the sky. Harper sticks out her tongue and closes her eyes. She whips her head from side to side, flicking the water into the air. She smoothes the water over her face and neck. The raindrops feel more like pebbles pelted from above.

Harper points to a cluster of boulders that create a protective tepee. Lucky has already found the shelter. She swishes her tail as the pair join her.

Harper rests her head on Beckett's shoulder, and he hides a kiss in her damp, ratty nest of hair. "We should thank the Great I AM for the rain," Beckett says.

"And the rocks," Harper adds. *And for saving you,* she thinks. Maybe he can truly forgive her and they can forget about Finch and Greta and live up here in solitude. Maybe Beckett's right. Harper is starting to feel something more, something bigger than the both of them.

They repeat the Evening Tune softly into the howling wind.

"Tonight's got promise
(Promise)
Tonight's got faith

(Faith)
Tonight's all we got
(For Sure)
(For Sure)
Tonight I got you
(And you got me)
Tonight's all I need."

They curl into each other and fall asleep.

A shrill scream erupts all around them. Harper's eyes spring open. It's morning. It takes a second to remember where she is and what has happened. Beckett's there and that's all that matters.

Another scream.

Harper's pulse rockets. Lucky leaps from her resting place on Beckett's lap and runs off to hide. Another scream and Harper and Beckett draw closer together. This scream doesn't stop. It feeds on itself and consumes the air around them. The sound tears at Harper's flesh as if it has teeth.

"Please. No." The words are repeated and jumbled among the screams.

"Greta." Beckett whispers her name and Harper's heart clenches. "We've got to help her."

Harper so wishes they could walk away. She was beginning to believe they could leave everything behind. But Greta's screams will not be denied. Beckett and Harper are being sucked back into the conflict that's based on hating what you don't understand and fearing an enemy you've only imagined.

TWENTY-THREE

Midnight leapt from her favorite spot on my chest and I woke with a jolt. There was someone in my room. My nerves jangled like they did when a telephone call came in the middle of the night. I held my breath so I could listen more intently. Every slasher movie I'd ever seen came flooding back. I imagined the flash of a knife, a wire pulled tight between fists, the sound of a gun cocked and ready to fire. But the strange thing was these thoughts didn't increase my pulse. A thought that couldn't possibly be mine sprang into my head. I tried not to think it, but it repeated over and over like a bazillion IM messages popping up all at once.

I wasn't scared of death. I was wishing for it.

We'd been locked in here for thirty-three days according to Tate's tally. I don't know when I changed, but at some point I'd stopped thinking about each day as being one day closer to freedom. Each day had become one day closer to death.

"Who is it? Who's there?" I asked. I sat up on my cot. I clutched the key in my fist. The key that I'd used to lock us in. Had one of them finally decided to come for it?

The darkness seemed to speak: "Icie, it's Chaske." I felt him bump my cot. "Can I sit down?"

"Whatever," I said. It sometimes felt like that was the only word in my brain. Nothing mattered.

The cot bounced as he sat. I thought I could hear him biting his nails.

"I don't want to be alone anymore." Chaske shifted so he was sitting right next to me. I slumped into him. He tilted so our heads touched. His long, silky hair fell like a curtain on my shoulder. He smoothed my dreadlocks and kissed me on the cheek.

I closed my eyes, feeling a rush of warmth. He kissed my forehead and my skin tingled where his lips touched and the feeling flashed like a firework through my body. Like the night sky on the Fourth of July, the darkness inside me was washed in a breathtaking array of color. And I started to live again.

When the lights in the tunnel were switched on the next morning, I was wrapped around Chaske. We'd held each other all night. That was enough.

This never would have happened out there. I'd lived my life in fast-forward. Everything was rushed and programmed. In here, we lingered. We had time to think, which wasn't always a good thing, but it meant that I could savor this moment with Chaske.

If he had showed up at my high school, we probably wouldn't have even talked to each other. Well, he wouldn't have had anything to do with the shallow, self-centered person I now realized I'd been. I'd like to think I would have given this quiet, mysterious guy a chance, but to be honest, I would have cared too much about what other people thought.

The even footfalls of Marissa on her morning run snapped me into the present.

"Wake up, sleepyhead," she called, and then she was standing in the doorway. "Oh, sorry." She turned away. She was wearing her hot-pink sports bra and ripped jeans. The jeans hung low on her thin hips. She'd lost weight, more than the rest of us with her insistence on exercise. We could see the electric-green elastic of her thong. Her skin seemed to have a grayish tint. Like always, she had her D&G bag slung over her shoulder.

Chaske and I sprang apart. "I-i-it's okay," I stammered. "We were just…it wasn't…is everything okay?"

"Yeah, fine. No problem," Marissa said, still facing away from us. "I've been thinking a lot and I thought I'd start a morning prayer service…I thought…you might want to… but you're…whatever." She rubbed her hand back and forth across her stubbly scalp. Chaske helped her shave her head with his hunting knife, but it hadn't worked so great. She looked like the love child of a guinea pig and a skinhead.

"Marissa, it's fine," Chaske said.

"I'll pray for you." She walked toward the entrance of the tunnel, then turned around and walked back the other way. When had Marissa found religion? The closest I'd ever seen her to spiritual was when she had demonstrated her cheer routine for us. She'd tacked on this plastic supermodel smile and struck the standard stiff cheerleader pose—fists on hips and legs spread in a sturdy *A*. "Ready! Okay!" she had yelled when she started every cheer. It was like a televangelist shouting "Amen!"

"You better go after her," Chaske said.

"Why?" I didn't want to leave him.

"She's getting worse."

We'd all noticed these weird changes in Marissa, not only her appearance but her behavior. We never really talked about it. If we didn't acknowledge it, then it wasn't happening. "Yeah, this prayer thing is new." I drew my body into a ball and picked at a hole in my jeans.

"Icie, it's more than that," Chaske said, and scooted away from me. "You know what I mean. I don't think the girl ever sleeps. Have you seen what she's done to the entrance?" I'd seen it for the first time yesterday. She'd taken a stone or something and drawn hundreds of faces, like emoticons, all over the walls. "She's doing that at night. I haven't seen her do it, but it's got to be her. The rest of us sleep."

"Why can't you talk to her?" I asked. "You know she

243

likes you best." I'd recently started to feel that she blamed me for everything, as if I'd somehow tricked her so I could lock her in this bunker with me. I felt this core of animosity as if she were a milk chocolate Easter bunny filled with red-hot chilies.

"I could but it's..." Chaske shifted on the cot.

"What?"

"It's awkward. She keeps..." His rosy cheeks said it all.

"She's coming on to you," I said.

"Yeah." He moved to the other end of the cot and crossed his arms and legs.

"So."

"It's more than that. She sort of stalks me."

"There's not much to do in here," I said, feeling guilty about my own pseudo-stalker behavior. I'd basically stolen his *To Kill a Mockingbird* and hadn't returned it yet. I thought about him nonstop. I was always listening out for him and secretly staring at him anytime the four of us were together. That was kind of stalkerish.

He stood up. "Just forget it."

"No, wait," I said. He'd come to me and we'd had this perfect night and I was sooo blowing it. I slowly lifted myself off the bed. My head always felt as if it were filled with cotton candy.

"Icie," Chaske said, staring after Marissa. "I think she's losing it. I mean seriously losing it. She keeps talking about me and her as if we are a couple. As if we've..."

"Oh." My body went cold. Why wouldn't Chaske and Marissa, you know? Out there they had been equally beautiful. They deserved to be on a movie poster in a mad passionate embrace.

"No. God, no," he said. "I don't want to hurt her feelings, but she's making me really uncomfortable."

"Okay, I'll talk to her."

He cupped my face in his hands. "Thanks," he said. Maybe I was going a bit crazy too. We inched closer; our heads touched. I could feel an electricity between us. He kissed my forehead and walked away.

"Hey, Marissa," I said as I entered the supply room with Midnight tagging along. Marissa was tallying our dwindling supplies. Luckily we had a renewable supply of water. Chaske and Tate had rigged a funnel and the canteens to collect the water that leaked from two of the fissures we'd found in the tunnel. We'd agreed on what we could eat and drink each day and used the honor system. At first I was hungry all the time, but my stomach had gotten used to my reduced caloric intake. Supplies were supposed to be my responsibility, but Marissa would double-check that we were all eating and drinking only our allotted amount. She kept precise track of what we had left. A few days ago I heard her screaming at Tate for eating a whole MRE by himself. She was also the vitamin police, making sure we each took a multivitamin every day.

She gave an exasperated and exaggerated sigh and made a dramatic production of starting her counting all over again. I waited until she was finished.

"Are you okay, Marissa?" I asked as she busied herself with counting the MREs. Midnight weaved in and out of the food piles.

Marissa huffed again. "Yeah. Fine. Fine. What's he been saying? I'm fine." But she wasn't fine. Well, none of us were. She was talking fast and her head twitched as if she were flicking phantom hair out of her eyes.

"He didn't say anything," I lied. "I thought we might do something together today. You could help me with a new exercise program or maybe we could whip up something interesting for dinner. Did you ever watch those cooking shows where they had to make three courses with, like, squid ink, some pasta, and chocolate sprinkles?"

"We can't use our resources that way. What are you thinking?" Her head twitched, but this time it was more like she thought she saw something behind her. She bent over the six piles of power bars. "Who put a peanut butter in with the summer berries?" she asked, not particularly of me.

"How about it, Marissa? We could see what makeup we still have and give each other makeovers."

"That's a waste of time. A complete waste of time. We could use that stuff for, well, I don't know, something useful." She was babbling in this stream of consciousness and then she just stopped. "You won, okay. I get it. You won. I lost."

"I don't understand."

She was freaking me out big-time.

"Chaske. You won. I lost." She started stacking the power bars against the wall.

"It's not a contest. We're all friends."

"The condoms." She extended her arm in this quick cheer action move. She pointed and shuddered. "The condoms are gone."

She was right. The three condoms were gone. We'd put them there along with the first-aid supplies. I remembered because it was a bit awkward how she explained to Chaske that they were there and how she'd smoothed down the foil packets in a straight line. "Well, I didn't—"

"You know, you're not so special." She was suddenly standing toe-to-toe with me.

"I never thought—"

Her face was glowing red. "Your parents are never coming. Do you hear me?"

Why was she saying that? I shook my head slightly, but as she continued my whole body trembled.

"Stop talking about them." She grabbed me by my shoulders and now she was shaking me. "Stop making me think there's hope. Don't you get it? This is it. This is all there is. We've lost everything. No one is saving us."

She shoved me hard. I stumbled, toppling piles of supplies. I hit the wall and slid to the ground. I covered my face and sobbed into my hands. Why did she have to say that? I knew in my head she was right, but in my heart I'd never, ever stop believing. I couldn't.

"Hey, guys!" Tate sang, appearing in the doorway. "Everything okay?"

I tried to stop crying. I wiped my eyes.

"Nothing. None of your business," Marissa said, cracking

her neck and bouncing like boxers do in the ring before the fight.

"Whatever, Baldy. I came for some food and to see if there were any empty containers I could use."

Marissa picked up a jug and downed the inch of water that was left. "Here." She wiped her mouth on her arm and handed the jug to Tate. That definitely wasn't like her. She usually savored and sipped the water.

"Uh, thanks," Tate said. He tucked the jug under his arm.

"I'm not sure if we should use—" I started, but Marissa interrupted.

She screamed at me, "It's one jug. One jug. Let him have it. Let someone have something other than you. You've got the key. You've got everything!"

Tate and I both blinked at the volume and force of her voice and hunched away from her.

"Whoa there, Baldy," Tate said, and raised his palms in surrender. "It's not that big of a deal. No need to get your panties in a wad."

"What are you making?" I asked Tate, giving Marissa a chance to calm down.

"Nothing. Just something. You know," he said, and picked up a peanut butter–flavored power bar. I had to give the kid credit. He kept himself busy with poker initially, then his own brand of queenless solitaire, and more recently with some top secret project he was constructing near his tent where the main tunnel dead-ended. He didn't complain much. I had expected him to crack first, not Marissa.

"You know you only get half a bar," Marissa said, eyeing the power bar in his hand.

"Yeah, why? You want to split it?" he asked.

"Okay," Marissa said, and clutched her D&G to her chest. "We can eat this in my room. We'll have to pray first."

Tate looked at me with a panicked expression.

"Have you been saved, Tate?" Marissa grabbed a fistful of Tate's shirt. "Well, I can save you." She had a wild look in her sunken eyes.

"Um, well, I don't know," he said as Marissa led him into the tunnel.

Maybe it was his turn to take one for the team. Marissa needed a project. Maybe saving Tate would save her too. I thought of that first day and Tate's comment about us having to repopulate the earth. An image of a baby with Tate's head and Marissa's muscular body flashed into my mind. If this was the future of the planet, we were going to be in serious trouble.

I should have talked to her, tried to help her. But I didn't know what to do. Every time I reached out to her it only made her more irritated. So I did what I always did and ignored it. I guess Chaske and I both did. It was easier, but it wasn't right. Maybe nothing could have saved her, but I felt seriously guilty later that I didn't try hard enough.

TWENTY-FOUR

GRETA

Greta's scream seems to circle the mountain. She looks out over the valley below and can't believe her brothers and Da don't hear her.

She screams because that's all she can do. She struggles against the vines binding her outstretched arms and legs to this wall-size thicket. Thorns dig into her back. The pain cloaks her almost desperate fear.

How could she be so stupid? She let her feelings for Beckett cloud her judgment. Da sent her on a mission and she let a few kisses become more important than the future of her people. She will never make that mistake again. Maybe she's been outwitted by a beautiful boy. Maybe Beckett was the bait in an elaborate trap.

Greta screams again out of helpless frustration. She throws her weight forward so her body is like a sail snapped taut by the wind. She projects the shrill sound at her captor. He doesn't even blink.

"Shut up," he growls, and slaps her across the cheek. The force slams her into the thorns. The vines that bind her shred the skin around her wrists and ankles. She bites her lip and stifles a scream.

She glares at the tall, bony figure looming over her. He wears a loincloth like Beckett, but that's where the similarities end. He is sharp in the way Beckett is solid. Hate radiates from him the way peace flows from Beckett. His bald head is pink and raw from the sun. Maybe he is the creature her brothers saw. If so, she hopes they will find and destroy him. "You shouldn't be on my Mountain. No one is allowed on the Mountain unless I permit it." So he is Beckett's leader. Da was right to be wary of these mountain people. "Beckett can't save you now."

"My people will come for me." She tries to squash the tremor in her voice.

"Let them come. I'll leave you here as a warning to anyone who dares to climb my Mountain," the monster says, and laughs. That sound is worse than his shouts, worse than his fist, worse than the blow that knocked her unconscious and allowed him to capture her.

He loops a vine around her neck and the thorny thicket. She

thrashes about, but he presses his body against hers. The thorns puncture her skin. He pulls the vine so she can barely breathe, and he smiles at her struggle. He ties the vine and walks away, still laughing. Greta flails like a fish flapping on sand, but every move strangles her. When he is gone, the sound of his laughter echoes in her ears. She looks out to Vega and feels the hopelessness of her situation. All she can do is sob. She hates herself for crying but it's not sadness. Her tears are hot with anger. The thorny brambles of the thicket vibrate with her rage.

"Greta." She hears her name whispered as if it's coming from the hedge.

"Greta."

"Beckett?" Her tears ebb as hope sneaks in. She may not die here. There may be time for her to warn her people.

"Is Finch gone?"

He must mean the monster. "Yes."

"I'm coming to save you," Beckett says.

His words trigger more anger. *He's saving me?* Her head and heart battle. She cares for him, but she must think of him as her enemy now.

She sees his silhouette through the thicket about ten feet from where she is tethered. He starts tearing at the vines with his bare hands. Every shift of the thicket causes more thorns to dig into her body. She doesn't flinch. She welcomes the pain to focus her, to claw out the part that wants to fall into his arms.

"Let me help." Another figure appears beside Beckett. They snap and splinter one vine after another, creating a gaping wound in the hedge.

Beckett slips through the opening. Greta recognizes the girl who follows him through. "Hurry," the girl says. "Finch could come back at any moment."

Beckett gasps when he sees Greta. She looks down at her body. Her pale white skin is swirled with yellow and green bruises. She tries to contract her body. She feels ashamed at what the monster did to her. She should have fought harder.

Beckett gently and methodically unties the knots at her wrists and neck. The girl is working on her ankles. She's ripping the vines free. The vines feel like blades slicing her skin. Her wrists have what look like bangles of blood.

When she is free, she tries to push past them. She has to get to Vega. She only walks a few feet before she collapses. Beckett's arms are around her before her body hits the ground. She wants to struggle but suddenly her body is weak. Beckett lifts her in his arms and she curls into him. The girl holds open the gap in the thicket, and Beckett carefully maneuvers through. She should object—but she doesn't have the strength. When Greta's hair gets tangled in the hedge, the girl picks it free. Beckett keeps looking over his shoulder. He shifts her higher in his arms. She remembers what it was like to kiss him and mourns that she will never feel that way again.

While Beckett carries her up the Mountain, the girl does her best to mend the thicket. Beckett lays Greta gently on the muddy ground. He brushes her hair, sticky with rain and blood, from her face. She feels a rush of affection for him. She wants to kiss him and forgive and forget everything that separates them. But she can't. She must build a thorny thicket around her heart.

"Thank you." Greta bows her head. "Both of you."

"That's Harper." Beckett gestures to the girl. As he sits next to her, Greta thinks she can feel him battling against his urge to hold her too. She looks at Harper and realizes how much they look alike. There's something between her and Beckett. She can't quite figure out their relationship. They are close. She could see it in the way they worked together.

"She can't stay here," Harper says, and faces Beckett as if Greta is not even there anymore.

Beckett glares at Harper.

"Well, she can't," Harper insists with a tone that reminds Greta of when she was a little girl and her brothers wouldn't listen to her.

"I've got to warn my family," Greta says, and tries to stand. She falls back hard on her butt.

"Greta will stay with us," Beckett tells Harper. "I don't want anything to happen to you," he says to Greta.

Greta hates it, but he's right. She couldn't make it down the mountain right now. She needs to gather her strength and plan her escape.

Beckett gets to his feet and reaches a hand to both of them. "I think we should keep moving."

Harper refuses his hand and adjusts the strips of cloth that cover her.

Beckett helps Greta up. She leans on him and he half carries her.

"Where are we going?" she asks as they head up the mountain. The pain is slowly subsiding.

"I think the only way to go is up," Beckett says. "Maybe we can find a vantage point to see what's going on and then decide what to do next."

As they climb higher, the terrain unnaturally and abruptly flattens. The ground is covered with tiny pebbles. Greta has spotted Lucky keeping pace with them.

"Is this some sort of road?" Greta asks, bending over to catch her breath. She's not used to mountain life, always standing at an angle. She's exhausted, but she will not show them weakness.

Harper twists left and right, stretching her athletic body.

"We've never been up this far," Beckett says.

"You live on the mountain. You never leave it, and you've never been this high before?" Greta can't believe what a limited life they've led.

"You wouldn't understand," Harper responds for Beckett. "We should keep moving."

A few steps more and they all see it at the same time. Rising from the path is a barrier constructed of rock. The rock wall seems to circle the mountain.

Greta plucks a stone at arm's height. Rocks cascade to fill the empty space. "What is this?"

Beckett walks straight up to the wall. "The Great I AM was here."

"Who?" Greta asks.

"The Great I AM." Beckett says it again as if it should mean something to her. He runs his hands over the sun-warmed rocks. "Can't you feel it?" Beckett shivers. He strokes the rock and bows his head and closes his eyes.

"Beckett—" Greta starts, but Harper quickly interrupts.

"Can't you see he's Saying?"

"What?" Greta asks. They have the same words but use them in such peculiar ways.

"Don't you Say?" Harper asks.

It takes a second to understand what Harper means. "You mean pray, like to some higher power?" Greta laughs in one quick burst. "People used to do that, but look where it led. Their higher powers led them to destroy everything." She shakes her head at Harper and her naïveté. "There's no one to help people like us."

"What do you mean, 'like us'?" Harper asks, and strides toward her, chest out, fists clenched. "I'm not like you. I've never been like you!"

Harper shoves Greta, then she stops and looks at her fists as if they've acted out of her control. Even with their higher power, they still use fists. Greta itches to shove her back and then knock her to the ground and make her pay for the sins of her people, but she doesn't. She might feel powerful and satisfied for the course of the fight. When it was over, she'd still be held hostage and her people would still be in danger.

"I'm sorry if I offended you," Greta lies, trying not to make matters worse. "But you are hardly one of them." She gestures to Beckett.

Harper crosses her arms high across her chest. "I may not look like them, but I'm a Cheerleader in here." She pounds her fist on her chest.

Greta shrugs. What do their riddles matter? They are so different from her people. They wish to something unseen while Da preaches that they and they alone are masters of their own fate.

"We're on the path," Beckett says when he opens his eyes.

"You mean the Great Ian's path?" Greta asks, trying not to laugh. She walks the perimeter of the wall, away from Harper.

"The Great I AM," Beckett corrects. "The Great I AM marked this Mountain as sacred. We have guarded it for generations."

"Why?" Greta asks, kicking at the pebbles. "Why this mountain, say"—she points—"and not that one over there?"

"We don't choose what's sacred...." Beckett falters. Greta imagines that no one has ever asked him these questions before.

"Don't you get it?" Harper shouts. "You are a complete and utter Tristan. Show her." She locks her arm around Beckett's. He tries to resist, but Harper shows Greta the birthmark on Beckett's wrist.

"No, Harper. Don't." Beckett is twisting away. "Please," he says, giving up the fight.

Harper releases him. "You will never understand."

Greta is standing well out of their way. "Won't understand what?"

"Can't you see who he is?" Harper says. She extends her arm parallel to Beckett's. Greta can see a thin scar that's the same as Beckett's birthmark. "He's our Cheer Captain. He was born with our sacred mark. He is a descendant of the Great I AM."

"Is that true?" Greta backs away. She doesn't know him at all. "Are you some sort of spiritual leader?"

Beckett nods ever so slightly. All this time she thought he was just a boy.

"The Great I AM has chosen him to lead us," Harper continues. She moves between them. "He must protect the Heart of the Mountain."

"Why didn't you tell me?" Greta asks, bobbing her head back and forth to get a line of sight around Harper.

Beckett brushes Harper aside and looks Greta in the eyes, but she can't stand what he's become. When she looks at him, she suddenly sees a stranger. She looks away. "Because of that," he says.

"What?"

"That look in your eyes. I'm not just Beckett anymore."

"Let's go," Harper says, and stomps off.

He looks different somehow, now that she knows what he really is. How can he believe in someone he's never seen? It all sounds so ridiculous.

"I've come this far...." And with that Harper effortlessly scales the rock pile. She pauses on top. "Come on," she says, and surfs down the other side.

Beckett gestures for Greta to go first. He stays close behind her as the rocks shift underneath her feet. She crawls up the pile and straddles the wall when she reaches the top. She scans the landscape below. Beckett is standing between her and Vega. She decides she'll continue to play along for now. What choice does she have? But she will find her moment and she will escape—no matter what she has to do.

TWENTY-FIVE

"Today's the day!" Tate actually sounded chipper as he trudged up the incline to the entrance where the rest of us were already gathered. Every few days, Tate would allow himself to listen to one tune on his iPod. Usually he would squirrel himself away in the farthest reaches of the bunker. He'd stay right where the light ended, on the wrong side of the boundary line Chaske had set for us. It was Tate's small you're-not-the-boss-of-me rebellion. "I've finally decided. 'Tonight' by Fame Sake."

"Really?" Chaske feigned interest. "Yesterday you said it was time for Collective Gasp." Chaske was sitting quietly a few feet from us. He could do that, just sit and think for hours.

"Wasn't last time," Marissa panted as she transitioned from sit-ups to tricep push-ups. "What's the awful band that's all death and destruction?"

"You'll have to narrow it down more than that," I muttered. "That's, like, his whole playlist." After Marissa's blow-up, I'd kept my distance. I was never alone with her or Chaske really. I think we were both concerned that if she caught us together, it might send her off the deep end.

"Nuh-uh. I have eclectic taste in music," Tate whined.

"It's that band that looks like they survived World War Thr..." Marissa started dipping faster and lower.

Tate cluelessly responded, "Oh, you mean A Pock O Lips." I put the sounds together and a lump rose in my throat. Tate sat halfway between Chaske and me. "And, no. A Pock O Lips was ten days ago. Last time I listened to 'Wha Eva' by Wha Eva. That's my fave." Then he insisted on singing the song word for word.

> *"Wha Eva*
> *Wha Eva*
> *The bad, the good*
> *Wha Eva*
> *I put my faith in Wha Eva*
> *Wha Eva alone."*

I laughed a little when he sang the really high parts. He squinted and tilted his head as if that might help him raise his voice an octave.

Midnight playfully batted at the cat toy I'd created from

one of Lola's jeweled skull earrings I found in the lining of my messenger bag and a thread that I unraveled from my already holey jeans. "Go on and play it already." I rolled my eyes.

When Tate wasn't talking about what tune he was going to play, he was reciting from memory the 1,496 albums he had on his iPod. He had scratched the names into the wall near the back. That was his project the first few weeks we were here. I dreaded to think what would happen if his battery died.

As crazy as it sounds, this had started to feel normal. This was our life. We had a routine and responsibilities. Everyone but Marissa had found a way to cope. We'd grown used to her constant motion—whether it was military-style calisthenics or the twitch she'd developed. I'd even grown to like the bizarre faces she'd drawn on the walls. At first they had felt somehow sinister, all those eyes looking down on me. But now I liked looking at the different expressions. She'd managed to capture almost every emotion. They reminded me of texting Lola and how we would communicate so much simply by selecting the right smiley face.

Today I'd brought along a surprise: my *Waiting for Godot* script. I was supposed to do a scene with Jazz Richardson for drama class the week after, well, you know. The script was crumpled at the bottom of my messenger bag. I'd picked up the script several times and thought about reading it, but I always decided to save it. Mrs. Lord couldn't have paid me to read the thing a few months ago, and now I cherished it like some sacred treasure. It was the same excitement I felt when I saw the commercial for each *Saw*. I'd want to see those movies on the first day of release, maybe even a preview if there was one in D.C. or any of the surrounding burbs. But usually I'd wait, savor the anticipation. 'Cause once you saw it, the thrill of the scare was gone.

I held that tattered copy of *Godot* and tried not to think of Jazz and Lola and Tristan and my parents. They had almost become like actors in a movie I'd seen a long, long time ago.

Sometimes I'd force myself to remember the time before. I'd recall a special memory: Christmas morning when I was seven and "Santa" had left me this wicked dollhouse. We'd stayed in our pajamas all day and arranged the new furniture in the dollhouse. We even had a tiny Christmas tree with miniature candles and bobbles stuck on it. Mum wrote our names on the thumbnail-size stockings that hung on the mantel of the mini fireplace, I experimented with moving the fireplace into the bathroom and the attic, but Mum wanted the fireplace in the main living room. We laughed when Dad put Barbie and Ken on the roof as if they were these giants attacking my dollhouse.

In that memory I knew that I was the girl in the *Nightmare Before Christmas* pj's, but I didn't feel anything. I'd make myself remember as much detail as I could. I didn't want to forget but I couldn't make myself feel.

"I thought maybe we could read this." I tossed the script in the triangle of space between Marissa, Tate, and me. "There are basically four main parts. Four of us."

"What's it about?" Tate asked, flipping through the pages as if he could speed-read.

I shrugged. "Just thought it might be fun."

"What is it?" Chaske asked, sitting next to me.

"*Waiting for Godot*." I checked the cover. "By Samuel Beckett. I was supposed to do a scene for my senior drama class and…"

Marissa, who was now doing lunges, froze mid-lunge and crossed herself as if she were Catholic. Chaske bowed his head. I'd broken one of our unwritten but completely understood rules: Never mention the past. I could see on their faces that I'd triggered memories of the time before and felt a pang of regret.

"What else are we going to do? Come on, guys. Paaaleeeeeeaz." I did this half whine, half plead. Midnight strolled over and sat smack-dab on the cover. "See, Midnight's in."

"Doesn't sound too exciting." Chaske stroked Midnight from nose to tail. Midnight leaned into each stroke.

Marissa was running in place, her head twitching as if it were part of her exercise regime. "Tate and I will do it." She wiped sweat from her head and her black, uneven hair spiked in all directions. With the chain-saw hairstyle, she looked a bit deranged. She'd lost so much weight that her cheekbones seemed pointed and her neck easily snappable. Her lips were still a deep red. She pulled my THIS PRINCESS SAVES HERSELF T-shirt into a knot at the base of her spine so her large breasts cast a shadow over her diamond-pierced belly button. The spark she used to have had been replaced by this dull, glazed stare—as if she were perpetually look-ing at something behind you.

"Oh, all right," Chaske said, scooping Midnight into his lap. Surprisingly, she curled up and stayed.

We leaned over the script so we could play our parts. The play was mostly these two guys talking. Doing nothing really. We took turns playing those two roles. Marissa kept twitching and glancing nervously at me.

Marissa was reading Vladimir and Chaske was playing Estragon. Marissa lowered her voice to sound more like a man. Chaske's voice boomed like an actor's, filling the space. They both spoke slowly, enunciating every word, and paused dramatically between lines. I soon realized this wasn't the right thing to read under the circumstances. The more the characters talked about waiting for Godot, the more I couldn't help but think of the parallel with my life. I knew logically that if Dad and Mum were alive and every-thing out there was fine, they would have come for me already. I'd created this way to believe and not believe simultaneously. I was so much like those guys in the play, waiting for someone who would never come. I was praying for the end of the first act.

Tate had started to read the stage directions out loud as if they were dialogue and it was annoying me. I held my hand up to halt Chaske from delivering his next line. "You know you're not really supposed to read that part," I told Tate.

"It's too boring to just sit here," Tate said.

Marissa read her next line. She—well, her character—

was saying that Vladimir and Estragon could part company if they wanted to. Chaske's character was disagreeing but they were all talking in a way that was getting jumbled in my brain. They were saying that they were going to leave, but they didn't move.

That's how the act ended.

Seriously? WTF.

"I don't get it," Tate said, tossing the script across the room.

"Not everything has a happy ending," Marissa said. She was twisting the studs on her ear. She stared at a spot just over my head, maybe the emoticon with the big ears and the tongue out.

"We can write our own Act Two," I said. "Maybe Vlad and Estro fall in love."

"They obviously care about each other," Marissa added, and I couldn't tell if she was serious or not.

"Yeah, and Godot shows up," Chaske interjected. "Everyone lives happily ever after."

And for some reason, that was the funniest thing I'd ever heard in my life and I started to giggle. I hadn't giggled since I was like five. I pinched my lips together, but this ticklish feeling started in my brain. Giggles kept bubbling out. Chaske full-on smiled. Then Tate started with this little girly snicker and I collapsed in a fit of laughter. I could hear Chaske and Marissa laughing. My cheeks hurt from the size of my smile. I tried to stop but instead I snorted, which got us going again.

We almost didn't hear it because we were laughing so hard. We were rolling around, tears streaming down our faces, gasping-for-breath laughing, and it felt amazing—the release and the loss of control. The sound filled the space and it wasn't so dark and we weren't so far underground. The world hadn't ended. And we could still laugh. I wanted to sweep them all in a big hug and squeeze them in gratitude. Midnight looked at us with her big yellow eyes as if we were crazy—and maybe we were.

Our laughs turned to exhausted sighs. No one said anything. Our eyes sparkled. It was good to feel human.

Then we heard it. It was a thud. And then another and another. We glared at Tate, but his hands were still.

There it was again.

We looked around, afraid to speak or even wonder about the source of the sound. I stuffed the script in my messenger bag and fiddled with the YOU'RE JUST JEALOUS THAT THE VOICES TALK TO ME button on the strap. Maybe I'd imagined the sound. We all had.

Silence.

We half laughed at our overreaction. Tate flipped his iPod over and over in his hand. Marissa raised her arms over her head, bending and pulling one elbow for a tricep stretch. Chaske lay down, butterflying his arms around his head. I opened and closed the fastener on the back of the button with a faint *click, click, click*.

There it was again, but this time the sound was the ping of metal on metal. We were on our feet. My ears strained.

Was that a muffled voice? Someone trying to shout through a foot-thick steel door? A voice couldn't penetrate that but I'd swear I heard something.

Someone was out there, pounding on the door.

My heart leapt. It was my parents come to rescue me at last. I ran to the lock.

Tate and Marissa spoke at once, throwing questions like hand grenades: "What if it's over?" "What if we were wrong?" "What if it's your parents?" "Maybe we're safe." "We could leave."

Marissa hooked her arm through Tate's and they did this weird square dance–like do-si-do.

Chaske was at my side

"Can you believe it?" I whispered to him. "It's over." I went to hug him, but his body was stiff. "What's wrong?"

"It can't be your parents, can it, Icie?" Chaske spoke slowly.

"Why not?" I said.

"Icie, you said your parents have another key, don't they? Why would they knock?" Chaske whispered to me.

"Maybe they lost it."

Chaske shook his head.

I knew he was right. My parents wouldn't pound wildly on the door like that. If they'd lost the key, they would knock in code. Mum always knocked in bursts of three. Dad rapped twice slowly and three times in quick succession. That's how they asked to enter my bedroom. I'd know who it was before I'd say "Come in." I desperately wanted it to be them outside knocking, but I knew it wasn't and I hated Chaske for being right.

"They *are* coming for me," I said, and shoved him in the chest. He didn't budge.

"What do we do?" I asked him.

"Nothing," he said. "We can't risk it."

"Someone's out there. We've got to let them in," Marissa said, walking to the door. She pressed her palms on the smooth silver metal and spread her fingers wide. "Believing is seeing," she said with almost a reverence.

Huh? My brain was too confused to decipher a Marissa-ism.

"Hey!" Tate called, and pounded on the door. "We're in here!"

The tapping and pounding from outside became frenzied. Midnight walked to the door and cocked her head at the sounds as if she was ready to be let outside.

"Ice." Marissa turned to me. "What are you waiting for? Open the door."

I shook my head and buried my face in Chaske's chest. He held me tighter. He knew I wanted more than anything to open that door. I needed to open it.

"Icie!" Marissa shouted. I felt a hard punch on my shoulder. "Icie, look at me."

I shifted away from Chaske.

Marissa came at me. "Open the door."

I shook my head.

"Icie!" Marissa's fingernails ripped at my neck as she slipped her fingers around the chain and yanked. The chain didn't give. She twisted the chain. The links bit into my skin. She squeezed tighter and tighter. It was hard to breathe.

Chaske grabbed her by the shoulders and threw her off me. "Stop it, Marissa," Chaske shouted. "We don't know who it is or what they want."

I clutched my neck and gulped air.

"They could have come to rescue us," Tate said, joining our huddle.

"They could have come to kill us," I said. I backed away until my shoulder blades dug into the rock wall.

"What if they need help?" Marissa's face was glowing red. Her body pumped up, like a rottweiler ready to attack.

"We are not opening the door." Chaske's response was firm but calm. "Whoever it is could be contaminated with that deadly virus. Marissa, you said you saw what it did to people. Do you want to end up like that? I'm not sure we have been in here long enough for it to be safe to go outside."

"How the hell do you know?" Marissa screamed, and raced down the tunnel.

The tapping continued. My heart was pounding. Someone was out there. How could I ignore that?

"We can't leave them out there," Tate said, looking from me to Chaske. "Can we?"

"We can't risk it." Chaske clapped his arm around Tate's shoulder. "Why don't we go play some cards in my room?" He was so calm. If this was eating him up inside, he gave no indication. He must have had training for the police or army or some special ops.

That noise was chiseling away the last of my sanity. There was someone out there. Maybe Tate and Marissa were right. Maybe there was no war. No threat. Maybe we could leave.

Then my thoughts flipped like a pancake.

What if it was terrorists come to kill the last survivors? Not for the first time, I wondered if it was an alien invasion. I pictured the slimy, screepy creatures from *Alien*. I saw the ripping and tearing of flesh. I'm sure no Hollywood special effects would come close to the horrors of a real genocidal alien race.

"Icie," Chaske repeated my name. I got the sense that he'd been speaking to me for a while and I hadn't heard him. "Let's go down to the supply room. I've been saving a Snickers bar for a special occasion."

"You've been holding out?" Tate said, giving Chaske a playful punch. It was as if Tate had tuned the sound out, forgotten someone was knocking. He'd so easily accepted Chaske's leadership.

Chaske shrugged. "It's a little melted but all the ingredients are still there." He tugged on my shirtsleeve and then guided us toward the tunnel.

Marissa barreled by Chaske, knocking his shoulder with hers. She grabbed me by the collar and dragged me toward the door. I flailed and tried to dig in my heels, but she easily overpowered me. She hooked her arm around my neck and pulled me forward. I stumbled beside her and felt the crush of her arm around my throat.

My olfactory senses had mostly deadened to the stench of this place—our unwashed bodies, the acidic earth, and our makeshift toilets, but because Marissa insisted on exercising nonstop, her skin was sour like sweaty gym socks left in a locker over Christmas break, mixed with rotten eggs. Over it all was the same citrus perfume I'd smelled the first time I met her.

She shoved me hard into the steel door. The force knocked the breath out of me and I bounced to the ground.

"Open this door!" she screamed.

I scuttled away from her.

With two strides she was on me again; she yanked me to my feet and slammed me with one hand against the door. She tightened her left hand around my throat and pressed my head into the door until I thought her force might actually meld my head to the steel.

"Open it, Icie," she said in a low growl.

Chaske whispered something to Tate and shoved him back toward the tunnel. "Marissa, calm down," he said as he approached us. "We are not going to open the door."

Marissa released me for a second and fumbled with something tucked in the back of her jeans, which used to be mine. She held me with one hand and Chaske's hunting knife in the other. She jabbed the knife at me. I flinched away.

"Open it now, Ice," she shouted, and shoved me toward the locking device. I glanced at Chaske. "Don't look at him. Look at me." She pressed the blade to my throat. When she twitched, its cold edge dug into my skin.

"Stop this, Marissa," Chaske said. "How is she supposed to do anything when you keep waving that knife at her?"

Marissa went for him. He stood his ground. She touched the blade to Chaske's chest. "Open the door, Ice. You think you know me, but I will do this." She dug the tip of the blade into him. He squeezed his eyes shut but didn't make a sound. A dot of blood seeped into his dirty white T-shirt.

Jagged, raw terror took hold. One of the things I hated about horror flicks was the token scene where the girl screams and does nothing to help the man battling the beastie—be it human, alien, criminal, or undead. I finally understood how fight or flight can create a bipolar symmetry that rendered you immobile.

"Don't you want to know what's out there?" Marissa asked, and burst into tears. "If someone's alive, don't we have the duty to save them? You saved me. You brought us here because you couldn't let us die. How can you just stand there when someone may need our help?" She wiped her runny nose on her arm. "Icie!" She blinked and blinked again, then opened her eyes extra wide as if she might pierce my soul with laser vision. "I've got to get out of here," she said, completely calm and in control again.

"Give me a second!" I screamed. I couldn't let her hurt Chaske. I couldn't open the door, but I had to do something, because the one thing I believed with all my heart was that she would do what she threatened.

Tate appeared at the entrance of the tunnel. "I couldn't find it, Cha—" He stopped when he saw the knife.

"Stay over there, Tate," Marissa said, pointing the knife at him. "Stay out of this."

I pushed my panic aside. My head cleared. I knew the only answer. "Marissa, I'll open the door on one condition."

She manically nodded to encourage me to go on.

"If I open this door, no one is coming in." My voice was shaking so badly I didn't know if the words had actually come out of my mouth.

"Okay. Okay," she responded quickly.

"Marissa, think about it." Chaske spoke as if he'd been a hostage negotiator his whole life. "This is a death wish. You don't know what's out there."

She trained her brown eyes on him. "You don't know what's out there either. I will die if I don't get out of here. Someone's out there and I can't take this anymore."

"Are you willing to risk our lives?" he continued. "We don't know who they are or what they want or what this means."

"What have you become?" Marissa thrust the knife at me and then back at Chaske.

"I want to make it through this, Marissa," I said. "I'll open the door, but no one comes in."

"You and Tate get out of here." She shoved Chaske away. "Now! You're making me nervous." She swung the knife. I dodged away from the blade.

"Go!" I shouted. "We shouldn't all get contaminated. We'll open the door a crack and check it out." I wanted him to survive. "It will be okay." The lie to end all lies. If someone felt the need to say it, odds were it wasn't remotely true. Maybe what was meant, maybe what my dad meant and what I meant, was that we will adapt and move on.

"Icie?" Chaske said.

"Please go," I begged. "Please."

Chaske and Tate turned.

"Run!" Marissa shouted. "I don't want to see you. Get out of here. Go or I don't know what I'm going to do."

Chaske called to Midnight and they disappeared down the tunnel.

"Are you sure?" I asked her.

She moved to the door and stared at it.

I turned the key in the lock.

The door seemed to consider whether it would open or not before it unlocked with a thud. I moved behind the door and pulled with all my might. She didn't take her eyes off the widening gap.

The door opened with a whoosh of air. Marissa peered into the darkness and gasped.

TWENTY-SIX

"Team equals together everyone achieves a lot."
—Just Saying 161

FINCH

"Shouldn't we search for Beckett?" Cal says, scanning the mountainside.

"I've told you, Beckett is gone," Finch replies. All the signs have aligned. This is his destiny. No one and nothing will stand in his way ever again. "Beckett has betrayed us. I saw him cross the Crown. I don't want to hear another word about him. The Great I AM has called us to avenge Atti's death. We must send a message to the Terrorists. They must leave our Mountain and our people alone."

They have built a fire on the Other Side of the Mountain. Tom and May will feed the fire and watch for any signs of Terrorists. If they extinguish the fire, everyone is to immediately return to the Mountain.

Finch's Cheerleaders have painted themselves black with the ash from Storytime. As the final glow of the sun fades, Finch's followers blend into the night. "Everyone knows what they need to do?" Finch cracks his knuckles, anxious to set his plan in motion. Everyone nods in response. "Then let's go."

They have one lit torch that they shield with their bodies. Finch doesn't want the light to announce their arrival. They need the element of surprise. They silently march in a disorganized blob down the Black River.

When they arrive at the outskirts of the Man-Made Mountains, they dart from building to building. Finch has always followed but now he can feel something greater directing him. All this time, he was the real Cheer Captain.

"For Atti," he reminds himself. He feels the slightest twinge of sadness. What's wrong with him? Harper was distraught by Atti's death. Why can't he feel that? Harper's gone now too. Finch knows that Harper helped Beckett escape, but he likes to imagine her back on the Mountain waiting for his triumphant return. She will look at him the way she always looked at Beckett.

He sees shapes dance among the Man-Made Mountains. *Terrorists*, Finch thinks. He flattens himself against a building and signals for everyone to do the same. His breath quickens and his adrenaline spikes. This place no longer has a hold over him. Finch will end the reign of terror.

He gathers the Cheerleaders together. He can see the fear in their eyes. "The Great I AM will protect us. Ours is a sacred mission." He lights his torch and lets it rest in the flame. One by one they all do the same and the fire grows into a crackling ball at the center of their circle. "Today we make a new Walk of Enlightenment. Generations will speak of our bravery."

Finch and the Cheerleaders divide and attack from all sides. He can't believe his luck. The Terrorists have scavenged everything useful from the buildings and organized their findings into huge piles. They offer the perfect kindling. Another sign the Great I AM is leading him. He lights fires in the rubble. Terrorists are beginning to spill from every building. Cheerleaders scatter.

Finch picks the highest tower. He has always wanted to climb the Man-Made Mountains. He watches the Terrorists flee and determines how to scale the building. He climbs the stairs to the very top. Wind whips smoke through the broken windows. He looks down on the tiny creatures' frenzy. Each Cheerleader is supposed to set a fire and then return to the Mountain. Strike like lightning was Finch's plan. All around him points of light flicker, small and insignificant, but then they grow and spread and morph into fiery beasties. He is mesmerized by what havoc he has wrought.

Heat washes over him in waves, cleansing him. Finch feels as if he is beckoning the fires forward. He cracks his knuckles one by one. Each click of bone on bone releases the tension.

He sees a Cheerleader toss a torch into a smaller building. The light vanishes into the dark space. The Cheerleader's shoulders slump, but suddenly the fire takes hold in a burst of light. Terrorists descend on the Cheerleader like vultures. They pick him apart until there's no life left. They have proven Finch right. These Terrorists are savages.

In his mind's eye, Terrorists assume their ghastly, scaly form.

He doesn't recognize their shape as similar to his or their resemblance to Harper. He paints claws on their fingertips and fangs in their screaming mouths.

The fires grow and spread—like hatred in the hearts of Forreal. To the east he sees what he believes are Cheerleaders returning to the Mountain. Below he watches and almost laughs at the Terrorists' attempts to extinguish his fires.

He plants his torch in a pile of cloth that appears to be someone's bed. He wants to stay longer, but the Man-Made Mountains are alive now. The fires roar. The Terrorists scream. His heart swells.

He slithers like a snake among the buildings, hiding in the shadows, and disappears in the black smoke. As he sets a course for his Mountain, he tells himself a story. How he ignited the fire and slipped through the flames untouched. How he fought bravely. How he walked through their streets with his head held high. How the black beasties bowed as he passed.

TWENTY-SEVEN

When I opened the door, Marissa lurched away from whatever she saw. She grabbed my shirt as she fell backward, nearly pulling me to the ground with her. Her gaze was fixed on the gap between the open door and the darkness beyond.

I saw it and screamed.

It was the only way to describe the thing that appeared in that sliver of light. It was as if an extra from *Night of the Living Dead* had leapt off the screen and come to life. Dried blood matted its hair. Its skin was wrinkled and peeling like the scales of a snake. It was a patchwork of scars that gaped to the bone below. Its bloodred eyes appeared to pulse from dark sockets. It reached a hand out toward me with blistered fingertips. The fingernails that remained were black ragged squares. Its pink, fleshy tongue quivered behind its parted, cracked lips.

"Help me," it whimpered, and took one belabored step closer. The beastie became a man. "Help me," he said again, a little more clearly. His whole body was trembling and he emitted this sound that was part growl and part moan.

I dragged Marissa away from the door before I realized that low guttural sound wasn't menacing. He was crying.

Chaske seemed to magically appear by my side. He raised his arms in front of him. The gun that had saved me from the snake a lifetime ago was pointed at the man.

"Move back! Back off!" Chaske shouted. The man raised both of his arms in surrender. "Close the door, Icie." Chaske shoved me toward the door. "Close it now before he contaminates us."

The man looked as if something was devouring him from the inside. Open, seeping sores dotted his dirt-brown skin.

"Wait," the man spoke in a hoarse whisper. "Please, you've got to help us." He sucked in a ragged breath. "Help us..." His voice trailed off.

"Shut the door, Icie," Chaske barked. I noticed that the gun was shaking in his hands.

"Chaske, are you sure?" I was being torn in two. I understood just how thin the line between living and dying was.

"Icie." Chaske grabbed my arm and yanked me to him. His ragged fingernails drilled into the soft flesh of my upper arm. "You've got to trust me. If we let this man in, we will die."

I didn't want to die. I had to see this man as a murderer. He would kill me as surely as if he held a gun to my head, except by the looks of him, his death would be slow and agonizing. I had to believe it was him or me.

I leaned my shoulder against the door and felt it give little by little under my weight. A breeze blew through the opening and with it the sour stink of rotting flesh and port-o-johns. This man was death walking, a zombie of sorts.

"Stop," Marissa shouted. She scrambled to her feet and stood in front of the open door. She pointed her knife at me and then at Chaske. "There are other survivors. Did you hear what he said? He said 'us.' We've got to help them."

"Get out of the way," Chaske yelled at her. "Icie, shut the damn door."

"Ice?" Marissa looked at me as if I were the beastie. I threw my weight behind the door.

Marissa wedged herself in the doorway. "This is a human being." I shook my head. I couldn't listen to her. I couldn't think of *that* as human. I didn't want to believe that what happened to it was happening to everyone out there. *It's a monster*, I told myself. A zombie. To think anything else was too confusing. Whatever it was, I couldn't let it in here. I couldn't let it infect us. I had to shut it out.

The zombie's hand clapped on Marissa's shoulder. She jerked free. Her shirt ripped as the zombie clawed to keep hold of her. My focus zoomed in on the two red jagged lines it had drawn on her skin. Chaske flinched and I knew he'd seen it too.

Chaske waved his gun at her. "Get out!"

"What?" Marissa's face blanched.

"You wanted to open the door, but I can't let whatever is out there in here. That...that..." He gestured at the zombie with the barrel of his gun. "It's scratched you. I can't let you stay here." He aimed the gun at Marissa.

"What are you doing?" Tate screamed. He was heading for Marissa. I stopped him and held him in a bear hug. This gave Marissa the chance to shove the door open a foot more.

"No!" Tate shouted. A black flash distracted me. Midnight was scampering between Chaske and me.

"You don't understand...you didn't see..." My mind wasn't functioning in complete sentences. I knew this was it. If I didn't do something, we could be in for slow and painful deaths. The look in that thing's eyes told me everything I needed to know about the suffering we'd locked out.

This princess saves herself.

"If you don't help me shut this door," I whispered to Tate, "we are going to die."

I forced our weight onto the door, but Marissa's body propped it open.

"We are going to help these people," Marissa said defiantly.

The diseased man looped his arm around Marissa's neck, pulling her through the door. She screamed and shoved him away, banging her arm into the doorframe and falling at the man's feet. He climbed over her. He was coming after us.

282

Chaske aimed the gun. "Stop," Chaske choked out. I rushed to his side. The creature took another step toward us and stood in the doorway. The gun was vibrating in Chaske's trembling hands.

"I've got to shoot him," Chaske whispered to me. "Right?"

"We can't let him in," I said, mirroring his stance.

The zombie shuffled forward.

"Chaske," I shouted. "Now. Do it now."

He nodded but everything else about him froze.

The zombie slowly approached, reaching an arm toward us. I had sacrificed everything and survived. The difference between life and death was the twitch of a finger. I couldn't stand here and allow this thing to infect me. I had to protect Chaske and Tate. I had come this far. I'd left others to die. I had to find the courage for one more act of survival.

I supported the gun in Chaske's hand. I looped my finger in the trigger, dislodging Chaske's grasp. The weight of the gun settled in my palm. I pointed it at the thing that stood between me and the ever-after.

I choose me.

I pulled the trigger.

The blast jolted my body backward. The explosion echoed through the tunnels and rang in my ears.

Blood exploded from the zombie's body and splattered on Marissa and the metal door. The force of the bullet propelled it back. It collapsed on the ground.

This felt like a scene from a movie. A movie that I wanted to switch off. But this was real; he was never getting up again. It was over in the blink of an eye, but one image froze and drilled itself into my memory: his face as the bullet smashed into him. It was as if my brain zoomed in on his eyes and the zombie morphed back into something human. I'd killed a man. I could see that but I couldn't believe it. That was someone's son, maybe someone's father or husband or friend. I had never done anything so final, so horrible. And what scared me most was that I didn't feel remorse.

"Icie, what have you done?" Marissa crawled to the bloody lump, which was coughing and spluttering.

I couldn't move. I was watching the scene around me but I was no longer in it. Chaske dived for the door, shoving with all his might. Midnight bolted through the crack and into the darkness.

"Chaske, wait!" I yelled, reaching for Midnight, but it was too late.

He shoved the door shut and twisted the key, which was still in the lock. The metal lock thudded into place. Marissa, Midnight, and the zombie were edited out of my story. I had saved us, but it didn't feel like that. It felt as though the bullet had killed me too.

Chaske took the gun out of my hand and gathered me into his arms. "You did the right thing," he whispered into my ear. "I couldn't do it."

I could. What had I become? Was I a murderer or a hero? Or both? But how could you be both?

"What have you done?" Tate asked, his face pale, his body slack. He was afraid of me now. I could see it in his eyes.

"We had to do it, Tate," Chaske explained. "You didn't see the man. He was sick. He scratched Marissa, infected her. . . . It was her own fault. She opened the door. If we'd let them in, we would have died." He sounded like he was trying to convince himself as much as Tate.

"You remember those people in the cars," I said to Tate. "We don't want to end up like them, do we? I did it to protect you."

The pounding started again. Muffled screams. Marissa was right there on the other side of the door. She was only a few feet away and probably dying. We stared at the door as if it were a window. I could picture her clearly—but it wasn't the Marissa who we just locked out. The twitchy, nervous girl with the yellow-gray skin and the dull eyes. In my mind's eye, it was the bald girl I met on the plane with the cheerleader smile.

The pounding stopped.

"There could be other survivors," Tate said, eyes glued to the door. "Marissa and Midnight could survive, you never know. They could."

"You never know," Chaske said.

More pounding. Tate burst into tears. I covered my ears and shut my eyes. I started singing Tate's favorite tune to drown out the noise: *"Wha Eva. Wha Eva. The bad, the good. Wha Eva. I put my faith in Wha Eva. Wha Eva alone."*

Tate sprinted down the tunnel, pumping arms and legs as if he were being chased by a beastie. An earthquake erupted within me, and my body gyrated with a force that caused my teeth to chatter. I was suddenly cold, as if I'd been plunged into the icy Potomac. Chaske carried me to his room. He laid me down on his cot and tucked his sleeping bag around me.

I thought I could still hear banging and shouting, even though it was impossible this far way. He left me there for minutes or hours, I couldn't say. I expected Midnight to jump up like she always did, but she would never do that again. She was gone. Midnight could survive. Marissa...I couldn't think of them anymore. I wouldn't let myself think about what I'd done. I was falling in a deep hole. I thought I couldn't fall any farther, but now I realized the pit was bottomless.

Chaske came back with two bottles of hand sanitizer— one from my purse and the one from Marissa's. He also had a jug of water and the cloth I used for my weekly spit baths. He doused his exposed skin with the sanitizer and did the same to me. He handed me a blue pill and a white pill. "Take these," he prodded. I opened my mouth and he placed them on my tongue. He handed me the jug of water.

"What are they?" I asked after I'd washed them down. I didn't care if they were cyanide. If we were infected, I'd prefer to go quickly.

"They were in the medical kit your parents sent...." He kept talking, explaining what they were and why he'd given some to each of us, but my mind grew fuzzy. My body had decided to engage auto-shutdown. Chaske slipped into bed behind me. As my world faded to black, I was conscious of two things: the warmth of Chaske pressed against my back and distant pounding, like the rumble of an impending thunderstorm.

From that day forward, it was as if Marissa never existed. Chaske divided her stuff among the three of us. Tate used her cheer captain shirt as his pillow. Chaske cleaned the clothes she had borrowed from me and folded them neatly in my backpack. I forced myself to forget the image of her in my THIS PRINCESS SAVES HERSELF T-shirt. I wanted to miss her, to feel something. I kept reminding myself: She tried to kill me. She would have killed Chaske. If it had ended any other way, we would be dead. I had to believe that. Every time my thoughts flashed to Marissa, my mind short-circuited and switched off. And then there was the phantom pounding. In the quiet before I fell asleep, I'd swear I'd hear a dull thudding. The only thing that helped was to distract myself with a song. Tate's tune was lodged in my brain. I'd sing it, sort of mumble it over and over until I gave in to sleep. "*Wha Eva. Wha Eva. The bad, the good. Wha Eva.*"

I kept seeing Midnight in every shadow. I'd see her scurry in and out of my peripheral vision. With each imagined sighting, my heart ached. She could survive in the wild. Maybe she was better off out there than trapped in here.

Chaske, Tate, and I became zombies, not like the one I'd killed, but the kind that looked human and healthy outside but decayed on the inside. None of us talked about what happened. Days and nights merged together. Chaske made sure we ate. Sometimes he had to force me. Tate continued to act as our human clock, but he called out the time at bizarre intervals: "It's nine forty-six." "It's almost seven o'clock." He kept tracking the days.

"Do you know what day it is?" Chaske asked me one day as I passed him on my way back from the necessary. He was standing, hands on hips, surveying Tate's jagged hash marks.

I shrugged.

"Today is our two-month anniversary."

It seemed longer.

"We've got to stop this," he said, nodding as if he was recounting the marks.

I didn't feel like responding.

"It may not feel like it, but we're the lucky ones. Let's draw another line right here and start again. Let's live for"—he paused—"for everyone who can't."

Sure, it was corny and felt a bit weird for him to say it, but it was true. I buried the past seventeen years in that dark hole and started to climb out.

We agreed to present something special to one another in celebration of our new beginning. Over the past weeks when I was sleepwalking, Tate had been busy building a drum set out of anything and everything he could find. He'd set it up at the very back of the tunnel near the pile of rocks, where the light ended. It was quite ingenious, really. I finally discovered what had happened to the condoms. Tate had blown them up and was using them as part of his drum set. He spent hours and hours putting it together and then every day he would practice, sometimes working out the drum arrangement for tunes on his iPod or creating tunes of his own. Tate had been working on a new version of

"Outta Time" by In Complete Faith. The song was incredibly sexist, and I tried not to cringe. I could hear one of my mum's feminist lectures playing on repeat in the back of my mind.

> *"Quit yo cryin' be-otch*
> *No time for lyin' we-otch*
>
> *"It's been good*
> *(Not all good)*
>
> *"Don't hold on to hate*
> *Accept your fate*
> *We had time*
> *(Not so much time)*
> *All you got is time*
> *Till it's gone."*

He'd added a ten-minute drum solo. Chaske and I sat and listened and gave him a standing ovation when he finally finished. I realized days later that Tate really did give the gift that keeps on giving, when I couldn't get that crupid song out of my mind.

Chaske gave us the best gift of all. He had found a pile of construction scraps and built a makeshift shower. With one less person, Chaske assured us we had enough water for each of us to take a shower this once. Chaske started the water flowing and left me alone. I stripped naked and let the water trickle over my body. It was better than the power shower I had at home with the ten strategically placed jets. This shower cleansed my soul. I told myself that I was washing away everything that was past—a baptism of sorts. I would be reborn from this minute. Brown rivulets snaked down my arms and between my breasts. Tate sneaked a peek, but I didn't care. If he could still feel something, then I wasn't mad, I was jealous.

Now it was my turn, but I had nothing to give. Tate said I should read them something that I'd written in my notebook—the one that was supposed to be my journal for English class—but I couldn't. It had doodles of emoticons all over the cover but was blank inside. Marissa had crept in at some point and drawn those. I thought about writing in it. Sometimes I'd sit with pen poised for hours, but I couldn't make myself write. I wasn't really sure I'd want to remember this place anyway. That is, if I survived. That is, if anyone was out there to read it.

I invited Chaske and Tate to my room. Tate thought that was my present. He spied my underwear pile, a tangle of silk and lace. I took great care of my underwear, setting aside part of my daily water supply for hand washing. Underneath the dirt and the loss of pretty much everything, clean underwear made me feel a little human.

Tate sat on the floor, a little too near my underwear. Chaske sat straight-backed on my cot. I settled cross-legged on the floor.

"I thought we could read this." I pulled Chaske's coverless copy of *To Kill a Mockingbird* from under my pillow.

"I wondered what happened to that," Chaske said, taking the book from me. Tears collected in his lashes. He stroked the title page.

"Is that okay, Chaske?" I asked. "I'm sorry." I'd robbed him of something. I could see that now.

"What?" Tate asked, looking from me to Chaske. "What?"

"It was my mother's book," Chaske said so softly. "It's the only thing I have of hers." He was giving us another gift—a tiny piece of his story. "I've never read it." He handed the book back to me. "It would be nice if you'd read it to us."

I cleared my throat and read. The book opened with the narrator reminiscing about the events leading up to some "accident." We didn't know what the accident was yet, but the narrator, her brother, and her dad all disagreed about what started it. One thought it started weeks before, while the other thought if you took a broad view, then the events that eventually led to the accident started a hundred years before.

When had my story begun? I wondered as I read. What had prompted terrorists to release the virus on some random day? Why that day? Why a virus? Was 9/11 the cause or the effect, or was it something else unrelated? I didn't understand the politics or the history or what drove people to kill other people they'd never met. I suppose it didn't matter what had started it all. Endings were beginnings and vice versa.

I tried to focus on the words on the page. Let Harper Lee take me and my mind someplace else where there was a loving father to watch over me and make everything all right. I read to them until I was hoarse. Tate passed me the water jug and begged me to read more. I only stopped when I noticed Tate asleep on my cot, snoring.

Chaske took my hand and led me out into the tunnel. Something was welling inside me. We walked down the incline and paused when we reached the archway to his room. Chaske tilted my face to his. Even in the low artificial light in the tunnels, I could see his eyeballs twitch as they studied me. I leaned in, casting my shadow over him. His pupils dilated.

That's how I felt. I was a pupil opening to let more light in. I placed my palm flat on his chest, which was expanding and contracting in time with my own. I moved closer until our lips were nearly touching, then pushed him away. How could this be happening in this place? Step. Push. Step. Push. Until his back was pressed into the wall. I didn't deserve this, but I needed it more than food, water, or shelter. I placed my palms against the wall on either side of his head. Our eyes were still locked.

"Chaske," I whispered. "I don't think I..."

He slipped his arms around me. Energy sparked in the air between us.

He pulled me close; I pushed away.

But he wouldn't let go.

His face so close. His body touching mine. It was almost too much to bear. After feeling nothing for so long it was overwhelming.

My arms relaxed and draped across his shoulders. He closed the distance until our bodies were pressed so tightly together I thought he might crush me.

I closed my eyes, and he kissed me.

TWENTY-EIGHT

"Greatness starts with one ginormous idea
and one small step."

—Just Saying 32

BECKETT

Beckett, Greta, and Harper trudge up the Mountain. Lucky scurries around their feet, her yellow eyes glancing up at them, unsure of which way they will go next.

Crossing the Crown has ignited something inside Beckett. Every step seems to heighten his senses. The edges of the boulders seem sharper. The moon brighter. The clouds whiter. The Mountain air smells sweeter, but there's a subtle acidic hint of ash.

Beckett spots a rocky ledge and climbs up, hoping for a view of Vega and inspiration from the Great I AM. But the vision below fills him with guilt and rage. Smoke gathers like angry storm clouds floating toward the Mountain. Gray streamers are tethered to Vega. Finch has carried out his plan. Vega is burning. Beckett wonders how long before the heat of war will follow.

He looks down at Harper and Greta. "What's wrong?" Greta asks, starting to climb up after Beckett, but Harper holds her back. Greta elbows her away, finds a foothold, and flings herself onto the ledge.

When she sees Vega, she lunges at Beckett, fists flying. "We finally find a home...." Her voice catches. "We survived everything...." Tears stream down her face.

Beckett hugs Greta away from Vega. She sobs into his shoulder. Harper propels herself onto the ledge, ready to defend him like always. He raises a hand to tell her to keep her distance.

"I am so sorry," Beckett tells Greta. "We will make this right."

She shoves him hard and for a second he teeters on the edge. The ledge overlooks a deep ravine. Harper grabs his arm and pulls him to safety.

"You could have killed him, you crupid Tristan!" Harper yells.

"It's okay, Harper." Beckett keeps the girls an arm's length away. He can feel them pulsing toward each other. "This won't help anything."

"I need to go home." Greta breaks free and faces Vega. "What's left of it."

"I don't think that's a good idea," Beckett says, reaching for her but stopping short of touching.

"Let her go," Harper mutters. She's staring out at Vega. "I think we need a bigger boat."

"What did she say?" Greta hauls her fist back to punch Harper.

"It's just something we say," Beckett explains. "It means we're in big trouble."

"Stop speaking in riddles!" Greta shouts. "Why can't you just let me go?"

He wraps his arms around her until she stops struggling. "I can't let anything happen to you." She pivots out of his grasp and in one swift movement she knocks Harper aside and is scampering back down the rock. He can't save Vega but he can protect Greta.

"I'll get her," Harper says, and leaps down and races after Greta.

Beckett hears their bodies smack the earth. They are shouting at each other. But his attention is drawn to the opposite edge. He stands so his toes curl around the rocky lip. He feels a push and pull. The edge beckons him closer to see what's below but also sends a shiver of fear at the long drop. He feels this lifting like the moment jumping turns to falling, as if he's on the verge of discovery.

Beckett peers straight down at the sheer drop below. He spots what looks like a skeleton among the rocks and it's as if he is transported someplace else. He spreads his arms wide and tilts his chin upward, drinking in the mountain air.

An image flashes into Beckett's mind. He sees a boy so much like him, with long black hair flowing down his back. The boy is bare-chested and stands in this same pose in this same spot. It's as if Beckett can feel the boy's spirit slip under his skin. Profound joy and desperate sadness knot in his chest. The boy takes flight and Beckett wants to soar with him. Beckett lifts his arms higher and he feels as if he's flying.

The image fades and Beckett falls backward hard onto the ledge. He's frightened by what might have happened. It takes a second for Beckett to shake the feeling.

As he climbs down, he sees that Harper has Greta pinned to the ground. Greta is writhing beneath her.

"What's wrong?" Harper asks. She must see the startled look on his face. Greta stops struggling and stares up at him too.

"I think the Great I AM has given me a television," Beckett says. He can't get the image of the boy out of his mind. He sees him flying but surely those are his bones below. Beckett thinks of the mass grave with the mix of pink and metal. He forces these images to make sense. The Great I AM is revealing the Mountain's secrets to him one by one. "The Great I AM wants me to find the Heart." It's the only answer. "'Everything happens for a reason,'" Beckett quotes the Great I AM.

"That's complete and utter bullshit." Greta bucks free. Harper leaps to her feet and grabs her by the wrist before she gets too far. "Sometimes horrible things happen and they are just horrible," Greta says. "Not signs. No meaning, just horrible." Greta pauses and glances at the gathering smoke in the distance. "But I suppose given enough time and distance, maybe someone somewhere will give this act meaning."

"We can't let bad things define us," Beckett says. He searches his soul and the words come to him. "We must learn what we can from difficult times and become better people. Maybe that's the reason. Maybe that's always the reason."

"What good can ever come from this?" Greta asks.

"All I know is that for the first time in my life, the Great I AM has given me a television. This has to be right. It has to." Beckett can feel Forreal and Vega colliding and slipping away all at once. "The Heart is up there somewhere and I'm going to find it. Maybe it holds the answer to our conflict." He takes off up the Mountain.

Harper follows, dragging Greta behind her. "He's doing this for you," Harper explains to Greta. "So can you stop fighting and go with us?"

"Do I have a choice?" Greta asks.

"No," Harper says.

Beckett wishes he knew what he was looking for. He's imagined the Heart as a giant glowing crystal. He wonders if it is a living creature. Or is it an organ, something beating like a human heart? Maybe it is as tiny as a speck of dust and as dull as a sun-worn rock. It could be energy like a ray of sun. He wonders if the Great I AM will be there, welcoming him with open arms. Whatever it is, he could have passed the Heart of the Mountain without realizing it.

His eyes strain as he explores the moonlit mountaintop.

He instinctively Says. "Great I AM..." He searches for the words.

And then there it is.

The Great I AM has led him here. For the first time since Finch imprisoned him, Beckett feels hope.

A huge round stone rests against what appears to be the opening to a cave. The stone is sandy brown and big enough that Beckett would have to stretch his body from fingertips to toes to fill the circle. The cave entrance has been packed tight with rocks similar to the ones used to create the wall that they scaled earlier. He looks closer; the infinity symbol is carved in the rock. *Believing is seeing.*

Beckett falls to his knees. He sends his thanks to the Great I AM. He's found the Heart of the Mountain. All the stories are true. The Great I AM marked the Heart of the Mountain with the symbol etched on Beckett's wrist.

To be at the spot where the Great I AM stood.

To be so close to the Mountain's secret.

He reaches up and traces the symbol with his finger, an unending loop. His mind races with what he might find inside. He has sacrificed his whole life for this. He thought he would feel more. No booming voice. No white light. Just a stone with a symbol. Maybe his simple human brain can't comprehend what this is and what it means.

"It's here," Beckett says as Harper, Greta, and Lucky catch up to him. "We've found it."

Harper now carries a torch in one hand and grips Greta's wrist in the other. One of her arms is bare where she's used her scraps of clothing to make the torch.

Beckett dislodges a rock from the pile that seals the opening to the Heart. As he pulls it free, rocks cascade down and spill at his feet. He removes another and another until he is shoveling them away in armfuls. When the hole is big enough, he slips inside.

He can see only a few feet before the light filtering around him fades to black. The smell of earth is overpowering.

Suddenly the space is illuminated in a flickering light. Maybe the Great I AM is here.

"Harper thought you might need this." It's Greta's voice. A torch is thrust through the opening.

He squints as his eyes adjust to the burst of light. He takes the torch and waves it around. There's a door. A door in the mountain. The earth has crumbled around it and it's tipped forward, leaving a gap between the doorframe and the earth. The Heart must lie beyond.

Beckett inches closer and closer to the door. His foot touches something rough. He shines his torch on the ground. It's not stones scraping the soles of his feet. These are bones. Human bones.

Beckett can tell there are two skeletons side by side. Wires are attached to a silver rectangle, which is embedded in the smaller skeleton. Beckett forces himself forward around the skeletons, toward the door.

Beckett's attention zooms to the symbol etched into the door. The circular shape is similar to the image on Greta's shirt. "Peace," Beckett murmurs.

Beckett wonders if death is always the price of peace.

TWENTY-NINE

Chaske and I made love every day. Out there I'd have laughed out loud at the phrase—making love. It's what soap opera characters did. Lola and I had made fun of our friend Tanz for saying she'd "made love" with Dirk after the homecoming dance. *Um, you can't make much in four minutes and fifteen seconds*, we'd said, and laughed. But now, in here, with Chaske, that was what it felt like.

We weren't doing it to pass the time. There wasn't pressure or guilt or embarrassment. He wasn't going to dump me for someone named Molly Andersen. It was something real and beautiful in this cold, dark place.

Chaske and I would zip ourselves snug in his sleeping bag

after. He'd lie on his back, and I'd curl into the crook of his arm. Our body heat would multiply and provide us the only warmth we would feel all day. I'd roll on my elbow and watch him sleep until Tate called ten something o'clock and switched off the lights. I'd memorize the slope of his nose and how his eyes were more squinty than opened. His broad nose and high cheekbones. I'd trace the scar on his eyebrow. I never mentioned the scars on the rest of his body and neither did he. His muscles drew well-defined lines on his earthy-brown skin. I loved the feel of his sculpted body holding me tightly until he finally relaxed with sleep.

I knew we weren't a perfect match. He was gorgeous and comfortable in his own skin. His thoughts and body flowed effortlessly. I was fake and plastic—a Barbie who thought she was original only to realize she was mass-produced. He was mysterious and dark like those modern comic-book superheroes—Batman and Spider-Man, full of tragedy and chivalry—which I guess made me the vapid damsel in distress. Not Catwoman or Spidey's Mary Jane Watson, but the ones who make a guest appearance in need of rescue and say something like "Golly, thanks, Batman."

In a very strange way, I was glad there was only one person around. I didn't want to share our romance with anyone. Tate was oblivious. I didn't want him teasing us or asking questions. I also thought it might make him uncomfortable. He saw us as a trio and that's how I wanted it to stay. I was afraid if he knew Chaske and I were a couple, he'd feel like the odd one out. Secrets were okay if they were to protect people's feelings, right? For all of his many annoying behaviors, I was beginning to think of Tate as a little brother.

"Chaske," I whispered one night after Tate turned out the lights.

"Yeah," he muttered.

"Why do you like me?" It was a stupid schoolgirl question, but I wanted to know. "Is it just because I'm here?"

"What?"

"Why do you like me?" I would have never asked this question in the light, never asked it out there. Those questions acted as repellent to high school boys.

"I don't like you," he said.

I felt the crush of rejection. Of course he didn't. How could I ever believe that someone like him could like someone like me? I made a move to turn over, but he pulled me in to him, kissing my eyebrow, the first bit of skin his lips could find. I didn't move, didn't help him navigate my face. His lips moved awkwardly to my nose, actually my nostril, and then slipped from one corner of my lips to my mouth, which I held stiffly shut.

He laughed this breathy laugh. "Isis, I don't like you, I love you."

I burst into tears. He loved me. How could *he* love *me*? He held me close and let me cry. When I finally caught my breath, I asked, "Why?" His answer would be undermined by the fact that as far as he knew I was the only woman left. Wouldn't a vegetarian love a hot dog if he was hungry enough?

He kissed me full on the mouth and I was lost for a second in his lips. Darkness magnified every sensation. I wasn't distracted by a stray hair stuck to his forehead or the sound of the TV in the background. The world had collapsed to the size of our lips and exploded in the way they moved together, gathering energy and electricity.

"That's not an answer," I said when his hands began to caress my body. He rolled me on my side, spooning my body. He kissed the back of my neck.

"I know I can't say anything to convince you," he said. "No matter what I say: You're beautiful and strong or I love your white dreads or you have the most amazing way of surviving. Nothing I say will be enough and also nothing I say will be the whole truth. I ache for you and all I do is think about you. I don't know why I like country music or this pair of blue jeans. It's something about the way they feel and something about how they make me feel." He snuggled me closer. "Does that make any sense?"

"Yeah." I was filled with this sense of profound happiness that I don't think I'd felt on the outside ever.

"Why do *you* love *me*?" he asked.

I should have anticipated this question, but I was completely unprepared. I wasn't very good at expressing things like that. Important words always got muddled in my mind. "I guess part of it is you saved me. You saved me from the snake." My body gave an automatic shiver at the word. "You save me every day in here with your calm, wise ways."

He laughed at that description.

"Shut up. You do," I said, and leaned in for another kiss. "Doesn't hurt that you're gorgeous." I felt the muscles in his face shift, I hoped to a smile. "You are strong in a way that makes me feel safe even in this place. I wish..." I paused. I didn't want him to pull away. "I wish I knew more about you. Your history. Your story before I met you."

He sighed. "That doesn't matter."

But his saying that meant that it oh so did. I remembered the scars that he was careful to hide from me.

"You know who I am now," he said.

"But don't you want to know—"

"No," he quickly interrupted. "I know everything I need to know and tomorrow I'll learn something new. Talking about it won't change it. Won't bring it back, it will just..."

I understood. "Hurt," I finished his thought.

"Yeah."

We had long philosophical discussions where I listened more than talked. I felt like a fridiot that I didn't know who Nietzsche (Mr. "what doesn't kill me makes me stronger") was or anything about Pascal's Wager—the idea that it was best to believe in God because you'd have less to lose if you're wrong. Or something like that. Chaske told me that his mom liked to talk about this stuff. I squirreled these tiny slips away. He wondered how the world worked, how the mind thought, and what happened when we died. I'd always been too tangled up in the day-to-day stuff. My world had to shrink to the size of a bunker to get me to think big.

Every night we'd gather with Tate like we had in my room

on our two-month anniversary for story time. When we finished *To Kill a Mockingbird*, we took turns telling stories to one another. Tate recounted classic action-adventure series. He'd change the names and fill in the blanks when he forgot the plot. We recognized James Bond, Jack Bauer, Jason Bourne, and Neo. Tate always lingered too long on describing the damsels in distress. I'd have to throw something at him when he detailed sexy stuff.

I started to tell one of my favorite movies, *The Shining*, but I couldn't do it. We'd lived through enough horror stories for a lifetime. So instead I decided to make them laugh. My stories were rambling and ridiculous, but Tate would quote one of my punch lines and chuckle for days after.

Chaske shared folktales that his grandfather had told him. My favorite was about why the North Star stands still. I loved to hear him tell it.

"One brave boy loved to climb," Chaske would start. He'd sit cross-legged, a hand resting on each knee. "He found the highest peak. He wanted to make his father proud, so he decided he would find a way to hike to the very top. It wasn't easy, because there was no path, no way to scale the sheer cliffs. He found a hole in the mountainside that sloped down and then up. He climbed in the dark with rocks slipping free and falling into the hole below. He was not afraid of climbing in the open air, but he was fearful of the dark space."

About this far into a story, Tate would fidget, but Chaske sat straight and filled the empty space with the sound of his voice. "He wanted to stop, but when he turned back he discovered that rocks now blocked his path. The only way to go was up. He followed a faint light and eventually emerged on the tip-top of the mountain. When his dad spotted him, he was very sad because he knew there was no way back down. His dad turned his son into a star. He became the North Star. A star that stays in one place to guide travelers."

"Onward and upward," I said, repeating the phrase Chaske often used. I was sitting right next to him but not touching.

"That's right," he said. "You must survive the dark to become a guiding light." I rested my hand on the ground next to his thigh. He slipped his hand on top of mine, casually so Tate wouldn't notice. Chaske was my North Star.

"It's my turn next!" Tate bounced. "Chaske, your stories need way more action."

"I think his story was perfect," I said, and squeezed his hand.

One night Chaske and I stayed up playing a new card game we'd created, which was a mix of truth or dare, strip poker, and the card game war. Each card and suit represented a, well, sensual act and a body part. We divided the queen-of-heartless deck and each flipped one card over. The person who had the higher card was the recipient of the action on the winning card. We leaned over the cards and kissed at every tie. One-eyed Jacks and twos were wild, if you know what I mean. Then whoever won the whole deck got to decide, um, the ultimate reward.

I had just finished kissing each of Chaske's toes, his five of spades trumping my three of hearts, when I swear I heard a *click* and then a *clack*. Chaske didn't seem to notice, mostly because I had trumped his ten of diamonds with a one-eyed Jack.

"Did you hear something?" I asked.

We both stayed very still.

"Never mind," I said, and puckered my lips as I considered if I wanted him to remove his shirt for the rest of the game or kiss my eyelids, which for some reason freaked him out a bit.

Click. Clack. Click. Clack. It was the faintest series of taps. We'd both heard that.

We dropped our cards and raced up the tunnel. I pressed my ear to the door. Nothing.

"You heard it too?" I asked.

He nodded. "Could it be someone knocking?"

I backed away from the door. A memory of the last time I opened the door flashed through my mind. *Please no*, I thought. *Not again.*

We waited and waited for the sound, but it never came.

"We must have imagined it," I said, and forced a laugh.

"Yeah," he agreed, even though a joint auditory hallucination was pretty much impossible.

A few nights later, it happened again. We were cuddled up together in the sleeping bag, waiting for Tate to turn out the light. *Click. Clack. Click. Clack.* On and on it went.

I covered my ears, exposing my shoulders to the chilly bunker air.

"Tate!" Chaske screamed.

I decided that warm was more important than eardrums, so I pulled the sleeping bag back around my neck.

"Tate! What are you doing?" Chaske sat up and shouted even louder. Cold air rushed in and robbed us of our cocoon of heat.

"Nothing!" he called back. "Nothing. It was nothing." I could hear his feet pounding up the tunnels.

Oh my God. I had to get dressed before he got here. He couldn't see me like this.

"I was just doing something but it's nothing. I'll stop," Tate was calling to us as he ran.

I shoved Chaske the rest of the way out of the sleeping bag and clumsily stumbled out of the cot. The rock was cold on my bare butt. I searched for my lavender I KNOW YOU ARE BUT WHAT AM I? shirt. Chaske pulled on his jeans in this smooth, ninjalike move. I snatched my shirt, which I remembered he'd tossed with great zeal earlier to the far side of the room.

Tate was babbling and running and getting closer and closer.

I pulled on my shirt and jeans and stuffed my bra and underwear deep in Chaske's sleeping bag. Chaske calmly combed his fingers through his hair and I used the cot to pull myself up, nearly ending up back on the floor with the cot on top of me. Chaske was helping me up when Tate appeared at the door.

"What were you doing?" Chaske asked, and stepped in front of me to distract Tate as I zipped up my jeans.

"Nothing. You know. I'll stop." He looked at me, sort of

hiding behind Chaske. "What were *you* two doing?" Tate asked, winking at Chaske.

I thought of the best lie I could. "I was doing some laundry, you know, washing my delicates, and I thought Chaske might give me a bit of his daily water." It sounded plausible. I stopped to see if the lie would soak in.

He squinted at me and then smiled the devilish smile that I had come to know and love. "I'll give you some of my water, Icie, if you'll let me help you."

"Not on your life, Roadkill," I said.

"I drank all my water today, Icie," Chaske said, showing me his empty water jug. "I'll save you some tomorrow."

"Yeah, fine. I better get back to my laundry," I said, and walked to the door. I gave Tate a friendly whack on the back of the head. "That's for being rude."

"Ouch." Tate rubbed his head. "I thought I was being helpful."

"Too much testosterone for me," I said as I left. I did this weird combination of mime and sign language and mouthed *My room later* to Chaske.

Chaske gave a subtle nod. It wasn't until I was back in my room that I realized it was Tate who had skillfully changed the subject from the clacking noises. He was probably just making the noise somehow with his mouth or armpit. I forgot about it. It was Tate being Tate. I never thought it would matter.

It mattered.

Maybe a week later Chaske and I were woken by the most horrible scream and crash. Chaske and I sprang to our feet, dressed without a word, and ran down the tunnel shouting for Tate, but everything was quiet.

We reached where the light stopped. Tate's tent was there, but he wasn't inside. Tate had added a few more drums to his drum set. I didn't know a lot about music, but I was sure most rock drummers didn't play upwards of fifteen drums. We switched on our flashlights and continued down the tunnel.

"Tate!" Chaske called.

"Tate!" I shouted almost in response.

We listened intently.

Nothing.

I wanted to turn back. I didn't want to know what I would find. "Tate!" I screamed again. We reached the place that looked like the tunnel had collapsed in a pile of rock. I remembered how that sight had unnerved me on that first day. I tried not to think about the tons of earth overhead. The rock pile wasn't solid anymore. Tate had deconstructed it, rock by rock. There was now a jagged opening, beyond which was pitch-black. The clacking noises suddenly made sense. Chaske climbed through.

"I don't like this," I told Chaske, and followed him.

He stumbled into a secret room. The temperature increased. The wall ahead of us had a metal door, more of a garage door, really. It was open. We stepped inside. The space was vast, but the air was warm.

Chaske sent a thin beam sweeping like a lighthouse over the sea ahead of us. Shiny silver canisters were stacked from floor to ceiling. A few of the columns had toppled over and the tops of the canisters had popped off, gaping at us like mouths opened in a scream. Chaske flicked his light here and there, not lingering or giving me time to really understand what I was seeing.

And there was Tate. He was lying lifeless on the ground. Dull rods and what looked like shattered black glass surrounded Tate. I rushed to him, but Chaske pulled me back. One of the stacks must have fallen on him.

As the scene soaked in, I realized what this was. But how could it be? I had started to believe that we could live in here together forever. I'm not sure I cared what was outside anymore. I stood there rejecting what I knew to be true.

I was never safe.

We never had a chance.

"Icie, look." Chaske shone his flashlight on the silver container closest to us. It was about a meter high and maybe sixteen inches across. The circle of light from Chaske's flashlight highlighted a round red icon. I went to move closer but Chaske held me back. I strained to see. The shapes shifted from random to symbol. I knew that sign. I knew what it meant. It was the universal symbol for radioactivity. A circle broken into three parts. I used to think it looked like an old movie reel until my dad told me what it stood for.

"Tate," Chaske said. Tate's eyes fluttered open.

"Hi," he murmured. "Don't be mad."

"We're not mad, Tate," I promised. But I was. Tate's discovery had robbed me of my safety and sanity.

Chaske brushed the dark glass off of Tate and picked him up. Shards of glass clattered to the ground. Chaske carried Tate and laid him right outside the door to the secret room.

"Tate, listen to me," Chaske said. "We need you to wake up and stand up when you're ready." Chaske turned to me. "Icie, shut the door and I'll be right back." His expression said that our situation had just gone from firecracker to supernova bad.

Chaske climbed out and took off up the tunnel. I reached for the bottom edge of the garage-like door. It was heavy and I'd grown weak and tired trapped underground. My head swam with the effort. I yanked the door down and staggered backward, feeling a little drunk with all the horrible thoughts rushing to my consciousness.

Tate slowly rolled over on his stomach and groaned as he rose to all fours. It took some time, but he stood like a scarecrow, arms out at his side. I could see hundreds of tiny red cuts all over his body. Tate's eyes begged me to say something.

"It's going to be okay," I said. Neither of us believed me.

I'd rescued this rich kid from the desert only to douse him with radioactive waste.

"Icie?" He asked a million questions with my name. "Is that…"

I nodded. "How did you…"

"At first I wanted to see what was hidden behind those

stones." He pointed. "I removed a few stones every night and then I discovered this hidden room." He shut his eyes. "You get so bored and you think maybe there's something in there. And it becomes like pirate treasure and a portal to the real world all at once."

"It's going to be okay," I said again.

"The door only had a padlock so I decided to crack its combination," Tate explained. "At night when I was sure you were asleep and this place gets deathly quiet, I'd turn that dial and listen. When that's all you have to do night after night, it wasn't so hard. Maybe I'll be a thief instead of a rock star." Tate tried to laugh. I fixed my gaze on the opening in the pile of rocks and begged Chaske to hurry.

Chaske fed armloads of stuff to me. "Maybe we should come out there too," I said, poking my head out.

"Stay still," he said to both of us, and then dashed off again. I stacked everything Chaske had given me: rubber gloves, Marissa's jeans, my hand sanitizer, two face masks, and Tate's Swiss Army knife. Chaske appeared again and dumped two jugs of water at my feet and then disappeared. We were going to scrub Tate down.

Maybe Chaske didn't understand how dire the situation was. Washing Tate down with soap and water wasn't going to make much difference. If he really had been covered in that stuff. If he'd really been spending night after night near that gunk, separated by a garage door. What good would soap and water do, but we had to do something.

I knew from my dad that radiation was like any chemical poison. It depended on the dose and the exposure time. He said it was like alcohol. If you downed a whole bottle of whiskey, then you'd feel sick and it might be life threatening. If you drank two bottles quickly, it might kill you. But if you drank a small amount once a day it might have no effect on your health. Radiation was like that; in the short term you could be fine, but it could increase your risk of cancer in the long run. I didn't know how much poison Tate had been exposed to.

"Tate, take off your clothes and put them in a pile in that far corner," I called.

He tugged his shirt over his head. I used the knife to rip Marissa's jeans into rags. I put the mask over my mouth and nose and pulled on the rubber gloves. I felt guilty shielding myself from him, but I wanted the protection. I wanted more protection than the gloves and masks were going to afford, but I couldn't turn my back on Tate.

Chaske continued to bring jugs of water. "You get started." He looked apologetically at Tate and handed me a half-empty bottle of green shampoo. "Rinse him and then scrub him down good with the shampoo. Rinse him and do it again. I'm going to get two more jugs and some clean clothes for him."

"Chaske..." I grabbed his arm, but I couldn't feel him beneath the slip of latex.

"Icie, we'll do our best," he assured me, and raced off.

I lugged a bottle of water over to Tate. "Shut your eyes," I told him, and slowly dumped the water over his head. It gushed down his face and twisted down his body. His skin looked red and irritated already.

"Sorry, Tate," I said, and I meant sorry about everything. I handed him a rag and dumped green shampoo on it, being careful not to waste a drop. I did the same to mine. "You do your face, and..." I indicated his private parts. "I'll start on your back."

I worked my way down, scrubbing and nearly pushing him over. He widened his stance and flexed his muscles. He'd grown taller in captivity. He wasn't a little boy anymore. Alarm bells were blaring in my head, but Tate didn't have to know how serious this was. And maybe I was wrong. Maybe this stuff wasn't deadly. My dad in one of the pop lectures he was always giving me said that radioactivity wasn't deadly forever and it depended on the type of radioactive waste it was. But it could be hazardous from ten thousand to a hundred-thousand-plus years. He also said that activists were always blowing the whole nuclear-waste thingy out of proportion. You could recover from contamination—a lot of people had. Yeah, except that one Russian spy guy in London. He was contaminated with some radioactive something and he...you know.

"I always thought my first shower with a girl would be different," Tate said. His teeth chattered as I dumped another jug of water over his head. "Can we stop now?" he begged.

Chaske's face peeked through the opening. "What, and miss a threesome with me?" He was carrying three water jugs. He quickly donned a pair of rubber gloves. He picked a rag and loaded it with shampoo. "I pictured you as a sing-in-the-shower type, Tate."

Tate's skin was red and raw. His lips were blue. Tears streamed down his face, but he started to sing "Tonight" by Fame Sake. Tate sang the main lyrics and Chaske and I provided the backup. We shouted it at the top of our lungs.

> *"Tonight's got promise*
> *(Promise)*
> *Tonight's got faith*
> *(Faith)*
> *Tonight's all we got*
> *(Fo Sure)*
> *(Fo Sure)*
> *Tonight I got you*
> *(And you got me)*
> *Tonight's all I need."*

THIRTY

GRETA

Vega is burning. All their work turned to ash. Greta was even starting to think of it as home. Now she will have nothing again. Worse than that, she knows her secrets have sparked this war. All she wanted was a few stolen moments with a boy. But that boy is gone. He never was just a boy. Beckett lied to her. They both lied. She was selfish and stupid to try to carve out something special for herself. She has to escape and help her family.

Beckett is exploring a hole in the mountain, but he believes it is some mythical place. She doesn't understand this side of him. Great Ian. Signs. Hearts. How can he believe in a higher power that lets the world come to an end? How can he put his faith in something that allows people to destroy one another? How can he abdicate choice to this unseen, unknown force? She can't believe in anything beyond the power of her own two fists. It makes it easier to do what she has to do.

She sees her chance when Harper's back is turned. Maybe Harper is giving her an opportunity to escape. She has made her hatred abundantly clear. She wants Greta off the mountain and out of their lives. Since Beckett disappeared into the tomb, Harper hasn't really been paying attention to her. She keeps looking in that dark hole and pacing. She loves him. That's obvious now.

Greta sneaks a rock from the pile that once sealed the opening of this tomb and slams it into Harper's temple. Harper flops to the ground. Her head bounces on the hard soil. Her limbs flail at odd angles. The tattered strips tied around her body slip and gap, exposing patches of white skin.

She can hear Da's voice in her head. It's telling her to kill them both. They have destroyed Vega. *An eye for an eye.* It's something Da says.

Greta has never killed before. But maybe she should. Maybe this sacrifice will absolve her of bringing the wrath of these mountain monsters on Vega. She finds a bigger rock, one with a sharp point. She raises it high above her head. She should bash Harper's head into the ground. It wouldn't be difficult. It might be more compassionate than letting her continue her small, sheltered, unfulfilled life.

Greta is continually amazed by how easily a life can end. She's buried her grandparents, her mom, and a sister. Their journey to Vega was littered with sickness and snakebites and human attacks.

She doesn't doubt that if the situation were reversed, Harper would deal the death blow.

Lucky saunters over to Harper and sniffs at the red puddle under her temple. She snuggles up in the space under Harper's chin. They look so helpless.

Greta cocks her arm back. It would be so easy. All she has to do is let the rock fall. She feels sorry for this girl, but not because she's slumped on the ground. She feels a kinship with Harper. They are both girls who don't belong anywhere, and they both love the same man. After this act, they will both be girls in love with someone who doesn't love them back.

She slowly lowers her arms, and the rock falls at her feet with a clack. She can't do it.

She peeks inside the tomb. Beckett appears to have vanished. Part of her hoped to see something awe-inspiring. In a strange way, she's jealous. What a comfort to believe that everything happens for a reason and that everything will be okay. She wishes she could pray and someone would tell her what to do. But she's got no one to blame, no one to rely on, but herself.

Lucky watches as Greta drags Harper to a nearby tree. Greta tears a wide strip of material from the hem of her shirt, erasing half of the peace symbol she drew there. She ties Harper's hands behind her back and secures her to the base of the tree. Lucky curls next to Harper again. They almost look peaceful, except for the blood dripping down Harper's face and the uncomfortable angles of her body.

Greta replaces the rocks that Beckett removed and seals him in the tomb. It won't keep him forever, but it will give her time to escape. She wishes this could end differently. She wedges a few more rocks into the pile so the wall is more secure, more solid. She tests to see if she could roll the stone across the entrance, but it's far too heavy and she's far too weak. She must go and see what's left of her home.

She bolts to the other side of the mountain. Through the thinning smoke, she sees that the landscape has changed. There's now a barrier between Vega and the mountain, as if a massive line has been drawn in the dirt. She squints through the gloom. This line is a human barricade. Maybe her family has survived Forreal's attack. Vega is lined up in neat rows facing the mountain. She can't tell numbers, but they advance in a slow, metered march. Vega is attacking. An eye for an eye.

THIRTY-ONE

"Something is better than nothing."

—Just Saying 3

BECKETT

Beckett stands in the pitch-black. One moment he'd made the most astonishing discovery of his life and then this nothingness...

Beckett had slipped through the metal door. The locking mechanism was still in place but the rock had shifted. He has felt the Mountain's tremors from time to time. Had the Great I AM shaken this free for him? His head ached with constant questions and the search for understanding. He felt a ticking like the second hand of the Timekeeper's watch. Time was running out.

Beckett knew he had to go deeper into the Heart. The future of Forreal and Vega depended on it. He had summoned his strength and held his torch high. He squinted through the darkness, expecting something. A blinding light. A voice. A swirling torrent of demons. The heat of a thousand flames. The electricity of a lightning bolt. He'd always believed the Heart was the source of the Mountain's power. Maybe in opening the space he had unleashed some unseen force.

The torch kept the darkness at bay. The black felt solid and endless beyond his protective bubble of light. He waved his torch to better gauge the size of the space. He was shocked to see hundreds of smiling faces looking back at him. The walls were filled with Facebook drawings.

Beckett spotted a tattered bag in the center of the space. All those smiling faces appeared to be staring at the backpack. He saw a shiny pin that winked in the torchlight. Beckett read the words on the pin: SAVE THE PLANET, ROCK THE WORLD. His breath caught in his throat. So many messages. He could feel the Great I AM's presence.

As he carefully picked up the backpack, the zipper burst and its contents spilled out. Beckett tried to catch the items before they hit the ground. His fingers caught a thick silver ring with a purple sparkling *I*, *A*, and *M*. Everything else seems to flutter in slow motion, down, down, down. He dropped to his knees. He was touching something that belonged to the Great I AM. He closed it in his fist and felt the connection between him and the Great I AM increase by a bazillion.

Among the items scattered on the ground, he noticed a small booklet with a yellowing cover and plain black text. The pages crumbled at his touch, but he could read three words clearly: *Waiting*, *for*, and *Beckett*.

He felt a rush of what he could only describe as joy ripple

through his body, mind, and soul. The Great I AM had been waiting for him to find the Heart.

He studied each item lovingly: a plastic card with a barely visible picture, two halves of a tiny glass pot, thin strands of tarnished silver loops that swirled and connected at a hook, and a silver C-shaped hoop. These must have belonged to the Great I AM. He stroked each item as if they might transfer some magical property. He returned them to the backpack to keep them safe.

The Great I AM had been here, stood where he stood. Smiled at these faces. Collected these treasures. Beckett had hugged the backpack to his chest. He felt the weight of something more inside. He dipped his hand in and pulled out a plastic bag that had been wedged at the bottom. His hands shook, rattling the plastic. Through the clouded, wrinkled bag he saw smiley faces scribbled all over the cover of a thin book. The original Facebook. He imagined walking back into Forreal with original Just Sayings from the Great I AM. Forreal would have to listen to him now.

The blackness beyond seemed to beckon. There was more to discover. But the strangest thing had happened. The flame on his torch shrank and then fizzled out. His eyes adjusted to the tiniest glow from the outside. But that light seemed to be fading too. Then darkness descended around him.

Now he stands perfectly still, waiting for another message from the Great I AM. The space is quiet except for a far-off drip, like rain plinking in a puddle. The sound seems to echo like a whisper in the vast space.

"Whatever," he says to the Great I AM, and tries to relax, but the darkness feels as if it's consuming him.

Beckett takes a deep breath and orients himself. He visualizes the space before his light was extinguished. Beckett slips the backpack's straps over his shoulders and inches along the cave wall toward the entrance. He's got to get out of here. He fumbles forward. His fingers find ragged rock. This must be the door. As he squeezes through, he thinks he sees twinkling stars up ahead. But that doesn't make sense.

Someone has walled up the entrance. What he thought were stars are only the tiny spaces where moonlight has found a path through the pile of rocks. He edges along the rocky wall, trying to avoid the skeletons beneath his feet. He claws at the rocks until he creates a hole and climbs out. He gulps in fresh air.

The first thing he sees is Harper slumped on the ground with Lucky standing guard. He rushes to Harper's side. A gash has opened up at her temple and blood is oozing down her face. He wipes away as much as he can.

"Harper," he says, untying her and taking her in his arms. Her body is limp and cold. "Harper, please be okay."

He can't do this without her. All this time, he thought he saved her, but looking at her lifeless body, he realizes it was she who saved him. Without her, he is a man with a birthmark. She's always made him a hero. She's always made him feel more than a man. She was propping him up, always right there behind him. "Not this," Beckett shouts at the top of his lungs. "This cannot be the sacrifice. Not whatever!"

Harper's eyes open a crack. "Thank the Great I AM," Beckett cries, and hugs her close.

She grimaces and presses her fist to her bleeding temple. "What..."

"Did Greta do this to you?" Beckett asks. Harper nods, and then her head lops to one side. "Harper, stay with me. Wake up." She needs to open her eyes again, to talk to him. "Harper," he says, and kisses her on her forehead. "Please, Harper."

Harper stirs ever so slightly. "Give me some air, would you, Becks," she whispers, and tries to sit up. She moans in pain and eases back down.

Beckett rests her against the infinity stone. "Are you okay?" he asks, easing himself down next to her.

Harper wrinkles her eyebrows together. "Seriously?"

Beckett half smiles at her sarcasm. She's going to be okay.

"We've got to stop Finch and Greta." Harper speaks slowly as if it pains her to say it. "As the Great I AM says, 'Desperate times call for outrageous measures.'"

A plan is beginning to form in Beckett's head.

Harper leans into Beckett. "What did you find?"

Beckett hands Harper the Great I AM's backpack. "I think it's the Great I AM's Facebook." Beckett wraps an arm around Harper.

"Beckett, what are we going to do?"

"I've got an idea," he says. "Let's give Forreal and Vega something to believe in."

THIRTY-TWO

After we cleaned him up, Tate spent the next hour in the necessary getting sick. Chaske held him upright while I placed cold compresses on his forehead. I tried not to gag each time he threw up. My body itched to run away. It took every ounce of courage to stay by Tate's side. Even after his stomach was empty he continued to heave. Eventually he collapsed in Chaske's arms. We tucked him into bed and took turns watching him sleep.

When he woke up the next morning, he was exhausted, but sort of fine. We let him eat a whole MRE. For a day it was as if we were almost back to our locked-underground normal. Even though I couldn't remember how I normally acted or what I normally did. Every second my brain was consumed by one question—are we being poisoned?

Chaske and I talked about leaving this place, but we were still more scared of what was out there than in here. Then Tate got too sick for us to even consider moving him. We watched this vibrant kid age before our eyes in agonizing stages. First came the diarrhea, then the nosebleeds. Next the chills and fever. He said he felt as if his head were being ripped in two. We gave him what medication we had.

"I don't know what more we can do for him," I told Chaske less than a week later. We had stepped out into the tunnel to discuss what to do next. Tate was bedridden. He couldn't eat or drink without getting sick. His hair fell out in fistfuls. He smelled as if he was decaying already.

"Should we, you know..." Chaske couldn't say it but I knew. "He's only going to get worse. More pain. It doesn't seem humane to watch him suffer."

I thought about the zombie and the weight of the gun in my hand. The trigger had clicked under the pressure of my finger and I remembered the look in the zombie's eyes as the bullet entered his body. How his eyes widened in surprise and then they squinted in pain. Then I always saw Marissa's face. We were both just trying to make it through this and remain human—which I knew now was impossible.

That memory made my body ache. My throat tensed. My stomach convulsed. My insides swam in a sickening swirl of guilt and anger and fear and sadness. I told myself again and again that I had to do it. It was him or me, but no matter how hard I tried to convince myself, I knew I'd taken two lives.

I told Chaske, "I can't. I know you're right, but I can't." I'd done it once in the heat of a life-or-death moment. I couldn't pull the trigger again, even if it was maybe for the best. I couldn't point the gun at Tate. I already felt as if I'd killed him by bringing him here.

"Icie, promise me. If I ever get that bad, you'll find the courage to put me out of my misery. You'll do it for me, won't you? I'm telling you it's okay. It would be what I'd want."

I shook my head. "We weren't exposed. We're fine. I mean, we'd be sick already, right?" but I knew it was impossible to say. I didn't know how much exposure we'd had and what type of radioactive waste it was. Also I knew from my dad that everyone reacted to poisons differently. Tate had been so close to that radioactive gunk for so long and he'd had direct contact too.

"I hope you're right, but promise me. Don't let me suffer."

I hoped it wouldn't come to that. I buried my face in his chest. My mass of dreadlocks fell over my face. "It's all my fault," I whispered, barely saying my confession. "I didn't know. My parents couldn't have known."

He stroked my dreadlocks.

"I thought we were safe," I said, and swallowed the thick saliva that had gathered in my mouth. "Why did Tate have to open that door anyway? Why couldn't he just leave it alone? We were better off not knowing, weren't we?"

"It doesn't matter," Chaske said. He brushed my hair aside so he could see my face in the soft glow of the solar lighting.

"My parents couldn't have known that stuff was here. Why would they send me here if that stuff was here? I mean—"

Chaske hugged me closer. "Icie, I saw those containers just like you did. They had no markings besides the radioactive symbol. Some company has taken advantage of this free storage facility or maybe the government is secretly storing the stuff here. Those canisters aren't marked with a company name or any fancy coding system. They must have been hidden here for a long time. Your parents couldn't have known."

"It doesn't make any sense." I buried my face again.

"It doesn't matter," Chaske said. "We would all be dead already if it weren't for you and this place."

"Yeah, I guess," I murmured into his chest, my lip nudging his bare skin with each word. I kissed his chest, his neck. I held his face and kissed him hard on the lips. I wanted to feel something. I didn't want to think about Tate anymore. I couldn't.

"Icie," Chaske said, and shifted away from me. "I can't. Not now. Okay?"

I heard his words but I couldn't stop. I had to make him understand. I wanted to feel what I'd felt so many nights with Chaske. I wanted that spark, that closeness. I kissed him on his cheeks. I ran my hands across his body, but instead of responding, his body tensed. I kept kissing him. He had to understand.

"Enough, Icie," he said, and pinned me against the tunnel wall.

"Chaske, stop it," I said, writhing against him.

"Icie, please," he whispered, and shook me until I stopped fighting. "It's not your fault," he said. I shut my eyes. "It's not your fault," he said again.

"Yes, it is. All this..." I started to cry. I hated these helpless tears. I wanted to pull my arms in and cover my face but he wouldn't release me.

"It's not your fault." He repeated it again and again and again.

"Then whose fault is it?" I shouted.

"If you want to blame someone, blame the people who made the stuff and put it here," he said slowly, but then the speed and intensity of the words increased. "Blame all the people who make things that are only designed to kill. Blame the governments for not making peace their only priority. If you want to blame someone, I guess you can blame me too. Maybe we are all to blame. We lived our lives and didn't care about anything bigger than ourselves. We are all to blame for not speaking up, standing up, shouting, kicking and screaming, and demanding better from the world, our leaders, each other, and ourselves. If we ever get out of here, let's do a better job. When you rule the world, why don't you preach peace and compassion and common sense?"

His fire, his passion, was contagious. And he was right.

"Maybe I will," I said.

330

Toward the end we let Tate listen to a few tunes a day, spacing it out and talking endlessly about what song to pick. Sometimes he didn't know who we were or where he was. He kept calling me Libby and calling Chaske Jaymo or something like that. We didn't correct him. We let him believe we were whoever he wanted us to be. When he stopped talking, Chaske and I carried on a discussion we thought Tate would like.

Chaske and I sat on the cold rock floor on either side of Tate's cot.

"Best rock singer of all time?" Chaske said, in a tone that if Tate were conscious, he would realize was too perky for Chaske. He tried so hard to keep the mood light. He had this too-wide smile plastered on his face. It was kind of freepy but I couldn't tell him that his smile was making me anxious.

"You mean besides Tate Chamberlain," I said, his name catching in my throat. Tears welled in my eyes. Tate wouldn't get his rock-star dream, or any dream, now.

We agreed to try to keep the mood happy for Tate, but that was nearly impossible. "Wha Eva's the best rock singer, of course," Chaske said, sticking to our lighthearted discussion.

I cleared my throat but I couldn't stop the tears streaming down my face. "Tate likes In Complete Faith and Fame Sake, don't you, Tate? What was the tune you played all the time?"

"Yeah, that 'Tonight' song," Chaske said, and started to sing: *"Tonight's got promise. Promise."*

I leaned in and whispered to Tate, "Chaske sure isn't the best singer of all time."

"Hey!" Chaske said. "I've got a good voice."

Chaske and I were acting too light and fluffy—like hosts on a children's television show.

"We already did best drummer and best rock tune...." Chaske struggled for another topic.

"And the best band of all time," I added. I was watching Tate slip away and all I could do was make crupid conversation.

"Tate, how about you and I list the top ten girls we want to be stuck in a bunker with?" Chaske asked, giving Tate a conspiratorial, but light, nudge.

"You've got me," I interjected. "What more could you..." But I knew if I said the rest of that sentence, I was going to lose it. I leapt to my feet and raced as fast as I could down the tunnel. I'd nearly reached the bottom before I burst into tears. That's what it felt like. Something inside of me had ripped open and I couldn't stop sobbing. I curled into a ball on the hard rock floor and cried. It wasn't only for Tate but for everyone I'd lost. I'd locked Marissa and Midnight out. I didn't know what was worse, watching Tate die or forever wondering what happened to my parents.

I told myself to suck it up. I couldn't be there for Mum or Dad or Lola, but I could be there for Tate. I wiped my eyes and marched right back to Tate's bedside. I mouthed *Sorry* to Chaske. "It's okay," he said. I slid down next to him. We sat in silence for a while, listening to Tate breathe.

Each of Tate's breaths was ragged and barely audible.

Chaske and I would hold our breaths until he took another, asking each other with the raise of an eyebrow if this was it.

Tate cracked opened one eye and stared at me.

"Hi, Tate," I said, and forced myself to stroke his arm. After we'd scrubbed him, his skin developed thousands of scabs, almost scales. I swallowed down the bile that rose in my throat. I didn't think he was contagious but I didn't know. I never paid attention in science class. I only half listened to my father when he talked his nuclear talk. It really didn't matter anymore, did it? We were already exposed.

"Icie?" Tate murmured.

"Yes, Tate, I'm right here."

After a long while he said, "I'm scared."

"I'm sorry." It was all I could think to say. I wasn't cut out for this. What do you say to a dying twelve- or was it thirteen-year-old kid? I should have really known his age. I should have tried to get to know him better.

Tate's eyes leaked tears. His lips trembled. I could tell it took great effort for him to speak, but he was determined. "I don't want to die." He opened his hand to me and I held it.

I knew he needed me to say something reassuring, but what could I say? I didn't want him to die—I didn't want to die. Tears flooded my vision. A sob clawed at my throat but I didn't want Tate to hear me cry. He was scared enough. He didn't need his final hours filled with me blubbering.

"Tate, we are right here," Chaske said. "We aren't going to leave you." Chaske took Tate's other hand. "I think we custom-make our own afterlife. You've lived longer than most everyone else out there. I think all the great rockers are up there waiting for you and you'll get to spend eternity jamming. You were going to be..." Chaske cleared his throat. "You are going to be the best drummer of all eternity." Chaske was talking in soothing tones as if everything was going to be fine. His voice wasn't full of questions and doubt like mine was. He sounded sure. "It's going to be amazing, Tate. I promise." Tears were streaming down Chaske's face but his voice never faltered.

"Icie," Tate whispered. I leaned in close so I could hear him. "My watch," he said, lifting his wrist less than an inch before it flopped back at his side. "You be the timekeeper."

"I couldn't." Part of me didn't want to take the watch, not only because it was admitting that his fight was nearing an end but also because a selfish part of me wondered if it was contaminated with radioactivity. It definitely felt infused with death. But I owed it to Tate to comfort him in any small way I could.

"Icie..." Tate struggled to speak. "Please."

Chaske slipped the watch off Tate's wrist and pressed it in my hand. Tate's body convulsed and he screamed in pain. I wanted to run but I forced myself to stay. All I could give him now was my presence.

"It's okay, Tate. We are right here. It's okay." Chaske continued talking in a steady, calming stream. Tate's body relaxed. His fingers loosened in our grasp.

I focused on Tate's watch. In my mind I counted the second hand. The ticks between breaths increased. I was sure each breath would be his last. I hoped it was. How horrible was that? I wanted his suffering to end, but also I knew once he died, I would have to try to block him out like I had so many others. I wondered if Chaske was right. Was a quick death better for everyone?

Looking at Tate when whatever it was that made him alive and not just a body disappeared, I realized that there was no such thing as a good death.

We wrapped Tate in Chaske's sleeping bag and carried him back to the end of the tunnels where light met dark. We used some of the stones Tate had removed from the secret storage area and built him a makeshift tomb.

"Wait a minute," I said. I took his iPod from my messenger bag. I gently placed one earbud in each ear. I dialed and selected "Shuffle Songs" and hit play. It was better than a eulogy.

I could already feel myself hardening. "I'm sorry, Tate." I zipped the sleeping bag all the way up.

"He would have died on that road without you," Chaske said. He tried to take my hand, but I batted it away. I was angry at him and everything.

"I'm not sure I did him any favors by bringing him here."

"Tate wasn't unhappy here," Chaske replied. I knew in a weird way he was right. Tate seemed to get on with it, better than the rest of us.

Chaske started humming. I recognized the tune to "Outta Time" by In Complete Faith. I joined in, and we sang the words we knew.

"Don't hold on to hate.
Accept your fate.
We had time.
(Not so much time.)
All you got is time.
Till it's gone."

I slapped an empty water jug in time to our out-of-tune and offbeat tribute. Chaske picked up one of the drumsticks Tate had fashioned from tightly twisting together the wrappers from our power bars. He wailed on Tate's drum set. That thumping sound would forever remind me of Tate, his blue twinkling eyes and his round face surrounded by a helmet of yellow curls.

We ended with a flourish that made my hands sting. Chaske reached for me, but I walked away. I kept walking until I was at the tunnel's entrance.

"Where's your gun?" I asked him.

"What?" Chaske kept his distance.

"Get your gun and let's get this over with. You're right. We are prolonging the inevitable." I rested my back against the cool metal door.

Chaske reached for me, but I held my hand up like some action figure creating a force field. "I don't believe all that shit you told Tate. Do you? What's going to happen to us... after?"

"God, Icie, I don't know. I've always felt there was something more. Not someone watching over me but a power or a force, you know. Something bigger than us. I want to believe I'll see my mom again. But at the very worst, it's just silence. I don't mind silence."

"Do you think I'm going to hell?" I asked. "For being a spoiled rotten brat who didn't know how good she had it. For killing that...man. For shutting Marissa and Midnight out. For everything."

"The one thing I don't believe in is hell. I believe in second chances and forgiveness." Chaske took me in his arms. "I think we've been punished enough, don't you?"

I nodded. Maybe he was right. This was hell. Maybe we were the only survivors on the planet. Everything and everyone we'd ever known was dead. Suddenly I could feel the radioactive waste penetrating my skin. I scratched my arms. It was inside me and I wanted it out. I tore at my skin until I created long, thin welts and bloodred tracks on my body.

Chaske hugged me tightly, pinning my arms to my sides. I writhed in his grasp. I broke free and looked him directly in the eyes. "Kill me now."

THIRTY-THREE

"Doubt is like awkward, certainty is like not possible."
—Just Saying 281

FINCH

Finch feels too big for his body. His skin is oily with sweat and ash. He smells of smoke. Every breath inflates him. Every step elevates him. He finds a vantage point on his Mountain and watches Vega burn.

Finch reclines on the rock. He dreams of his Forreal homecoming. He wants to wait until sunrise, until he's sure the Cheerleaders have returned from Vega. He wants them to wonder and worry about him. He wants the stories to circulate of his heroic acts. He hopes that some might start to grieve for him and despair about the future of Forreal without Finch to lead them.

He should think of a speech, something that will be quoted for generations to come. Terrorists will never threaten Forreal again.

He has purged and purified. He can almost feel the warmth of Forreal's gratitude and admiration.

Finch wishes Beckett were here. He would like to see Beckett bow down before him. Finch recalls the look on Beckett's face when he attacked him. Beckett was always so smug, so calm. The Great I AM has punished him. What Beckett once worshipped ultimately claimed his life. He wishes he could see Beckett's body, know that he is gone, but he won't let thoughts of Beckett spoil his triumphant return.

Finch rises to his elbows. It's almost time. He surveys the valley below. Maybe he will expand his domain toward Vega. They can protect but not be trapped by the Mountain.

He notices movement below. He sits up. A line in the distance seems to shift forward. It can't be. He has defeated the Terrorists.

He stands and glares through the smoke.

Terrorists are heading toward the Mountain. They should be running away, not charging forward.

Panic packs a powerful punch.

"Whatever. Whatever. Whatever," he mutters, and hopes the Great I AM will show him the way. This was not what was supposed to happen.

He doesn't want to admit it but he's scared. He starts to walk and then run up the Mountain. He tells himself he's climbing to get a better view, to commune with the Great I AM, but part of him is considering running down the other side and leaving the Mountain like his mum.

When he reaches the Crown, he remembers Beckett's girl. She is exactly what he needs. He can barter her life for peace.

He reaches the spot where he tied her to the Crown. He sees the remains of the vines that bound her wrists and ankles. The thorns are tipped with her blood, but she has vanished. She can't have gotten very far. He notices the Crown has been ripped open. Up ahead, through the Crown, something glows.

"Do you think this will work?"

It's Harper. Finch walks toward her voice.

"Something is better than nothing." That sounds like Beckett's voice. He's quoting the Great I AM. But it can't be. Beckett's dead.

Harper laughs. "It's not exactly the vote of confidence I was looking for."

Finch sneaks closer and sees Beckett and Harper through the Crown. How have they survived? They've built a small fire and stand warming themselves. Lucky darts outside the ring of firelight. Her fur is suddenly bushy. Her tail seems to have doubled in size. As if the cat has sensed Finch's presence, she skids to a stop and crouches, preparing to pounce. Her ears are pulled back, her yellow eyes wide. She makes a low, throaty growl and then darts back to Beckett and Harper.

Finch finds a place to hide where he can still see them and overhear their conversation. He doesn't know whether to be scared or angry.

"Do you think future generations will call it the Crown of Fire?" Harper asks.

"Yeah, oh great one." Beckett laughs. "And you will be known as the Fire Mistress."

"How about Fire Warrior or Flame Bearer or She Who Carries a Torch?"

"Or Fridiot Who Set the Mountain on Fire."

Their conversation doesn't make any sense. How can they laugh? They have disobeyed the Great I AM. They should have been punished. But they sit there as if nothing has changed.

They are quiet for a long time. Finch has never understood how the two of them can do that. He finds it unnerving, as if they are communicating telepathically, and he's being left out again. He clenches his fists. The tension is building again. He aches to crack his knuckles, but he can't risk any sound.

"Do you think Mumenda will ever come?" Harper asks. She's staring into the flickering flames.

How can Harper blaspheme? Finch wonders, especially when the Great I AM has spared her.

"Now more than ever, I believe in the Great I AM. We have crossed the Crown and been to the Heart. I believe the Great I AM is leading us to end the conflict with Vega." Beckett takes Harper's hand. "Are you ready?"

Harper's eyes sparkle with tears. "If he..."

"If she..."

"Goes, I go," they both say, and cling to each other. Finch is surprised that he can still feel jealousy at their connection.

Beckett kisses Harper tenderly on the mouth. She is surprised and reacts too late; her puckered lips follow his as he pulls away. She cups his face in her hands. "I..." she starts, but doesn't finish her sentence. Finch twists to get a better view between the vines, but he can't decipher what passes wordlessly between them.

Beckett leans in so they are cheek to cheek. Finch inches closer.

"This is it," Beckett says. "You know what you need to do and when you need to do it."

She nods. "Get out of here already." She pulls him back when he tries to leave, as if she might say something. If she does, Finch doesn't hear it.

She lets Beckett go. He parts the opening of the Crown that Finch spotted earlier. Harper picks up Lucky and cuddles the cat. Beckett looks back at her one last time through the knotted brambles.

"I love you," she whispers into the tangled thicket. "I love you," she says again. Finch hears but Beckett is already rushing down the Mountain. Finch wishes she would say that to him.

He doesn't understand what they have planned. He is torn between chasing after Beckett and confronting Harper. He can almost feel the Terrorists as they draw closer and closer to his Mountain. He's come this far, sacrificed so much. If there must be more blood on his hands, so be it.

THIRTY-FOUR

I begged Chaske to kill me. Everything felt like a dead end. He said the only thing that could save me. "I love you, Icie."

What did it matter?

Maybe it shouldn't.

But it did. He loved me.

It was something to hold on to.

Something to live for.

But was it enough?

"All this, as awful as it is, brought me to you." He brushed my dreadlocks aside. "Endings are beginnings. Every ending a beginning and every beginning an end.

God, I know that sounds horrible. The world ends so we can be together. But it's like you rose out of the ashes to save me."

I wondered who saved whom. We slipped into each other's arms. I rested my head on his chest and listened to his heartbeat.

"Icie, that day...the day you found me...on the mountain. Well, I'd...I'd come to the mountain to..." He paused. He covered his mouth with one hand, and he shook his head. His fingernails had jagged edges, but they were longer and the skin around his fingernails was smooth. He lowered his hand. "Icie, I need to tell you...I mean..."

Chaske had become a mythical creature to me. He had no past. Part of me wanted to stop him. I soooooo didn't want him to be human. I needed him to be something more. Something that I could continue to believe in and someone who could save me. As he struggled for words, I knew he needed to climb down from the pedestal I'd put him on and be human with me.

"I'd come to the mountain to"—he paused again—"kill myself."

What? That didn't make any sense. Chaske was strong and confident. He saved me. He kept us grounded in this bizarre place. I tried to look at him, but he held me so close and wouldn't release me.

"But there you were," he continued, "and you needed saving more than I needed to die."

I didn't believe him, but then I thought about all those scars. Chaske was always at peace with our situation, but maybe that was only because he was already prepared to die. "But you had survival gear and food."

"I stole it from my foster dad's army supply store. I wrecked the shop and stole what I needed to get away from him." Something wet hit my cheek. I smoothed it away. I glanced up at Chaske's face. His cheeks were wet with tears. His pain seeped into me. Seeing this strong, proud man's agony was worse than any hurt I'd ever experienced.

"It's okay," I said, that stupid, untrue, unhelpful phrase. Nothing was okay. Nothing was ever okay. "You don't need to tell me."

"I think I do," he said, and kissed me on the top of the head. "I don't know who you think I am, but out there, if I kept doing what I'd been doing, I would have ended up in prison or dead. I wasn't going to graduate high school. I was on probation for stupid shit." He sniffed and wiped his eyes.

"I just wanted to run away." He couldn't stop now. "I thought I would live on the mountain for a while. My grandpa—my mom's dad—used to take me camping out in these mountains when I was younger. But once I got here, I didn't see the point. I wasn't living. I was just surviving. I couldn't go back and I didn't know how to go forward. The moment I found you, I had the gun and I was finally ready to pull the trigger and then it was as if you'd been dropped from the sky."

What was so awful about his life that suicide was his only answer? Before I got that 911 text from my parents, I couldn't imagine anyone's life being so hopeless that death was the only answer. I understood it now.

He released me and shifted so he was cuddling my back. He rested his chin on my shoulder. "I thought you were a sign."

I closed my eyes and listened to his steady breath in my ear. I didn't ask the question that felt almost solid in the air between us: Why? Why had he given up on everything out there? If he wanted to tell me, he would. I waited and eventually Chaske spoke.

"It all seems so trivial now. All the reasons—big and small. How do I explain it to you? You had two parents who loved you. All I had was my mom and she died a few years ago. She was this wonderful, kind woman who taught me all about the philosophers and asked me what I thought and listened to me. I was shuffled from family member to family member and then eventually put in foster care. The last family was the worst. They didn't treat me like a human and I guess I stopped feeling like one. You had this golden, sparkly future that lay ahead of you like the yellow-brick road to a glittery Emerald City. My future was heading toward a brick wall."

"I'm sorry, Chaske." It was all I could say and it wasn't enough. It felt like my fault. I had a great life that I didn't appreciate. How come he had gotten such a tough life, and, up until recently, I had gotten such an easy one?

No matter what happened before, we'd both ended up here.

I leaned back into him. "What now?" I asked, because I didn't really know. "Should we go outside?"

"Is that what you want?" he asked.

"No." I was surprised by my answer. "I'm not ready yet."
The longer we stayed here, the more terrified I'd become
about what we would find when we opened that big metal
door and resurfaced. We were running out of food. We
couldn't stay here much longer. I should have been more
worried that what had killed Tate was slowly killing us, but
I wasn't. I just wanted to stay here locked away with Chaske
for as long as we could.

"Let's just live in the moment," he said.

I tilted my head and he kissed my cheek. I could try to
live his way, but I wondered if his strategy was because he
knew our days were numbered.

We moved to the front of the tunnel, as far away from the
radioactive material and Tate's dead body as we could. We
spent every minute together. We had meals at regularly
spaced intervals. We slept. We played cards or told each
other stories. The only difference now was we didn't have the
constant tug-of-war to escape. I wasn't on pins and needles,
expecting, hoping, praying that my mum and dad would
come knocking on the door. We just lived in the moment.

He finally told me details about his life before but in
small dots of information that I had to connect. An incom-
plete image was evolving, but I didn't care. I let my life have
spaces too. I left out parts that I'd sooner have forgotten.
We developed the one-inch rule. We weren't allowed to be
more than one inch apart—except for trips to the necessary.

But the poison at the heart of the mountain seemed to

pulse its presence. I never forgot for one minute it was there. Every cough, every scratch, every pain, I wondered if it was the poison taking hold.

One night I woke up shivering. I didn't have to move to know that Chaske wasn't there.

"Chaske?" I called quietly, as if I might disturb someone else's sleep.

Then I heard the sound that was like a rusty dull knife to the heart. I realized it must have been what woke me. Chaske was coughing. The sound echoed in the tunnels. It grew and folded in on itself. I wanted it to stop. I waited for the next wheezing breath.

"Chaske?" I screamed. I wanted to hold him. Rub his back. Give him the air that settled so comfortably in my lungs. I could calm him. I would breathe for him.

The coughing stopped. He was trying to call to me, but he couldn't catch his breath.

"Where are you?" I yelled, and felt around for the flashlight that was always within reach every night. He must have taken it with him.

More coughing. I thought I heard him moving, shuffling toward me.

Then came the most awful silence.

"Chaske!" I screamed. "Don't leave me!" It was a selfish thought, but in those moments I had a glimpse of life without him and I was terrified in a way I'd never been before—not when I said good-bye to my parents, not during the

348

panic at the airport, not on that long ride with Marissa or when the taxi left us behind. Not on our hike up the mountain or even when we shut that heavy metal door behind us.

"Chaske!"

"I'm okay, Isis." His voice was hoarse. "Go back to sleep. I'll see you in the morning."

"But, Chaske..."

"Please leave me alone." His words weren't harsh, but they knocked the wind out of me.

"Is there anything I can do?" I asked him. I wanted to hear his voice. I desperately wanted him to talk to me, say anything, just talk. He felt so far away.

"No, I'll be fine tomorrow."

A lie, but I loved him for saying it. I only wished it were true.

I scooted myself to the nearest wall and sat up. I couldn't go back to sleep. I thought if I stayed awake, then he wouldn't die. He could never die. In my head I delivered a stream-of-consciousness monologue. I recounted every single thing I missed from the outside—sunshine, junk food, fresh air, TV. I missed my iPhone, Facebook, Twitter, and anything else that could take my mind off what was happening. I missed those inane text sessions with Lola: What R U doin? Nuttin. U? Nuttin. Wassup? Same stuff. Meet u @ Bucks? I thought of all the things I wanted to show him from my old life: from the Washington Monument lit up at night to my favorite purple shoes that I'd bought for the prom I'd never attend. I wanted to slow-dance with him while a disco ball cast white polka dots on the gym wall.

I must have fallen asleep because I woke to the most

god-awful roar. He was half screaming, half retching. I could hear the splash as the contents of his stomach splattered onto the floor. The acidic stink filled the space and my stomach convulsed. He vomited again. Bile rose in my throat. He continued to retch until all that was expelled were dry, choking gags.

"I'm sorry, Icie," he whispered.

"Oh, Chaske," I said. I tried to keep the sound of sadness out of my voice. "Turn on the light and let me help you."

"No." Even the one word sounded weak.

There was no need to talk. The sounds. The smell. We'd lived through them before with Tate, but we wouldn't both live through them again.

It must have been a day later when he crawled in next to me. I hadn't moved. He had switched on the light and cleaned himself up. He was hot and sweaty. I held him as his body shook so violently that I was bruised from his elbows and head thrashing about. I forced water down him.

"Should we leave?" I'd asked him. "Maybe we could get you some help." Maybe all he needed was fresh air and sunshine. I hoped there was at least still fresh air and sunshine.

He shook his head. "Just talk to me, Isis," he said. "Tell me a story. Anything."

It was impossible to think of something to say when the only thoughts circling in my mind were how terrified I was of losing him. But I needed to find something to take his mind off the pain.

"My favorite place ever used to be a movie theater. You know that moment before the movie begins when the lights go out and everyone gets quiet. In that dark stillness I could be transported anywhere. I used to love horror movies. That bunched-up feeling you'd get when the music got all screepy and you knew something terrible was going to happen..." What was I saying? I stuttered and stammered as I searched for a transition to something happier. "I don't think I'd like scary movies anymore. It's funny that when we'd turn off the lights each night and everything would be quiet and so dark in here, I'd get that same feeling. I'd think maybe I'd wake up tomorrow and it would have all been a bad dream. Or maybe tomorrow would be the day that my parents would..." *Argh!* I was doing it again. "But now I wake up and all I want to do is be with you. Nothing else matters as long as you're always there." I stroked his hair. "I used to love a skyline at night. Vegas has a great skyline with all those big neon signs. I thought I'd always live in a big city. I loved the buzz of having so many people around me all the time. Did you ever ride the subway or a bus or an airplane and look around and think of the bazillion stories that these people have to tell? I mean, each one has these secrets and stories that I'll never know. I loved that noise of the city. But I've gotten used to the quiet. I'm okay with being with you and my thoughts. It's as if I can hear myself for the first time. You know out there my phone was always beeping with texts and ringing with calls and I never really sat still. I can do that now. Weird, isn't it?" I half laughed. "I used to imagine us on the streets of D.C. walking hand in hand. I imagined that we'd go on dates, you know, dinner at my favorite Mexican restaurant—wait, I think we'd go to a steak place. I wouldn't want salsa breath if you were going to kiss me, right?" I think he smiled. "Then we'd go to a movie and maybe to Starbucks later for a coffee, but then lately I've been thinking that I'd like to take you to a beach. Someplace sunny. Remember how the sun used to feel on your skin? Remember the way the sun would warm you like a blanket and make you all drowsy? You'd get dozy and hover in this place between awake and asleep. Then a breeze would come and kind of wash it away. I could close my eyes and hear the ocean and later even when I left the beach I could still hear that sound in my ears, that *whoosh, whoosh,* as the waves crashed on the shore..."

On and on I went, letting one topic morph into another. I tried to recall all the peaceful and beautiful places I could. I spoke until my throat was raw.

We never said a word about how quickly he was deteriorating. That stuff was making him sick. Maybe it had been poisoning us all along, leaching into the water, secreting its poison as we slept. I couldn't understand why it was happening to him and not to me.

"Isis," he whispered, and shook my shoulder. "Isis."

My eyelids flew open. Was this it? *Oh shit, don't let this be it.* I sat up, nearly knocking heads with Chaske. He was dressed in a clean pair of jeans and a fresh T-shirt.

"I want to go outside," he said.

"Okay," I said. "Let's go."

"You don't have to come." He put a little pressure on my shoulder to keep me sitting. "I just want to know, you know, before I…"

"I'm coming with you."

"I'd rather you stayed here," he said, kissing my forehead. "We don't know what's out there."

"We know what's in here."

His face whitened and he slid back against the wall. He'd used all his energy getting ready.

"Why don't you sleep a bit? I'll change and pack up a few things." I stroked his long black hair. He closed his eyes. He now swam in the clothes that used to cling to his muscled body. He was more bones than flesh.

Maybe I could find him help. Maybe everything hadn't ended.

THIRTY-FIVE

GRETA

Greta's anxiety grows with each passing minute. She managed to make her way past the Crown and into the cover of the pine, but her energy is fading. Adrenaline masked her injuries at first, then anger at Finch spurred her forward. Blind determination kept her moving down the mountain. She can't see her people approaching anymore. Have they already reached Forreal? Greta's body is throbbing with pain, but she has to find her family and fight alongside them. She knows Da will be leading the charge.

She makes a steady descent, ducking and hiding and resting, until she realizes that the mountain is deserted. Greta quickly shifts strategies. She will not join the Vega army. She will make her way to Forreal and plan a counterattack. If she's given the chance, she will destroy their homes like they destroyed hers. An eye for an eye.

She sees the shelters that must be Forreal and cautiously invades. Clothes are soaking in washing tubs. A bucket half full of water has been dropped. Chuckwallas scamper from the dried meat someone has left on an abandoned plate. A fire smolders in the biggest structure. It's no more than poles, a roof, and a few benches. She picks up a branch from a pile of timber near the fire pit at the far side of the structure. One end of the branch has already been wrapped in cloth. She takes the ready-made torch and rams it in the fire. She will burn Forreal to the ground. It won't take much. The branch is smoking. She waits to make sure the fire takes hold.

She spots a thin slab of wood abandoned on one of the benches. She leaves the branch to burn in the fire for a minute. She examines what has been etched into the wood. Smiley faces. Hundreds of them. She touches the face with the googly eyes and squiggly mouth. She smears dirt, ash, and blood across the faces. She imagines rubbing it smooth, erasing those smiling faces. That's what she's planning, isn't it?

All around her she sees the remains of a simple life, of a people who work and worship together. There aren't any weapons. These are a peaceful people, like Beckett. Finch could be the only thorn. She wouldn't think twice about killing him, but she can't exact her revenge on the rest of them.

She carefully places the slab of wood back where she found it. Her branch has ignited but she leaves it to burn. Greta sees footprints—big and small—leading down the mountain. She follows the trail. She hears raised voices and the rumble of a fight—of bodies colliding with bodies.

"Greta."

The sound startles her.

Beckett steps from the shadows. Even after everything, her heart reaches out to him. He lunges for her. They clumsily crash into each other and he presses his lips to hers, knocking heads and teeth. She cringes in pain but tries to find the rhythm that used to come so naturally. She has a fistful of his dreads and is holding him close. The sounds of fighting seem to mute.

She shoves him away. He looks at her with those big, trusting eyes. "I forgive you, Greta," Beckett says.

"How can you?" She wants to be angry at him. If it weren't for him, there would be no fires or fighting. But she has forgiven him too.

"The Great I AM believes in second chances and forgiveness," Beckett says, and takes her hand as if nothing's changed.

"It must be wonderful," Greta says. "To believe in something outside yourself. To know you are not alone. To think that you have a higher purpose. The only person I ever trusted was myself. The only thing I'm sure about is that one day I will die, just like everyone else I have ever known."

"Let me show you a miracle," he says.

She kisses his cheek. "It's too late for miracles. Don't you hear that? Vega has already attacked Forreal. What can we do now?"

"It's never too late for a miracle."

She strokes his shock of white hair. "I wish we weren't enemies."

"We don't have to be enemies. Trust me one last time. Let me show you the power of the Great I AM." He doesn't wait for her answer. He laces his fingers among hers. "Don't let a few bad people ruin it for everyone."

"That's really all it has ever taken," Greta says. She knows the story of how it all ended. A small terrorist cell created a virus. They unleashed it on an unsuspecting world. There were attacks and counterattacks until only handfuls of humans survived.

Beckett looks at her as if her comment has triggered something deeper. "Evil wins when good men do nothing."

She can tell he's quoting someone. "What's that from?"

"It's a Just Saying from the Great I AM."

Maybe she should give Beckett's god a chance. What does she have to lose?

Beckett climbs onto the highest boulder he can find and pulls her up after him. The first rays of the rising sun flicker on the horizon. Below a battle rages. The sky shifts to a hazy pink. "It's time," he whispers in Greta's ear.

He stands tall and pulls his shoulders back. "Stop!" he shouts at the top of his lungs. Everyone freezes, startled by his booming voice. "The time for fighting is over. It's time for reconciliation."

Vega outnumbers Forreal nearly three to one. Her people are stained black from battling the fires. They quickly try to resume the fight, but Beckett's people refuse to engage. The way they look at him, it's as if they are seeing a ghost.

"Please," Greta says, searching the crowd for her family. "Listen to him. Give him a chance." She spots her father and brothers. "Da. Bungle. Joe. Tinker. Buzz. This has to stop before we destroy what we've worked so hard to build."

Beckett raises his and Greta's hands into the air. "I've asked the Great I AM for a sign."

Greta turns her face toward Beckett and whispers, "I hope you know what you are doing."

He looks toward the top of the mountain. And Greta prays for Beckett's miracle.

THIRTY-SIX

Even though I dressed in exactly the same clothes I wore when I arrived, I had changed in every way imaginable. My T-shirt still proclaimed HAVE A MEDIOCRE DAY. That would be an improvement.

I unlocked the bunker door and helped Chaske out. It seemed to have grown heavier and took all my strength to pull it open. I held my breath, wondering what awaited us. I braced myself for the worst.

We had to sidestep the rotting remains of the zombie. The stench of decay lingered in the air. I was relieved to find only one set of bones. Maybe Marissa and Midnight had survived. Maybe they were still alive and out there somewhere.

We stepped into the world. The light was so bright it hurt my eyes. The feel of fresh air on my skin took my breath away. Neither one of us could speak. The sky was a bright shade of blue I'm sure I'd never seen before. We squinted and shielded our eyes. We blinked back tears that glimmered in the sunlight. We drank in the pine scent. The breeze rustled through leaves. Animals scurried about. Birds called to one another. Joy welled up in me at this orchestra.

But this felt unnatural. Too much to take in all at once. It felt as if the volume on the world had been ratcheted up. The colors were too vivid. The sounds too loud, the smells too strong. Being in such a vast space made me feel vulnerable.

I'd expected an ashen landscape, void of color and sound. Everything looked miraculously the same as when we'd gone underground. Maybe we'd gotten it all wrong. Maybe the world hadn't ended. Had we been locked away for nothing? But I remembered the madness that day we locked ourselves in and the zombie. We'd escaped something, but a new hope was beginning to glisten inside me. Maybe we weren't the only ones to survive. I just needed to take it one step at a time. The most important thing was to get Chaske healthy again.

I propped Chaske by the stone with the infinity symbol carved in it. I traced the sun-warmed lines with my finger. There was no infinity for anything except that awful poison. I told him to rest for a while. I placed the loaded gun on his lap, just in case.

I had to go back in. I stood at the entrance for a long time. My body refused to move. I was scared to leave Chaske. I also couldn't bear the dark again. I shuffled, one foot in front of the other. *Don't think, just do*, I told myself. The stale, rank smell of the tunnel hit me. I didn't realize how much my senses had dulled underground. After so long, we didn't smell the foul odor or realize how dim the light or how claustrophobic the space was.

I forced myself forward, even though every cell in my body screamed to leave this place. I wanted to salvage as many supplies as possible. I didn't want to return ever. I also wanted to mark this space. I wished I could make a ginormous "Do Not Disturb" sign so no one else would enter these tunnels as people and leave as ghosts. I wanted to write a message, but how do you communicate when you don't know the language or symbols of future generations? I thought about writing "Do Not Enter." I only knew English. Was that good enough? Not everyone spoke English. This poison could be deadly for ten thousand years, which was longer than humans had existed. I thought of the evolution from cave drawings to cursive. Would language continue to morph and change? Would the language we spoke today be as difficult for future generations to understand as Homer's epic poems in the original Greek were for me?

If I marked the mountain in some way, would others be curious? Think this place was special? Wonder if it held treasures? I thought of all of the Egyptian "Do Not

Disturb" signs—the threats of curses—that hadn't stopped anyone from entering sacred tombs and looting the treasures. Modern-day museums were filled with Egyptian relics that were never supposed to have been uncovered. Locked doors and "Keep Out" signs sometimes tempt rather than repel. How could I ever convince future generations that what was buried in this mountain was deadly, not special?

I felt powerless. There was nothing I could do or say. This poison would continue to kill forever. My body tensed and a scream started at the tips of my toes and jolted through my body, gathering momentum and volume. A primal scream erupted from me and filled the space. I hoped somehow it would embed in the rock.

Then I did something I hadn't done since we entered the tunnels: I prayed. I prayed to any god that was listening. I prayed to the ghosts that might be lingering and any angels watching over me. I prayed to anyone who was still breathing in any far corner of whatever was left of my world and to those who had passed on. I asked for Chaske to be spared. I asked that they guard this place of death and keep the living away.

I wished I had explosives to collapse the tunnels. But even that didn't seem enough.

I filled Chaske's backpack with our remaining food and hauled jugs of water outside. I kept Chaske's copy of *To Kill a Mockingbird*, but left *Godot* behind. Samuel Beckett might be right about the absurdity and futility of it all, but I didn't need the reminder. I dragged Tate's body wrapped in the sleeping bag and laid it parallel to the zombie's decaying corpse. It wasn't easy, but I couldn't bear the thought of him all alone, so close to the poison that killed him.

I took one final look at this place that had somehow grown to be my home. I felt no nostalgia. I didn't know if this place had saved or killed me. I locked the door. I used Tate's pocketknife to scratch the symbol for radioactivity onto the door. I scribbled those lines over and over. Would it even mean anything to anybody in a few hundred years? But it was something; something was better than nothing.

By the time I resurfaced the sun was setting. I built a fire and snuggled up to Chaske for the night. We were finally warm. I thought I'd never be warm again. Chaske and I split an MRE, but this time we warmed it over the fire. I fed him as best I could. We both needed to keep our strength up.

"Do you think it's smart to have the fire?" Chaske asked. He didn't have the energy to open his eyes. "What if someone sees it?"

"What can anyone do to us now?"

He rested his head on my shoulder and fell sound asleep. I lost myself in the crackling of the fire and the dancing orange flames. It was beautiful. Even with Chaske dying in my arms, the tiniest spark of life was rekindling in me, but what was waiting for us out there?

It took Chaske and me hours to walk to the vantage point we had climbed to the night we closed ourselves in. There was a poetic symmetry to standing there, staring out over the silent, barren landscape. There wasn't a crater where Las Vegas used to be, but the skyline wasn't the same. The buildings appeared broken. The landscape dull and dead. There were cars lined along the road, but it was obvious even from this distance that they were abandoned, some even burned out. We strained to see any signs of life. Nothing moved or sparkled. There was no whoosh of airplanes or helicopters overhead.

"This doesn't mean anything," Chaske said. I knew what he meant; there could still be life out there.

As the final rays of the sun faded, Chaske raised a weary finger. "There." He pointed.

I followed the line from his finger. A thread of smoke twisted skyward, blending with the low-hanging clouds that looked heavy with rain. I kissed him on the cheek. "Maybe" was all I said.

I woke with a jolt. Chaske was riffling around in my backpack.

"What do you need?" I scrambled to his side, my body dull with sleep and my eyes barely able to focus.

I instinctively inched away when I saw Tate's knife. "What are you doing with that?" I swiped at it but he moved it out of my reach.

"I had an—" His thought was interrupted by a hacking cough. "An idea." He panted, but he was intent on continuing. "When I was sitting by that..." He mimed the infinity symbol.

"Yeah," I said, my eyes focused on the blade.

"I want us..." *Gasp.* "To be..." *Cough. Deep breath.* He finished with a blurt, "Together forever."

My stomach lurched. Was he proposing joint suicide?

"Is that what you want?" I asked.

"Trust me," he whispered. His brown eyes held the same fire I'd seen when he'd shot the rattlesnake and saved my life.

He took my wrist, palm up, in his hand. He gathered his strength. He traced the symbol on my wrist across the bulging artery and the crisscrossing blue veins. I bit my lip to mask the sting of the cut. A slip of the knife and we could end it here together. Red lines emerged where the tip of the blade had broken the skin. I didn't dab it away; I let the blood collect and drip onto the ground.

He handed me the blade and I carved an identical symbol into him.

"Now no matter what..."

"We're together forever."

We lay on our backs and dozed in the warm desert sun. Every muscle and bone was drained of energy. I memorized every inch of Chaske. His long black hair was fanned out under his head. His broad nose. The scar that split diagonally through his left eyebrow. High cheekbones that flushed pink when he smiled that half smile of his. His full, rosy lips that gave his smile substance and softness.

"What are you thinking?" I asked.

"Something my mom said: 'All that is necessary for the triumph of evil' "—Chaske took a deep breath—" 'is that good men do nothing.' "

"Who said that?" I asked as the words plunged deep into my soul.

"I don't know, some Irish guy, I think." He bit his lower lip. "Edmund Burke. That's it."

I stared at the sky, now dotted with a million stars. The night sky looked the same as it did that night we buried ourselves alive. Still beautiful and mysterious. All those dots made me feel less alone, as if maybe those lights were living beings out in the universe.

"What made you think of that?" I asked after a while.

I felt Chaske shrug. My eyes were closing and my thoughts blurring with sleep when Chaske whispered, "I was thinking of you. Do something, Icie. Don't let evil triumph."

I fought sleep. I didn't want to waste a minute with Chaske. But my body felt heavy, as if I were wearing one of those sumo wrestler suits. My eyelids slid shut. I tried to open them, but my eyelashes felt magnetized. The rhythm of his breath eventually lulled me to sleep.

I woke up to the image of Chaske standing naked, arms open wide against a field of blue. His long black hair fluttered down his back. His once muscular body had withered, but he still looked majestic as he lifted his face to the sky. His skin glistened.

Then he took flight.

"No!" I screamed, and scrambled to the edge. At the last moment, I pulled back. I didn't want to see his broken body below.

I didn't wonder why. He'd told me already. A flood of grief the size of a galaxy-wide tsunami crashed over me. I collapsed into sobs that I was sure made the mountain quake. I cried until everything else faded away. I don't know if I slept or lost consciousness, but when I opened my eyes, grief hit me all over again. The sadness hollowed me out. My eyes were open but I wasn't awake.

I searched the pale blue sky for a cloud or bird or anything. But the sky seemed vast and lonely. I inhaled but the air soured in my nostrils. I could somehow smell the damp, stale air of the bunker and the sour scent of Chaske's decay. The once warm sun now seared my skin. The pasty white of months underground was being toasted into a harsh pink.

I didn't want to move. Leaving this spot felt like leaving Chaske behind. I closed my eyes. I could picture him vividly. This spot couldn't hold him, only his death and whatever remained of his flesh.

I walked back to the bunker. I studied the symbol that had already scabbed over on my wrist. Chaske's body was at the bottom of the ravine, but I felt as if he were still walking beside me.

A wave of nausea overwhelmed me. I dropped to my knees. My stomach convulsed and my mouth and eyes watered. I gagged and retched but nothing came out. My stomach rolled as if something had found its way inside of me and was knocking like a pinball into my internal organs. This was it. The poison had finally grabbed hold.

The next thing I remembered was waking up on the

ground, my limbs sprawled at awkward angles. I drew my knees into my chest. My breasts felt tender and sore. I didn't want to die here like this, defeated, curled like a baby in a womb. If I was going to die, I was going to do it my own way.

As the sun set, I ate a whole power bar and gulped water, no longer worried about conservation. I felt exposed and helpless on this mountainside now. I went back in the bunker but kept the door open. I sat in that space with its walls covered in Marissa's faces.

I took out my pen and notebook. I finally knew what I wanted—no, needed—to say. I wrote our story. I wrote until my hand cramped. I wrote in long, rambling sentences with no punctuation and questionable spelling. It took me days, but I wrote until I'd said everything I needed to say. The ink was fading and the last few words were only indentations on the paper. I wrapped the notebook in heavy plastic bags. The Egyptian-like relics that would remain in my backpack would include candy corn–flavored lip gloss, a key ring with my purple sparkly initials, my Capital Academy ID card, four stale Tic Tacs, and two mismatched earrings. I shoved the notebook to the bottom of the backpack and folded the canvas around it. My shiny SAVE THE PLANET, ROCK THE WORLD pin glinted in the flashlight.

And I waited for death to find me like it had everyone else.

THIRTY-SEVEN

"Endings are beginnings."
—Just Saying 156

HARPER

Harper touches her torch to the dry branches and waits until they start to smoke. She watches the flames lick at the surrounding branches. Her seed of fire blossoms into a red rose. Without this sign, Beckett's just a man whispering "Peace" into the abyss.

She tries to look through the flames and rolling smoke as if she might see Beckett ascending to lead Forreal and Vega.

She is bathed in firelight but darkness snakes around her. She hears cracking but it's not coming from the fire. She sees a creature rising out of the flames. She staggers away from the Crown. The creature is gaining on her.

Harper trips and crashes to the ground.

"Harper," it says, squinting down at her. She tries to crawl away. Pain rips through her brain. Stars flash in her eyes with every move. The creature advances at a steady, hobbled pace. She tries to pull herself upright, but the creature curls his fingers around her ankle and pulls her back. She claws forward, and he drags her back toward the flames.

She flips over and stares up at her attacker.

"Finch," Harper shouts, and lands a kick squarely on his beak-like nose.

He screams and releases her. He covers his nose, now gushing blood.

Harper springs to standing. Her head swims with pain.

"You found the Heart, didn't you?" Finch growls. "What was in the Heart? Tell me!"

She doesn't mean to, but she glances in the direction of the Great I AM's backpack. She realizes too late what she's done. Finch follows her gaze. She can't let him have it. She dives for it and rolls away, pinning the backpack to her chest. She flings it free, a safe distance up the Mountain.

"It doesn't matter." He laughs and begins to stamp out Harper's fire.

Harper knows what she must do. She walks straight toward him. She pivots and kicks him hard in the stomach and thrusts him into the burning Crown. He clutches her wrist and pulls her into the flames. Her clothes ignite and the fire burns with the bite of a million fangs. As the flames engulf him, his grasp melts away. Harper tumbles on the ground, smothering the flames that cling to her.

Harper can feel the fire eating holes through her skin. She can feel the darkness again. It's coating her. With her last ounce of strength, she finds the Great I AM's backpack and rests it near the fire she and Beckett built. Lucky curls up on the backpack.

The entire Crown is alight now. The flames stretch skyward and create a wall of heat that shimmers against the morning sky. The kindling sputters and spits sparks and ash. Harper imagines her burned and broken body as part of the Crown. Beckett will usher in a new era of peace. She's sure that one day people will praise him.

Smoke is rolling off her, creating a cloudy gray halo. She would give anything to see him one last time. She whispers through the pain: "Whatever. Whatever. Whatever."

THIRTY-EIGHT

"Knowledge can suck."

—Just Saying 257

BECKETT

The top of the Mountain glows in an eerie ring of light. The Great I AM sent a sign. Forreal and Vega stand transfixed.

"I have come to deliver a message of peace and hope," Beckett calls from atop his rocky perch. "We must set aside our differences and discover how we can live together."

The Cheerleaders' faces are pale with surprise. Finch must have told them he crossed the Crown. Where is Finch? He started this. Beckett can't believe Finch would abandon Forreal.

He can see the way Greta's people are looking at her. It's similar to the way the people of Forreal used to look at him.

Greta squeezes his hand. "This is Beckett," she tells her people. "He is a prophet and the leader of Forreal."

She tells how he saved her from Finch. She talks about how he's seen the sacred Heart of the Mountain. "We can't let bad things define us," Greta says. "We must learn what we can from difficult times and become better people."

Beckett realizes she's quoting what he said to her on the Mountain. She is elevating him to mythical status. He and Greta can never go back to the way things were before, but maybe together they can lead and be the link between their two cultures.

Beckett's thoughts flash to Harper. She was supposed to light the Crown and then make her way back to Forreal. Beckett scans the crowd. He can't see her anywhere. She should be here by now. Worry sneaks in.

"The Great I AM has sent a sign," Beckett shouts. "We will work together. We will rebuild Vega. We will find peace."

Beckett invites the man Greta calls Da and the other leaders of Vega to the Mall tomorrow to outline a plan for working and living together. He asks the Cheerleaders to pass around baskets of berries, nuts, and dried meats. They share cool water from the Mountain spring.

He should be enjoying this moment, but something's wrong. He can feel it. He moves through the crowd, hoping to glimpse Harper's scraggly dreads.

Greta strides up next to him. "You were wonderful," she says, and hugs him, giving a little yelp of pain when he squeezes her back a little too tightly.

He looks around again. Everyone is staring at them. He still doesn't see Harper.

"I haven't seen her," Greta says. She doesn't say it, but he can tell she knows the secret behind his miracle. "I think you are right. We all need to believe in something greater than our-selves." She touches his cheek. "Go find Harper. She deserves to celebrate too. Even if she is a…what did she call me? Even if she's a Tristan from time to time."

As he walks through the crowd, people reach out to touch him. It's like walking against the wind. People search his eyes as if they hold the answer. The Cheerleaders tell of Beckett's birth-mark. Whispers follow him as he heads up the Mountain.

He has ended the conflict, at least for now. But what he hadn't anticipated was that now he is part of the miracle. He has always considered himself a conduit for the Great I AM, but now he's afraid his miracle has made him the message, not the messenger. Now more than ever, he needs Harper.

He races up the Mountain. The air is heavy with smoke. He stops when he sees the glowing embers of the Crown. The once great barricade is a smoldering pile of ash. It feels strange to see beyond to the mountaintop. The Mountain feels naked.

"Harper!" Beckett shouts as he crosses the blackened line of ash.

"Harper, where are you?" he yells again, standing motionless, ears straining to hear her reply. He feels trapped in this smoky fog.

"Beckett." His name is more breathed than spoken.

"Harper?" he asks, not sure if he's imagined his name in the rustling ash.

"Beckett."

He's sure he heard it that time. A breeze clears the smoke and he sees her. Even in the dim light, Beckett can see her body and clothes are burned. It's as if she's turned to ash too.

"Beckett," she says again.

374

"I'm here, Harper. I'm right here." He kneels down beside her. He reaches out but he doesn't make contact.

"Harper, what happened?" Beckett's heart begins to pound.

"Finch," she says slowly, as if the effort to speak his name is exhausting. "Did it work?"

"Yeah, Harper, just like we imagined." He tells her about everyone gathering and the future that now seems possible.

"I told you so," she says, and there's a hint of a smile on her blistered lips.

"I will listen to you more from now on," Beckett says, but the words catch in his throat. He thought he'd lost her.

"Finch is dead," she says.

"It's over, then," Beckett replies.

"I think it's only beginning." Her eyes flutter and then close.

"Harper," Beckett whispers. "I love you." He doesn't mean the romantic kind that he had started to feel for Greta. This love is etched into every cell of his being. It helps him stand. It lets him breathe. It makes him a better man.

"Save Harper." Beckett whispers his demand to the Great I AM. He will not lose her. She is the greatest miracle in his life. He needs her by his side in this new, uncertain future they have created.

Beckett sits beside her. Her hands are too burned to hold, so he strokes the singed stubble of her hair. "I won't leave you, I promise," he tells her. He needs to get her down the Mountain and cool her skin in the Mountain spring. He will move her when she's had the chance to regain her strength.

Lucky stretches and Beckett sees the backpack he found in the Heart.

He pulls the notebook from its protective shell and slowly opens the cover. He reads:

> The property of Isis Ann Murray.
> Please don't read because I'm such
> a loser in English.
> If found, please destroy.
> My life is humiliating enough
> without someone posting my
> drivel on Facebook.

He can let what's in this notebook remain a mystery or he can read it and know the truth—as if there is such a thing. This book could offer the secrets of life and the meaning of everything. Beckett believes it's his destiny.

"Isis Ann Murray." He says the name out loud. "I. A. M."

Beckett reads every word in the tattered notebook. The enlightened journey of the Great I AM transforms into one girl's desperate attempt to survive. The mountain, no longer sacred but poison. The last few words have been lost to time but he understands.

He Says even though he now knows he is speaking to a girl, an inert speck of dust that was caught in a big bang. Tears are streaming down his face. He realizes the true power of what he's discovered. If a girl could become a god, then he, Harper, and Greta have the power to create a new future for Forreal and Vega.

THIRTY-NINE

In that cold, dark cave, I begged death to come.

Death was the only thing that would end this pain.

I even sat with Chaske's gun in my hands for a while, but I couldn't do it.

I let memories of Chaske fill me.

And I cried.

And cried.

And cried.

Until I felt empty.

But instead of death, a furry black head peeked through the door. Bright yellow eyes gleamed.

"Midnight," I whispered, and she leapt into my arms.

And I realized I wanted to live for Chaske and everyone who had gone before.

Resurrected. That's how it felt. I'd been brought back from the dead.

I wanted to leave the mountain, but I couldn't. Chaske was here. I could feel him shining down on me like my own personal North Star. And even after everything and beyond all logic, I thought my parents might find me one day. If they were alive, they would not stop until they returned to the mountain.

Maybe I'd lost my mind, but I finally thought I'd found my calling. I was destined to protect future generations from the poison at the heart of the mountain. I sealed my backpack with my story inside the bunker. I hoped it would explain everything when I was no longer around to warn people. After locking the door, I piled rocks in the opening that was once covered by the infinity stone. I built a wall, wedging pebbles in every crack to create a solid barrier. I vowed to never return to this place. I tossed Chaske's gun down a deep ravine and watched it smash against the rock walls until it disappeared from view. I would never kill again.

Midnight and I moved into the cave Tate had found on our trip up the mountain. As I patrolled the base of the mountain, I sang Tate's songs: *"Wha Eva. Wha Eva. The bad, the good. Wha Eva. I put my faith in Wha Eva. Wha Eva alone."* Why those fragments stuck with me, I'll never know.

As much as I didn't want to admit it, I was getting sick. I was nauseated and exhausted. I was sure it was the radiation. I dressed in one of Chaske's T-shirts and covered myself with Marissa's cheer captain button-down. I wore Tate's watch so that I would remember all three.

But then they came. They saw my fire and they pilgrimaged to the mountain. It was a group of young kids about Tate's age. They had been at one of those isolated schools for troubled kids. All the administrators and teachers had abandoned them or died. These kids had survived in their compound, which was near Lake Mead. But then they saw my fire, and they thought it was a sign.

"You can't stay here," I told them. "It's not safe."

They didn't seem to hear me. They hugged me and warmed themselves by the fire. They were dirty and exhausted and I couldn't turn them away, not yet. A few of them were sick. I segregated them in the cave and brought them food and water. I made them as comfortable as I could and prepared myself for more death.

But these kids survived and thrived. I couldn't explain it. They had what I assumed were the lingering effects of the virus that had ravaged the world, but these kids slowly recovered, completely recovered, and no one else got sick. They thought that I and the mountain had cured them. Nothing I could say or do would change their minds. If I believed in such things, I might have thought it was a miracle too. But I had stopped believing in anything but myself.

We organized into teams and I handed out assignments. We took turns venturing into the outskirts of Vegas and scavenging anything we could find. We built a gathering space, which I jokingly referred to as the mall.

I gathered them together and told them stories about my journey to the heart of the mountain with a cheerleader and a rock star. I couldn't bring myself to tell them about Chaske. He was mine and mine alone. I told them my mum and dad would come one day because I wanted to believe it and I wanted to give them hope.

When I had finished my story, a little girl, who I had nicknamed Lola for her spiky hair and tough-as-nails attitude, asked, "Is this for real?"

"Yes," I said, "this is for real." Even though my story was starting to feel like something that happened to someone else. "You must never cross the thorny hedge or..." I wanted to tell them the truth, and I would someday, but I needed them to believe me now. "If you cross and go up the mountain, something horrible will happen."

"Like, you mean you'll die or something," a boy everyone called Beckett asked.

For simplicity, I decided to go with their version. "That's right. You'll die."

"Freepy," Lola said, which made me laugh.

And they believed me. They obeyed me. I'd saved them, and they looked up to me in a way that made me feel uncomfortable and responsible and not human, but what could I do? I thought about telling the truth about our home, about me, but we were all happier believing this mountain was special and that we'd survived for a reason.

I wanted to believe it too because I thought I'd be gone

soon. My health didn't deteriorate as fast as Tate's and Chaske's did, but my body was changing.

Over the next months I realized that my body wasn't preparing for death—quite the opposite. I gave birth to a son. I called him Chaske after his father. I told them he was special and he was. He was part Chaske and part me. This horror and tragedy had produced a precious, perfect life. He made me believe in miracles again.

I watched over them for as long as I could. And I watch over them still....

FORTY

"It's going to be okay."

—Just Saying 301

BECKETT

Beckett picks up Icie's notebook. He rips out page after page, tossing each one like confetti into the smoldering embers of the Crown. He throws the empty notebook shell on top. Black dots spread and eat into the paper. The flames take hold and the pages disintegrate.

He knows the truth. He will keep the Great I AM's secret.

It's funny but Beckett feels as if Icie is watching over him. And maybe she is. Maybe she gave him the vision of Chaske's death. Maybe she blessed him with a birthmark that mirrored the symbol Chaske etched on their wrists before he died. He will let these mysteries go unexplained.

Beckett vows to return to the Heart with Harper and close it for good. He will create an avalanche somehow. He will bury the

Heart so no one can enter it again. He will scrape out the infinity symbol until he has erased it.

As the sun rises, he Says to the Great I AM one last time. He thanks her for her sacrifice. He promises to carry out her mission—to do what she couldn't.

Harper's eyes open.

"You're going to be okay," he tells her. "We will join with Vega and we will leave the Mountain."

"What about Mumenda?" Harper asks.

Beckett bows his head. He grieves for the loss of the Great I AM and for a girl who lost so much. "Mum and Dad"—he pronounces it as Icie would have—"aren't coming. They are never coming."

Harper looks up at him in surprise. "How can you be sure?"

"I know, Harper. You'll have to trust me. I just know." The weight of Icie's secret weighs heavy on him, but it is a burden he is prepared to bear. He will let Forreal keep the faith, but he will have to look within for inspiration. He will have to ask Harper and Greta for guidance. No more looking for signs.

Beckett looks out over Vega, just like Icie did once. He tries to imagine the time she walked on this earth. He would have liked to have known this girl who built Forreal.

She wasn't a god.

She was just a girl.

But it doesn't matter. She has proved one person can change the future. Now it's up to him.

THE END

AUTHOR'S NOTE

In November 2009 my Little, Brown editor, Alvina Ling, dropped me a quick e-mail. She was listening to a fascinating discussion on Slate.com's podcast The Culture Gabfest. She felt the topic could be the inspiration for a young adult novel. She wrote: "And then I was thinking, 'But who could write this...' and I thought of you."

Well, I was flattered. I dropped everything and read the article and listened to the accompanying podcast. The article was titled "Atomic Priesthoods, Thorn Landscapes, and Munchian Pictograms: How to communicate the dangers of nuclear waste to future civilizations." It discussed how a United States Department of Energy (DOE) panel planned to label the site of an underground nuclear waste repository.

(When last I checked, you can still find the article at http://www.slate.com/articles/health_and_science/green_room/2009/11/atomic_priesthoods_thorn_landscapes_and_munchian_pictograms.html.)

It may sound a bit dry and boring, but think about it. Some types of nuclear waste are deadly for more than ten thousand years. The article noted that: "China, the planet's oldest continuous civilization, stretches back, at most, 5,000 years. And the world's oldest inscribed clay tablets—the earliest examples of written communication—date only from 3,000 or 3,500 B.C. It's impossible to say what apocalyptic event might separate 21st-century Americans from our 210th-century successors. Successors, mind you, who could live in a vastly more sophisticated society than we do *or* a vastly more primitive one."

I never told Alvina—until now—that my first response to her suggestion to base a teen novel on this issue was *absolutely not*!

But the article sparked something in my brain and I couldn't stop thinking about it. The idea that we are creating a substance that will be deadly for tens of thousands of years definitely seemed like science fiction, something right out of a superhero comic book. And then there was the added conundrum of how to communicate with future generations, which most likely will not speak the same language or understand our symbols. Fascinating!

That was the seed that would blossom into this story about the nature of faith and the power of miscommunication— and above all, the strength of the human spirit to adapt and survive.

The mountain and abandoned nuclear waste repository in *Half Lives* are fictional. I based my setting on both the deserted nuclear waste repository at Yucca Mountain in Nevada and the ongoing construction of the Onkalo Waste Repository, a long-term storage facility for highly nuclear waste in Finland. Although my nuclear waste repository is located in Nevada, the mountain I have created is not in the same geographic location nor does it have the same geological makeup as Yucca Mountain. According to the state of Nevada, the Yucca site is nothing more than a single boarded-up, empty tunnel, approximately five miles long.

The deterrent system outlined in the DOE report—titled "Expert Judgment on Markers to Deter Inadvertent Human Intrusion into the Waste Isolation Pilot Plant"—inspired the crown of thorns and the rocky wall in *Half Lives*. But the actual recommendations created by the panel of thirteen linguists, scientists, and anthropologists, at a cost of approximately $1 million in 1993, included a berm with a salt core and granite monoliths.

And truth is strange than fiction...over the course of the three-plus years it took to imagine, research, and write *Half Lives*—the situation at Yucca Mountain changed. The Yucca Mountain project was abandoned by the DOE. As of this writing, the debate for where to house nuclear fuel rods in the United States continues.

A recent editorial in the *Washington Post* outlined the issue: "Nuclear power holds great promise to provide electricity with practically no greenhouse emissions, if government can deal with the radioactive byproducts. But the not-in-my-back-yard-ism of [politicians] has all but killed the waste-disposal project at Nevada's Yucca Mountain, the site Congress chose in 1987 for a permanent repository. Instead, waste is piling up in the back yards of dozens of communities across the United States, at sites that weren't designed for long-term storage.

"Under existing law, the federal government can't begin accepting spent nuclear fuel for even an interim storage site in the absence of Yucca or some other permanent repository. So waste continues to accumulate at reactor sites—72,000 tons so far, three-fourths of it sitting in cooling pools like those that overheated at the stricken Fukushima Daiichi nuclear facility, threatening Japan with much more radioactive contamination" ("Nuclear waste need not be a radioactive debate," *The Washington Post* editorial board, June 13, 2012).

This issue is not unique to the United States. Countries around the world with active nuclear power stations must find a long-term solution. As of this writing, plans were being discussed for Britain's first nuclear research and disposal facility.

The bottom line is that *Half Lives* is a work of fiction. I have taken a few creative liberties to enhance my futuristic tale. But the issues it raises are real, and the debate is ongoing.

For more information, check out the following resources:

- *About a Mountain* by John D'Agata
- *Nuclear Eternity* (UK; released in the US as *Into Eternity*), a documentary written and directed by Michael Madsen
- Yucca Mountain: www.yuccamountain.org/new.htm
- World Nuclear Association: www.world-nuclear.org

Wishing you a long and healthy life!

Sara Grant
London, England
June 2012

ACKNOWLEDGMENTS

First and foremost I should thank my Little, Brown editor, Alvina Ling. She planted the seed that would blossom into *Half Lives*.

I was also blessed with a wonderful editorial team in three countries—Alvina Ling, Amber Caraveo, Tim Sonderhuesken, Bethany Strout, and Jenny Glencross. Not only are they exceptional editors but they are also lovely people. Thanks is not enough for their editorial feedback and collaboration!

I must also acknowledge all the fine work by my champions at Andrew Nurnberg Associates—my agent, Jenny Savill, and her assistant, Ella Kahn. Jenny challenges, listens, and encourages. I couldn't ask for a better partner in my literary life.

A special thanks to my dear friend Sara O'Connor for always being on the other end of the phone, text, or e-mail to offer advice, ideas, and enthusiasm!

Every writer needs a support group—not only to offer editorial guidance but to talk you off the fictional ledges you sometimes create along the way. Thanks to my fellow writers and friends Kate Scott, Jasmine Richards, and Karen Ball.

A huge thank-you to Jim and Liz Boone. I found Jim's website online—http://www.birdandhike.com/index.htm—when I was researching mountains near Las Vegas. Wonderfully and bizarrely, he and Liz spent a scorching hot morning hiking the mountains around Las Vegas with a writer they'd never met before and answering all my strange questions.

I give eternal thanks to my family and friends for their love and encouragement. Growing up, my parents provided a safe place from which I could let my imagination run wild. And to Susan—my big sister and best friend—she is the person I know will always come to my rescue.

And every writer should have a spouse like mine. He makes roast dinners when a deadline is looming. He brainstorms with me when I'm having plot problems. He's read this and all my prose countless times. He's my cheerleader and my rock star!

This book is dedicated to my writing companion of seven years, Margaret Carey. She passed away in 2011, but not before giving me editorial guidance and endless support on *Half Lives*. Her time on this earth was cut short, but so many wonderful memories of her live on in the hearts and minds of her friends and family.